TEMPEST

By Troy Denning

TEMPEST

TROY DENNING

BALLANTINE BOOKS • NEW YORK

Star Wars®: Legacy of the Force: Tempest is a work of fiction. Names, places, and incidents either are products of the author's imagination or are used fictitiously.

A Del Rey Books Mass Market Original

Published in the United States by Del Rey Books, an imprint of The Random House Publishing Group, a division of Random House, Inc., New York.

DEL REY is a registered trademark and the Del Rey colophon is a trademark of Random House, Inc.

This book contains an excerpt from *Star Wars®: Legacy of the Force: Exile* by Aaron Allston. This excerpt has been set for this edition only and may not reflect the final content of the published book.

ISBN: 978-0-345-47752-1

Printed in the United States of America

www.starwars.com
www.legacyoftheforce.com
www.delreybooks.com

OPM 9 8 7

For Connie and Mark
Good friends who live in a city far, far away

acknowledgments

Many people contributed to this book in ways large and small. I would like to thank them all, especially the following: Andria Hayday for her support, critiques, and many valuable suggestions; James Luceno, Leland Chee, Howard Roffman, Amy Gary, Pablo Hidalgo, and Keith Clayton for their fine contributions during our brainstorming sessions—initial and otherwise; Shelly Shapiro and Sue Rostoni for *everything,* from their remarkable patience to their insightful reviewing and editing to the wonderful ideas they put forth both inside and outside of the brainstorming sessions—and especially for being so great to work with; to my fellow writers Aaron Allston and Karen Traviss for all of their hard work—coordinating stories *and* writing them—and their myriad other contributions to this book and the series; to all of the people at Lucasfilm and Del Rey who make being a writer so much fun; to Laura Jorstad for her outstanding copyediting; and, finally, to George Lucas for letting us take his galaxy in this exciting new direction.

THE STAR WARS NOVELS TIMELINE

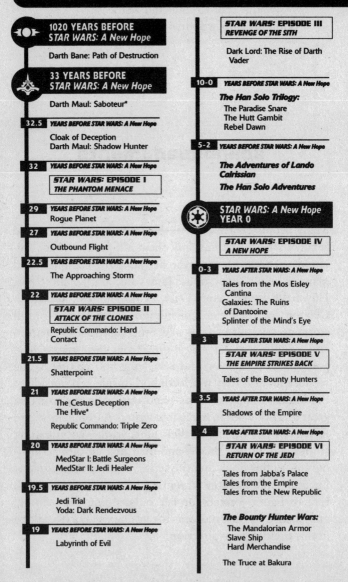

1020 YEARS BEFORE
STAR WARS: A New Hope

Darth Bane: Path of Destruction

33 YEARS BEFORE
STAR WARS: A New Hope

Darth Maul: Saboteur*

32.5 *YEARS BEFORE STAR WARS: A New Hope*

Cloak of Deception
Darth Maul: Shadow Hunter

32 *YEARS BEFORE STAR WARS: A New Hope*

**STAR WARS: EPISODE I
THE PHANTOM MENACE**

29 *YEARS BEFORE STAR WARS: A New Hope*

Rogue Planet

27 *YEARS BEFORE STAR WARS: A New Hope*

Outbound Flight

22.5 *YEARS BEFORE STAR WARS: A New Hope*

The Approaching Storm

22 *YEARS BEFORE STAR WARS: A New Hope*

**STAR WARS: EPISODE II
ATTACK OF THE CLONES**

Republic Commando: Hard
Contact

21.5 *YEARS BEFORE STAR WARS: A New Hope*

Shatterpoint

21 *YEARS BEFORE STAR WARS: A New Hope*

The Cestus Deception
The Hive*

Republic Commando: Triple Zero

20 *YEARS BEFORE STAR WARS: A New Hope*

MedStar I: Battle Surgeons
MedStar II: Jedi Healer

19.5 *YEARS BEFORE STAR WARS: A New Hope*

Jedi Trial
Yoda: Dark Rendezvous

19 *YEARS BEFORE STAR WARS: A New Hope*

Labyrinth of Evil

**STAR WARS: EPISODE III
REVENGE OF THE SITH**

Dark Lord: The Rise of Darth
Vader

10-0 *YEARS BEFORE STAR WARS: A New Hope*

The Han Solo Trilogy:
The Paradise Snare
The Hutt Gambit
Rebel Dawn

5-2 *YEARS BEFORE STAR WARS: A New Hope*

*The Adventures of Lando
Calrissian*

The Han Solo Adventures

STAR WARS: A New Hope
YEAR 0

**STAR WARS: EPISODE IV
A NEW HOPE**

0-3 *YEARS AFTER STAR WARS: A New Hope*

Tales from the Mos Eisley
Cantina
Galaxies: The Ruins
of Dantooine
Splinter of the Mind's Eye

3 *YEARS AFTER STAR WARS: A New Hope*

**STAR WARS: EPISODE V
THE EMPIRE STRIKES BACK**

Tales of the Bounty Hunters

3.5 *YEARS AFTER STAR WARS: A New Hope*

Shadows of the Empire

4 *YEARS AFTER STAR WARS: A New Hope*

**STAR WARS: EPISODE VI
RETURN OF THE JEDI**

Tales from Jabba's Palace
Tales from the Empire
Tales from the New Republic

The Bounty Hunter Wars:
The Mandalorian Armor
Slave Ship
Hard Merchandise

The Truce at Bakura

dramatis personae

Allana; Chume'da, heir to the Hapan Throne (human female)

Alema Rar; Jedi Knight (Twi'lek female)

Ben Skywalker; junior GAG member (human male)

C-3PO; protocol droid

Dur Gejjen; Five Worlds Prime Minister and Corellian Chief of State (human male)

Han Solo; captain, *Millennium Falcon* (human male)

Jacen Solo; Jedi Knight (human male)

Jagged Fel; bounty hunter (human male)

Jaina Solo; Jedi Knight (human female)

Lady Galney; chamberlain (human female)

Lalu Morwan; former flight surgeon (human female)

Leia Organa Solo; Jedi Knight (human female)

Luke Skywalker; Jedi Grand Master (human male)

Lumiya; Dark Lady of the Sith (human female)

Mara Jade Skywalker; Jedi Master (human female)

Nashtah; assassin (female; human/unknown)

Nek Bwua'tu; Galactic Alliance admiral (male Bothan)

R2-D2; astromech droid

Tenel Ka; Hapan Queen Mother (human female)

Zekk; Jedi Knight (human male)

prologue

The object of her desire was walking down the opposite side of the skylane, moving along a pedwalk so choked with vines and yorik coral that even the zap gangs traveled single-file. He was two levels below and ten meters ahead, and he kept stopping to study door membranes and peer into the windows of coral-crusted buildings. Then he would just stand there in the gloom, alone and empty-handed, as though no Jedi need fear the dangers of the undercity . . . as though *he* ruled the twilight depths down where Coruscant changed to Yuuzhan'tar.

Jacen Solo was as arrogant as ever—and this time, it would be his undoing.

The angle was perfect, almost *too* perfect. If she struck now, he would be dead almost as soon as he hit the pedwalk. Even if corpse robbers did not drop the body into the skylane, the only hint of what had killed him would be a tiny barb in his neck and a trace of venom in his nervous system. Nobody would know that his death had been an execution . . . not even Jacen.

But Alema Rar needed them to know. She needed to see the shock of recognition in Jacen's eyes when he collapsed, to feel his fear burning in the Force as his heart cramped into an unbeating knot. She needed to hold him dying in her arms and suck the last breath from his lips, to hear his father roaring curses and watch his mother wailing in grief.

That last part, Alema needed more than anything.

She had spent years pondering what she could take from Leia Solo that would be the equal of everything Leia had taken from her. An instep and five toes? That would be a fair trade for the half-of-a-foot Leia had cut off on Tenupe. And the Princess's eyes and ears would do for the lekku she had severed aboard the *Admiral Ackbar*. But what of the giant spidersloth to which Leia had fed her in the Tenupian jungle? How was Alema to match *that*?

Because this was not about revenge, not about cruelty. It was about *Balance*. The spidersloth had nearly *killed* her, had bitten her almost in half and left her slender dancer's body roped with white scars, an ugly lopsided thing that only a Rodian would desire. Now Alema had to take something equal from Leia, something that would shatter *her* to the core . . . because that's what Jedi *did*. They served the Balance.

And the first thing Alema wanted to take was Jacen, who was moving along the pedwalk toward the corner of an intersecting skylane. She had wanted to take him for a long time, since the day he had returned so mysterious and powerful from his five-year sojourn to study the Force. And now she would have him—perhaps not in the way she had once desired, but she *would* have him.

Eager to keep her prey in sight, Alema hurried back toward the nearest pedestrian bridge. It was fifty meters away, but she could not risk Force-leaping across the sky-lane after Jacen rounded the corner. This region was teeming with Ferals, the half-wild survivors of the Yuuzhan Vong invasion who continued to live a primitive existence deep in the undercity. If they saw Alema do something that remarkable, Jacen would sense their shock.

As Alema drew near the bridge, a faint nettling came to the stump of her amputated lekku. She stopped and slipped as far into the shadows as the coral would allow, then stood motionless, listening to the Ferals murmur behind their door membranes. When no danger appeared, she extended her Force-awareness a few meters and felt a pair of nervous presences behind her.

Alema turned to find the sunken-eyed faces of two young humans smirking up from the floor. They were hiding along the back of the pedwalk, in a shadowy stairwell so ringed with yorik coral that she had not noticed it. When they realized she was looking at them, the boys snickered and started to slip back down the stairwell.

Alema caught them in the Force. They cried out in shock and grabbed at the wall, cutting their hands on the yorik coral as they tried to keep from being pulled back into view. With thin brows and small, round-ended noses, they were clearly brothers. She raised her lip in a twisted half smile, enjoying the sense of power that rushed through her veins as their shock changed to fear.

"And what did you two have planned for us?" Alema always referred to herself in the plural. It was a habit she had acquired when she became a Killik Joiner, and one that she had no interest in losing. Using the singular would mean admitting that her nest was gone—that Jacen and Luke and the rest of the Jedi had destroyed Gorog—and that was not true, not while Alema still lived. "Robbery? Murder? Ravagery?"

The brothers shook their heads and started to open their mouths, but were clearly too repulsed by her deformities to speak.

"You're staring." Alema Force-pinned them against the wall. "That's rude."

"Put us down!" the larger ordered. With a lean face and a shadowy line of mustache fuzz on his upper lip, he was probably a year or two into human adolescence. "We didn't mean nothing. It's just . . ."

His gaze slid from Alema's face toward the lekku stump hanging behind her shoulder, then quickly began to drop. Alema had traded her provocative attire for more traditional Jedi garb, but even those shape-concealing robes were not enough to hide her disfigurements—the lopsided twist of her body, and the way one atrophied arm hung at her side. As the boy's gaze fell, she sensed in the Force his growing revulsion—actually experienced the disgust he felt when he looked at her.

"It's just *what*?" Alema demanded. In her anger, she was pressing both boys against the wall so hard they began to wheeze. "Go ahead. Tell us."

It was the younger brother who answered. "It's just . . ." He nodded at the lightsaber hanging from her belt. "You're a Jedi!"

Alema smiled coldly. "Aren't you clever? Pretending you've never seen a Jedi Knight before." She glanced ten meters down the pedwalk, to where a knobby-scaled radank had backed a screeching Falleen into a tangle of slashvines, then looked back to the boy. "But we have the Force. We *know* what you were looking at."

Allowing the older brother to fall free, she pointed down the pedwalk and Force-hurled his younger sibling into the slashvines next to the Falleen. The startled radank reared back on its hind legs, front feet raised and claws unsheathed, then extended its thin proboscis and began to sniff the new prey. The boy whimpered and called for help.

Alema looked back to the older one, who was already trying to inch his way toward his brother, and waved him on.

"Go." She gave a cruel little laugh. "After the radank is finished with you, you'll know how *we* feel."

The boy's eyes flashed with fear, but he pulled a shiv of sharpened durasteel from his sleeve and raced down the pedwalk to help his brother. Alema turned toward the bridge and, as the snarl and shriek of combat erupted behind her, allowed herself a small smile of satisfaction. The boys had mocked her disfigurement, and now they would be disfigured themselves. The Balance had been preserved.

She continued up the pedwalk, then started across the bridge. Her stump began to nettle again, and she wondered if someone was watching her. Jacen had seemed to be alone when he left his apartment, but—as commander of the Galactic Alliance Guard—he would know to expect assassins. Maybe his young apprentice, Ben Skywalker, had followed a few moments later to watch his back.

Alema gently extended her Force-awareness into the shadows behind her, searching for that flicker of pure bright power that always betrayed the Force presence of earnest young Jedi Knights. She felt nothing and decided that maybe the cause of her uneasiness was a raucous zap gang ahead. They had claimed the middle of the bridge for their own and were taking turns trying to push a frightened Gamorrean female over the safety rail. As Alema approached, they spread across the bridge and leered at her twisted form. They were all young human males, all wearing white tabards over various pieces of plastoid armor.

"What do you think you are?" the leader asked, eyeing Alema's black robes. He was a large youth with a three-day growth of beard and a badly swollen cheek. "Some kind of Jedi?"

"We have no time for your games," Alema replied coolly. "Go back and play with your Gamorrean." She made a shooing motion with the backs of her fingers, at the same time touching his mind through the Force. "You might have more fun if you let *her* do the pushing."

Swollen Cheek frowned, then turned to his companions. "She doesn't have time for us." He started after the Gamorrean, who was lumbering toward the far end of the bridge as fast as her thick legs could take her. "Get her! We'll try something new this time!"

The zap gang spun as one and raced away. Alema followed, catching up as they surrounded the Gamorrean and began to argue about who would be shoved into the safety rail first. Alema slipped past and smiled to herself. *Balance.*

At the other end of the bridge, Jacen was nowhere to be seen. He had either rounded the corner of the building or entered a doorway while Alema was dealing with the city's riffraff. She drew her lightsaber and advanced up the pedwalk, half expecting to feel the emitter nozzle of a lightsaber pressing into her ribs just before Jacen activated the blade.

The most dangerous thing Alema met was a foraging skrat pack, which skittered away into a tangle of slash-vines almost as soon as she saw it. The only other oddity was the sporadic stream of Ferals disappearing through a door membrane near the corner of the building. They were of many species—Bith, Bothan, Ho'Din—and they were all bearing the carcasses of dead animals, including hawk-bats, granite slugs, a few slimy yanskacs. Once, there was even a Chevin clutching what looked like a dead Ewok in its huge claw. They were probably just Ferals returning home with the day's hunt, but as Alema passed in front of the doorway, she kept her lightsaber at the ready.

No one leapt out to attack her, but she sensed a trio of Force presences on the other side of the membrane. Alema did not bother to investigate; had it been Jacen lurking behind the door, she would have sensed nothing at all. Instead, she exchanged her lightsaber for a short blowgun and armed it with a small cone-dart from a sealed container in her utility belt. She had eight more such darts— one for each of the Solos and the Skywalkers, plus two extras—all fashioned from the stinger and venom sac of a deadly Tenupian wasber.

The poison was fairly quick—at least on human-sized creatures—but more important, it was certain. It co-opted the white blood cells sent to fight infection, turning them into tiny toxin-producing factories. Within moments of being struck, all of the victim's organs would fall under attack, and within moments of *that,* his vital systems would start to fail. Jacen would live just long enough for Alema to reveal herself; he would probably die even before he realized that his Jedi poison–neutralizing techniques could not save him.

Alema raised the blowgun to her lips and stepped around the corner, her body already purring with the sweet tingle of murder.

But Jacen seemed determined to disappoint her. The pedwalk was empty and dark, and there was not a sentient soul in sight. Thinking he had lured her into a trap after all, Alema whirled back around the corner, her lungs filled with the air that would send the lethal dart shooting into her ambusher.

There was no ambush. That pedwalk was empty as well, and the only danger Alema sensed was the same faint tingle she had been feeling since before crossing the bridge. Could Jacen Solo be *hiding* from her?

Alema's anger welled up inside. It was those boys. They

had made her hurt them, and Jacen had always been so sensitive to such things. She cursed the brothers for making her lose control. Her plan had just grown more complicated, and that meant the pair would have to pay—but later. Right now she needed to go after Jacen. The poison on her dart would lose its effectiveness in less than an hour.

Alema returned to the door she had just passed, the one all the Ferals had been entering with their carcasses. Dark and ringed by a thick crust of yorik coral, it looked more like a cavern mouth than a doorway. She pressed a nerve bundle on the doorjamb, and the membrane pulled aside. Standing opposite her was a brawny Nikto with a scaly green face and a ring of small horns encircling his eyes. He kept one hand in the pocket of his soiled jerkin, obviously holding a blaster, and Alema could sense two more guards beside him, hiding on either side of the door.

He studied her for an instant, then rasped, "Wrrrong doorrr, lady. Nothing inside to interest *you*."

Alema started to reach for the guard in the Force, but stopped when her danger sense grew so strong that her remaining lekku began to tingle as well. She pointed her blowgun at the Nikto's feet and—using a Force suggestion to ensure he would obey—commanded, "Wait."

The expression in the Nikto's eyes changed from threatening to surprised to obedient, and Alema extended her Force-awareness in all directions.

To her astonishment, she brushed a cold presence—something dark and bitter—back up the pedwalk near the bridge. But when she turned to look in that direction, all she saw was the zap gang cheering on the Gamorrean as she belly-bounced their leader into the safety railing.

And the presence did not belong to any of the zappers. It was much too strong in the Force, too focused . . . then the darkness vanished, and the danger tingle in her lekku subsided as quickly as it had come.

Alema continued to study the pedwalk for a few moments, trying to digest what she had felt. Someone was definitely stalking her, but it could hardly be Jacen. Even had he been careless enough to let her detect him—and he wouldn't have been—the Jacen she remembered was anything but bitter: solemn and brooding, certainly, but also devoted and sincere.

So who *was* stalking her? Not Ben. He was too young to be so bitter. And not Jaina. Her temperament was too fiery to feel so cold. Besides, the presence had felt dark . . . and it made no sense for a dark-sider to be watching Jacen's back. It had to be something else.

Another possibility dawned on her: Maybe *Alema* was not the one being followed. Maybe it was *Jacen*.

Could someone be trying to steal her kill?

Alema turned back to the Nikto, gesturing past him with her blowgun. "Did Jacen Solo go in there?"

"Jacen Solo?" The Nikto shook his head. "Don't know any Solos."

"Come now." Alema used the Force to draw the Nikto out onto the pedwalk. "The news holos reach even down here, and every third report contains his image. The commander of the Galactic Alliance Guard? The savior of Coruscant?"

"Why would someone like that come here?" The Nikto tried to sound uncertain, but Alema could sense his lie in the subtle tremor of his Force presence. "There's nothing inside but housing—"

"You dare lie to *me*?" Alema used the Force to raise her crippled arm, then grabbed him by the throat. "To a *Jedi*?"

Still calling on the Force, she lifted him off his feet and

squeezed until she heard the happy crackle of crushed cartilage. The Nikto's mouth fell open and a terrible gurgle came from his throat. Alema continued to hold him aloft until his eyes rolled back and his feet began kicking; only when she sensed the other two guards stepping into the doorway did she drop the Nikto on the balcony and turn to find a pair of tentacle-faced Quarren bringing their old E-11 blaster rifles to bear.

Alema waved her blowgun, using the Force to turn their weapons aside, then touched their minds with hers to search out the doubt she knew would be foremost in their thoughts—the fear that they could not stop her from entering, that *they* would be the ones who died.

"You do not *need* to die." Alema spoke in a Force whisper so soft and compelling that it sounded like a thought. "You do not *need* to stop anyone."

The guards relaxed. Alema stepped over the dying Nikto and went through the doorway. "No one is coming through the door," she purred.

As Alema passed between the Quarren, she noticed that one of them had only three face-tentacles. Their beady eyes began to focus on her, and their old E-11 blaster rifles started to swing back toward her.

"You do not *need* to die." Alema tapped the muzzles of their weapons aside. "You do not *need* to see me."

Their eyes grew unfocused again, and they turned their attention back to the door. Once Alema was safely inside, she faced the two Quarren.

"You know me well," she said, continuing to speak in her Force whisper. "We have been talking for several minutes."

The Quarren shifted their stances, opening a place for Alema, and turned their heads slightly toward her.

Now Alema spoke in her normal voice. "Where do you suppose *he* was going?"

Three Tentacle turned to face her. "Who? Solo?"

Alema nodded.

"Where do you *think* he was going?" Three Tentacle retorted. "To see It, of course."

"*It?*" Alema had spent enough of her life wallowing in the underbelly of the galaxy to know that illicit enterprises were often referred to only in vague terms. Did Jacen have a secret vice—an addiction he was hiding, or a compulsion he had picked up in captivity and been unable to shake? She looked back to the Quarren. "What are we talking about? Spice dens? Death games?"

Now the second Quarren turned toward her, his tentacles straightening in his species' equivalent of a frown. "Is that supposed to be a joke? He's here for the same reason everyone is. To see It. The friend."

"The friend—of course."

Alema knew the kind of "friends" males kept hidden in places like this . . . the kind they would dare visit only in the anonymous depths of an undercity. Jacen's time with the Yuuzhan Vong must have left him more bent than even she had realized. She pointed her blowgun out the door, gesturing at the fallen Nikto, then spoke in her Force whisper again.

"Your companion was attacked by an intruder," she said. "You *saw* the intruder kill him, and soon the intruder will want to come inside."

"To kill It?" the second Quarren gasped.

"Yes, to kill It," Alema agreed. "You must stop the intruder from entering."

Three Tentacle pressed a nerve bundle, closing the door, then both Quarren pointed their blaster rifles at the heart of the membrane.

"Good," Alema said.

She turned away from the door, confident the two Quarren had already forgotten her. During her time with the Killiks, the queen of her nest—a Dark Jedi named Lomi Plo—had helped her develop a slippery presence in the Force. Now, as soon as Alema vanished from some-one's sight, she also vanished from memory.

Alema left the vestibule and entered a warren of wind-ing, tunnel-like passages lit by the bioluminescent lichen typical of Yuuzhan Vong–converted buildings. She se-lected the largest, most heavily trodden corridor and started forward at a brisk pace. She had to work fast if she wanted to be the one who killed Jacen; whoever was behind her would not be delayed for long by the Quarren.

The air quickly grew hot and dank, and puffs of what smelled like ammonia and sulfur started to roll up the passage. Alema wrinkled her nose and began to wonder just what kind of pleasure den this was. No spice she had ever used was so harsh; if the odor grew any stronger, it would be foul enough to quell a rancor in rut.

She had just reached a short side passage when the dis-tant shriek of blaster rifles sang down the corridor—the vestibule guards opening fire on her mysterious stalker. Alema peered down the side passage and saw that it opened into something vaguely reminiscent of a Kala'uun joy cave: a central chamber surrounded by a number of privacy cells. Was that where she would find Jacen and his *friend*?

A strange chorus of *snap-hiss*es erupted from the entry vestibule, and the blasterfire ceased as suddenly as it had begun. By the sound of it, whoever was following Alema was using some sort of strange lightsaber technology—and using it well. The Quarren had bought Alema even less time than she had expected.

But which way had Jacen gone—into the joy cave, or deeper into the building? Searching for him in the Force would do no good—indeed, would probably prove disastrous. Even if he wasn't concealing his own presence, he would feel her looking for him, and Alema could not best Jacen Solo in a straight duel—not with one half-useless arm and one clumsy half foot.

Fortunately, Alema knew males, and males—especially important males who pursued their secret passions in low places—did not like to wait for their pleasure.

She went down the side passage and was surprised to find no panderer there to greet her, nor any spice dealers, nor any glitter girls waiting for new clients. There wasn't even a beverage center, only a fountain gurgling in the center of the room and a refresher tucked away into a rear alcove. The doors to most of the privacy cells were open, revealing small dens containing beds, nesting basins, or simple raised pallets.

But a handful of the cells were closed, and Alema could sense beings in them all. She went to the first and, holding her blowgun ready to shoot, pressed the nerve bundle beside the door. The membrane retracted to reveal a pair of Jenet curled up on large floor cushions, their limbs pulled in tight and their snouts tucked close to their legs. Neither opened an eye, even when Alema grunted in disbelief.

There were no spice pipes in the cell, no aphrodisiacs, not even an empty ale mug. They were sleeping—just sleeping.

Alema moved on, opening two more doors. She found a lone Duros behind one and a trio of Chadra-Fan behind the other—all *sleeping*. Apparently, she had stumbled into some sort of staff dormitory. She cursed under her breath. What kind of pleasure den had its staff quarters in *front*?

Alema started back toward the main corridor and glimpsed her pursuer's shadow on the far wall. She ducked out of sight and made sure that her Force presence was damped down, then peered around the corner and watched as a thin woman in a scarlet robe came down the corridor.

The woman was middle-aged, with red hair and a thin nose, and she kept the lower half of her face concealed behind a black scarf. In one hand, she held a coil of strands—leather and gem-studded metal—attached to what looked like the hilt of a lightsaber.

Alema was so shocked that she almost let her feelings spill into the Force. At the Jedi academy on Yavin 4, she had studied the story of an Imperial agent named Shira Brie: how Brie had attempted to discredit Luke in the eyes of his fellow pilots, only to be shot down and nearly killed; how Darth Vader had rehabilitated her, turning her into as much a machine as he was, then training her in the ways of the Sith; how she had constructed her lightwhip and returned to trouble Luke Skywalker time after time in her new identity as Lumiya, Dark Lady of the Sith.

Could it be that Lumiya had returned once more? Alema saw no room to doubt. The woman was the right age and appearance, she concealed her lower face beneath the same dark scarf that Lumiya wore to hide her scarred jawline, and she carried a lightwhip—a weapon unique in the era of modern Jedi.

And she was hunting Jacen Solo.

Alema drew back around the corner, her thoughts whirling as she struggled to sort through the implications. She knew from the histories she had studied that Lumiya hated the Skywalkers and Solos almost as much as Alema herself did, so it seemed likely their goals were the same—to destroy the Solo-Skywalker clan. But Alema could not permit Lumiya to steal her kills. If the Balance was to be served, Alema had to destroy the prey herself.

She filled her lungs with air, then raised the blowgun to her lips and spun around the corner to attack.

The corridor was empty.

She stepped back around the corner, expecting Lumiya to attack from the cover of a Force blur or drop off the ceiling at any instant.

When nothing happened, Alema stood and stepped away from the door. Still, Lumiya did not appear. Alema expanded her Force awareness, searching for the Sith's dark presence.

Nothing.

She cautiously peered around the corner again. When no attack came, she studied the walls, ceiling, and floor carefully, searching for any odd shadows or blurred areas where Lumiya might be hiding. When there was still no attack, she advanced up the short side passage to the main corridor and did the same thing.

Lumiya was gone, vanished as quickly as she had appeared.

Alema grew cold and empty inside, and she began to wonder if she had really seen Lumiya at all. Maybe it had been a Force-vision . . . or maybe her fever had returned. Once, near the end of her first year marooned in the Tenupian jungle, she had spent days exploring the Massassi temples on Yavin 4 with her dead sister, Numa—only to find herself stranded high on a Tenupian mountain when the fever finally broke.

But another explanation seemed just as likely: Lumiya had continued after Jacen.

Alema started down the corridor at a run, growing more worried with each step that Lumiya would beat her to the kill, no longer taking the time to move quietly, barely paying attention to which way she was going, just moving deeper into the building, deeper into the heat and the dankness and that horrid smell of ammonia and sulfur.

Twice she ran headlong into surprised Ferals, and twice she had to kill them for attempting to lie to her before finally pointing the true way to It. Another time, she heard a large group of armored Ferals clattering up a ramp she was descending. She pressed herself against the wall between two patches of glow-lichen, then drew a Force shadow over herself and watched impatiently as they rushed past to search out the intruder.

Finally, the ammonia-and-sulfur smell grew almost overpowering, and Alema began to hear strange gurglings and splashes. She emerged onto a narrow mezzanine balcony and found herself gazing across a huge well of yellow fog. It looked nothing like the pleasure den she had been expecting, but she stepped out of the passage and crossed the balcony without hesitation. In typical Yuuzhan Vong fashion, there was no railing to keep pedestrians safe. The yorik coral floor simply ended twenty meters above a vast pool of steaming slime.

A constant supply of bubbles was rising from the depths of the pool, speckling the surface with flashes of light as they burst into scarlet and yellow glimmers. The surrounding walls were mottled with patches of bioluminescent lichen, barely visible through the thick fog. Higher up, several tiers of balconies curved away on both sides and vanished into the steam. Scattered along the balcony edges were the shadowy silhouettes of Ferals, usually in the process of tossing animal carcasses—or even lifeless bipeds—into the pool below. The splashes were always followed by a short gurgle, as though the bodies were too heavy to float on slime.

Alema furrowed her brow, trying to decide exactly what she was looking at. In Coruscant's savage undercity—especially the part that was still Yuuzhan'tar—dead animals were invariably devoured by Ferals or other scavengers long before the meat spoiled. So it seemed unlikely the pool was some sort of garbage pit. Instead, the Ferals had to be feeding something—something that Jacen was interested in, as well.

Alema was about to back away when a voice murmured up through the fog. It was impossible to make out what it was saying over the gurgling of the pool, but Alema didn't care. She recognized that voice: its dark timbre, its careful rhythms, and—unmistakably—its patronizing inflections.

Jacen.

Alema focused all her attention on that voice, trying to pinpoint its source. The fog and the pool worked against her, muffling Jacen's words and drowning them out with gurgles. But eventually she grew attuned enough that she shut out everything else and began to understand what he was saying.

". . . let me worry about Reh'mwa and the Bothans." Jacen sounded irritated. "Leaving the Well was foolish. I can't protect you here."

The only response Alema heard was a long liquid purl, but Jacen responded as though he had been spoken to.

"That's ridiculous. I'd *know* if I had been followed. Not even Bothan assassins are that good."

Ever so carefully, Alema used the Force to clear the fog between herself and Jacen. She was running the risk that Jacen would feel her drawing on the Force, but she would have only one shot, and she needed to see her target. Besides, Jacen was likely too preoccupied with his conversation to notice such a subtle disturbance.

After another long purl, Jacen's voice grew concerned. "*Inside* the building? You're sure?"

There was a short gurgle.

"Of course I'd care," Jacen replied testily. He snapped his lightsaber off his belt. "You're the Guard's most valuable asset. Without you, we couldn't track a *tenth* of the terrorist cells we do now."

The fog cleared, and Alema was astonished to see Jacen addressing a fleshy black monstrosity that had come up from the slime. The thing was so large, she could not even tell how much of it she was seeing. Its eye had a pupil the size of a Sullustan's head, its tentacles were as big around as Alema herself, and—like everything in this part of the undercity—its appearance was distinctly Yuuzhan Vong.

The creature blinked . . . and thrashed its tentacles across the surface.

"I *can't* ban Bothans from the planet," Jacen replied. "That would push Bothawui straight into Corellia's camp."

Alema began to suspect what this creature was. While Jacen had been held captive by the Yuuzhan Vong, he had supposedly struck up a friendship with the World Brain, a sort of genetic master controller whom the invaders had created to oversee the remaking of Coruscant. Before escaping, Jacen had persuaded it to thwart its masters' plans, to cooperate only partially in their efforts to reshape Coruscant. Later, during the final days of the war, he had convinced his "friend" to switch sides and help the Galactic Alliance retake the planet. Now he was using it to spy on Corellian terrorists.

Clever boy.

Alema raised the blowgun to her lips and, using the Force to hide the cone-dart, expelled her breath.

The dart had just left the blowgun when, somewhere

above Alema and to her right, a throaty female voice cried out, "Jacen!"

Jacen spun, igniting his lightsaber as he turned. But the dart was tiny, swift, and still hidden in the Force, and Alema realized with a bolt of satisfaction that his blade was not rising to block.

Then Jacen cried out and flew backward, as though hurled by an invisible hand, and the dart flashed past, eliciting a liquid roar of pain as it disappeared into the enormous eye of the World Brain.

Alema was astonished, dismayed, angry—but she was not stunned. She had been in too many death fights to let herself be paralyzed by *any* surprise. She pivoted toward the voice that had alerted Jacen.

Five meters across the Well's edge—and one balcony up—stood the fog-blurred silhouette of a thin woman in a scarlet robe. Her arm was still extended toward the slime pool, leaving no doubt that she had been the one who Force-hurled Jacen to safety.

Lumiya.

As Alema backed away from the balcony's edge, Lumiya pointed toward her. "There, Jacen!"

Alema turned to run, but the fog suddenly flashed blue, and a tremendous crack sounded from behind her. In the next moment she found herself sliding across the floor, snakes of Force lightning dancing across her anguished body until she finally passed from her attacker's sight.

Alema did not understand what had just happened— had Lumiya really *warned* Jacen? had he been the one who hurled the Force lightning at her?—but there was no time to figure it out. She forced her cramped muscles to drag her into the nearest corridor, then rose to a knee and drew a Force shadow over herself. She reached into her pocket for another dart . . . and that was when she realized the Force lightning had made her drop her blowgun.

Jacen alit on the edge of the balcony, so obscured by yellow fog that he was barely more than a silhouette. But he was burning with a rage that Alema had not thought possible for him, an anger so fierce that it warmed the Force like fire. He ignited his lightsaber, casting a green reflection that made his eyes shine with murderous intent. His gaze fell on the blowgun, and he started forward.

An ear-piercing screech rang out from the Well of the World Brain, then a dozen black tentacles rose out of the fog. They began to thrash about wildly, gashing themselves on the balcony and spraying the walls with blood. Jacen's eyes darkened to the color of black holes, and he started forward, his gaze shifting to the corridor where Alema was hiding.

Though Alema knew she lacked the power to kill Jacen with one attack—and that she would not have time for two—she opened herself to the Force, preparing to blast him with lightning.

Then a second silhouette—this one a slender woman with a veiled face—dropped out of the fog, landing on the edge of the balcony and dancing past the thrashing tentacles as only someone trained in Force acrobatics could.

Alema extended her hand. Lumiya was *not* going to steal her kill.

But instead of attacking Jacen, Lumiya merely caught him by the arm and spun him toward the thrashing tentacles.

"Jacen, those are convulsions," she said. "We have to slow the poison *now,* or your spy is dead."

Alema's jaw dropped. Lumiya's tone was one of command—a Master to a student.

"But the assassin—"

"Would you rather have vengeance or preserve an intelligence asset?"

"This isn't *about* vengeance." Jacen looked toward the corridor where Alema was hiding. "It's about justice. We can't let the assassin—"

"The assassin is only the tool," Lumiya interrupted again. "It's the hand wielding her we need to stop. It's Reh'mwa and his lieutenants."

Jacen continued to stare at Alema's corridor, his fury and desire to kill pouring into the Force.

Lumiya released Jacen's arm, pulling her hand away in disgust. "I can see it was a mistake to pick you. Go on." She waved him toward Alema's hiding place. "You are a servant to your emotions, not a master to them."

"This has nothing to do with my emotions."

"It has *everything* to do with your emotions," Lumiya countered. "You're angry because your friend was hurt, and now you can think of nothing but bringing the attacker to 'justice.' You're hopeless."

Lumiya's last comment seemed to sting Jacen. He continued to glare into the corridor for a moment, then glanced away long enough to summon her blowgun.

"Tell Reh'mwa we're coming," he said, pointing the blowgun in Alema's general direction. "This won't go unanswered."

Jacen turned away. He and Lumiya danced past the thrashing tentacles of the World Brain and dropped into the fog. Even after they were gone, Alema remained in hiding, too shocked to move.

Jacen Solo, apprenticing with a Sith.

Had the galaxy gone mad?

chapter one

The air aboard the *Thrackan Sal-Solo* was filled with new-vessel smells—the acrid bite of ventilation fans burning off packing grease, the sweetness of escaped actuating gas, the ozone tinge of fresh-air exchangers. As Han and Leia Solo passed through hatchway after hatchway, Han still found himself touching the durasteel bulkheads to be sure he wasn't dreaming.

The *Sal-Solo* was the flagship of a secret assault fleet that the Corellian government had put into construction nearly ten standard years before, under the leadership of Han's recently deceased cousin, Thrackan Sal-Solo. Nobody would say what Sal-Solo and his cohorts had been planning for the mysterious armada, and Han didn't care. The fleet was ready to deploy and large enough to shatter the Alliance blockade, and that was all that mattered. The blockade had been extended to all five planets in the Corellian System, choking their economics and threatening their off-world facilities.

When the Solos reached the Command Center, Han did not need to be a Jedi to feel the excitement in the air. The door guards inspected everyone's passes with more than the usual cursory nod, and they even ran a security scan on C-3PO. Inside, the support officers had forsaken the caf dispenser and were actually at their duty carrels, studying data displays and coding orders. The only individuals who did not seem busy were half a dozen civilian security agents waiting on steel benches outside the Tactical Planning Salon, and even they sat in tense silence.

Han leaned close to Leia and asked in a whisper, "Will you be okay with this?"

Leia looked up and arched a brow. The lines at the corners of her dark eyes only made her gaze that much more penetrating . . . and, well, *wise*.

"Okay with *what*, Han?"

"Being married to a Corellian admiral." Han smirked and ran his fingers over his chin, clean-shaven now that there was no longer a need to hide his identity from his cousin's assassins. "Look around. Wedge is getting ready to bust the blockade, and he's going to need me to take one of the Dreadnaughts."

Leia surveyed the busy cabin, allowing her gaze to rest on the security agents outside the planning salon. "I don't think we need to worry about that, Han."

Han frowned. "You think I'm too old for a line command?"

"Hardly. You're not even seventy yet." Leia lowered her voice, then added, "I just have a feeling."

"Oh dear," C-3PO said. "It's never good when Mistress Leia has a feeling."

They reached the door to the planning salon and had to end the conversation. Instead of admitting them immediately as he had the previous day, the door guard—a square-jawed petty officer in a blue duty uniform—blocked their way.

"The admiral will be with you as soon as he can, Captain Solo."

"As soon as he *can*?" Han was starting to think Leia's feeling might be right. "He called *us*."

"Yes, sir, I'm aware of that." The door guard studied Han with the weary smirk that Corellians reserved for grandstanders and blowhards. "Admiral Antilles is a very busy man."

"Yeah?" Han was growing embarrassed by his earlier confidence—and nothing made him testier than embarrassing himself in front of Leia. "Well, so am I."

Before Han could turn to leave, Leia caught him by the arm. "Tell Admiral Antilles to take his time," she said to the guard. "We understand how busy he must be right now."

Han did not resist as she pulled him to one side of the door. Wedge Antilles had been appointed Supreme Commander of the Corellian forces some ten standard days earlier—the day after Thrackan Sal-Solo's assassination—and Han knew as well as anyone how hectic his schedule had to be right now.

That was why the Solos had been so surprised to receive a message asking them to rendezvous with Antilles in the Kiris Asteroid Cluster. The Kirises were so far out on the fringes of the system that they were almost free floating, and so obscure that even Han had been forced to ask for coordinates. The Solos had spent the better part of the trip—made even longer by the necessity of evading the Galactic Alliance blockade—debating what the blazes Corellia's new Supreme Commander was doing so far from the war.

All their questions had been answered when they rounded Kiris 6 and saw the *Sal-Solo* floating in her hidden dock. The Dreadnaught was a typical Corellian design—innovative, austere, and configured for vicious, close-in combat, with turbolaser turrets and missile tubes arrayed heavily and uniformly over a blue, egg-shaped hull. Han had known the moment he saw her that the ship was exactly what Corellia needed, a vessel capable of plunging into the core of the Alliance blockade and tearing it apart from the inside.

But Han's pulse had not quickened until a couple of hours later, when Antilles had informed them that the *Sal-Solo* had two sister ships and an entire support fleet hidden in the Kiris Cluster's *other* shipyards. Given the obvious element of surprise, Antilles felt sure the fleet would be powerful enough to smash the blockade and convince the Alliance to reconsider its war plans. What he had wanted to know from Han was whether he and Leia considered an early end to the war a strong enough possibility to serve in the Corellian military.

Han and Leia had spent the night agonizing over Antilles's question, worrying about whether Han would eventually find himself in battle against his own children. Jaina was now serving with the Jedi instead of the military, and Jacen was supposedly back on Coruscant torturing Corellians, but war had a way of bringing about the unforeseen. If Han ended up killing one of his own children, he would shatter into more pieces than there were stars in the galaxy.

The question posed a dilemma for Leia, as well. Four years ago, when her Master, Saba Sebatyne, had proclaimed her a Jedi Knight, she had sworn to obey the Jedi Council even when she disagreed with it, and the Council was supporting the Galactic Alliance. So far, Saba and the other Masters had been tolerating her insubordination out of respect for who she was. But that would certainly change if Han openly took arms against the Alliance. The

Council would have no choice except to demand that she choose between Han and the Jedi.

Still, the only other alternative was to stand by and watch the war blossom without them, and the Solos had *never* been the type to do nothing. In the end, they had decided the best course of action was to put Coruscant in a more reasonable frame of mind by helping Antilles prove that a war would be as costly for the Galactic Alliance as it was for Corellia. After the blockade was smashed, the new administration would be in a position to negotiate from strength, and Leia would secure the peace by volunteering to act as an envoy.

That was why Han had been so disappointed to be denied admittance to the planning salon. He and Leia had made up their minds to risk everything to help Antilles end this war quickly. Now it looked as though their help was no longer wanted.

The wait was shorter than Han had expected. He had barely started to consider a trip to the caf dispenser when Wedge Antilles arrived in his white admiral's uniform. His tapered face was creased with wrinkles and worry lines, and his neatly trimmed hair was now more gray than brown.

"Han, Leia—I'm sorry for the delay," Antilles said. As the door slid shut behind him, Han glimpsed the back of a civilian head nodding vigorously as someone else spoke in sharp tones. "Have you decided?"

"Yeah." Han began to feel a little more optimistic; perhaps Antilles was just having a difficult meeting with a couple of civilian bigwigs. "I was kind of thinking of signing on."

"Glad to hear it!" Antilles smiled and stuck out his hand, but there was more apprehension in his face than warmth. "We have an important job for you."

Han clasped the offered hand, but Leia continued to study Antilles with an expression of reserve. "We're looking forward to hearing about it," she said, "so we can make a final decision."

Antilles did his best to look disappointed, but made the mistake of quietly letting his breath out through his nose. It was an old sabacc tell, and one that Han knew always meant relief. Whatever was going on here, it was beginning to smell like a Hutt's belly.

"That's right," Han said. "Why don't you tell us what you have in mind?"

"Fair enough." Antilles drew them away from the door guard and lowered his voice. "We need you to negotiate a coalition."

"Negotiate?" Han scowled. "I thought you wanted me in the military."

"Maybe later." Antilles did not sound too serious. "Right now, this is more important."

"I must say, trusting Captain Solo to negotiate anything other than an asteroid belt seems foolish," C-3PO said. "His temperament is poorly suited to diplomacy."

"Han is a man of hidden talents." Antilles kept his gaze fixed on Han. "There's no one else I would trust with this mission."

Han pondered the compliment only a moment before deciding his friend was feeding him a load of bantha poodoo. "This is about Jacen, isn't it?"

Antilles frowned. "Jacen?" He shook his head. "Han, we *both* have kids fighting on the other side of this thing."

"Syal isn't torturing Corellians on Coruscant," Han countered. As angry and ashamed as he was about what Jacen had become, he wasn't going to hide from it. "Look, I don't like what Jacen is doing any more than you do, but he's still my kid, and I'm not going to disown him. I'll understand if you've got a problem with that."

"Han, I *don't*," Antilles replied. "Jacen has lost his way, but it's only because he believes in what he's fighting for. Sooner or later, he's going to remember that you and Leia taught him right from wrong, and he's going to find his way back."

Leia reached out and squeezed Antilles's hand. "Thank you, Wedge," she said. "I know that's true, but it feels good to hear someone else say it."

"Yeah, it makes you think maybe you're not crazy after all." Han turned away so he could blink a tear out of his eye, then looked back to Antilles. "So what do you *really* want me for?"

"I told you," Antilles said. "To negotiate a coalition."

As he spoke, the admiral's eyes shifted toward Leia, and Han realized the truth was he wanted *Leia* to negotiate the coalition.

Han shook his head. "For once, Threepio is right—you don't want to ask me to negotiate any kind of coalition. I might start a war or something."

Antilles gave a theatrical sigh. "Come on, Han." He briefly shifted his gaze to Leia again. "You understand what I'm asking."

"Then *ask*," Han said. "You know how I hate games."

"Very well." Antilles turned to Leia, and his eyes began to blink more rapidly—another old sabacc tell that usually meant your opponent was trying to pull a fast one. "You understand this can't be an official request—"

"Why not?" Han interrupted.

"Because *I'm* not Corellian," Leia said. "And I'm a Jedi Knight. It would look suspicious for me to conduct negotiations."

"So you want me to be the front man?" Han continued to look at Antilles.

Antilles nodded. "Exactly."

"Not interested," Han said, not even pretending to consider the request. He could not ask Leia to negotiate on behalf of a cause that even he knew she supported only partially, especially when Antilles himself so clearly had reservations about what he was asking. Besides, Han had a sneaking suspicion that his old friend was deliberately trying to discourage the Solos from accepting the assignment. "Call me when you need someone to do some fighting."

He turned to leave, but Leia caught him by the arm. "Han, shouldn't we hear Admiral Antilles out?"

"What for?"

"For Corellia." Leia fixed him with a stern-eyed gaze that worked better on him than any Jedi Force suggestion. "You're always talking about the importance of preserving Corellia's independent spirit. Is sitting at a negotiating table really so much to ask?"

Han's jaw dropped. Leia had renounced her role as a senior diplomat during the war with the Yuuzhan Vong, when it had grown apparent that the political process was only undermining the New Republic's ability to win the war. That she would volunteer to resume the role *now*— on Corellia's behalf—seemed very suspicious.

He scowled. "You *want* to do this?"

"I'm willing to consider it." Leia turned back to Antilles. "But we're not making a decision before we hear the details—*all* the details."

"No one expects that." Antilles smiled, but the note of disappointment in his voice was unmistakable—at least to someone who had known him for forty years. "My orders were simply to find out if you'd be willing to consider it. Prime Minister Gejjen will brief you on the rest."

Han's brow rose. Dur Gejjen had risen to power by helping Han and Boba Fett assassinate Han's megalomaniac cousin, Thrackan Sal-Solo. Afterward, Gejjen had abolished the office of President of Five Worlds, which Sal-Solo had created for the sole purpose of exerting his personal dominion over the entire Corellian system. Had Gejjen stopped there, Han would have admired his integrity and wisdom. But Gejjen had proved to be just as bad as Sal-Solo, establishing his own hold by arranging to have himself named both Chief of State of the planet Corellia *and* Five Worlds Prime Minister.

"Gejjen is here?" Han asked. "You have *got* to be kidding."

"I'm afraid not."

Antilles led the way into the planning salon, a spacious cabin lined with the latest battle-coordination technology: half-wall display screens, a ceiling-mounted tactical holoprojector, automatic caf dispensers in each corner. Dur Gejjen and two others sat talking at a large oval conference table with a combination data/comm station at every seat.

As soon as Han and Leia entered the room, Gejjen ended the conversation and extended his hand. "Captain Solo, welcome." He was young and good looking, with dark skin and black hair worn in a short military-style cut. "I'm so pleased you agreed to accept this assignment."

"Yeah, well, don't be too pleased," Han said. "I haven't accepted anything yet."

He gave Gejjen's hand a single pump, then looked past him to the others. They were older—the first a sandy-haired man with a blocky jaw and graying mustache, the second a middle-aged woman with a round face and cold gray eyes. Han wasn't familiar enough with the new government to recognize them by sight, but he was guessing by Antilles's displeasure and the number of security agents waiting outside that they were Gavele Lemora and Rorf Willems. Along with Gejjen, Lemora and Willems were the heart of the Five Worlds government, with Lemora serving as minister of intelligence and Willems as the minister of defense.

Gejjen frowned in Antilles's direction. "I thought you weren't to bring them in here unless—"

"Admiral Antilles's request was necessarily rather vague," Leia interrupted. "Han will need to know a few more details before he can agree to serve as your emissary."

"Ah—of course." Gejjen glanced over his shoulder at the cold-eyed woman—Lemora—and looked relieved. "We'll be happy to give him a basic briefing."

"*After* the droid leaves," Lemora added, staring at C-3PO.

"I can't leave!" C-3PO objected. "I won't be able to record the briefing."

"That's the point, chiphead," Willems said. He had a gravelly voice and a thuggish demeanor. "We don't *want* it recorded."

"Are you certain?" C-3PO inquired. "Captain Solo's memory circuits have been showing signs of fatigue lately. Just the other day, he told Princess Leia that with her new short haircut, she didn't look a day over thirty-five."

"I *meant* it," Han growled. "And stop eavesdropping."

"He doesn't have a choice, Han—it's in his programming," Leia said. She turned to C-3PO. "But I'm sure Han can still keep a few basic facts straight. You can wait outside."

C-3PO's chin dropped. "Very well. I'll be available if you need me."

After C-3PO left, Gejjen motioned Han and Leia to chairs. Antilles took a seat at the end of the table, a choice that suggested he really did not like being a part of this conversation.

"I assume you recognize ministers Lemora and Willems."

Han nodded. "Yeah—I was just wondering what could bring the entire High Cabinet all the way out *here*."

"We're on an inspection tour." Lemora did not even bother trying to sound plausible. "What matters to *you* is that a unique opportunity has presented itself."

Before Han could threaten to leave because he didn't like being lied to, Gejjen dropped the bombshell. "Queen Mother Tenel Ka has agreed to meet a Corellian delegation."

"Yeah, sure."

"You *can't* be serious!"

Han and Leia spoke at the same time, for the only thing that might have surprised them more—or caused more doubt—was to hear Gejjen claiming that their son Anakin had not really died fighting the Yuuzhan Vong. Tenel Ka was a vocal and very loyal supporter of the Galactic Alliance, and any suggestion that she might be willing to discuss changing sides was crazy.

"I assure you, we *are* serious," Gejjen said. "The High Cabinet did not come out here to play a practical joke on you."

"Then someone fed you a bad set of coordinates," Han replied. "There's no way Tenel Ka is going to support Corellia. She's already assigned two battle fleets to Alliance command."

Gejjen was not deterred. "And if that were to change,

the Galactic Alliance would be forced to reconsider its position regarding Corellia."

"The invitation is real," Lemora assured them. "The Queen Mother has half a day available on the twentieth. Can you reach Hapes by then?"

"Sure." Han glanced toward the end of the table and found Antilles gazing into the corner, apparently contemplating the wonders of automatic caf dispensers. "If there's any sense in going."

"I think what Han means to say is the offer sounds suspicious." Leia looked to Han as though for confirmation, but she was really signaling him to play along. "We both know Tenel Ka well enough to be certain that she'll never change sides."

"You see, that's why you're perfect for this job," Willems said. "If anyone has a chance of talking some sense into her, it's you two."

Han did not like the menacing note he heard in Willems's gravelly voice. "You'd better not be sending us there to threaten her," he said. "Because that would steam me about as much as it would Tenel Ka."

Gejjen waved a calming hand. "Nobody's making threats, Captain Solo. But we *do* have some intelligence that suggests her support of the Alliance is straining her relationship with her nobles."

"We assume that's why she's willing to talk," Lemora added. "Perhaps she's merely putting on a show to placate them or trying to buy some time, but we can't afford to ignore the opening."

"No, of course not," Leia said. "But Admiral Antilles said you were asking Han to negotiate a coalition. You do understand there's no chance of that happening, don't you?"

"If there is any hope, you're it," Gejjen replied. "But we

don't need a coalition—and neither does Queen Mother Tenel Ka."

"If Hapes were to make an open statement of neutrality and withdraw her fleet from Alliance command," Lemora said, "Corellia's position would be strengthened both militarily and politically. Other governments might be emboldened enough to support us openly."

"And Tenel Ka's nobles would no longer have grounds to challenge her decision—or her throne," Leia surmised. "Is the threat to her that severe?"

"We hear there are rumblings." Gejjen leaned forward and deliberately locked gazes with Leia. "It might not be an exaggeration to say that persuading the Queen Mother to assume a favorable stance toward Corellia would be as much a service to her as to us."

"I see." Leia studied Gejjen for a moment, then turned to Han. "The prime minister does have a point, dear. We might do Tenel Ka *and* Corellia a lot of good."

"Yeah, maybe." Han looked back to Antilles, who was continuing to study the caf dispenser as though it could help him divine the secret plans of the Galactic Alliance. "But something about this smells like Hutt breath."

"Fine—you don't like it, we'll find someone else." Willems pointed toward the exit. "Thanks for—"

"Minister Willems," Gejjen interrupted, "why don't we hear Captain Solo's concerns *first*?" He turned to Han with a lifted brow.

"All this would sound fine, if we were talking about it back on Corellia," Han said. "What I don't get is why Wedge had me come all the way out here, just so *you* three could come all the way out here to ask us to take the assignment."

To Han's surprise, Gejjen turned to Antilles. "Perhaps *you* should explain, Admiral."

"All right." Antilles finally looked away from the caf dispenser. "You were already on the way here when the prime minister received Tenel Ka's message. I had originally intended to ask you to take command of the Home Fleet and prepare to counterattack the blockade."

"Counterattack?" Han frowned. The Corellian Home Fleet was spread across the system's five habitable planets, either pinned in their berthings or playing moog-and-rancor with Alliance vessels carrying double their firepower. "Are you spacesick? We'd lose half the fleet just trying to rendezvous."

Antilles shook his head. "Not likely. We're almost ready to launch the real attack from here."

Han frowned, thinking, then demanded, "I was never going to see action?" He didn't know whether to be angry or hurt. "I was going to be a *decoy*?"

"Sorry, Han," Antilles said. "I had to do *something*."

"We've been getting intelligence intercepts indicating that Alliance High Command is worried about where Admiral Antilles is," Lemora explained. "I suggested we needed a diversion."

Leia rested a hand on Han's arm. "Think of it as a compliment, Han," she said. "There's no one else the Alliance would believe crazy enough to try something so risky."

"Thanks a lot." As Han said this, he was looking at Antilles. "It's always good to feel needed."

"As you obviously are," Gejjen said quickly. "Admiral Antilles is not happy about losing you to a diplomatic mission."

"And that's the reason *three* of you chased me all the way out here?" Han asked. "To bully Wedge into letting me go?"

"Not entirely," Lemora admitted. "The Queen Mother didn't give us long to select an envoy. If *you* won't go—"

"—*I* will," Willems finished.

"It hasn't come to that yet," Gejjen said. The look that passed between him and Lemora suggested they both hoped it wouldn't. "But with strict comm silence being maintained here, we'd have to wait for a messenger to return to Corellia with your decision. It just seemed safer to come out here and talk in person."

"And we really did want to inspect the Kiris fleet before we gave the go-ahead to launch the surprise attack," Lemora added. "Corellia's future is riding on it."

"That's understandable," Leia said. She turned to Han and shot him her best *do-it-for-me* pout. "Satisfied?"

"Sure." Han frowned and curled his lip at her—he *hated* it when Leia used her female powers on him. "Count me in."

Leia only smiled and patted his hand. "Me, too."

"Excellent." Gejjen looked relieved. He rose and stretched his arm across the table. "The Five Worlds are grateful."

As he and Han shook hands, Lemora removed a data card from her pocket and passed it to Leia. "I took the liberty of preparing a vidbriefing. You can look it over when you return to the *Falcon*."

"Our instructions are on it?" Leia asked.

"Of course," Gejjen said. He extended a hand toward the exit. "You'll need to get under way quickly if you're going to reach Hapes in time."

"I'll show you out." Antilles stood and led the Solos into the outer cabin. As soon as the door closed behind him, he clasped Han's shoulder. "Sorry, old buddy. I was looking forward to ordering you around."

"Why?" Han retorted. "You don't think I'd have obeyed, do you?"

Antilles laughed. "I suppose not." He turned to Leia

and said, "Thanks for helping. If we have any hope of getting the Alliance to back off before this war gets ugly, you're it."

"I'm glad to help—you know that." Leia studied Antilles for a moment, then her voice grew sober. "Wedge, what aren't they telling us?"

Antilles looked back toward the door and shook his head. "I don't know, Princess—and I don't like it any more than you do."

"Well, whatever it is, it's got to be better for us to talk to Tenel Ka than Willems," Han said. "That guy could drive *me* into the Alliance's arms."

"I think that's what Gejjen was counting on," Leia said. "He knew you'd have to say yes if you saw the alternative in person."

"It worked." Han turned to Antilles. "That and finding out *my* alternative was being your decoy."

"Glad I could help you make up your mind, then." Antilles smiled wearily, then shook hands with Han and kissed Leia on the cheek. "I should be getting back, or they're going to think I'm trying to talk you out of this. May the Force be with you."

"Thanks, Wedge," Leia said, turning toward the door. "We'll need it."

chapter two

Jaina Solo did not want to leave her dreambubble. She was with Jagged Fel deep in the heart-warmth of their nest, their heads still throbbing to the rhythm of the Little Dawn Rumble, their bodies filled with the sweet heat of Killik mating pheromones. All the galaxy's troubles seemed far away, and their battle in the skies of Tenupe had never happened. For once, they were together and at peace, with nothing to do but listen to the sweet sound of . . . *alarm bells*?

The bell was chiming inside Jaina's skull, shaking the dreambubble until it popped, calling her back from her Force-hibernation into the icy free fall of reality. She opened her eyes and found herself staring at the frost-rimed interior of a StealthX canopy, her teeth chattering so hard she thought they might shatter. She felt queasy and sore and muddleheaded, and even in the frigid conditions, the cockpit smelled stale and sour.

"Okay, Sneaker, I'm awake," Jaina said. "You can turn up the heater. And the air scrubbers."

The astromech, a replacement for Sneaky—whom she had lost when Jag and his squadron shot her down on

Tenupe—beeped an acknowledgment, and warm air began to pour into the StealthX's cockpit. Jaina expanded her Force-awareness. As her mind cleared, she felt her wingmate, Zekk, also awakening. He had resigned his commission in Rogue Squadron a couple of weeks earlier, when Jacen had attempted to court-martial Jaina for refusing to fire on a helpless blockade-runner. Now he and Jaina were part of a Jedi reconnaissance team spying on the secret Corellian shipyards in the Kiris Asteroid Cluster.

Though Jaina could feel Zekk's Force presence floating a dozen meters ahead and a little below her own position, it took several moments to locate the cross-shaped silhouette of his StealthX. Basically a configuration of the formidable XJ3 X-wing, the StealthX starfighter had a fiberplast body that was all irregular planes and angles, with a matte-black finish camouflaged with an eye-deceiving pattern of tiny blue points that rendered it almost invisible against a starry background. It also had a gravitic modulator, photon absorbers, thermal dissipators, and an entire suite of specialized signal negators that made it almost invisible to sensor sweeps. Even its fusial engines burned a special Tibanna isotope whose efflux turned dark a millisecond after fusion.

About a kilometer ahead of Zekk's StealthX tumbled the inky darkness of Kiris 17, which marked the "upper" limit of the Kiris Asteroid Cluster. The Corellian sun was just visible beneath the asteroid's belly, a yellow pinprick barely brighter than the surrounding stars. Next to the star was the slow-growing dash of an efflux trail.

"What do we have, Sneaker?" Jaina asked.

A message appeared on the now-defrosted display, informing Jaina that a light transport was departing the cluster.

Jaina frowned. "You pulled us out of hibernation for a single vessel?"

Sneaker displayed another message. CONTACT PROFILE IS UNIQUE. VESSEL IS OVERPOWERED CEC YT-1300, EXHIBITING SUDDEN CHANGE TO POSSIBLE *OUTBOUND* TRAJECTORY. EFFLUX SIGNATURE SUGGESTS MILITARY-GRADE EXHAUST NOZZLES.

"The *Falcon*?" Jaina was not all that surprised—of course Han and Leia Solo would be in the thick of things. She just hoped they did not return to the Kirises before Admiral Bwua'tu sprang his trap. So far, the Corellians did not seem to realize that the Galactic Alliance knew of their secret fleet, and when the Kiris fleet finally left base, the Corellians were going to be in for a nasty shock. "Are you *sure*?"

AFFIRMATIVE. TRAJECTORY IS NOW CONFIRMED OUTBOUND.

"I mean about the efflux signature," Jaina growled. "Is that the *Falcon* or not?"

UNCERTAIN. CURRENT DATA YIELDS AN IDENTITY COEFFICIENT OF ONLY 94%.

Jaina sighed. For the R9 unit to be "sure," he would have to be plugged into one of the *Falcon*'s data sockets, swapping data with the primary control brain.

"Keep watching and plot a list of likely . . ."

Zekk's StealthX suddenly started after the *Falcon*, and Jaina let the sentence trail off.

A LIST OF LIKELY DESTINATIONS? Sneaker inquired.

"Right."

Jaina shoved her own throttles forward and shot after Zekk, at the same time reaching out to him in the Force. Though their telepathic Joiner bond had finally dissolved a couple of years before, she and Zekk remained so acutely attuned to each other that they could often communicate through the Jedi battle-meld more clearly than most people conversed, and she quickly understood his intentions.

Equal parts spy and assault craft, StealthX starfighters were equipped with eavesdropping equipment so sensitive it could intercept stray signals from a vessel's internal computers. If Zekk could close the distance before the *Falcon* jumped to hyperspace, he might be able to capture enough data from the Solos' nav computer to determine their destination.

What Zekk did not intend to do, he assured Jaina, was vape her parents. She answered with a cynical concern for *him*. If there was any shooting, he was the one who would need worrying about—not her parents. This elicited a warm feeling of satisfaction from Zekk—a *sincere* feeling of satisfaction.

The meld nearly shattered beneath the harshness of Jaina's frustration. She wished Zekk would just give it up. He would never be more than her best friend. Why couldn't he just accept that and go find a nice Falleen girl to fall for?

Even without mind sharing, the message was clear enough. Zekk withdrew into himself, maintaining barely enough contact to keep the meld open, and they closed the rest of the distance in cold isolation. Jaina hated hurting him like that. He was the best wingmate she'd ever had, but he just did not seem to get it. She didn't want to be in love, not with him, not with Jagged Fel, not with anyone. She was the Sword of the Jedi, whatever *that* meant; she probably wasn't even *supposed* to be in love.

Kiris 17 slid past above, drawing a momentary curtain of darkness over Jaina's canopy; then there was nothing between the StealthXs and their target except a hundred kilometers of empty space. The *Falcon* was really moving. Jaina's throttles were pushed to the overload stops, and still the old transport yielded her lead only grudgingly.

The inky mass of Kiris 3 tumbled past beneath the

chase, its dark surface and frigid heat signature betraying no sign of the shipyard concealed within. The *Falcon*'s efflux trail slowly changed from a tail to a solid bar. Jaina activated her eavesdropping array, then instructed Sneaker to inform her when he began to pick up signals. But several more seconds passed, and Jaina began to think she and Zekk would not catch up before the *Falcon* escaped the Kiris Cluster's weak gravity and entered hyperspace.

Finally, the outline of the *Falcon*'s sensor dish grew visible above the brilliant glow of her ion drives, and Sneaker reported that the eavesdropping array was picking up stray signals. Jaina and Zekk strengthened their contact and swung out to opposite sides of the target—then felt a wave of astonishment roll through the meld as Leia discerned its presence.

Jaina pulled out immediately and, astonished by her mother's Force sensitivity, tried to make her presence very small. Her eavesdropping array lit up as it began to capture and record electronic pulses from inside the *Falcon*. An instant later she sensed Leia searching for her and tried to draw in on herself even further, but there was no hiding from one's own mother—not when that mother was Leia Solo, anyway. Jaina felt a brief moment of warmth, followed by an overwhelming sense of relief and—oddly— reassurance.

Then the battered old transport shot away, her ion tail thinning into nothingness as she vanished into hyperspace.

The meld filled with a sense of puzzlement as Zekk reached out for an explanation, but Jaina understood no better than he did. Her mother had obviously sensed their presence, which meant she now knew the Jedi were keeping a watch on the Kirises—and that they had probably captured the *Falcon*'s destination.

Zekk wondered if Leia had been relieved because she

thought he and Jaina would not report the contact. The Solos were, after all, high-value targets, and what kind of daughter would sic a hunter-killer squadron on her own parents?

Sneaker beeped for Jaina's attention, then scrolled a message across the display announcing that he had analyzed the intercepted data and used his superior computing power to develop a list of the *Falcon*'s most likely destinations.

"So stop bragging and show me," Jaina ordered.

DROIDS DON'T BRAG, Sneaker replied. THEY INFORM.

A list of planet names began to scroll down the display: ARABANTH, CHARUBAH, DREENA, GALLINORE—

"Those are all in the Hapes Consortium!" Jaina cried.

Sneaker confirmed that they were, then apologized for not pinpointing the destination more exactly. The Transitory Mists that enveloped the Consortium made hyperspace lanes such a tangle that once a vessel entered Hapan territory, evaluating what course it would follow was statistically impossible.

"That's okay," Jaina replied. "You're close enough."

Zekk's surprise flooded the meld, and Jaina knew that his R9 had just reported the same thing to him. His surprise changed to urgency. Whatever the *Falcon*'s reasons for traveling to the Hapes Consortium, it could not mean anything good for the Alliance. Someone had to leave the observation post to report the intercept—and the possibility that the Corellians might soon know that the Galactic Alliance was watching their secret shipyards.

And Jaina knew who that had to be. Expecting Zekk to omit the *Falcon*'s name from his report was out of the question. Sometimes he was just too much of a steady blade for his own good—or, in this case, for her *parents'* good.

chapter three

It was the moment Mara had been dreaming of—and dreading—for years, the first time father and son entered the Jedi Temple Sparring Arena with live blades. But she had never imagined it would be like this, with Luke so determined to *teach* rather than train, with Ben so resentful and frightened. It made her fear for them both, made her wish that she could be down on the arena floor instead of up here in a hot control booth packed with glide-levers, toggle switches, and actuating buttons.

The far door of the arena opened and Luke entered. Walking to the center of the floor, he glanced up at the control booth and flashed Mara a reassuring smile, then stood waiting for Ben. The Sparring Arena was basically a bowl-shaped chamber filled with balance beams, various kinds of swings, and repulsor-floated wobble balls. Interior conditions such as temperature and lighting could be changed from the control booth, and an automatic safety field caught anybody who started to fall out of control.

The near door opened, and Ben entered, his blue eyes sweeping the vault, examining everything in the chamber but his opponent. In contrast to the simple gray robe in which Luke was dressed, Ben wore a sparring suit made of a lighter, more flexible version of the vonduun-crab-shell armor that had proven so difficult to penetrate in the Jedi's first encounters with the Yuuzhan Vong.

Despite his obvious apprehension, Ben marched straight to the center of the vault, and Mara was struck by how mature her thirteen-year-old son had become. He was wearing his red hair in a helmet-friendly crew cut with a single braid of longer hair, and his face was losing its roundness. But the biggest change was in his raised chin and square shoulders, in his resolute stride and proud expression.

He bowed formally, then said, "Apprentice Skywalker reporting for sparring instruction as ordered, Master."

Luke raised his eyebrows at Ben's use of the title *apprentice,* but did not correct him. "Very good." He studied Ben's sparring armor for a moment, then motioned at the breastplate. "Take it off."

Ben's brow rose, but he undid the side closures. The breast- and back plates fell away in his hands, and he placed them on the floor beside him.

Next, Luke motioned at the arm and leg guards. "All of it."

Ben lost enough of his composure to let his feelings show, and Mara began to sense through the Force how nervous their son really was to be formally summoned to a private sparring match with his father—and how disturbing he found it to be ordered to remove his armor. But she could also feel his courage. Despite his confusion, Ben was determined to present himself well, to set aside his anxiety and prove himself worthy of the trust that was being placed in him.

And *that* made Mara remember why her nephew was

good for Ben. It had been Jacen who had drawn her son out of his shell and helped him embrace the Force, who had taught him to face his fears and look beyond himself. Jacen was teaching Ben responsibility, giving him a sense of himself as someone other than the son of Luke Skywalker, Grand Master of the Jedi order.

Ben removed his last shin guard and placed it on the floor beside him. Then, as he straightened up again, Mara experienced a profound sense of certainty. It was as powerful as a Force-vision, except that its source was standing ten meters below her, in the form of her own son. The Force had drawn him to Jacen for a reason, and if she and Luke dared interfere, it would be at Ben's peril.

Luke snapped the lightsaber off his utility belt and looked up toward the control booth.

"Start with basic obstacles," Luke ordered. "Then work up to a class-five environment."

"Full hazard?" Mara asked in astonishment. Even Masters found class-five environments trying. "Are you sure?"

"I'm sure," Luke answered in his best *are-you-really-questioning-the-Grand-Master* voice. He looked back to Ben. "How else can I test what Jacen has been teaching him?"

"Don't worry, Mom." Ben met his father's gaze evenly, but the crack in his voice betrayed his apprehension. "I can handle it."

Not likely, Mara thought. But Luke would be in there, too, and he wasn't going to let anything terrible happen to their son—at least nothing physical.

"If you say so." Mara had to let Ben make his own mistakes and learn his own lessons . . . Luke, too. Wasn't that what the Force was telling her? "We'll start with variable gravity, and I'll add something every ninety seconds. Ready?"

Ben's face paled, but he snapped the lightsaber off his belt. "Ready."

Mara reached for the gravity-control glide-switch. They had to trust Ben to find his own way, to learn from his own experiences. If they didn't, he would become resentful and angry and withdrawn, and all he would ever be in life was the *son* of the great Luke Skywalker.

That's what the Force was telling her—wasn't it?

Luke felt his knees tense as Mara pushed the gravity to two g's. He could sense through the Force that she doubted he was doing the right thing, that she believed he should just talk with Ben and help him see how Jacen was slipping toward darkness. But Luke had tried talking, had been patient, and their son was still going on raids with the Galactic Alliance Guard. Ben had even killed a man in self-defense—and the fact that he had been in so much danger only made it more disturbing.

Luke did not want his son to grow up believing that such things were common necessities for Jedi. The time had come to show Ben that there was another way, a better way for someone strong in the Force to use his power.

"All right, son," Luke said. "Let's see how well Jacen has been training you."

Ben brought the hilt of his lightsaber into the salute position, but did not ignite the blade. "You know I don't want to do this, right?"

"It's hard to miss." Luke remained where he was, holding his own weapon at his side. With round eyes and pudgy cheeks, Ben still looked like a little boy to him, like a child playing Jedi apprentice. "Why not?"

Ben shrugged and refused to meet Luke's eyes. "I just don't."

"Are you afraid I'll hurt you?"

"Yeah, right." Ben's voice was sarcastic. "The greatest sword handler in the galaxy accidentally cuts up his own son. Like *that's* going to happen."

Luke had to force himself to keep a serious expression. "Then you're afraid you'll hurt *me*. Is that it?"

"Maybe." Ben nodded uncomfortably. "By accident."

Luke waited for Ben's gaze to return, then said, "You won't. Have some faith, okay?"

Ben's cheeks reddened. "I do," he said. "But I'm still afraid. Something feels wrong about this."

"Something *is* wrong about this," Luke said. "You shouldn't be going on hunts with Jacen, you shouldn't be a member of GAG, and you sure shouldn't be busting down doors and killing people. You're too young."

Ben's face hardened—not with the resentment Luke had expected, but with resolve. "I save lives every time I go on a mission. Isn't that what Jedi are supposed to do?"

"Ben, you're *not* a Jedi," Luke said. "You're not even a true apprentice. You haven't completed any of the academy tests."

"I've been kind of busy catching terrorists." Ben's tone was pointed without being angry. "Besides, Jacen says I'm stronger in the Force than any of the academy's apprentices."

"That's not for Jacen to judge." Luke was relieved to discover how hard Ben was to anger—it made him hope that maybe Mara was right, that maybe Jacen wasn't leading their son down such a dark path after all. "If you want to continue helping Jacen and GAG, you'll have to prove to *me* that you're ready."

"I'm not quitting GAG," Ben insisted. "Jacen needs me. The *Alliance* needs me."

"Then show me you're ready."

Luke brought his lightsaber to guard, but did not activate it.

"If I have to." Ben ignited his own blade, then frowned when Luke did not do the same. "Aren't you going to turn on your lightsaber?"

"When I need to," Luke said. "When you *make* me."

A gleam of understanding came to Ben's eye, and he stepped forward with a high slash. The double gravity slowed the attack, and Luke had plenty of time to contemplate the hesitation he saw in his son's eyes. Ben was not comfortable sparring. He hadn't done it often enough to trust himself not to hurt his partner—or his partner not to hurt him. Luke evaded the attack by dropping into a squat, then thrust his foot out to sweep Ben's leading leg out from beneath him.

Ben slammed to the floor, then cleared the area by whipping his blade in a circle around his body. The boy might not be much at sparring, but he *did* know how to fight. Had Luke not already launched himself into a backward spring, the attack would have taken his legs off at the knees. He landed just beyond reach and allowed Ben's blade to sweep past, then stepped forward again and deadened the brachial nerve bundle by kicking Ben under the arm, hard.

Ben's hand opened, and the blade of his lightsaber fizzled out as the hilt went spinning across the vault. Luke somersaulted three meters up to land atop a balance beam.

"You'll have to do better than that, son," he said. Though his tone was light, inside he was cringing at how hard Ben had thumped the floor. The safety field would not allow anyone to hit hard enough to suffer any real harm, but no good father enjoyed bruising his own child— even if it *would* make that child wiser and stronger. "You won't force me to ignite my blade by swinging short."

Ben's face reddened more from embarrassment than ir- ritation. Then he sprang to his feet and tried to reach toward his lightsaber. When his sword arm failed to rise—the nerves would still be numb from Luke's kick— he extended his other hand and summoned the weapon back to it.

He activated the blade and took a few test swings to make sure his one-handed grip was dry and firm, then looked up at the balance beam where Luke was standing. "I don't understand why you're doing this."

"Yes, you do," Luke said. "I need to know you can de- fend yourself."

"Then why am *I* doing all the attacking?" Ben de- manded. "That's not going to tell you anything."

"It'll tell me plenty." Luke pointed at a wobble ball floating nearby, then used the Force to send it hurling at Ben. "There are many kinds of danger."

Ben ducked the projectile and Force-sprang into the air. Luke hurled another wobble ball, and this time Ben had to block, bringing his lightsaber around to slice the ball in two. He landed on the far end of the balance beam . . . and that was when Mara turned on the wind.

The sudden blast was nearly enough to knock Luke from the beam, but Ben merely leaned into the wind and started cautiously forward.

Luke frowned up at the control booth, wondering whether Mara had used the Force to give Ben a little warning.

The thought had barely crossed his mind before he

sensed her touch, assuring him she had not—but urging him not to be too hard on their son.

Yet Luke *had* to be. He had to know what lessons Jacen was teaching Ben. He rooted himself to the beam through the Force, then glanced up at another wobble ball and brought it flying down at his son from behind.

Ben's eyes widened as he sensed danger through the Force, and he flattened himself atop the beam. In the next moment he used a Force shove to accelerate the heavy wobble ball into Luke's chest and send him tumbling toward the floor.

On the way down, Luke caught the support cable of a nearby swing and hooked a leg over the seat—then saw Ben descending toward him in a series of somersaults, his lightsaber weaving a wild snarl of light. This time Luke sensed no hesitation. Ben intended to make him activate his lightsaber—even at the risk of cutting something off.

Luke released the swing and dropped toward the floor, barely bringing his legs around in time to land on his feet—sinking so deep into a crouch that his knees hit his chest.

Ben used the Force to adjust his own trajectory, descending headfirst with his lightsaber held out in front of him. Luke rolled into a backward somersault, an eerie tingle erupting over his entire body as the safety field reacted to Ben's uncontrolled plunge.

But the safety field did not prevent Ben's lightsaber from puncturing the floor. A loud electrical pop echoed through the arena, and suddenly the air was filled with the acrid stench of melted circuitry. A terrible thump sounded, and when Luke completed his somersault he found his son lying in a heap, facing the opposite direction and groaning.

The roaring wind died, and Mara's voice came over the loudspeaker. "Ben!"

Luke rushed up behind Ben. "Ben! Say something."

When there was no answer, Luke started to kneel . . . then heard the familiar *snap-hiss* of an igniting lightsaber.

Ben whirled into a shoulder roll, and Luke sprang up, launching himself into a full Force flip to buy some distance. When he came down five meters away, Ben was still kneeling where he had landed, staring at Luke in astonished frustration.

Luke smiled. "Nice move."

Ben pursed his lips skeptically. "Still didn't make you ignite your lightsaber."

"Almost, though," Luke said. "Did Jacen teach you that?"

Ben rolled his eyes. "Come on, Dad. Playing dead is pretty basic stuff."

Luke raised his brow. "Nearly got *me*."

"Just using your fatherly love against you." Ben shut down his lightsaber and rose to his feet. "I'm not sure that's fair."

"Me, either." Luke chuckled, then pointed to the hole in the floor. "And that's not good, either. You probably put a gap in the safety field."

Ben studied the hole for a moment, then looked back to Luke. "You can't blame *me* for that," he said. "You're the one who didn't block."

"I will next time, I promise." Luke assumed a fighting stance and motioned him forward. "Come on."

Ben's face sagged with discouragement. "What for? We already know I can't touch you—and I'm not learning anything."

"You're sure of that?" Luke started to slip slowly forward. "Ben, I'm not doing this to be mean. If your sparring is any example, it's clear that you need to devote more time to your Jedi studies and less to helping GAG."

"Sparring isn't fighting," Ben said. "When my life is on the line, I can take care of myself."

"Against most people, yes." Luke reached striking distance and stopped advancing. "But do you remember the woman I told you about? Lumiya?"

Ben's eyes widened. "The crazy Sith woman?"

"That one," Luke confirmed. "I still don't know when she returned or why, but I *have* learned a little about her—and I've been meditating on it. I'm convinced that if she can, she'll strike at me through you."

"Me?" For the first time, Ben began to look frightened—and Luke began to hope he might actually get through to his son. "How?"

Luke could only shake his head. "I wish I knew. But you need to be ready—and that means you need to be properly trained."

"I *am* being trained."

"Not by a Master, and not well." Luke paused, trying to choose his next words carefully, to make Ben do what thirteen-year-old boys never did: think about the future. Finally, he said, "You're right about one thing, Ben. Jacen and the Alliance do need you. You're helping them save lives, and that's a good thing."

Ben eyed him warily. "Dad, it'd be really nice if you just stopped there."

"Sorry, I can't," Luke said. "What you're not seeing is that the Jedi need you, too. We need you to prepare yourself now, because Jacen and the Alliance and the rest of the galaxy are going to need you *tomorrow* even more than they need you today. Ben, you need to take a Master."

"I have a Master," Ben retorted. "Jacen is training me—and he'll protect me from Lumiya, too."

Luke shook his head. "Jacen can't protect you all the time, and he's *not* training you. I've sparred Rontos who are better."

Despite the affront—*Rontos* were eight- to ten-year-old academy students—Ben remained surprisingly calm. "I'm not sure I believe that. I'm pretty sure I'm better than any kid who's still working with a training prod."

"Then prove it," Luke said. "You don't even have to make me ignite my lightsaber. Just make me move my feet."

Ben scowled, obviously suspicious. "Dad, come on. We both know—"

"Do it!" Luke ordered. "If Jacen is training you so well, prove it. Just make me move *one* foot."

Ben furrowed his brow but slipped into a fighting stance and began to circle behind Luke.

Luke closed his eyes and concentrated on the drone of the lightsaber, all the time tracking Ben's presence through the Force, waiting for the telltale flicker of resolve that would mean his son was attacking. It did not come until Ben was directly behind him, where Luke would be forced to pivot to see the attack.

But Luke didn't need to see. He merely listened until the drone of the lightsaber began to change pitch, then raised his free hand and made a grasping motion, grabbing the hilt of Ben's weapon through the Force and holding it motionless two meters away.

Ben grunted in surprise, but he was both resourceful and quick. Luke heard the lightsaber deactivate as the hilt was released, then felt his son flying toward the center of his back. He dropped his own lightsaber and turned his weapon hand toward the floor, rooting himself to the

Force. Ben struck an instant later, kicking out with both feet in an attempt to send Luke flying.

Luke did not budge, and Ben hit the floor with another loud thump.

"Rodder!"

Luke remained motionless, but he opened his eyes and summoned Ben's lightsaber into his grasp. "Does that mean you give up?"

"Not . . . yet."

Luke sensed another flicker of excitement in the Force, then glanced over his shoulder to see Ben summoning the lightsaber Luke had dropped just a moment earlier.

When it arrived, Ben hefted its weight a couple of times, then scowled and opened the base.

Nothing came out.

Ben turned to Luke in astonishment. "You *couldn't* activate the blade!" he complained. "There's no power cell!"

"No, there isn't." Luke turned to face his son full-on. "A Jedi's greatest weapon is his mind."

Ben's face grew red. "So I've heard." He rose and handed Luke's lightsaber to him. "Thanks for rubbing my nose in it."

Luke returned Ben's weapon to him. "That's not what I was doing."

"I *know* what you were doing, Dad. You had to test me." Ben returned the lightsaber to his utility belt, then added, "But I'm not going dark. Anger has no control over me—and neither does fear."

Luke nodded. "I can see that, Ben. I still want you to take a proper Master."

"Then make *Jacen* a Master," Ben replied. "He knows more about the Force than anybody."

"That's not going to happen, Ben," Luke said.

Ben considered this a moment, then spoke in a resigned voice. "I guess that's your decision, Dad. You're the Grand Master." He started to gather up his sparring armor. "I've got to get going—we've got a raid at twenty hundred."

"Ben, I wish you—"

"I *have* to, Dad. They're counting on me." Ben stood and started toward the door, then suddenly stopped and faced Luke. "But I *could* use some more sparring, if you've got the time."

"Sure." Luke was as surprised by the peace offering as he was delighted. "I'd like that, a lot."

"Me, too." Ben turned away, then called over his shoulder, "But you'd better bring a power cell. Next time, I won't go so easy on you."

Mara entered the Sparring Arena to find Luke kneeling in the center of the floor, staring at the hole Ben had made, but not really examining it. She could sense that he was more worried than ever, though whether it was about Ben's training or something else, she could not tell.

"Does it really bother you that much?" she asked.

Luke furrowed his brow. "What?"

"Ben passing your test," she said. "Whatever he's learning from Jacen, it's *not* turning him to the dark side. I didn't feel any anger in him."

"Neither did I." Luke's gaze grew distant and thoughtful. "He was almost *too* calm."

Mara let out her breath in exasperation. "When could Jacen have prepared him?" she demanded. Luke had intentionally summoned Ben at a time when Jacen would be tied up in a meeting with Cal Omas and Admiral Niathal. "And you'd better not be telling me you wouldn't sense an act in your own son."

"No, he wasn't acting." Luke stood and led the way

toward the exit. "But I'd still like to see Ben apprenticed properly. His training is suffering."

"That's true," Mara said. While Ben's self-defense skills might be adequate, his sparring *had* shown a lack of confidence in his control. "But has it occurred to you that Ben might be right? Maybe you *should* make Jacen a Master."

Luke stopped at the door and scowled at her as though she were a fool or a traitor—or both.

"Come on, Skywalker," Mara said. "You can't dispute Jacen's Force knowledge. And being a Master might pull him back into the Jedi order. It might give you *some* control over him—at the least, you'd have a formal means to oversee how he's training Ben."

The disapproval vanished from Luke's face. "There's something to what you're saying, but I just can't do it. Jacen isn't ready to be a Master . . . and I don't think he ever will be. The sooner we get Ben away from him, the better."

He started through the door toward the changing rooms, but Mara caught him by the arm.

"Actually, Luke, I'm not so sure of that." She told him about the profound sense of certainty she had experienced earlier, about how convinced she was that the Force had drawn Ben to Jacen for a reason. "Whatever is going on with Jacen, we need to be careful about interfering. I think his destiny and Ben's are linked."

Luke's face grew clouded, and Mara could sense that while he did not doubt what she was telling him, he was having a hard time accepting it. Jacen was walking very close to the dark side—even Mara had to admit that—and yet here she was, telling him that their thirteen-year-old son had to walk that line with him.

"I know it's a lot to ask," she said. "But everything

I feel is telling me that we have to let Ben learn from his own experiences—even if those experiences involve Jacen. If we don't, Ben is going to grow resentful and withdraw again—from us *and* the Force."

Finally, Luke nodded, but his expression remained clouded. "Okay, as long as he keeps sparring with me."

"That shouldn't be a problem. It was *his* idea." Mara continued to hold Luke in the door. "But I get the feeling there's something you're not telling me."

Luke frowned. "I'm not sure how it relates."

"But you think it might?"

He nodded. "My dream has been getting worse."

"I see," Mara said. For some time now, Luke had been having dreams about a faceless, cloaked figure that he believed to be Lumiya. "Define *worse*."

"She's sitting on a throne," Luke said. "Sitting on a throne and laughing in a man's voice."

Mara swallowed. She couldn't dismiss what Luke saw in the Force any more than she could deny the certainty of what she had felt just a few moments earlier. "Did you see—" Her throat closed with dryness, and she had to try again. "Was Ben—"

"No," Luke said. "Nobody else was there. Just her—him, *it,* whoever—looking down and laughing."

"But it has *something* to do with Ben?" Mara pressed. "That's why you wanted to test him today?"

"It's why I wanted to test him, but I don't know how much the dream has to do with him," Luke said. "I'm beginning to feel that it's bigger than Ben and Jacen."

"Well, that's a relief—sort of," Mara said. "I don't like that throne, though. It smacks of empire."

"It certainly does," Luke said, nodding. "So I think it's time to break out my shoto."

Mara raised her brow. The shoto was a special half-length lightsaber that Luke had built after nearly losing his life the first time he encountered Lumiya's lightwhip. The shorter blade allowed him to fight in the Jar'Kai style—with a weapon in each hand—which counteracted the advantage of the lightwhip's dual-natured strands of energy and matter.

"So you're going after her?" Mara asked.

Luke nodded. "I think it's time to find Lumiya and get to the bottom of this."

"Then I'd better build a shoto, too," Mara said. "Because you're not going after her alone."

chapter four

After a long mission Force-hibernating in the cold, cramped cockpit of a StealthX, what Jaina *wanted* was a hot sanisteam and a nerf steak as large as her plate. What she *got*, as she passed the fastidious officers on the command deck of the *Admiral Ackbar*, were sudden glances and—sometimes—wrinkled noses. She was still wearing the same black flight suit in which she had spent the last week, and the climate-controlled warmth of the Star Destroyer was doing nothing to mask the fact.

Jaina stopped at the edge of the Tactical Salon and waited for Admiral Bwua'tu to free himself. After a decade of off-and-on service in Rogue and various other X-wing squadrons, it was hard to avoid saluting or reporting her arrival in a clear, sharp voice. But she was no longer in the military—she had been discharged for refusing to obey Jacen's order to fire on a fleeing blockade-runner—and Jedi Knights seldom needed to announce themselves.

The tactical holodisplay in the center of the salon suggested that the Corellian situation had not changed during her week at the observation post. Fleets enforcing the Alliance Exclusionary Zone still surrounded Centerpoint

Station and all five of Corell's habitable planets, and the Kiris Asteroid Cluster continued to glow in faint, cautionary yellow. The location of Bwua'tu's ambush fleet—lying in wait three light-years from the edge of the system—was indicated by a simple blue arrow and a distance marker. Were the situation to remain static for another year, the two sides might actually have time to work out their differences.

But the galaxy was not going to be that lucky. There were too many schemes under way, too many factors on a collision course—and Jaina was about to bring another big complication into play. When High Command learned that the Corellians were in contact with Hapes—one of the Alliance's most supportive member states—spies would be tasked to investigate and diplomats sent to make inquiries. Forces would be mobilized and assets moved into position, and the war would grow that much harder to stop.

Jaina did not even want to consider what might happen if High Command heard that her parents were involved. There would be a lot of unjustified concern, perhaps even panic. Scouts would be dispatched to locate them, and a task force assigned to capture—perhaps even destroy— the *Millennium Falcon*. That possibility had run through her mind over and over during the long journey back from the Kirises, reinforcing the notion that her report might not need to include certain things.

Jaina looked from the holodisplay to a niche high on the salon's back wall, where a larmalstone bust of the great Admiral Ackbar kept watch over his namesake. She knew enough about the political instincts of Bothans to realize Bwua'tu was only displaying the statue to curry favor with the Alliance's new Mon Calamari Supreme Commander, Cha Niathal. But the effigy struck her as deeply ironic. Ackbar had been a firm believer in the benevolent power of a united galaxy, and no one could be more disturbed to see the Galactic Alliance going to war against one of its own member states than he would have been.

The trouble was, Jaina just did not see how Omas could have avoided it. Thrackan Sal-Solo and his cohorts *had* been trying to bring Centerpoint Station back online, and they *had* been building a secret invasion fleet in the Kiris Asteroid Cluster. Clearly, Corellia had been preparing to attack *someone*—and the inability to discover the intended target did not excuse the Alliance from its duty to intervene.

Jaina sensed Bwua'tu approaching and turned her attention in the admiral's direction. With small burning eyes and graying chin fur, the Bothan cut a feral and surprisingly dignified figure in his white uniform.

"A reminder," Bwua'tu said in his gritty voice.

Jaina frowned in bafflement. "Sir?"

Bwua'tu pointed a finger at the bust of Admiral Ackbar. "The statue," he said. "It has nothing to do with Admiral Niathal, as you were thinking. It's there to keep me humble."

Jaina was too surprised to ask Bwua'tu exactly how he knew what she had been thinking. Perhaps that was what *everyone* thought when they saw the statue—or perhaps he was just that good at reading faces.

"Humble?" she asked. "How is that, sir?"

The fur rose along the back of Bwua'tu's neck. "Jedi can't possibly be *that* poorly informed. I was the laughingstock of the entire space navy over the incident in the Murgo Choke."

"Not the *entire* space navy, sir," Jaina said. During the recent peacekeeping operations in the Unknown Regions, the *Ackbar* had been captured by a swarm of Killik commandos—smuggled aboard in busts of Admiral Bwua'tu himself. "I'm pretty sure Admiral Pellaeon didn't find it at all funny."

Bwua'tu's ears came forward; then he seemed to recognize the humor in Jaina's tone and snorted in approval. "No, he didn't," Bwua'tu said. "As a matter of fact, I'm surprised the old battlecat let me keep my command."

"The Killiks certainly wished he hadn't," Jaina said.

Bwua'tu studied her with narrowed eyes, no doubt wondering whether there remained enough Joiner in Jaina to wish that the Killiks had prevailed in their war against the Chiss.

"What I'm trying to say is that your performance after the *Ackbar*'s capture was brilliant," Jaina clarified. "Nobody else could have stopped those nest ships in the Murgo Choke."

Bwua'tu's expression grew pleased. "Probably not. No one else would have moved so quickly to exploit the enemy's uncertainty, especially in the face of such overwhelming . . ." The admiral stopped and glanced up at Ackbar's bust, then flattened his ears in embarrassment. "Well, I *was* taking a substantial risk. But that can't be the reason you need to see me. What's this about a transport leaving the system?"

Jaina swallowed, then stepped close enough to speak in a hushed voice. "It was bound for the Hapes Consortium, sir."

"The Consortium." The fur on Bwua'tu's brow pulled forward. "You're sure?"

She nodded. "Very sure. The accuracy of the intercepts is beyond doubt."

"Well, how . . . *alarming.*" Bwua'tu avoided asking any specifics about the intercept method. StealthX eavesdropping technology was highly classified, and there were too many ears without the proper clearance to discuss the matter in the TacSal. "The Hapes Consortium is a big gob of space. Were you able to determine which planet?"

Jaina shook her head. "I'm afraid not. The Transitory Mists make Hapan hyperspace lanes too tangled to tell, but Hapes is definitely the direction that the vessel was headed."

"I see." Bwua'tu fell silent for a moment, his gaze growing distant and thoughtful. "So, the Corellians are hoping to draw the Hapans into the war on their side."

"That's very hard to believe, Admiral," Jaina said. It *was* the obvious conclusion, but given who was involved, it just didn't make sense. "We might want to consider alternative explanations."

"I already *have,* Jedi Solo." Bwua'tu studied Jaina carefully, his eyes slowly growing beady and suspicious. "*This* one is a near certainty. Naval Intelligence reports that both Nal Hutta and Bothawui have refused to ally—at least openly—against the Galactic Alliance, and Corellia knows she can't defeat us alone."

"They may be desperate, Admiral, but they're not fools." Jaina had grown up in a household where Heads of State and Supreme Commanders were everyday guests, but there was something penetrating in Bwua'tu's gaze that made her feel exposed and uneasy. "The Galactic Alliance has Tenel Ka's full support, and the Corellians know it. She's sent us two full battle fleets."

Bwua'tu's look of suspicion changed to one of disappointment. "I didn't say they were going to meet the *Queen Mother,* Jedi Solo."

Jaina frowned, digesting his remark for a moment, then asked, "You think Corellia intends to overthrow Tenel Ka?"

"I think Corellia intends to *help*," Bwua'tu corrected. "The Queen Mother's support of the Alliance is unpopular among her nobles, so I'm sure they have their pick of potential usurpers."

"No." Jaina's stomach knotted with outrage—with the refusal to believe her *parents* could betray such a good friend. "That just doesn't make sense."

Bwua'tu studied her with a cocked head for a moment, then asked, "Exactly *what* doesn't make sense, Jedi Solo? There's something you're not telling me."

"What makes you say that, sir?" Jaina knew as soon as she had spoken that it was the wrong question to ask. Bothans were renowned throughout the galaxy as masters of treachery—and that meant seeing through lies as well as telling them. "I mean, I have good reason to believe that's not what the Corellians are intending."

Bwua'tu looked at her expectantly.

"I'm only sorry that I'm not at liberty to reveal it," she said. "It's, um, a secret of the order."

"I see." Bwua'tu tugged at his graying fur, then turned away and motioned for Jaina to follow. "Come with me, young woman."

Jaina gulped and did as she was ordered.

Bwua'tu led her into his private office at the rear of the Tactical Salon. Like everything else aboard his Star Destroyer, the cabin was austere and tidy, with another bust of Admiral Ackbar sitting on one corner of his desk. There were half a dozen sturdy plastoid chairs in front of the desk and a pair of gray couches in one corner, but Bwua'tu did not invite Jaina to sit on any of the furniture. Instead, he opaqued the transparisteel wall that separated the cabin from the salon, then turned to face her.

"The transport was the *Millennium Falcon*." The admiral stated this as fact, not question. "Jedi aren't technically under my command, so I won't bother ordering you to answer me. But you should know that this is what I assume."

Jaina's heart fell. Her parents were about to have a pair of very big targets drawn on their backs. "The exact identity of the vessel didn't seem relevant at the time."

Bwua'tu's voice grew sharp. "Obviously, it was. You don't believe Han and Leia Solo would betray your friend."

"I *know* they wouldn't," Jaina insisted.

"You would have a better idea of that than I, of course." Bwua'tu's reaction was surprising in its mildness. "But the fact remains that they're on their way to the Hapes Consortium, and this is a very crucial moment for Corellia. We must at least *consider* the possibility."

He laid a furry hand on Jaina's shoulder, then continued in a voice as gentle as it was raspy. "I want you to take a moment and think this over very carefully. I'll believe whatever you tell me . . . but please remember that the lives of your parents are only two of the many billions that may depend on your accuracy."

"I'm aware of that, Admiral," Jaina said. "But thank you for the reminder."

As much as Jaina wanted to leap to her parents' defense again, she forced herself to do as Bwua'tu asked. The truth was, Jaina had no idea how her mother and father might be reacting to the change in Jacen. At one time, her mother had vowed never to have children because one of them might grow up to become another Darth Vader. With the holonews reporting that Jacen had imprisoned hundreds of thousands of Corellians, her parents might well have decided that Leia's old fears were justified.

But Jaina had not felt any hint of guilt when her mother touched her through the Force earlier—and had the Solos been planning to betray Tenel Ka, she believed she would have. Besides, her parents had always been loyal to their friends—especially friends who were loyal to *them*—and she could not see that changing now.

Finally, Jaina sighed and shook her head. "I know it looks bad, but I just don't think they would do something like that."

Bwua'tu stared into her eyes. "You are sure?"

"It's what I believe, Admiral. That's the best I can do." Jaina looked away. "Given what a monster my brother is becoming, I don't think I can be *sure* of what anyone is capable of."

Bwua'tu's lip curled at the mention of her brother. "Yes, your brother is driving dissenters into the enemy camp even faster than he is killing them."

Jaina raised her brow in surprise.

The admiral winced visibly, then waved the comment off with a flip of his hand. "Waste no time fretting over my loyalty," he said. "I swore a vow of *krevi* the day I became a fleet admiral. Even when Bothawui finally enters the war, I'll continue to serve the Galactic Alliance."

"When Bothawui enters the war?" Jaina asked. "Not if?"

"When," Bwua'tu confirmed. "My people prefer treachery to war, but we *do* occasionally let outrage dictate our actions."

Jaina frowned. "What are you talking about?"

A gleam of understanding came to Bwua'tu's eyes. "I'm sorry—you wouldn't have heard. Your brother has started assassinating Bothans."

"Assassinating Bothans?" Jaina gasped. "Jacen isn't that stupid."

"No, but he *does* protect his assets," Bwua'tu said. "The World Brain is near death because of a recent attack, and it is Jacen's best means of tracking Corellian terrorists through the undercity."

Jaina frowned. She was hardly surprised to learn that her brother was employing the World Brain as a spy, but she *was* shocked to hear Bwua'tu talking as though they had discussed the matter personally. "I can't imagine Jacen sharing that information with the military."

"He didn't," Bwua'tu said.

"So your sources are . . . ?"

"Accurate," Bwua'tu replied. "That's all you need to know."

"Okay," Jaina said slowly. "And these sources think the *Bothans* are the ones who attacked the World Brain? The True Victory Party?"

"No." Bwua'tu hesitated, then said, "According to my sources, the True Victory Party can't even find it. But Jacen believes that Reh'mwa ordered the attack, and so my species is becoming an endangered one on Coruscant."

Jaina's stomach grew hollow and queasy. This was one more force pushing the galaxy closer to war, and—as usual—her brother was in the middle of it.

"I don't see how your informants can know what Jacen believes," Jaina said, still probing for the source of his intelligence. "I have the Force and I'm his twin sister, and even *I* couldn't tell you what he believes."

"*You* aren't a Bothan, Jedi Solo."

Jaina raised her brow. "So your sources are inside the True Victory Party?"

Bwua'tu looked away for a moment, obviously debating how much to tell her.

"You asked *me* for an honest answer." Jaina sent him a little Force-nudge. "And I gave it to you."

Bwua'tu nodded. "Very well. We both have divided loyalties here, so we'll just have to trust each other." He waited for an affirming nod from Jaina, then continued, "For some time now, the Bothan government has been asking me to resign my commission and return home. The intelligence regarding the assassinations is their latest attempt to persuade me."

"They have a source inside GAG?" Jaina gasped.

"I don't know the nature of their intelligence," Bwua'tu replied carefully. "Only that it has proven accurate so far."

"That doesn't mean you should believe their denial," Jaina said. "I mean, the Bothan government has a vested interest in convincing you that the attack on the World Brain wasn't Bothan."

"True, but there is other evidence," Bwua'tu replied. "Had True Victory been behind the attack, it would not have failed."

Jaina chose to ignore his species conceit for the moment and treat the statement as fact. "Okay. If Bothans weren't responsible, who was?"

"My guess is Corellian terrorists. If the World Brain has been helping Jacen track them, then they're the ones who have the most to gain by killing it." Bwua'tu retreated toward his desk, then clasped his hands behind his back and stared at the galactic vidmap hanging on his wall. "But that's hardly our concern at the moment. Whatever your parents are doing in Hapan space, their trip has *something* to do with a coup attempt. Perhaps they are only going to warn Tenel Ka about the consequences of supporting the Alliance."

"You mean, to threaten her?"

"A threat is a warning," Bwua'tu replied. "At the moment, that is what we must assume. It's really Corellia's only hope."

"Which means the Corellians aren't going to send the Kiris fleet against our blockade," Jaina said, guessing Bwua'tu already realized this. "They'll use it to support the Hapan coup."

"Exactly," Bwua'tu replied. "My fleet is badly out of position."

"So you'll reposition?"

"I'll certainly suggest it to Admiral Niathal," Bwua'tu said. "But she's a very domineering fish. She's laid a trap for the Corellians, and she won't abandon it easily."

"So?" Jaina asked. "You're going to move anyway, right?"

"And disregard my *krevi*?" Bwua'tu sneered at her as though she had suggested cheating at dejarik. "Who do you think I am—your father?"

"S-sorry," Jaina said, taken aback by his harsh tone. "I didn't mean anything by it—but there's something else you should know. When the *Falcon* departed, my mother sensed my presence. She must know the Jedi are watching the Kirises."

"I see." Bwua'tu grew thoughtful. "Do you think she would tell your father?"

"We have to assume that," Jaina said.

"And we must also assume *he'll* tell the Corellians that we know about their secret fleet." Bwua'tu's expression grew pensive. "And yet, we can't be certain. This does add an interesting twist to the problem."

"That's an understatement," Jaina said. "But now you'll *have* to move the fleet."

Bwua'tu frowned at her. "Haven't you been listening? Admiral Niathal's mind is made up."

"But when she hears—"

"She isn't going to change her plans because of a few

feelings between a mother and daughter," Bwua'tu said. "She'll dismiss it as soft intelligence."

"Then what are you going to do?"

"I don't know yet." Bwua'tu wrinkled his muzzle and returned his gaze to the galactic vidmap on his wall. His voice assumed an absentminded tone. "How interesting."

When he did not elaborate, Jaina went to his side and stared up at the vidmap. It was a standard galactic projection, with the luminous white cloud of the Deep Core near the center of the upper frame and the Unknown Regions not shown at all. Corellia was a small dot on the opposite side of the Deep Core from Coruscant, forming a large triangle of space with Bothawui and Nal Hutta.

"It looks more frightening to me than interesting," Jaina said. "If you're right about Bothawui joining Corellia, it won't be long before Nal Hutta follows. The rebels will control a quarter of the galaxy."

"Not that." Bwua'tu pointed a finger at Duro, which was located just beyond Corellia on the Corellian Trade Spine. "It appears that Chief Omas's fears were rather well justified."

Jaina scowled, still not understanding. "I'm happy to hear that, but—"

"The mines." Bwua'tu tapped a control key below the display, and the map zoomed in until it showed only the Corellian system. He pointed at a tiny yellow blip near the outer edge of the system. "In a few weeks, the Kirises will be in a direct line between Duro and the Corellian star. With all that electromagnetic blast in the background, it would be impossible for the Duros to detect the launch of the Kiris fleet."

Jaina's jaw dropped. "Sal-Solo was going to attack Duro?"

"The timing is certainly right," Bwua'tu said. "And Duro still has large deposits of baradium and cortosis."

Jaina did not know whether to be sickened or relieved. As the primary component of explosives ranging from thermal detonators to proton bombs, baradium had become the commodity of choice among the galaxy's ever-growing number of arms smugglers. And woven cortosis fibers could be used to short-circuit lightsaber blades.

"Well, at least Chief Omas and Uncle Luke can stop double-guessing themselves about the blockade," Jaina said. "The last thing the galaxy needs is someone dumping a million tons of baradium into the black market."

"Or to start selling lightsaber-proof armor," Bwua'tu added. "But that's not our concern at that moment. Someone needs to warn the Queen Mother about the situation—and we can't trust this to a holocomm. Even if the signal isn't intercepted, we can't be sure the message will reach Tenel Ka without passing through the wrong hands first. The Consortium is a real flooger-bed of intrigue."

"I can reach out to her through the Force," Jaina said. "That will give her *some* warning."

"A *specific* warning?"

Jaina shook her head. "She'll know there is danger, but not from where."

"Then someone needs to see her in person," Bwua'tu said.

"So you're sending me?" Jaina asked.

"I'm *asking* you," Bwua'tu corrected. "You're a Jedi, remember?"

"Of course," Jaina said. "I mean, I'll be happy to go."

"Good." Bwua'tu checked his chrono, then said, "And I think you should pick up Zekk on the way. This isn't the sort of thing we should take chances with. I'll ask Lowbacca and Tesar to go out early and take over the observation post."

"Very good." Jaina would need to carry some extra fuel for Zekk's StealthX, but it was doable—and it would give her a chance to figure out what the blazes her parents were doing. "Thank you."

"No, thank *you*," Bwua'tu said. "I'll send a message up the chain of command, too, but this will be faster—and maybe you can find a way to keep your family name out of this mess. I doubt anyone back on Coruscant would want HoloNet News accusing Han and Leia Solo of running across the galaxy arranging coups."

chapter five

The Queen Mother's Special Salon was equipped with every modern convenience, from flavor-optimizing beverage dispensers to auto-massaging furniture to participatory holo-drama booths. So Han did not understand why the only chronometer in the room was an ancient pendulum clock, the kind with a long, weighted arm that swung side-to-side and emitted a loud *tock* every second. By his estimate, he had heard that *tock* more than twenty-five thousand times already, and each one seemed louder than the last.

"One more *tock*, and I'm going to smash that thing," Han growled.

"I don't think the Queen Mother would take that very well, Captain Solo," C-3PO said. Not for the first time, Han wondered why they hadn't left him behind on the *Falcon* with Cakhmaim and Meewalh. "It's pre-Lorellian, probably looted from a Balmorran colony ship by the very pirates who abducted Tenel Ka's ancestor."

"So it's about time Tenel Ka got another." Han eyed the salon's rare byrlewood paneling and gilded ogee molding, searching for the spycam that just *had* to be there. "By the

looks of this place, she oughta be able to afford something a little quieter."

"Han!" Leia, who had been sitting on the floor meditating, opened her eyes. "That clock is worth more than
the *Falcon*. A lot more."

"Yeah, and it's noisier, too."

Han stood, then grabbed a priceless larmal-topped end
table and started across the room.

Leia jumped up to block his way. "Han, what are you
doing?"

"I can't take it anymore." He gave Leia a quick half
wink, then started around her. "That *tock*ing is driving
me nuts."

"So I see." Leia caught him by the arm. "But the crazy
act won't get us an audience any sooner. We're not under
surveillance."

"Of course we are. This is Hapes, remember?"

"It's *Tenel Ka*'s Hapes." Leia turned him around to face
her. "And she respects us too much to spy on us."

Han rolled his eyes. "Yeah, right."

"She knows we'd notice the surveillance, so why risk
insulting us when she won't learn anything? This way, she
can let us know that no matter what our differences, she
still considers us friends."

"Let me see if I've got this straight." Han continued to
hold the table up by his shoulder. "She keeps us cooling
our heels seven hours to make sure we know we're still
friends?"

"Exactly," Leia said. "It's the same reason flight control
had us land the *Falcon* in the Royal Hangar. She's trying
to let us know politely that she won't be able to see us."

Han's stomach sank. "Tell me this isn't one of those
diplomatic code things."

Leia gave him an apologetic smile. "Afraid so. You

know how Coruscant would react if she gave us an audience. Omas and Niathal would think she was considering the possibility of recalling her fleets—possibly even helping Corellia."

"Then how come she told Gejjen to send us?"

"To placate her nobles, I'm sure," Leia said. "She needed to buy some time to maneuver, and now we've served our purpose."

"So she used us," Han said. "I *hate* that."

"It wasn't personal, Han." Leia took the end table from his hands and used the Force to float it back to its place. "We'll just have to wait. Eventually, she'll find a way to see us without the spies knowing."

"*Eventually?*" Han went to the intercom panel next to the door. "She can do better than that."

"Han, you can't keep—"

"Sure I can."

Han pressed the call button, and a moment later the peevish face of one of Tenel Ka's male social secretaries appeared on the vidscreen.

"Captain Solo," he said, obviously exasperated. "Is there something I can do for you?"

"Yeah," Han said. "You can tell Tenel Ka I'm tired of waiting."

The man's expression grew weary. "As I've already explained, the Queen Mother is unavailable. She asked me to assure you that as soon as she can break free—"

"*Break* free?" Han cried. "We were supposed to have half a day with her. We've already been here twice that—"

"Excuse me, Captain," the secretary said. "Were you under the impression that the Queen Mother was *expecting* you?"

"Of *course* I'm under that impression. We had an appointment!" Han was ready to crawl through the intercom and choke the man. "If you think we came all the way from Corellia just to drop in—"

"Are you saying we're *not* expected?" Leia interrupted, coming to stand next to Han.

"Indeed I am," the secretary replied. "The Queen Mother canceled the conference when Prime Minister Gejjen insisted it had to be held on the same day as the Queen's Pageant."

Han scowled. "The Queen's Pageant?"

"To pick the most handsome man in the Consortium," C-3PO explained. "After the Queen Mother's Birthday and the Marauders' Masquerade, it's the largest ball of the year."

"Precisely." The secretary nodded. "*Of course* the Queen Mother is unavailable today."

"You don't say." Han was starting to have a bad feeling about their assignment. "And it's *always* on the twentieth?"

"On the last day of the third week," C-3PO corrected. "The tradition is more than four thousand years old. It seems that the first Queen Mother threw the original pageant as a parody on the slave auctions once held—"

"Enough, Threepio," Han said. "We don't need the history of the whole cluster."

"Your droid is correct about the ancient history of the tradition," the secretary said from the intercom. "I explained all this to Prime Minister Gejjen myself."

"To Gejjen personally?" Leia asked. "Not to his assistants?"

"There's no use acting surprised," the secretary sniffed. "He understood me very well."

A cloud came over Leia's face. "I'm sure he did. Please accept our apologies. The mistake is clearly ours."

"Obviously," the secretary replied. "Please be patient. The Queen Mother will see you at her convenience."

The vid display went blank.

"How rude!" C-3PO said. "He didn't even wish us a good evening."

"He wouldn't have meant it." Han deactivated their end of the intercom and turned to Leia. "Do you get the feeling this is a setup?"

"Absolutely," Leia said. "But I don't understand what Gejjen expects to gain by embarrassing us."

"There's no logic to it that *I* can see," C-3PO said. "Captain Solo can be quite embarrassing enough on his own."

Han was too busy trying to figure Gejjen's angle to retort. Gejjen had to know that sending them to negotiate on a celebration day would only irritate Tenel Ka and make her even *more* unlikely to cooperate with Corellia . . . and that could only mean that Gejjen did not care whether he irritated Tenel Ka.

Han began to feel worried. With the Bothans and Hutts both refusing open alliance, Corellia was growing more desperate by the day—and desperate governments took dangerous gambles. Maybe Gejjen did not care about irritating Tenel Ka because he expected to be dealing with someone else in the near future . . . in the *very* near future.

Han turned to Leia. "What if it's not *us* Gejjen is setting up?"

Leia's eyes grew narrow. "You think he's using us to draw Tenel Ka out?"

"Or positioning us to take the blame," Han said. "If Tenel Ka gets killed, whoever's getting ready to take her place will want to point the finger at someone pretty kriffing quick. Otherwise, an investigation might uncover *them*."

Leia thought for a moment, then shook her head. "Possible, but Tenel Ka is bound to have a first-class security team, and—as a former Jedi Knight—she's formidable in her own right. Whoever's behind this, they're smart enough to realize they'll need a professional—and a good one."

"Sure, but I don't see where *we* fit in," Han said.

"I don't either—yet." Leia thought for a moment, then asked, "Why was it important for us to arrive on the day of the Queen's Pageant?"

"Oh!" C-3PO raised his hand. "I think I know!"

Han turned to the droid. "So spit it out."

C-3PO's photoreceptors flickered. "Droids are unable to salivate, Captain Solo. But the palace will be filled with handsome young men today, most of them unknown to the staff. It would be the ideal time to slip an assassin onto the premises."

"Which means security will be even tighter than normal," Han pointed out.

"Which is why *we're* important," Leia said. "Gejjen knows Tenel Ka will find time to see us—and that will interrupt the security routine."

"So we're bait," Han grumbled. "That really burns my jets."

Han turned to the intercom and started to reach for the call button, but Leia caught his arm with the Force.

"Han, we can't," she said.

Han frowned in confusion. "Sure we can," he said. "I love Corellia, but Tenel Ka is practically a daughter. If you think I'm going to let Gejjen assassinate—"

"Han, *that's* not what I think," Leia said. "But if their plan depends on a change in routine, they must have someone close to Tenel Ka to alert them to that change."

"Right." Han dropped his hand and tried to hide how foolish he felt for not realizing the same thing. "I knew that."

"Of course you did." Leia smiled and gave his arm a re-assuring pat. "And you also know that their informant would just intercept your warning and let the assassins know that we're on to them."

"Oh, yeah," Han said. "I knew *that*, too."

Leia nodded. "I thought so."

She took a deep breath and closed her eyes, obviously preparing to reach out to Tenel Ka in the Force.

It was Han's turn to grab *Leia's* arm. "Can't do that either, sweetheart."

Leia opened her eyes again. "We can't?"

"What about their backup plan?" Han said. "You *know* they have one—and the minute their informant sees Tenel Ka acting weird, they'll activate it."

Leia sighed. "And we'd blow any chance Tenel Ka has of trapping them."

"Right," Han said.

"So what *are* we going to do?"

Han stepped closer and opened Leia's robe.

Leia raised her brow. "Han, I don't think we have time right now."

Han gave her a roguish grin. "Don't worry—this won't take long." He opened one of the pouches on her utility belt and removed an automated lock slicer. "And then we can go find Tenel Ka. That should throw a hydrospanner into their plans."

Han went to the hand-carved double doors through which the social secretary had disappeared after dumping them in the salon, then knelt on the floor and slipped the unit's input/output card into the crack between the doors.

C-3PO clunked over to stand behind him. "Captain Solo, may I ask what you're doing?"

"No."

The lock slicer emitted a short beep, announcing that it had made contact with the security system.

Before Han could activate it, Leia reached over his shoulder and covered the instrument panel. "Han, we need to be—"

"We can't afford to wait around," Han said. "Tenel Ka's a good kid. She isn't going to keep us sitting—"

"I was going to say *quiet*," Leia interrupted. "There are two sentries on the other side of these doors."

"Oh, dear," C-3PO said. "It looks as though Captain Solo is going to embarrass us again."

"It's okay, Threepio." Leia pulled Han away from the door and took the lock slicer from his hands. "In fact, we need you to return to the *Falcon*."

C-3PO cocked his head. "Return to the *Falcon*? Whatever for?"

"Just do it, chiphead," Han said.

An indignant *harummph* sounded from the droid's vocabulator, but he turned and left through the other door, which opened into the Royal Hangar. Leia returned the slicer to her utility belt and began knocking loudly. It took several moments before an electronic buzz sounded and one of the doors opened partway.

"I'm sorry, Princess Leia," a Hapan voice said, "but the royal guard isn't allowed to converse with guests. If you require assistance—"

"Actually, I don't."

Leia used the Force to jerk the sentry through the door, at the same time sticking a leg out to catch him across the ankles. He landed at Han's feet in a huge purple-cloaked heap reeking of musky Hapan cologne.

Han leapt onto the sentry's back and smashed the man's helmet into the stone floor to disorient him. The Hapan was extremely large for a human, nearly the size of a

Barabel and just about as tough. Despite repeated hammering, the fellow managed to rise to his hands and knees.

Realizing he was in trouble, Han hooked his legs around the sentry's waist and planted his feet on the man's knees, then *pushed*. The fellow dropped to his belly again. Han got in a quick face-slam that actually stunned the Hapan long enough to pull off his helmet.

The sentry started to rise again, one hand reaching back to grab Han's leg. Han delivered a powerful hammer-fist to the base of the jaw. The big Hapan went limp for a second—then his fingers dug into Han's thigh so hard that Han had to cry out.

He struck with the hammer-fist again, and the sentry finally dropped to the floor in an unmoving heap.

By this time Leia was hauling the other guard—also unconscious—into the room. Though the fellow was just as large as the one Han had handled, his hands and feet were already bound, and Leia was using only one hand to drag him. Han would have liked to believe she was using the Force, but he knew better. After four years of Saba-style Jedi training, she was just that strong.

"Everything okay?" Leia asked. "Do you need help?"

"I'm . . . fine," Han panted. "How about a little warning next time?"

"Why?" Leia pursed her lips in mock disapproval. "You getting old or something?"

"No." Han tore a strip off the sentry's cloak and began to tie the man's wrists. "Just not used to following your lead, that's all."

Leia smiled. "How can you say that, dear?" She dumped her sentry on the floor next to his, then bent down, took the man's security card, and kissed Han's cheek. "Breaking into Tenel Ka's palace was *your* idea."

chapter six

Located in the heart of the Senate District between the Jedi Temple and the Galactic Justice Center, Fellowship Plaza was usually abandoned after dark. But tonight, Alema was hardly alone. Jacen and Ben stood just a few meters away, talking in the shadows beside a neatly trimmed row of blartrees.

And she was not the only one eavesdropping on them. First she had spotted Lumiya, standing in a tall privacy hedge on the opposite side of the walkway, so quiet and motionless it was impossible to be certain she was still there. Then there was the dark blur that had come creeping through the fog after Ben arrived. It was about twenty meters away, crouching behind the hedge on Alema's side of the walkway, pointing what appeared to be a small parabolic dish through the blartrees toward where Ben and Jacen stood talking. Whoever it was, the shadow had to be a Jedi—and a fairly adept one, at that. Like Lumiya and Alema herself, he—or she—had drawn in on himself until he no longer seemed to have a Force presence at all.

". . . have the sparring sessions been going?" Jacen asked. "Is he still trying to make you lose your temper?"

Alema thought she saw Ben shaking his head. The two cousins were taking care to stand out of the light, and in such foggy conditions even dark-sensitive Twi'lek eyes could see little more than silhouettes.

"No," Ben said. "I think he's really trying to teach me something."

"You couldn't ask for a better instructor," Jacen said. "But be careful. Your father is just looking for an excuse to send you back to the academy."

Ben remained silent for a moment, then asked, "Is he going to find one?"

"That's up to you," Jacen replied evenly. "Do you think the techniques I've been teaching you are dark?"

"It depends on how I use them," Ben replied.

"Exactly." Jacen's voice grew warm, and he clasped Ben's shoulder. "But the older your father grows, the more conservative he becomes. He's afraid he hasn't done a good job preparing the modern generation of Jedi—that they aren't strong enough to employ all aspects of the Force."

"What do you think?" Ben asked.

"I think he's done a better job than he realizes. Many Jedi Knights *aren't* strong enough to use the whole Force, but some are." Jacen laid both hands on Ben's shoulders. "*You* are."

Ben poured pride into the Force. "You're sure?"

"What do you think?" Jacen demanded. "You're just asking because you want me to say it again."

"I guess so." Ben's tone was chagrined. "You wouldn't be teaching me to use my emotions if you didn't think I was strong enough."

Alema's heart swelled with an awe that was almost religious. Unless she misunderstood what she was hearing— and that did not seem possible—Luke Skywalker was losing his only son to the thing he feared most: the dark side. And his own nephew was going to be the instrument of that loss.

"That's right," Jacen said to Ben. "I'd never teach you something you're not ready to use. Now I need you to tell Captain Shevu that I won't be able to join him on tonight's raids. You'll have to handle the Jedi duties alone."

"Can do," Ben said. "But Captain Girdun is starting to worry about not having enough Jedi to run two teams. Maybe you should consider asking the Council for some help."

Jacen tipped his head at a cynical angle. "And how do *you* think that request would be received?"

"Yeah, I know—Dad runs the Council." Ben's tone was more conspiratorial than apologetic. "But Captain Girdun wanted me to suggest it."

"I see." Jacen considered this for a moment, then said, "You'd better tell Girdun that I'm considering the idea. We don't want our subordinates worrying about our relationship with the Jedi Council, do we?"

"Probably not," Ben agreed. "Should we hold the interrogations for you?"

Jacen shook his head. "Girdun may have to start without me," he said. "I'm meeting someone else, then I have some business with Admiral Niathal."

"The GAG Star Destroyer?"

"Maybe." Jacen pointed up the walkway toward the Galactic Justice Center. "Go on to headquarters. I'll tell you about it at home."

"You better."

Ben turned and started up the walkway, passing first Lumiya's hiding place, then Alema's. Once he was past, Alema turned her attention to the back side of the hedge and found the eavesdropper creeping toward her, still holding the parabolic antenna in one hand.

As the shadow drew nearer, its silhouette sharpened into that of a Jedi in a standard hooded robe, then into the form of a tall *woman* with the pale face and heavy brow of a Chev. A couple of steps more, and Alema realized that this was not just any Jedi following Ben. It was Tresina Lobi, one of the Masters who had served on Cal Omas's Special Council during the war with the Yuuzhan Vong.

Alema dropped her hand to her lightsaber, at the same time willing Lobi not to make the mistake of letting that parabolic antenna swing past her hiding place. At this range, the antenna was sensitive enough to pick up sounds as faint as heartbeats, and the last thing Alema wanted was to have her presence detected.

She needn't have worried. Lobi was still two meters away when Lumiya's sharp voice sounded from the other side of the hedge. "Jacen, I'm impressed."

Alema risked looking away from Lobi and saw Lumiya stepping onto the foggy walkway, her long robes seeming to flow out of the hedge as though they were nothing but shadow.

"You have him very well under control."

"It's not a matter of control." There was just a hint of hostility in Jacen's voice. "Ben is my cousin. I care about him very much."

Lumiya studied Jacen from behind her veil, then said, "Caring is fine—as long as you don't let it stand in your way."

"There's a difference between letting something stand in your way and destroying it needlessly," Jacen countered. "I'm beginning to think maybe I *should* send him back to his father."

Lumiya's voice grew as alarmed as it did disapproving. "Why would you do a foolish thing like that?"

"To complete his training," Jacen said. "I'm having trouble finding the time to do it myself, and that leaves him vulnerable. You saw how he tried to manipulate me into feeding his ego."

"I did, and that kind of weakness *will* make him a servant to his emotions," Lumiya said. "It will also make him *your* servant, if you use it wisely."

"That's not what I want for my cousin," Jacen said, sounding slightly disgusted.

"What you want doesn't matter!" Lumiya retorted. "What you *need* does—and you need an apprentice."

"I need an *assistant,*" Jacen countered. "And there are several Jedi Knights who would serve me better and require less time from me—Tahiri Veila, for example."

"Tahiri is not a descendant of Anakin Skywalker," Lumiya replied. "She does not have Ben's potential, and she will not serve you as well in the long run."

Jacen remained silent for a long time, then finally asked, "Don't you mean serve *you*?"

"It's the same thing," Lumiya replied quickly. "We serve one cause—though I am having doubts about *you,* Jacen. You seem more committed to your friends and family than you do to our mission."

"If that means protecting them from needless harm, then yes, I am," Jacen said. "We're supposed to be doing this for the good of the galaxy—and the galaxy *includes* my friends and family."

"Of course it does, Jacen. I don't mean to imply that it doesn't." Though Lumiya's words were conciliatory, her voice remained stern and demanding. "But the galaxy is bigger than your family. You must be willing to sacrifice what you care about to a greater purpose."

"I've already proved that I'm willing to do that," Jacen said coldly. "I'm proving it every day."

"Indeed you are." Lumiya's voice softened, and she took Jacen's elbow in her hand. "All I'm saying is that we need to keep Ben near; I don't know how yet, but I have a sense that he will prove the key to our success."

Jacen considered this for a moment, then let out his breath and nodded. "Okay—for now. But the minute I begin to suspect that you're only using him to get even with Uncle Luke—"

"You won't, because I'm not," Lumiya said. "Everything I do, I do to bring peace and justice to the galaxy."

Alema's admiration for the woman was growing by the moment; Jacen Solo wasn't easy to deceive, and she was using Jacen's own idealism to destroy him *and* his family. Delightful.

Lumiya glanced up and down the walkway, no doubt reaching out in the Force to make certain no one had wandered into the area while they were talking, then asked, "Why did you want to see me *here*?"

"Because I didn't have time to go to your apartment," Jacen said.

Alema glanced back to the other side of the hedge. Lobi had dropped into a crouch and was running a feed line from the antenna to a recording rod on her belt. Now Alema began to feel less awestruck by the Balance than betrayed by it. Since her failed attack on Jacen, she had spent her time spying on him and Lumiya, and it had slowly dawned on her that just as Luke was losing Ben to what he feared most, Jacen was *becoming* what Leia hated most: a Sith Lord.

But if Lobi revealed that to Luke *now,* Jacen's training would never be completed. Luke would hunt Lumiya down and kill her, Leia would redeem her son through her love, and the Solos would live happily ever after.

And where was the Balance in *that*?

Jacen recaptured Alema's attention with an angry rebuttal to something she had missed.

"I don't have time to be *that* careful tonight. Niathal is about to give me my own Star Destroyer." His voice grew calmer, yet also more cold and demanding. "I was supposed to meet her five minutes ago, but I need you to take care of something for me. Now."

"What is it?" Lumiya asked. Her tone made clear that she wasn't agreeing to anything. "And you might try asking in a civil manner."

Alema kept her gaze fixed on Lobi, who was continuing to record every word.

After a moment, Jacen spoke in a calmer tone. "Sorry. I lost a friend today."

"I see." Lumiya's voice held just a hint of disapproval at Jacen's sadness. "That must be why the Ferals are rioting."

"Yes. The World Brain died this afternoon." Jacen's voice actually cracked. "But the Ferals aren't exactly rioting—they just don't have any impulse control without the World Brain to guide them."

"And you want me to provide some?"

"No, Coruscant Security can handle that," he said. "I need you to finish that list I gave you."

"The Bothans?" Lumiya asked. "Jacen, you can't let your personal feelings—"

"I'm *not*," Jacen interrupted. "The Corellians finally figured out how GAG has been tracking them. They're planning to send their whole network after the World Brain."

"But not if they realize it's dead already," Lumiya surmised.

"Right," Jacen said. "And I *need* them to attack. It will bring the terrorists out in the open."

"And GAG will be waiting?" Lumiya asked.

"GAG will be *watching*," Jacen corrected. "Coruscant Security will handle the actual ambush. Our agents will concentrate on the terrorists who escape. Some are bound to panic, and with any luck we'll be able to follow them back to their ringleaders."

"So, many Bothans must die to bait your trap," Lumiya said.

"No one would understand the necessity better than Bothans," Jacen said.

As Jacen said this, Lobi was pulling her comlink from her utility belt. Alema watched with increasing despair as the Chev carefully set the parabolic antenna on the ground and donned her headset and throat mike. This could not be in the interests of the Balance—not when Alema still owed Leia so much.

After a moment's pause, Lumiya said, "You know that finishing this list will force Bothawui to declare war. Their *ambassador* is on it."

"Do him first," Jacen said. "Bothawui is going to declare war anyway. Niathal says they're already outfitting three cruiser fleets for Corellian crews."

"Fine," Lumiya said. "The ambassador first . . . if you're sure."

"Don't I *sound* sure?" Jacen snapped. A pair of military boots began to clack down the walkway as he departed. "Just do it. I can't keep the admiral waiting any longer."

Tresina Lobi reached for her throat mike and started to depress the SEND key in rhythmic sequence, using a click code to begin a silent broadcast to whoever was on the other end. Alema could see her finger movements just well enough to make out some of the message.

". . . Skywalker he was . . . Lumiya IS following Ben—"

That was as far as Lobi made it before Alema understood the reason the Force had brought the Chev so close to her hiding place.

". . . is more . . ."

Alema jerked her lightsaber off her belt. She was a Jedi—and Jedi served the Balance.

". . . Lumiya is—"

Alema sprang from her hiding place, activating her blade as she flew through the air. Lobi was already rolling, her hand flying from her throat as she reached for her own weapon.

Alema stretched her jump into a Force leap and brought her mangled half foot down between Lobi's shoulder blades . . . then felt a crushing pain as the Chev continued to roll, smashing the back of an elbow into Alema's knee and knocking her legs out from beneath her.

Alema landed flat atop a chrysanthus shrub, surprised and hurting. Lobi had never been a flashy fighter, but she was powerful and effective—and clearly deserving of her rank. Alema whipped her lightsaber around to protect herself, half expecting to feel the death slash before it reached middle guard.

But the Chev had been disoriented by the unexpected assault and decided to buy some reaction time by leaping into a high Force flip. Alema arched her back and sprang to her feet—then nearly fell when her aching knee buckled. Instead of leaping into another attack, she extended her hand and used the Force to pluck the headset off Lobi's head.

The Chev landed an instant later, her eyes wide with rage and disbelief, but she wasted no time acknowledging

Alema's identity. She merely ignited her own lightsaber and raced forward to attack.

Alema barely had time to slash the headset apart before the Chev was on her, driving her back toward the hedge with a combination of high slashes and powerful front thrust kicks. The first kick that landed drove the air from Alema's lungs. The second doubled her over, making her an easy target—until she used the Force to accelerate herself off Lobi's foot and deep into the hedge where she had been hiding a moment earlier.

As Alema crashed into the blartrees, she heard Lumiya on the other side, calling down the walkway to Jacen.

"Go on! I'll handle this."

No! Alema wanted to yell. *Lobi is too dangerous—we need all the help we can get!*

But of course, she did not dare. During the early stages of the Killiks' conflict with the Galactic Alliance, her nest—the Dark Nest—had attempted to assassinate Jacen's daughter, and she was quite sure that he'd be happy to let Lobi kill her. So she pushed out onto the walkway just far enough to reveal herself to Lumiya.

The Sith scowled and ignited her own weapon—an exotic one that seemed equal parts whip and lightsaber, with long flexible strands of metal and bright hissing energy.

"Who are you?" Lumiya demanded. "Why are you—"

"No time!" Alema launched herself back through the blartrees; if Lobi had not yet followed, that could only mean she was fleeing. "Come, before the Jedi spy escapes!"

Alema emerged from the hedge to find Lobi twenty paces away and already fading into the night. Alema dropped her lightsaber and pointed in the Chev's direction, opening herself completely to the Force, using her anger and fear to draw it deep down inside. A moment later its power began to burn, and she released it in a long crackling bolt that caught her target square between the shoulder blades—and drove her to the ground.

Lumiya emerged from the hedge, her lightwhip burning a bright-colored hole in the fog. She glanced at the blue bolts coming from Alema's fingertips, then asked again, "Who *are* you?"

"We're a friend." Continuing to pour Force lightning into Lobi's prostrate form, Alema limped forward on her throbbing knee. "One who doesn't wish Master Sky-walker to learn what you are doing with his nephew."

Lumiya followed. "*We?* I don't see—"

"*Later!*" Alema snapped. They had closed to within five meters of Lobi. "Right now, we are in too much trouble to . . ."

Lobi suddenly stopped writhing and extended a hand toward a nearby patio. A decorative urn came flying out of the fog.

Alema let the Force lightning sizzle out and tried to redirect the urn, but Lobi's Force grasp was too secure. The urn caught her full in her crippled shoulder and sent her flying. She landed in the chrysanthus shrubs several meters away, her body throbbing with pain and her mind numb with shock.

The hum-and-sizzle of clashing weapons slowly brought her back to her senses, and she sat up to find Tresina Lobi spinning and parrying, slowly forcing Lumiya back, probing and feinting, trying to work her way past the crackling strands of Lumiya's exotic lightwhip—and into the striking range of a lightsaber.

Alema summoned her own weapon back into her grasp, then stood and limped forward to help.

Lobi sprang into a backflip and sailed over a crackling whip strike. Then, as she was still descending, she extended a hand in Alema's direction and used the Force to pull her into the path of the flashing strands. Lumiya barely managed to shut down the weapon before it struck, and even then the hot filaments cut through Alema's robe, burning a rainbow of hot welts into her thigh and ribs.

Alema was still screaming when Lobi landed at Lumiya's side. The Chev brought her lightsaber down, and Lumiya's weapon arm—one of her many cybernetic parts—fell to the ground trailing sparks and hydraulic fluid.

Lobi reversed her blade instantly, angling for Lumiya's torso, but Alema was already leaping forward to catch the Chev's attack on her own lightsaber.

Lobi whipped her lightsaber around low, aiming at Alema's knees and forcing her to leap back.

Alema pointed at Lumiya's severed arm, then used the Force to send it spinning toward Lobi's head. The Chev woman ducked easily, but that gave Lumiya time to call her lightwhip into her remaining hand and strike again. Lobi pivoted away from the attack. Alema sprang at her from behind, striking for the Chev's thick neck, then cried out in surprise as a huge foot glanced off her ribs . . . and *still* sent her staggering back.

Lumiya seized the opportunity to launch a flurry of attacks, fanning the strands of her whip to make it more difficult to block, striking right and left to prevent the Chev from pivoting away again, slowly driving Lobi back toward Alema's droning lightsaber.

Then, finally, Lobi faltered, gathering herself for a Force leap, but hesitating and retreating another step toward Alema instead.

It was the moment Alema had been waiting for.

"You are good, Master Lobi—but not that good." Alema spoke in a Force whisper so soft that it was little more than a thought. "Even you cannot defeat two of us."

Lobi's head snapped around, her eyes filled with confusion and doubt, and she spun into a whirling charge of crescent kicks and horizontal lightsaber strikes.

Alema held her ground, ducking a lightsaber strike and letting a kick slip off her shoulder, then Force-slammed the hilt of her lightsaber into the pit of the Chev's stomach and spoke again in her Force whisper.

"No good."

Amazingly, Lobi stumbled only one step back . . . but that step was one too far. Lumiya's lightwhip caught her across the back of the legs and severed them both at the knees. The Chev roared first in anger, then—as she dropped onto the stumps and pitched forward onto her hands—in agony.

It was a terrible sound to hear. Alema stepped forward and spoke once more in her Force whisper.

"There is no need to suffer." She swept her blade across the back of the Chev's neck, and the head tumbled away. "Your fight is done."

Lumiya stepped into view at the other end of the body, but her gaze remained on Alema, and she did not deactivate her lightwhip. "Do I know you?" she asked.

"Not yet." Alema knelt beside Lobi's headless body and rolled it over, then removed the recording rod from the Chev's belt and tossed it to Lumiya. "But we hope you will let us serve you. What you are doing with Jacen is so delicious—and so right for the Balance."

chapter seven

The Hall of Masters was as long and fancy as all the others down which the Solos had sneaked, with red qashmel carpeting and some of the finest artwork in the galaxy hanging on the walls. Between each masterpiece, an ornate trefoil arch led into another equally opulent corridor, while a white alabas staircase at either end of the hallway ascended a vaulted turret into the higher reaches of Tenel Ka's immense palace.

"Oh, boy," Han said. "Which way *now*?"

"Good question."

Han frowned. "Can't you just follow the Force or something?"

"I could, if I wanted Tenel Ka to feel me searching for her." Leia glanced at the security card she had stolen from the guard she had left lying in the Queen Mother's Special Salon, then started down the hall. "But I have a better idea."

Han followed her to the end of the hall, where they found a small data terminal tucked away beneath one of the staircases. Leia inserted the security card and selected

QUEEN'S PAGEANT: HER MAJESTY'S PUBLIC SCHEDULE from the menu that popped up.

Tenel Ka had finished the Preliminary Judging of Muscles half an hour earlier and was due to host a banquet in two hours, but there was nothing scheduled for the moment.

"Look for a private schedule," Han suggested. "This doesn't tell us anything."

"Sure it does," Leia said. She called up a map of the palace, then pointed to a blacked-out area marked simply ROYAL RESIDENCE. "That's where we'll find her."

"I don't mean to sound skeptical, but—"

"It'll take her an hour to dress for the banquet," Leia said. "And she's been judging the pageant all day. Where do *you* think she'll spend her one unscheduled hour?"

"With her kid," Han agreed. He should have known better than to doubt Leia; having grown up in a palace herself, she would have an instinctive understanding of Tenel Ka's life. "So where's the playroom?"

"Good question." Leia plucked the data card from the terminal, then turned her face upward and closed her eyes for a moment. "Stairway's clear."

Han and Leia ascended side by side, passing portrait after portrait of Tenel Ka's royal ancestors. The staircase was wide enough to accommodate a landspeeder, with room left for pedestrians, and it seemed to go up forever. After a good minute of climbing, a muffled murmur began to spill out of an unseen doorway onto a landing above.

Thinking they would need to find another way, Han took Leia's arm and started to pull her back down the stairs.

"No time," she whispered. "If Tenel Ka's going to see us, it will be after she's visited Allana and before she starts dressing for the banquet."

Leia pulled Han close to the wall and continued to ascend, slowly and silently. When they had drawn to within a few meters of the landing, she stopped and pointed out into the emptiness on the other side of the banister. An instant later a loud *clunk* echoed up the turret, as though something had fallen onto the floor of the lowest level.

A pair of royal guards rushed out onto the landing to investigate. As they peered over the balustrade, Han and Leia pressed their backs to the wall and crept up the last few steps in silence, then slipped into an extravagant waiting room filled with cologne-heavy Hapan males. They were attired in elegant shimmersilk tunics and fine tavella doublets. All were holding plasticlear cases containing orchids from across the galaxy—sometimes more exotic than beautiful.

Leia slipped her hand through Han's arm. "They're probably suitors hoping to escort the Queen Mother to tonight's banquet," she whispered, leading him into the room. "Tenel Ka certainly likes to play games with her nobles."

"As long as they don't play games with *us*," Han answered. "I really wish you hadn't made me leave my blaster aboard the *Falcon*."

"This is *supposed* to be a friendly call."

"Then how come you're wearing your lightsaber?"

"That's different," Leia replied. "This is Hapes, and I'm female."

As they moved deeper into the room, the young nobles turned to study them, sneering at Han's travel-worn flight jacket or frowning at Leia's Jedi robes. The Solos paid little attention, holding the gazes of the courtiers just long enough to suggest they belonged here as much as anyone—and for Leia to reinforce the idea with a Force prod.

The trick must have worked, because by the time the Solos reached the perimeter of the seating area, the courtiers were turning back to their sabacc games and private conversations. Han and Leia weaved through the crowd to a large, spitting-rancor fountain that dominated the center of the room. Opposite them, a dozen royal guards blocked the mouth of a large ceremonial arch, beyond which lay a long white corridor. The hall was lined with displays of antiquated weapons and ancient blast armor, but its most spectacular feature was a glistening wind-crystal chandelier the size of an A-wing fighter.

"Guess we know where the Royal Residence is," Han muttered, looking away from the guards. "But to get past that bunch, it's going to take a pretty big—"

Leia's fingers bit into Han's arm. "Han, she's here."

"Here?" Han glanced casually around the room and saw nothing out of the ordinary, just a couple of young nobles arguing over the stakes of a dejarik game and a middle-aged bachelor lecturing a pasty-skinned youth about the propriety of wearing a hat indoors. "*Who's* here?"

"The assassin."

Leia's gaze went to the pasty-skinned youth and stayed there. With a slim beardless face and a bald head crowned by a fashionable—if ridiculously tall—top hat, he had a dangerous-yet-feminine appearance. His eyes were dark and sunken, his nose as straight as a knife, his mouth a small, ruby-lipped gash. He was wearing a ruffled dress jacket that had to be six sizes too large for him, and he was careful to keep his hands balled inside the outer pockets, as though afraid of what they might do on their own.

"You mean him?" Han whispered in disbelief. "He's just a kid."

The *kid's* eyes slowly slid away from his lecturer and found Leia. When she did not look away, he gave her a short, almost imperceptible nod, then turned back to his conversation.

Leia grabbed Han's arm. "That's no kid." She pulled him toward the guards waiting beneath the ceremonial arch. "In fact, she's older than you are."

"*She?*"

"It's not important right now," Leia said. "She's not working alone. We need to warn Tenel Ka."

As they neared the arch, a rough-featured guard wearing the golden cuff-hashes of a sergeant of the royal guard stepped out to meet them, blocking their way with a bulky Hapan power blaster.

"The Hall of the Wind Crystals is closed to visitors."

"Of course it is." Leia lifted her hand in one of those little waves that Jedi used when they were making a Force suggestion, then spoke so softly the sergeant had to lean down to hear her. "But the Queen Mother is in danger. You need to seal the chamber."

The sergeant's eyes widened, and he repeated, "The Queen Mother is in danger." He was too well trained to react hastily, however—even under the influence of a Force suggestion. "What's the nature of this danger?"

"From people in this chamber." Leia's voice was impatient. She made another little wave. "The Queen Mother is in danger. You need to seal the chamber and sound the alarm *now*."

The sergeant nodded. "The Queen Mother is in danger." His eyes flicked past Leia's shoulder, and then he turned to face his subordinates. "Seal the chaaaraggh—"

The command ended in a strangled gasp when something long and white hissed past Leia's head and planted itself in the side of the sergeant's neck. Han cried out and

instinctively shielded Leia, throwing himself onto her—
and nearly losing an arm as her lightsaber blade snapped
to life.

They had barely hit the floor when more of the strange
projectiles hissed past overhead, coming from all corners
of the chamber and filling the air with a sound like ripping cloth. An instant later the rest of the guards dropped
to the floor amid a cacophony of strangled outcries and
clattering armor.

Leia pressed her hand to Han's chest. "Han, you've *got*
to stop doing that." She rolled him off with surprising
ease and came up kneeling, then plucked at her robe.
"*Jedi*, remember?"

"Sorry—old habits."

Han rose to his knees. Half the suitors in the room—a
couple of dozen—were charging across the chamber,
leaping and dodging furniture, either holding a white
throwing knife or drawing another from their sleeves. He
spun around, reaching for the fallen sergeant's weapon,
and found the entire complement of guards lying in the
archway, most dead already, but a few writhing in pain
with a plastoid hilt protruding from their throats or faces.

A cold knot formed in the pit of Han's stomach. The
assassins were good—organized *and* well trained. He
crawled forward and grabbed the sergeant's bulky power
blaster, then began to fumble with the unfamiliar Hapan
safety.

"Blast! I don't care what you say, next time I'm
bringing—"

Leia's lightsaber droned behind him, then the smell of
burned flesh filled the air and a body thudded to the floor.
The rest of the attackers were already racing into the
archway to either side of the Solos. Most paid no attention at all to Han, simply grabbing weapons from the

fallen guards and continuing up the corridor at a sprint.
But one, a heavy-jawed man with blond hair, looked over
and caught Han's eye.

"You okay?" he asked.

"Uh, yeah," Han answered. He finally found the power
blaster's safety catch—a small nub inside the trigger
guard—and depressed it. "Thanks for asking."

He pulled the trigger, blasting a fist-sized hole into the
center of the man's chest. The Hapan tumbled over backward, his brow still rising in surprise.

Han turned to find Leia behind him, standing over a
dead Hapan and frowning in the direction of the man he
had just killed.

"You ever get the feeling we don't have the vaguest idea
what's going on here?" Han asked.

"We're not the only ones."

Leia pulled Han to his feet, in the process turning him
back toward the waiting chamber. A dozen young noble-
men were standing over the middle-aged bachelor who
had been lecturing the pale-skinned "kid" about the hat.

Another fifteen suitors were watching in slack-jawed
astonishment as the "kid" dived and rolled toward the
same door through which the Solos had entered, dodging
a constant stream of blasterfire from the guards posted
there. Now that the assassin had discarded her oversized
coat—revealing a skintight bodysuit and a utility belt
lined with throwing knives—it was very clear Leia had
been right about her being female. And she *did* have
hair—at least a little of it. The top hat was also gone, revealing a bushy topknot that made her look wild, unpredictable, and very dangerous.

Han started to shoulder the power blaster, but Leia put
a hand on the barrel.

"Not yet," she said. "She's Force-sensitive."

"Force-sensitive?" Han understood what Leia was saying. The woman would not be a quick kill, and they could not afford to get tied up here. "Will someone please tell me what the blazes is going on?"

"Maybe later." Leia turned up the corridor after the assassins. "After I have time to figure it out myself."

Han grabbed a couple of spare power packs off the dead sergeant and raced after Leia. By the time he caught up to her, they were two dozen meters down the white stone corridor and not gaining on their targets. Han stopped and knelt at the side of the corridor, taking cover behind the pedestal supporting a blue-sheened suit of early durasteel blast armor.

"We need to slow them down," he said.

"Good idea." Leia continued running. "Try not to hit me!"

"Hey!" Han called. "Not what I meant!"

But Leia was well down the corridor, already passing beneath the great chandelier and picking up speed. Han cursed her foolhardiness, then took three deep breaths and shouldered the power blaster.

Before he could open fire, the assassins suddenly stopped running and glanced uncertainly back toward Leia. Even without the Force, Han could sense their confusion. Either they had come to an unexpected dead end, or they had not seen her attack their fellows and could not understand why she was charging them. Maybe both.

"What the blazes is going on?" Han asked again. He set his sights on the Hapan in front and blasted him between the shoulder blades, then swung the muzzle to the next man and fired again. That one bounced off a display pedestal, then staggered into the middle of the corridor and collapsed. The surviving assassins dived for cover, finally starting to return fire.

Leia caught up to the rear of the group and launched herself into a whirling lightsaber attack, cloaking herself behind a basket of sapphire light and batting blaster bolts back toward their source. Han dropped another assassin and she killed three; Han blasted a man's leg and sent him somersaulting across the corridor; Leia used the Force to crush two more beneath a flying suit of heavy plexoid armor.

Then the deafening bang of a concussion grenade echoed down the corridor. Han was momentarily blinded by a brilliant flash of yellow. Leia cried out in surprise, and the air resonated with the piercing shriek of blaster-fire. Hapan voices began to scream and abruptly fall silent, and blaster bolts flew down the corridor so furiously it took a moment for Han to realize his vision had cleared.

Leia was Force-tumbling back toward him, somersaulting and twisting through the air, arcing from one side of the corridor to the other, batting blaster bolts aside and taking momentary shelter behind the display pedestals. Behind her, the surviving assassins—if there were any—were nowhere to be seen, and a wall of royal guards was charging into the far end of the corridor, power blasters blazing.

Han rose just high enough to show his shoulders and head above the pedestal he was using for cover. "Knock it off, you rodders!" he yelled. "We're on—"

A volley of blaster bolts brought his protest to an end, blowing the armor display off its stand and sending him to the floor beneath a crashing avalanche of durasteel.

"Han!" Leia's voice was barely audible over the screech of blasterfire, and the burned-meat stink of blaster combat had grown so thick in the hall that Han felt like retching. "Keep down!"

"Like I have a choice," Han grumbled—or would have grumbled, had there been enough air in his chest to do so.

He pushed a twenty-kilo breastplate off his shoulders and head, then rolled to his knees. His breath still would not come, but the ache in his chest was dull and general, suggesting he'd simply had the air knocked out of him. Leia was on the opposite side of the corridor and a little ahead of him, trapped behind a display pedestal by a torrent of blasterfire so bright and constant it resembled an ion drive's efflux.

Han looked back to the royal guards, who had already advanced halfway down the corridor. "Okay," he growled. "I've had it with you guys shooting at my wife."

He dropped back behind the display pedestal, pointed his blaster at the ceiling, and fired into the heart of the giant chandelier. It took only a handful of shots to bring the huge fixture down in a chiming crash of wind crystals and metal, and the torrent of blasterfire coming down the corridor immediately faded to a fraction of what it had been. He raised his head again and saw that the chandelier had landed squarely in the midst of the charging guards, leaving the largest part of the company sprawled on the floor—injured, trapped, or just too dazed to move.

But nearly a dozen guards had been far enough down the corridor to escape the chandelier. They were concentrating their fire on Leia, driving her back behind the pedestal every time she tried to make a break for Han's side of the corridor. And Leia was not helping matters much, simply deflecting their bolts instead of batting them back into her attackers. Clearly, she was trying to avoid hurting Hapans still loyal to Tenel Ka.

Han cursed her scruples, then took aim at the guards' feet and began to bounce blaster bolts off the floor. More than half of them immediately turned their attention to

Han, but one—an angry-browed man with the weathered face of a veteran—repaid the Solos' courtesy by pulling a concussion grenade off his equipment belt.

"No!" Han cried, more to himself than anyone else. "Don't—"

The guard thumbed the activation switch, and Han had no choice but to take aim at the man's chest.

Before he opened fire, a string of bolts flew up the corridor from behind him, catching the guard full-on and knocking him off his feet. The grenade tumbled from the Hapan's hand and rolled free. Han swung around in shock—or maybe it was fear—and had just enough time to glimpse the pale-skinned assassin standing in the archway, firing a cumbersome Hapan power blaster with each hand.

Then the concussion grenade detonated behind him, filling the corridor with light and thunder and fire. The assassin barely blinked. She simply continued firing with one of her weapons and used the other to wave the Solos toward her.

"Come on!"

Too astonished to do anything else, Han looked across the corridor at Leia—who merely looked back and shrugged.

A few of the guards trapped beneath the fallen chandelier began to recover and fired down the corridor again, at the assassin as well as the Solos. She dropped into an evasive roll, then came up firing and suppressed their attacks to almost nothing. She gestured to the Solos again, this time leaving the power blaster pointed in Han's direction when she finished.

"Come on," she repeated. Her voice was high but cold. "If you want to live."

Han glanced over at Leia.

She nodded vigorously. "Who doesn't?"

Leia rose and raced toward the archway spinning and tumbling, batting the few blaster bolts that came her way back up the corridor. Han mirrored her progress, scrambling along sideways and laying suppression fire back toward the chandelier. He still had no idea what was happening here, but it was growing more and more apparent that nobody else did, either—and when that happened, the only rule became survival by any means possible.

As they passed through the archway, the pale woman pointed her chin toward the entrance by which they had arrived. "Stairs!"

"Fine by me," Leia said, leading the way.

They met no resistance as they crossed the chamber, for the suitors who had *not* taken part in the attack were cowering behind furniture or cringing in corners, unwilling to risk their lives without weapons of their own. From what Han had seen of the assassin so far, it was probably a smart decision.

On the landing outside the chamber, the two door guards lay sprawled and motionless—as did two more on another landing on the opposite side of the turret. So far, there was no sign of any more guards—but Han knew that would be changing very shortly. He led the way down the stairs and into the corridor that led back toward the salon he and Leia had occupied earlier.

The assassin called out behind him. "Wait!"

Han stopped and glanced back to see her kneeling at the entrance to the turret. She was pointing both power blasters up the stairs, but looking toward Han and Leia.

"Where are you going?" she demanded.

"Back to the hangar," Han answered. "We've got to get out of here."

"No." The pale woman glanced back into the turret

and began to fire up the stairs. "We have a contract to finish."

"*We?*" Leia asked.

"Maybe you're not getting paid, but you're part of this." The woman continued to fire with one weapon, but pointed the other at Han's chest. "And don't look so surprised. This isn't exactly the way *I* expected it to happen, either."

The knuckles on Leia's weapon hand went white, but luckily Han was the only one who saw. The royal guards had reached the top of the stairs, and the assassin was busy exchanging fire with them.

"Look," Leia said. "I don't know—"

"You obviously know who *we* are," Han interrupted. He was beginning to see why the fight had seemed so crazy—the assassins had mistaken him and Leia for people who were supposed to help them get to Tenel Ka. "How about returning the favor?"

The assassin looked away from the stairs long enough to scowl at him. "You don't know?"

"We haven't exactly been in the loop," Leia pointed out, picking up on Han's strategy. "We just got in from Corellia."

A flurry of blaster bolts flashed into the corridor, nearly taking off the assassin's head. She merely rolled out of the doorway and pressed her back against the wall, then glanced over at Leia's lightsaber.

"Why don't you call me Nashtah?" She almost seemed to smile. "I'd like that."

For some reason Han did not understand, the name sent a chill down his back—or maybe that was just the growing stream of blasterfire pouring through the doorway.

"All right, Nashtah," he said. "In case you haven't noticed, someone set us up."

"Tenel Ka obviously knows about the assassination attempt," Leia added. "And that means we have *no* chance of getting to her right now. All that can happen is we get trapped and killed."

"I don't think she knew *we* were involved until this started," Han said. "But that's changed. We've only got about two minutes to get back to the *Falcon*—if we're lucky. After that, the hangar is going to be sealed up so tight even a lightsaber won't be able to cut our way back inside."

Nashtah's eyes seemed to grow darker and more sunken as she considered this possibility. Suddenly she dropped into a squat, then whirled back into the doorway and poured a volley of blasterfire up the stairs. There was a chorus of anguished screams.

"Lead!" Nashtah rose and waved them down the corridor, then tapped Leia's arm with a blaster barrel so hot that it singed the fabric of her robe. "And this had better not be a double cross. There is nothing I love more than killing Jedi."

chapter eight

The Consorts' Sitting Room stank of smoke, scorched fabric, and seared flesh, and the floor was strewn with charred furniture and blaster-burned bodies. Emergency crews were evacuating the injured while palace security agents holorecorded the dead. On the far side of the chamber, a group of dazed-looking nobles was being sequestered by a detail of the Hapan royal guard.

Jaina began to have a bad feeling about the CEC light transport that had jumped to hyperspace just as she and Zekk entered the system. It had been accelerating away from Hapes at a rate few freighters could achieve, and the fact that there had been two squadrons of Hapan starfighters on the vessel's tail only tended to confirm that it had been the *Millennium Falcon*.

Zekk leaned close. "Han and Leia Solo did *not* do this," he whispered. He was still in the same flight suit he had been wearing for more than a week, but the smell was nothing to the acrid stench that already filled the room. "It's not their style."

"I don't need *you* to tell me that." Jaina realized that Zekk was only trying to comfort her, but comfort was not what she needed right now. What she *needed* were facts. "Don't you think I know my own parents?"

Zekk ran a hand through his sweat-matted hair, then shook his head and let out a disgusted snort. He started across the room without another word, leaving Jaina to stand there wondering what was wrong. It was not like Zekk to be short with her, and she did not understand why *he* should be upset. After all, it wasn't *his* parents they had seen fleeing the scene of an assassination attempt.

When Jaina did not immediately start after Zekk, the sergeant in charge of their escort nudged her in the back. "Stay together." He motioned Jaina toward the vestibule. "We've had enough Jedi tricks for one day."

Jaina turned to face the Hapan. He was tall and typically handsome, with chiseled features and dark blue eyes. "My mother didn't have anything—"

"Tell it to Prince Isolder." He rested a hand on the butt of his holstered blaster, then used the other hand to point after Zekk. "Go."

Tempted as Jaina was to Force-slam the sergeant into the nearest wall, she recognized that now would be a less-than-ideal time to adjust his attitude. She settled for a smirk of disdain, then followed Zekk toward the corner, where Prince Isolder was watching a female security officer interview a shaken-looking noble.

As Jaina and Zekk approached, two bodyguards stepped out to block their way. Isolder touched the arm of one.

"No, Brak." Though it had a few new—and well-placed—lines, Isolder's strong-featured Hapan face was as handsome as it had ever been. "They're fine."

Brak did not retreat. "They're *Jedi,* milord. After what just happened—"

Isolder clamped down on Brak's arm and physically

pulled him back. "They're probably the reason my daughter *survived* what just happened." He turned his attention to Jaina. "Unless I miss my guess, you were the source of the Queen Mother's recent uneasiness."

"I did reach out to her, yes," Jaina said.

"I thought as much." Isolder opened his arms, inviting an embrace. "It's good to see you again, Jaina."

"And you as well, Prince Isolder." Jaina hugged him, then stood aside as he clasped arms with Zekk. "I'm only sorry we couldn't arrive earlier."

"Nonsense. We're thankful for your, uh, warning. It prompted the Queen Mother to increase her guard."

"And to seal the residence's inner blast doors," Tenel Ka said, arriving behind Jaina and Zekk. "You have nothing to be sorry for."

Jaina turned and saw Tenel Ka standing two meters away, surrounded by a small company of attendants and royal guards. Her rust-colored hair hung loose down her back, and she was dressed in a frock of green shimmersilk that managed to appear as practical as it did elegant. The effect was so striking and regal that Jaina had to consciously remind herself she was looking at an old Jedi academy classmate and comrade-in-arms.

"Your Majesty."

Jaina bowed, and Zekk along with her. Tenel Ka's eyes flashed with embarrassment at being exalted by her friends, but she was careful to hold herself tall and still to hide her discomfort from her subjects.

"Jaina, Zekk. What an unexpected pleasure." She motioned them upright, then glanced over her shoulder, toward the great hall where most of the devastation had taken place. "I assume your visit has something to do with *that*."

"Right—we came to warn you." Jaina did not mention

the Corellian assault fleet that Bwua'tu suspected would soon be on its way to help with the coup; she would share *that* intelligence later, once they were alone. "We didn't think it would happen so soon."

"I know you did everything in your power." Tenel Ka's face grew troubled. She continued, "What I *don't* understand is why your parents were involved."

Jaina felt like she had been kicked in the stomach. "Involved?" She glanced around at the devastation, unable to believe her parents would participate in an attack against Tenel Ka. "You're sure?"

"More than we'd like to be," Isolder said. He sounded more disappointed than angry. "Your mother and Captain Solo arrived unannounced and asked for an audience with the Queen Mother. Before she could find time for them, they slipped out of the guest salon and disabled the entire palace security system."

"We're still trying to learn how," Tenel Ka said. "As close as we can estimate, they did it in less than two minutes—and they had to travel nearly half a kilometer through unfamiliar corridors."

"Maybe you're having trouble because they didn't do it," Zekk suggested.

"Of course they did it!" The woman who said this was a stately looking aide of perhaps forty or fifty—it was hard to tell, given how hard Hapans worked to stay young and attractive. "Such a feat is nothing for a—"

"Thank you, Lady Galney." Tenel Ka silenced the woman with a polite flip of two fingers, then turned to Zekk. "Do you have another theory?"

Zekk furrowed his brow, then said, "Maybe they were here for the same reason we are—to warn you."

The suggestion was greeted only by doubtful—in many

cases scornful—Hapan expressions, and even Jaina had trouble seeing the basis for Zekk's assertion.

Finally, Tenel Ka asked, "Then why were they seen leaving with the leader of the assassination squad?"

"They were?" Jaina gasped.

"I'm afraid so," Tenel Ka said. "A pale woman with a shaved head and a topknot. When my guard managed to pin your parents down, she even risked her own life to rescue them."

Jaina's heart sank. It certainly *sounded* like her parents were working with the assassins.

"There must be an explanation." Zekk gave her arm a reassuring squeeze. "Jaina, you need to trust your feelings."

Jaina pulled away, irritated and confused and . . . shaken. She found it hard to believe that her parents would participate in *any* kind of assassination attempt . . . but she just didn't know. There were all kinds of rumors suggesting her father had helped Boba Fett assassinate Thrackan Sal-Solo, and her mother had experienced firsthand the evil wrought by Darth Vader. Was it too much to think Leia might kill a friend to keep Jacen from following the same path?

"I don't know what my feelings *are*," Jaina said. She turned to Tenel Ka. "Tenel—er, Queen Mother, I don't know what to say."

"I'm having a hard time believing it myself," Tenel Ka replied. "First appearances are against them, but the investigation is far from complete, and there *is* some conflicting evidence."

"Such as?" Zekk demanded.

"Some eyewitness accounts suggest the Solos may have *attacked* a few assassins when the fighting began." Tenel Ka turned and extended her arm toward the great hall where most of the fighting had taken place. "We can go have a look, if you'd like."

"I'd like." Zekk's voice was hardly hostile, but it did not take a Jedi to sense that he was angry. "Why are you ignoring these accounts?"

"We're not ignoring them," Isolder said. He stepped to Zekk's side, and they all started toward the ruined hall. "But eyewitness accounts are notoriously unreliable—as I'm sure you were taught in your investigation courses at the Jedi academy."

"And some eyewitnesses claim that the men the Solos attacked were actually trying to defend the Queen Mother," Lady Galney said. "Some very *credible* witnesses."

"I'll judge that for myself," Zekk said. He turned to Isolder. "When can I speak to these witnesses?"

Isolder stopped and turned to Zekk. "You want to interrogate Hapan *nobles*?"

"That's right," Zekk said. "There's something wrong here, and I—"

"That's enough." Jaina grabbed the back of Zekk's arm and squeezed. His tone was bordering on the rude—especially to the sensitive Hapan ego—and harsh accusations would only make the official investigators more likely to overlook evidence that might exonerate her parents. "I'm sure the Queen Mother and her staff will discover the truth."

"Fact," Tenel Ka said. "The investigation will give the Solos every benefit of the doubt—and I *do* intend to interview every eyewitness personally."

That was enough to quiet Zekk's protests, and to assure Jaina that her parents would not become convenient scapegoats. Though family duties on Hapes had forced Tenel Ka to leave the Jedi order, she retained all the talents and Force skills she had learned as a Jedi Knight. If anyone tried to lie about the Solos' involvement, the Queen Mother would know.

"Thanks, Your Majesty," Jaina said. "I appreciate it. If there's anything we can do to help—"

"There is," Isolder said instantly. "We know the *Falcon* often travels under false transponder codes. A list would prove *very* helpful."

Jaina's mouth grew dry. She was being asked to choose between her loyalty to her family and her duty to the Jedi order, and she was well enough trained to realize that her decision really did not hinge on whether her parents were guilty of anything. A member state of the Galactic Alliance was asking for information regarding an attack on its government, and as a Jedi Knight she was obliged to provide it.

When Jaina was slow to answer, Lady Galney reminded her, "The Hapes Consortium is an important part of the Galactic Alliance—a very important part—and your parents are terrorists."

"Alleged terrorists," Tenel Ka corrected. She fixed her gray eyes on Jaina, then said, "It would be better for everybody. My commanders will be more . . . *careful* if they know when they're actually dealing with the *Falcon*."

"And the information will be useful only as long as they remain inside the Consortium," Isolder pointed out. "If they *aren't* a danger to the Queen Mother, I'm sure they'll be departing Hapan space as soon as possible."

"In which case, we *won't* pursue them beyond our boundaries," Tenel Ka added. "We'll leave them to the Alliance authorities—whom I'm sure already have the false codes."

"I'm not sure I know all the false codes," Jaina said, forcing herself to answer. Tenel Ka's deal was more than

fair. The Hapan Royal Navy was going to be boarding—
or destroying—every YT-1300 it found. This way, at least
Tenel Ka could issue orders instructing her commanders
to capture the *Falcon* and her crew in one piece. "But I'll
give you the ones I do."

"Thank you," Tenel Ka said. "I know how hard that
must be for you."

"Just tell your commanders to be patient," Jaina said.
She glanced in Galney's direction and was a little sickened
by the smug satisfaction she sensed in the woman, but
that changed none of the basic facts of the situation.
"Mom and Dad won't give up easily—but they're *not*
going to kill anyone they don't have to, either."

"I've already instructed my commanders that we need
your parents alive," Tenel Ka said.

"Good," Jaina said. "We should go someplace and finish our briefing. On our approach, Zekk and I saw the
Falcon jumping into hyperspace. If we hurry, we may be
able to spare your commanders the trouble of capturing
them."

"By going after them yourselves?" Isolder asked. "In
Hapan space?"

Jaina frowned. "Assuming they're still *in* Hapan space,
yes."

"Oh, that won't do." Galney stepped in front of Jaina,
then turned her back as she addressed Tenel Ka. "We
can't have Jedi Solo pursuing her own parents. It will look
as though *you* staged the attack as a pretext for property
seizures. You'll end up driving more nobles into the
enemy camp."

Tenel Ka sighed, then looked over Galney's shoulder at
Jaina. "Lady Galney is right, my friend. It would look
very strange to Hapan eyes."

"No one has to know," Zekk said. "We're Jedi."

"*Everyone* would know," Isolder said. He waved a hand around the chamber, allowing it to linger a bit on Tenel Ka's retinue. "Look about."

A sheepish look came to Zekk's face, and Jaina realized she had to yield to Tenel Ka's wishes. The Hapes Consortium was indeed a flooger-bed of conspiracy and intrigue . . . and sending a daughter to bring her own parents to justice would have raised eyes even on Coruscant.

"Right, but this is a matter of Alliance security, too," Jaina said. "We could help by identifying that assassin and trying to trace her travels. That shouldn't offend—"

"Actually," Tenel Ka interrupted, "I've already asked your brother to help us with that investigation."

Jaina's jaw dropped. "Jacen?"

"I know you've had your differences of late, but this is what Jacen *does* now." Tenel Ka's voice was apologetic but firm. "Can you honestly say you would do better?"

"That depends on what you mean by *better*," Jaina retorted. She could not believe Tenel Ka intended to turn her brother loose inside the Consortium. "Do you have any idea what he's been *doing* on Coruscant?"

"Protecting the populace from Corellian terrorists, by all accounts I have seen." Tenel Ka's tone was defensive and stubborn. "I'm sorry to distract him, but there may be a connection between the terrorists and this assassination attempt—and Jacen is the only one with the knowledge to investigate it."

Jaina exhaled in frustration. "Okay. I can tell when we're not wanted."

"What about Allana?" Zekk addressed himself to Tenel Ka. "Anyone trying to remove you will also want her eliminated. Until things settle down, maybe she should have a couple of Jedi babysitters."

"That won't be necessary." Tenel Ka's expression remained calm, but her alarm poured into the Force. She had been keeping her daughter out of sight since the day of Allana's birth, to the point that rumors of a birth defect had begun to circulate through the Jedi Temple. Perhaps there was something to those rumors, after all. "Her security is better than my own."

"Like I said, I can tell when we're not wanted." Jaina could not help feeling a little angry and hurt; she had just agreed to provide one of her parents' most closely guarded secrets, and still Tenel Ka refused to trust Jaina with the nature of Allana's vulnerability. "Maybe we should just finish the briefing and be on our way. But we really need to do this in private." She cast a pointed glance at Tenel Ka's retinue.

"Of course," Tenel Ka said. "Come with me."

The Queen Mother motioned the two Jedi to her side. When they had obeyed, she drew gasps from Galney and several other noble ladies by slipping her arm through Jaina's, then leaning close.

"And you *are* wanted, my friend." Tenel Ka's whisper was so soft that Jaina heard it inside her head more than in her ears. "There is something else I must ask you to do for me . . . something I can trust only to my oldest friends."

"Of course," Jaina replied. Her heart had sunk clear to her knees. Whether or not her parents had been a part of the attempt on Tenel Ka's life, the fact remained that Jaina had to consider the possibility . . . and that struck her as a sadness nearly as great as her brother Anakin's death. "The Jedi are always at your disposal."

chapter nine

Though dawn had come bright and golden several minutes earlier, a sense of darkness and danger still hung over Fellowship Plaza, and the closer Luke and Mara drew to the crime scene, the heavier and more sinister that sense became. A squad of dark-visored policebots blocked access to the walkway at both ends, while a team of spiderlike forensics droids swarmed over the tall privacy hedges to either side. Two detectives—the first a huge-headed Bith in a rumpled tabard, the other a green-scaled Rodian in a sharply creased zingsuit—stood inside the security cordon comparing notes.

"*This* doesn't look good," Mara said. "I'm afraid we're about to find out why we can't find Tresina in the Force."

"Me, too," Luke answered. "I didn't like the way that security dispatcher sounded this morning."

Mara glanced over and scowled. "How did she sound?"

"Surprised," Luke said. "Maybe even disbelieving."

The security force dispatcher's first words when Luke answered the comm half an hour before had been to assure him that his son was "not involved" in the incident.

Refusing to answer any questions herself, the dispatcher had asked whether Luke knew where Master Lobi was, then instructed him to meet a pair of detectives in Fellowship Plaza. Of course, Mara had immediately commed Ben; to their relief, he was quite safe and on his way to an important rendezvous with Jacen.

They reached the security cordon and were stopped by a policebot, who did a quick retinal scan on Luke and stepped aside.

"Detectives Raatu and Tozr are expecting you." The policebot pointed first at the Rodian, then the Bith. "Please remember that the law requires you to answer all questions truthfully, or not at all. Refusal to answer may be considered grounds for an interrogation warrant."

"Since when?" Mara demanded.

A scanning beam shot from the policebot's visor into Mara's eye, then it asked, "Mara Jade Skywalker?"

"Just answer the question, chiphead," she said.

"Take that as an affirmative," Luke said quickly. "When did silence become a suspicious act?"

The policebot kept its visor trained on Mara. "The Suspicious Silence Provision was added to the Galactic Loyalty Act at oh three twenty this morning."

"In the middle of the *night*?" Mara asked. "How'd they ever get a quorum?"

"Under the Law Enforcement Tools Provision of the Galactic Loyalty Act, quorums are no longer required to approve anti-terrorism legislation."

"And when did *that* pass?" Mara asked sarcastically.

"Yesterday at eighteen twenty-seven," the policebot answered. "By five votes, under reduced quorum requirements due to the boycott of the Bothan delegation."

"Thanks for the information," Luke said. He took

Mara's arm and started toward the detectives. "It's always good to know the law."

"Especially when they keep changing it," Mara added under her breath.

"The latest legal updates are available from any law enforcement droid," the policebot said behind them. "All inquiries will be noted in your file."

"Wonderful," Mara grumbled.

Luke found her attitude a little surprising. Mara usually supported a stern response to terrorism. But as a former Emperor's Hand, she also knew how easy it was to abuse the kind of information the government was now gathering under provisions of the Galactic Loyalty Act. Every year, she gave a special seminar at the academy, teaching young Jedi how to use the galaxy's vast data banks to track their quarry.

As the Skywalkers drew near, the two detectives stopped talking. The Bith extended a delicate-fingered hand in greeting to Luke, then to Mara.

"Master Skywalker and Master Skywalker, thanks for coming. I'm Chal Tozr." He waved at his green-scaled companion. "This is my partner, Gwad Raatu."

Instead of offering a hand, Raatu twitched his scaly snout in suspicion. "Do you know a Tresina Lobi?"

"Of course they know her," Tozr said. "She's a Jedi Master."

"That's correct," Luke said. He could sense Raatu's excitement through the Force; the Rodian's hunting instinct had been triggered, and he was eager to find his prey. "She sits on the Jedi Council, as a matter of fact."

"Not anymore." Continuing to study their faces rather obviously, Raatu waved a hand toward the hedge on the near side of the walkway. "A gardener droid found her."

"Gwad! Show some respect." The edges of Tozr's cheek folds turned blue with embarrassment. "Sorry about that. My partner thinks everyone is a suspect."

"Everyone *is* a suspect." Raatu's dark eyes remained fixed on Luke and Mara. "Where were you early last night?"

Tozr let out his breath in whistled exasperation. "Gwad!" He turned his huge head toward the Skywalkers. "You don't have to answer."

"No, it's fine." A knot of anger was forming in Luke's stomach, but it was not Raatu he was upset with. The Jedi comm center's night tech had left a message detailing Master Lobi's interrupted transmission, so he *knew* what had happened to Lobi—and who was responsible. "I had an important meeting with Chief Omas that lasted until after midnight. Mara was with me."

"If you'd like to confirm that, you can comm his office." Mara's voice was particularly sharp and sarcastic— a sign of the sorrow and anger that Luke could feel in her through the Force. "Ask for the Chief of State."

Raatu rotated his dish-shaped sensory antennae toward her. "Would I be able to speak with Chief Omas personally?"

"No!" Tozr said. He turned to Luke. "Look, someone assassinated the Bothan ambassador last night, and the chief of detectives wants as many of us on it as he can get. So if you want to handle this matter yourself, just say—"

"*We're* the law on Coruscant," Raatu objected. "Not the Jedi."

The Bith whirled on his partner. "Someone killed a Jedi *Master,* you laserbrain!" He was so irritated that his voice warbled. "Even if we solve the case, are *we* going to make the arrest?"

Raatu's snout widened in excitement. "You're afraid of a challenge?"

"Maybe we should all work together for now," Luke suggested. He waved at the forensics droids swarming over the near hedge. "You've already started collecting evidence, and the Jedi can bring some unique resources to bear."

Raatu cast a resentful glance in Tozr's direction, then let out a disgusted snort. "We call the shots," he said. "Technically, you're just observers."

"I guess that's better than suspects," Mara retorted. She turned to Tozr. "Why don't you show us the scene?"

"You're standing on it." Tozr nodded at the walkway, then waved at the blartree hedges lining either side. "It looks like they were waiting in ambush—"

"*They?*" Luke asked.

"You think that's wrong, Skywalker?" Raatu kept his bulging eyes fixed on Luke. "Something maybe you need to share?"

"No, go on," Luke said. The interruption had been a mistake, and not only because it had aroused Raatu's suspicions. He could feel Mara studying him, too, wondering what he knew that *she* didn't. "I was leaping to conclusions—no one has anything to gain by that."

"Right," Tozr said. He pointed down the walkway to a blartree on the far side, where a forensics droid appeared to be making resin casts of a set of footprints. "One ambusher was waiting there, and another over here."

He pointed to a bush on their side of the walkway, a little closer, where another droid was casting footprints.

"What species?" Mara asked.

"Human or near-human," Raatu answered. "The shoes made it hard to tell, but both ambushers were probably female and fairly light—the prints were small and shallow."

"And one had a deformed foot—she didn't put any

weight on the front part of her shoe," Tozr added. Motioning the Skywalkers to follow, he stepped through the hedge. "We think your Jedi realized something was wrong and tried to come up on them from behind."

"Too bad they saw her coming," Raatu said from the back of the group. "But it doesn't look like she suffered long."

They emerged from the hedge into a bed of knee-high chrysanthus shrubs. A pair of medical droids were waiting on the far side with a stretcher and a hoversled, while yet more forensics droids were swarming over the area, making casts of footprints and holorecording every detail of the crime scene.

In the center of the bed, still dressed in Jedi robes, lay the torso of a large Chev woman. Both lower legs and her head lay a couple of meters away. The lifeless eyes in the head were still open wide in surprise. There was no sign of her lightsaber or other equipment.

Luke's stomach grew hollow. "This is a message." He started to move closer to the body, but a forensics droid quickly cut him off. "She's toying with me."

"Toying with you?" Raatu repeated. "Who would that be?"

"In a minute." Mara touched Luke through the Force, making sure that he felt her suspicion—and growing irritation. "*How* is this a message, Luke? From Lumiya?"

"I'm afraid so," Luke said. "I think she's telling us she can take Ben anytime she wants."

"What does this have to do with Ben?" Mara demanded. "You'd better not be telling me you were using our son as bait."

"Not bait, exactly," Luke said. He had not told Mara about asking Tresina Lobi to follow Ben, in large part because of their disagreement over whether Jacen was good for him. "But I *did* ask Tresina to keep an eye on him, because I thought Lumiya might try to use him against me." It looks like I was right."

"And *that's* why you told me to bring my shoto?" Mara asked, referring to the half-length lightsaber she had built as a defense against Lumiya's lightwhip. "Because you knew Lumiya had something to do with Tresina's death?"

Luke shrugged. "It looks like I was right."

"Being right is no excuse," Mara said. "You should have told me."

Luke sighed. "I *said* it would be a good idea to keep an eye on him. You accused me of looking for an excuse to spy on Jacen." He paused to collect himself and sensed the keenness of Raatu's interest in their conversation. He gave Mara a Force-nudge, reminding her of their audience, then said, "Besides, *that's* not what you're really angry about."

Mara flashed him a look that said this conversation wasn't over, but took the hint. "No, I suppose it's not."

"I take it this *Lumiya* is our prime suspect?" Tozr asked. "Who is she?"

"One of Luke's old girlfriends," Mara said sharply.

Raatu's antennae snapped upright. "Ah—that explains it." He lifted his hand and dictated a note into the datamike clipped to his cuff, then gestured at Lobi's body. "And Master Lobi is the new girlfriend?"

Instead of answering, Mara merely lifted her brow and looked to Luke.

"Not at all!" Luke answered. "Mara is—er, Mara is my wife. I don't have a girlfriend."

Raatu shrugged. "What do I know about you Jedi?" he asked. "With *most* humans, it's usually sex or love."

Tozr nodded sagely. "Eighty-seven percent of the time," he said. "Spice is a distant second."

"Not *this* time," Luke insisted. "This time, it's revenge."

"Revenge for what?" Tozr asked. "And how is your son involved?"

"Lumiya was a Sith apprentice," Luke explained. "She wants revenge because I shot her down and helped overthrow the Emperor. Ben is just a means to an end."

"Sure, Master Skywalker," Raatu said. "Whatever you say—but for now, we'll keep all motives on the table."

"Any idea who the accomplice might be?" Tozr asked.

Mara's voice suddenly rose behind Luke, sharp and angry. He turned to see that she had stepped away from the group and was not quite shouting into her comlink.

"I'm a lot more than Ben's mother, Corporal Lekauf," she was saying. "I'm *Master* Mara Jade Skywalker of the Jedi order."

The corporal's reply was not quite audible to Luke.

"If you *know* who I am, then you also know that you'd better tell me why my son's comlink is being jammed—or spend the next six weeks in a bacta tank trying to regrow all the parts I'm going to cut off." Mara looked across the plaza toward the giant silver cylinder of the Galactic Justice Center. "I can be there in three minutes."

There was a short pause.

"*Of course* this comlink is scrambled," Mara said.

The corporal spoke again.

"He's *what*?"

The corporal repeated whatever he had told her, then Mara's anger began to fade from the Force.

"I see. Well, have him get in touch with me the moment he returns." Mara paused, then added, "The *moment*, Corporal Lekauf. Do I make myself clear?"

Mara closed her comlink, then seemed surprised to find Luke and the others watching her. She frowned. "I just want to be sure that Lumiya isn't delivering the rest of her message."

"And you're sure she *isn't*?" Luke asked.

"Corporal Lekauf was very convincing," she said. "Apparently, Jacen took Ben up to Crix Base."

"Crix Base?" Raatu echoed. "What for?"

Mara shot the Rodian a *don't-be-stupid* look. "He wouldn't say."

More properly known as the General Crix Madine Military Reserve, Crix Base had been constructed during the first wave of fleet reorganizations undertaken in the wake of the war with the Yuuzhan Vong. It was a huge complex of orbital hangars currently serving as home port to the Third, Eighth, and the mysterious Ninth Fleets. It also housed the headquarters of two elite fighting units, the Space Rangers and Gamma Corps, and—as Chief Omas had revealed during their meeting last night—a brand-new *Imperial*-class Star Destroyer secretly assigned to GAG, the *Anakin Solo*.

"Maybe that's a good thing," Luke said, guessing that Jacen had taken Ben to the base to go on the *Anakin*'s shakedown cruise. "At least we know Lumiya won't get him there."

"Do we?" Mara asked. "Base security wouldn't stop *me*."

"No, but it *would* take time for you to defeat it," Luke pointed out. He didn't mention the possibility of a shakedown cruise because Raatu and Tozr lacked the necessary security clearance to even hear of a vessel named the *Anakin Solo*. "And it would entail risks you wouldn't need to run elsewhere."

Mara thought about this a moment, then nodded. "Okay. Your point?"

"That *now* is our chance," Luke said. "Until Ben gets back, it's just her and us."

"And *us*," Raatu reminded Luke. "This Lumiya woman is *our* suspect."

"Do you think you can identify your old girlfriend?" Tozr produced a large datapad from a pocket of his wrinkled tabard and began to enter codes. "There was a lot of fog last night, but the security cams have pretty good imaging filters. We're in a blind spot here, but we might be able to catch her on the way in."

"I'd recognize her if I saw her." Luke went to the Bith's side and saw that he was calling up last night's video feed from the anti-terrorist cams that had been installed to protect Fellowship Plaza. "But she won't be visible."

"She won't?"

"No. She's too skilled for that." Mara joined them and held her hand out for the datapad. "May I?"

Tozr ruffled his cheek flaps, then reluctantly passed over the datapad. Mara began to punch keys, bringing up the feed from the entrance closest to the Jedi Temple. It didn't take long to spot Ben entering the park and Master Lobi trailing him, following a discreet distance behind and taking care to remain in the shadows. But they spotted no hint of Lumiya—or of the second killer—even when Mara brought up the feeds from the next two cams.

Luke checked the time stamp at the bottom of the screen, then said, "It's too early. Tresina's message didn't come in until nineteen twenty-two."

"What message?" Raatu asked.

"She clicked in with a partial message saying she had spotted Lumiya," Luke replied.

"What else?" Raatu demanded.

"That's it," Luke said. "Just that I was right, Lumiya was watching Ben. Then she cut it short."

"But it doesn't look like this Lumiya was following your son when he left the Temple," Tozr said. He reached

over to tap the screen of the datapad. "So she was waiting for him *inside* the plaza."

"It would seem so." The edge in Mara's voice was as
cold as the knot in Luke's stomach. "I don't like it. She
knew where he was going to be."

"We *said* this was an ambush," Raatu reminded them.
"Both killers were waiting for Master Lobi in the hedges."

"That's the way it looks, all right," Luke said. He turned
back to Mara. "Lumiya had to enter the plaza somewhere."

Mara began to bring up feeds from the other entrances
and run through them at high speed. Finally, a line of
static flashed across the screen, and she froze the picture
and checked the time code.

"Nineteen fourteen," she reported.

"Eight minutes before Tresina's message," Luke said.
"That fits."

"But that's just a power glitch," Tozr said, still looking
at the datapad.

"It's a Force-flash," Luke corrected. "And it can be
used to prevent a security cam from recording your image
as you pass through its field of view."

Mara checked the cam code at the bottom of the screen,
then asked Tozr, "Is that the Galactic City entrance?"

Tozr nodded. "That's right."

"Then we're in luck," Raatu said. Without asking, the
Rodian took the datapad from Mara and called up a
schematic of the cam net. "Galactic City is dignitary central. There are security cams all over."

He scrolled through the feeds from each of the adjacent
cams until he came to a line of static similar to the last
one.

"Nineteen oh six." Raatu led the way back through the
hedge, then started up the walkway toward the Galactic
City entrance. "Looks like we're on the scent."

chapter ten

Within a few hours of discovering Lumiya's trail in Fellowship Plaza, Luke, Mara, and their two detective companions were following a Neimoidian building manager down a larmalstone hall on the three hundredth floor of the opulent Zorp House apartment tower. Luke had talked Raatu out of calling an enter-and-capture team—but just barely—by pointing out that SWAT-droids were hardly inconspicuous. Lumiya would have sensed the agitation of any bystanders who happened to see them moving into position and fled before they could capture her. But Saba Sebatyne and two other Jedi *were* stationed outside as backup, posing as maintenance workers on a hoversled just around the corner.

The building manager stopped next to an expensive homogoni side table, then pointed down the hall to a double sliding door of polished brass.

"That's three hundred seven twelve," he whispered.

"You're sure it's theirs?" Tozr asked. Like Raatu, the Bith was convinced that Lumiya had an accomplice. Luke and Mara were not arguing the point, especially since there *had* been two sets of footprints in the hedges.

The Neimoidian spread his leathery hands. "There are twenty-five thousand apartments in Zorp House," he said. "I can't know who lives in them all."

"But this is where the security cam keeps malfunctioning?" Luke asked.

The Neimoidian nodded his flat-faced head. "And that is the only apartment whose door never opens when the cam *is* working."

Mara commed Saba, telling her they were about to go in. Raatu drew his blaster and started down the hall, pulling the Neimoidian along beside him.

"Buzz them," Raatu ordered. "Say you've been getting a smoke alert for their apartment, and you want to be sure they're okay."

"Me?" The Neimoidian glanced warily at Raatu's blaster, then at Luke and Mara. "Isn't the tenant dangerous?"

"Are you refusing to cooperate with a criminal investigation?" Raatu demanded.

"You won't have to go inside," Tozr said, speaking to the manager over his partner's shoulder. "We're just trying to find out if they're home."

The Neimoidian's pace remained unenthusiastic, but he did go to the door and do as he was asked. As they waited for a response, Luke extended his Force-awareness into the apartment, searching for any glimmer of a presence that would suggest someone hiding inside. He felt nothing, but that meant little. Lumiya would certainly be capable of hiding her Force presence.

When no answer came after the second buzz, the Neimoidian said, "It seems they're not home." He turned to leave. "If you need me, I'll be down in my—"

"Not yet." Raatu caught his arm and pointed at the security panel. "The universal code."

The Neimoidian's relief flooded the Force. "Of course."

He extended a finger and reached for the keypad. "If you'd be kind enough to avert your eyes."

A prickle of danger sense raced down Luke's spine, and he and Mara cried out in unison, "Don't!"

Luke used the Force to pull the Neimoidian's hand away from the panel, then stepped forward. "I think it's been altered."

"Altered?" the Neimoidian asked. "That's impossible. No one but our maintenance personnel can . . ." He let his explanation trail off when Luke ignited his shoto's short blade and carefully began to cut the security panel out of the wall.

"Have you gone spacesick?" the Neimoidian cried. "Who's going to pay for that?"

"I hope you're not trying to deny us access to the apartment," Raatu said. "Harboring terrorists results in a total property forfeiture."

"Who's harboring terrorists?" The Neimoidian threw up his hands. "Fine. I'll write it off as tenant damages."

Luke finished cutting, then deactivated his weapon and carefully pulled the unit out of the wall. Attached to one side was a small thermal detonator, with a thin signaling wire running from the security pad to its trigger.

"Well, at least we know we're at the right apartment," Mara said.

She reached over and depressed the detonator's safety, then broke the signaling wires, detached the casing from the security panel, and slipped it into her pocket for safekeeping.

Luke held the security panel out toward the Neimoidian. "*Now* you can enter the code."

The Neimoidian stared at the keypad for a moment, then began to shake and looked toward Luke. "Red seven, blue twelve, green zero zero."

Luke entered the code, and the doors slid open. Without waiting to be dismissed, the Neimoidian spun around and tried to leave again.

Luke caught his arm. "Wait here," he ordered. "You'll be safe in the hall—and I'll know if you try to leave."

The Neimoidian's face paled to ivory. "Of course. I'm happy to assist the Alliance any way I can."

Raatu patted the fellow's cheek. "That's a good citizen. Coruscant needs more like you."

Luke led the way into the apartment. It was smaller than he had expected and surprisingly cozy, with a sunken seating area in front of the entertainment wall. The rest of the walls were decorated with reproductions of famous artwork from across the galaxy—including a holographic copy of Leia's own *Killik Twilight*. But the thing that most surprised Luke were the mirrors. There was at least one on every wall, all carefully arranged so that it was possible to see any corner of the room by looking into the appropriate combination of mirrors.

Luke motioned to Raatu and Tozr to remain where they were, then he and Mara went into the bedroom and checked the closet and refresher to make certain Lumiya was not hiding anywhere. By the time they returned to the main room, the two detectives were already emerging from the kitchen area.

"Didn't I ask you to stay by the door?"

"You asked," Raatu replied. "She's not in the kitchen."

"Not in there, either," Mara said, hooking a thumb toward the bedroom. "Looks like we missed her."

"She'll be back." Tozr pointed to a bouquet of blue, long-stalked puffballs sitting in the middle of the dining table, then smiled and stepped over to smell them. "Nobody puts out fresh flowers unless they're coming—"

"No!" This time, it was Mara who Force-jerked a potential victim out of danger. She floated him to the opposite side of the room, then said, "I wouldn't do that."

Tozr flared his cheek folds in irritation. "Why not?"

"Sith specialize in tricks and traps." Luke took Raatu's datapad, then snapped an image of the flowers and requested an identification.

"That's why we wanted you to stay in the main room," Mara explained. "Everything in this place is a potential trap."

The datapad beeped, and Luke looked down to find a name and description of the flower. "Nerfscourge," he reported. "An overdose of pollen causes nerve damage in most species."

"Oh." Raatu glanced around the room a couple of times, then followed Tozr out into the hallway to wait with the building manager. "You can just dictate a record of what you find into the datapad."

"Good idea." Mara pointed Luke toward the kitchen. "You take the galley. The last thing I want is you rooting around in an old girlfriend's bedroom."

"No worries." Luke flashed a roguish grin. "Nothing in there I haven't seen before."

Mara shot him a look that could have melted a comet, then waved him into the kitchen. "Get busy. This woman is after our son, remember?"

Luke went into the kitchen and began to look through processing units and storage containers. He quickly learned that Lumiya lived almost entirely on juice and protein drinks—not too surprising given the challenges of maintaining a body that was as much cybernetic as flesh. But he found nothing to suggest how she had known Ben would be in Fellowship Plaza last night—no eavesdropping equipment tucked away in a cabinet, no electrobinoculars hanging from a drawer knob, no holocam recharger sitting on the counter. Nothing.

Luke turned back toward the living room and saw Mara's reflection staring at him out of a mirror. She seemed more beautiful than ever, her hair a deeper red, her face a little fuller and less lined.

"Notice anything?" She was speaking from the bedroom, but thanks to the reflection, Luke felt as though he were looking directly into her eyes. "About the mirrors, I mean."

"Of course," Luke said. "They're everywhere—and you can see the entire apartment from anywhere."

Mara appeared disappointed. "Not that," she said. "They distort your image—make you appear more attractive from every angle."

"Okay, now I see it," Luke said.

"Like you said, Sith are all about illusions and deception," Mara said. "Even when they're alone. Know what else I found?"

"Her datapad?" Luke asked hopefully.

"Sorry." Mara emerged from the bedroom empty-handed, and he turned to face her—the *real* her, which he thought was even more beautiful than the enhanced reflections. "Nothing. No luggage, no power cells, no tool kits."

Luke frowned. "No replacement parts?"

Mara shook her head. "Not a one."

"Replacement parts?" Raatu asked from the door.

"Cybernetic replacement parts," Luke answered. "Lumiya is as much machine as human, and that means she needs to maintain herself."

"Exactly," Mara said. "All Luke has is one mechanical hand, and he has to keep half a kilo of parts handy or risk not being able to cut his own nerf steak. Lumiya must carry a small workshop around."

Tozr raised his brow. "So if her tools aren't here—"

"Then neither is Lumiya." Raatu let out a vile Rodian curse. "Someone warned her we were coming!"

"No." Mara went into the bedroom, then returned with an elegant taffeta skirt-and-tunic set. "She intends to come back sometime. No woman would take her luggage and leave *this* behind—at least not one who has so many of *these* mirrors."

"So she's just taking a trip somewhere," Raatu said. "That means she had to arrange transport."

He entered the room, took the datapad from Luke, and went over to the entertainment wall. He started to jack it into the central comm port—then suddenly stopped and looked over his shoulder for reassurance.

Luke did not sense any danger. "It's safe," he said. "But I don't see what—"

"The Law Enforcement Tools Provision," Raatu explained. "I can recall all data accessed from this origination point anytime in the last month." He jacked in, then began to punch the keypad furiously. A moment later a section of the entertainment wall activated, displaying a record of data accesses from that location. He selected TRAVEL, and a map showing the location of the Bothan embassy appeared.

"What the blazes?" Tozr cried. "That doesn't make any sense!"

"It does if *Lumiya* killed the ambassador," Mara said. "See what other locations she's looked up."

Raatu tapped a few more keys, and a long list of addresses in the Bothan quarter appeared. Before Luke could request it, Raatu had already asked for a list of corresponding names.

As soon as names started appearing, Tozr gasped, "It's her! She's the one who's been killing Bothans!"

Luke and Mara shared a glance, silently asking each other if they needed to share something that Omas had told them the night before about the Bothan murders.

As Raatu continued to scroll through the long file, Tozr pulled out his comlink and started to open a channel.

Mara reached over and stopped him. "You might want to wait until you're back at headquarters."

Raatu craned his green neck around, the lips of his green snout pulled back into a threatening snarl. "This is a law enforcement matter."

"It's also a political minefield." Luke pointed at the names on the screen. "Those dead Bothans were all members of the True Victory Party."

Raatu's snarl vanished, and Tozr immediately snapped his comlink shut.

"We'll wait," the Bith said.

"Good idea," Mara said. "What I want to know is *how* Lumiya got their membership list."

"Let's see if I can sniff that out," Raatu said. He typed a few more commands, then a message came up asking for a password. He tapped the keys some more, and another message appeared. GAG ACCESS ONLY.

Raatu disconnected his datapad so fast that its speaker popped, and Tozr let his chin fall to his chest.

"Crimey," the Bith said. "Now we're just borked."

A second message appeared on the wall screen: YOUR ATTEMPT TO BREACH SECURITY HAS BEEN NOTED.

"How did Lumiya slice into GAG files?" Mara asked.

Luke didn't bother guessing. He was beginning to fear the answer was a lot less complicated than they realized— and the thought was causing an icy lump to gather in his belly. He stepped over to the apartment door and motioned the building manager over.

"What's the name on this lease?"

"Defula," the Neimoidian informed him. "Bant Defula."

"Defula?" Mara asked, coming up behind Luke. "Who's his employer?"

The Neimoidian removed a small datapad from his robe pocket and tapped in a command. "My records indicate that he's a senior executive with Astrotours Limited."

"Never heard of them," Mara said. "What's their comm code?"

The Neimoidian turned his datapad so she could see.

Mara frowned. "That's the same suffix as GAG's code."

Luke looked at the number and frowned himself. "Maybe it's just a coincidence," he said. "Just because two comm codes have the same suffix doesn't always mean they're related."

"No—but it usually does," Mara said. She turned to Raatu. "See what you can find out about Astrotours."

Raatu kept his hands away from the datapad. "Does it have anything to do with GAG?"

"That's what we're trying to find out," Luke said. "Go ahead. You've already tripped their security gate."

The Rodian let out a reluctant nose-whistle, but quickly brought up a poorly done information page advertising Outer Rim adventure cruises with stops at rugged worlds such as Hoth, Geonosis, and Dagobah.

"Who'd want to go to Geonosis?" Tozr asked scornfully. "It's nothing but a bug nest!"

"I think that's the point—*nobody* would," Mara said. "And Hoth and Dagobah aren't exactly vacation paradises, either."

"I don't know," Luke said. "Dagobah's all right."

"Only if you enjoy feeding leechwings," Mara retorted. She shook her head in disgust, then entered the comm code the building manager had provided for the renter. A moment later she arched her brow, then turned to Luke with a worried expression—but spoke into the comlink. "Corporal Lekauf—why am I not surprised?"

Luke suddenly found himself very angry. If Astrotours Limited was a GAG front company, then Lumiya had not sliced into the GAG files—she had been *given* access to them.

He pulled his own comlink and tried to open a channel to Ben, but Ben's comlink was still being blocked, probably because he was still in the security zone around Crix Base—or already aboard the *Anakin Solo.*

"Don't bother denying it," Mara was saying to Lekauf. "I recognize your voice."

Luke took the comlink from Mara, then said, "Corporal, this is Grand Master Skywalker of the Jedi order. Do you know whether Colonel Solo and my son have already boarded the *Anakin Solo?*"

"The *Anakin Solo,* sir?" Lekauf did his best to sound confused.

"Don't play stupid." Luke held the comlink between him and Mara so she could hear, too. "This is my son we're talking about."

Lekauf hesitated, then said, "I believe they have, yes. GAG was scheduled to take her out on a short shakedown."

"Then contact Crix Base and tell them to delay the *Anakin*'s departure," Luke said. If Lumiya was working with GAG, then she was working with Jacen, too. "My son is not going *anywhere* with Colonel Solo. Do you understand?"

Lekauf's only reply was a nervous silence.

"He *asked* if you understood!" Mara snapped.

"I understand, ma'am," Lekauf said. "But I'm afraid what Grand Master Skywalker asks is impossible. The *Anakin* left for Hapes an hour ago."

"Hapes?" Luke asked. He felt Mara take his comlink from his belt—since he was still speaking to Lekauf on hers—then saw her slip away to start making arrangements to follow. "Did I hear you correctly?"

"You did," Lekauf confirmed. "Apparently, the terrorists have attempted to assassinate Queen Mother Tenel Ka. She's requested Colonel Solo's aid in rooting them out."

Luke fell silent for a moment, trying to decide whether Lekauf was telling the truth or trying to throw him off the track of some other operation.

"Your son will be safe, sir," Lekauf said. "He's very well trained. I've worked with him myself."

Seeing that he had little choice at the moment but to accept what Lekauf was telling him, Luke said, "This had better be the truth, Corporal."

"It is, sir." Lekauf paused, then added in a reassuring tone, "Colonel Solo took a quarter of GAG along. I'd be with them myself, except I'm on desk duty because I twisted my knee a couple of days ago."

"Very well."

Luke glanced back at Raatu and Tozr, who were still staring at the last message on the wall screen and having a hissed debate about what they should do.

"There was an accidental attempt to access GAG files from your safehouse on the three hundredth floor of Zorp House," Luke said. "I'd like you to ignore it."

"Consider it done," Lekauf said. "And don't worry about your son. He'll be fine."

"I hope so, Corporal."

Luke closed the channel and turned to find Mara already talking on the comlink she had taken from him.

". . . hangar in twenty minutes," she was saying. "I want the *Shadow* prepped and ready to go."

chapter eleven

Jacen stood at the viewport of the *Anakin Solo*'s Command Salon, staring out at the cloud-mottled face of the planet Hapes. It was a world of splendor and abundance, covered in sparkling oceans and verdant islands, but Jacen was too troubled to enjoy looking at it. Someone had tried to kill Tenel Ka and his daughter, Allana. His hands were shaking and his stomach was knotted, and as he awaited the arrival of their shuttle his thoughts kept careening back and forth between fantasies of mass vengeance and eruptions of self-reproach.

Jacen *knew* he could not be Allana's first line of defense. So far, his relationship to her remained secret. If he spent too much time at the Fountain Palace, Tenel Ka's nobles would begin to suspect that the heir to the Hapan throne had been fathered by a Jedi foreigner, and that would only endanger Allana further. Besides, Tenel Ka was more than capable of protecting their four-year-old daughter, and he could not give up his anti-terrorism work back on Coruscant without letting the whole galaxy suffer.

But Jacen could not help feeling guilty and frightened.

Every instinct in him wanted to send Allana away to be raised somewhere safe—perhaps among the Fallanassi or Jensaarai. Only the experiences of his own childhood, which had proven again and again how fallible such strategies could be, prevented him from considering it.

That—and the fact that *no* place was truly safe. Jacen had spent most of his life trying to bring peace to a brutal and chaotic galaxy, and matters only seemed to be growing worse. There was always some unseen war about to spill over from the next system, some hate-filled demagogue ready to slay billions to assure the "greater good." Sometimes Jacen wondered if he was having any effect at all, if the galaxy would not have been just as well served had he never returned to the Jedi and remained among the Aing-Tii, meditating on the Force.

As Jacen contemplated this, the Hapan oceans began to sparkle more brightly. Some of the sparkles steadied into lights and began to shine in a hundred lustrous colors. Others turned red or gold and began to blink at regular intervals. They flowed together into narrow bands and began to circle the planet, like the rivers of flowing traffic that had once girdled Coruscant.

Jacen took three deep breaths, exhaling slowly after each, and consciously stilling his mind. While he could not yet summon Force-visions on command, he had learned to welcome them when they came. They were a manifestation of his unity with the Force, a sign of his growing power, and the increasing frequency with which they came reassured him that he would succeed, that he was strong enough to hold the galaxy together.

On the planet below, the island rain forests darkened to a deep, night-colored purple. Two white dots began to glow up from the heart of one of the shadowy islands, and Jacen found himself staring into the spots. They were larger and brighter than any of the lights on the oceans, and the longer he looked, the more they resembled eyes— white, blazing eyes staring up at him from a well of darkness.

A few wisps of cloud drifted across the face of the shadowy island, creating the impression of a lopsided mouth and a spectral face.

The mouth rose at the corners. "Mine."

The words were breathy and cold and rife with dark side power . . . and the voice was familiar. It sounded like Jacen's. He leaned closer to the viewport, studying the wispy features below, trying to decide whether he was seeing his own face.

But the clouds were not cooperating. The wisps drifted into a new arrangement, and a lumpy brow appeared above the eyes. The cheeks grew sunken and smashed, while the mouth became gaping and twisted. Then the entire face began to expand, drawing a veil of shadow over the rest of the planet and dimming its sea of scintillating lights.

The mouth rose at one corner, and the smile became a sneer. "Mine."

This time, the voice was too low and harsh to be Jacen's. He felt relieved, since the mangled face could not be a vision of his future if the voice did not belong to him.

The shadowy head continued to expand, swelling beyond the edges of the planet and engulfing the Hapan moons. The face became long and gaunt, its features now defined by patterns of the half-obscured light shining through from the surface of the planet.

"Mine."

This time the word was crisp and commanding, and the head continued to grow, becoming round and coarse. It swelled beyond what Jacen could see through his viewport, dimming the stars to all sides of Hapes and engulfing—as far as he could tell—the entire known galaxy. Most of the face vanished into unrecognizable patterns of light and shadow, but the eyes remained, expanding into a pair of blazing white suns.

"*Mine!*"

The white eyes flashed out of existence with all the brilliance of a pair of exploding novas, and Jacen felt as if an incendiary grenade had detonated in his head. He let out an involuntary groan and whirled away, hands clamped to his face.

But his head did *not* explode. The pain vanished as quickly it had arrived, and when he pulled his hands away, it was to find himself staring down at the reassuring pearliness of the Command Salon's luxurious resicrete deck covering. There weren't even any spots swimming before his eyes.

"I hope that expression doesn't mean you left something back on Coruscant," Lumiya said. She was sitting across the spacious cabin at Jacen's equipment-packed intelligence station, poring over the latest data on Tenel Ka's unpredictable nobles. "We have an opportunity to position you as the savior of the Galactic Alliance—but only if we move fast."

"*Positioning* me isn't what matters here." Jacen did not want Lumiya to see how shaken he was—at least not until he understood what the Force was trying to tell him. "Catching the terrorists who attacked the Queen Mother—*that's* important. Making certain it doesn't happen again—*that* matters."

Lumiya frowned. "What *do* you see down there?"

She rose and started across the cabin, wearing a black flight suit that matched exactly the color of the scarf that covered the lower half of her face. The pilot disguise was appropriate to the berthing she had demanded down near the hangar decks, and when she was in public areas, it also allowed her to conceal her disfigured face behind a darkened visor. On any other Star Destroyer, a pilot walking around in an identity-concealing helmet would have raised a security flag, but the *Anakin Solo* was a GAG vessel—and most GAG visitors had valid reasons for concealing their identities.

"What's wrong?" Lumiya inquired again. She stopped at Jacen's side and looked out on Hapes, which had returned to its normal placid appearance. "I see nothing disturbing."

"It's gone." Jacen could think of only one reason for the succession of dark faces he had seen, and he retained enough of his childhood indoctrination to shudder at the thought of a Sith dynasty. "Don't worry about it."

"Don't worry about *what*?" Lumiya pressed.

"Nothing."

Jacen continued to look out the viewport, watching distant smoke trails rise and fall as interplanetary traffic entered and departed the Hapan atmosphere. Was the Force telling him that he was making a terrible mistake, that the Sith way would lead the galaxy into a long era of darkness and tyranny?

"Come, Jacen. There can be no secrets between *us*." Lumiya slipped her hand under Jacen's arm and gently turned him toward her. "Tell me what you saw. I sense how it worries you."

"I'm *not* worried," Jacen insisted. He started across the cabin toward the intelligence station. "Have you found out who's behind the attack on the Queen Mother?"

"Silly boy—you won't fool me by changing the subject." Lumiya pulled him back around to face her, this time more forcefully. "I know how troubled you are. The veins in your neck are throbbing like drum worms."

"I doubt that very much," Jacen said. Like all Jedi Knights, he had been trained from childhood to conceal such obvious signs of his feelings—and he was far better at it than most. "I'm not troubled at all."

"Oh—I can *see* that," Lumiya mocked. "Then your pupils must be dilated because you are so excited." She looked out the viewport and allowed her gaze to linger on the face of the planet. "Is there some reason visiting Hapes would make you *happy*?"

"I'm always happy to come to the aid of an old friend," Jacen said carefully. The last thing he wanted was for Lumiya to keep probing and discover his feelings for Allana and Tenel Ka. "Tenel Ka and I were classmates at the Jedi academy."

"I see." Lumiya's voice assumed a knowing tone. "*Now* I understand why you are so concerned."

Jacen's heart leapt into his throat, and he began to worry that he had given away too much already. He had promised Tenel Ka that he would never reveal the secret of Allana's paternity to *anyone*—and when it came to Lumiya, he considered that promise doubly binding. The Sith regarded love as a blessing that must be sacrificed in order to balance the attainment of power, and there were some things Jacen would never be willing to sacrifice.

Jacen met Lumiya's gaze. "Actually, I don't think you do." He had to give her something else to think about, something that she would find even more engaging than whether or not he had a relationship with Tenel Ka. He exhaled slowly, then said, "I saw faces."

He went on to recount his vision, describing how the cowled heads had covered a little more of the galaxy each time he saw them. When he finished, Lumiya arched her thin eyebrows.

"And this future frightens you?" she demanded.

"I have a hard time thinking of a Sith *dynasty* as a good thing," Jacen admitted. "Call it family prejudice."

"Your family's opinion has been shaped by Darth Sidious." Lumiya's tone was surprisingly patient. "And he cared more about personal power than his responsibility to the galaxy. That is not the Sith way—as I had believed you to know by now."

"I know what you claim," Jacen said. Despite his tone, he was relieved to have changed the subject. "That the Sith way is the way of justice and order."

"The Sith way is the way of peace," Lumiya corrected. "To bring peace, first we must bring justice and order. To bring justice and order to the galaxy—"

"First we must control it," Jacen said. "I know."

Lumiya ran her fingertips down the inside of Jacen's arm. "Then why do you worry about what you saw?"

"You know why I worry." Jacen pulled his arm away—not sharply, but firmly enough to let her know he would not be distracted by her games. "You saw what Palpatine and my grandfather became."

"And that is how I know you won't fall to the temptations that undid them." Lumiya paused to think, then added, "Vergere certainly didn't think so, either . . . or you wouldn't have been the one she chose."

Jacen raised his brow. "There were other candidates?"

"Of course," Lumiya said. "Do you think we would select someone for such an important role without considering all our options? Kyp Durron is too stubborn and unpredictable, Mara too committed to her attachments, your sister too ruled by emotion—"

"You considered *Mara*?" Jacen gasped. "And *Jaina*?"

"We considered everyone. Your mother was too frightened by Darth Vader's legacy, your uncle was . . ." Lumiya's voice turned hard and cold. "Well, he wouldn't have listened. He was too bound by Jedi dogma."

"And old grudges," Jacen added. The long history of malice and betrayal between his uncle and Lumiya was one of the reasons he still had doubts about his decision to become a Sith. He was well aware that all Lumiya's talk of saving the galaxy might be a ploy; that turning him and Ben into Sith would be a vengeance on Luke that surpassed even murder. "What about you or Vergere? Why bother making me a Sith when you *were* Sith?"

"Because *we* wouldn't have succeeded," Lumiya said. "I'm as much machine as human, and you know how that limits me."

"I know the theory," Jacen said. "The Force can be tapped only by living beings, so people with largely cybernetic bodies can't use it to its full potential. But, frankly, your Force powers don't seem all that limited."

"Neither did your grandfather's—except to the Emperor, whose power *had* no limit," Lumiya replied. "You have the potential to succeed. I don't."

"And Vergere?" Jacen asked. He needed to know that Lumiya wasn't using him to get back at Luke; that he really *was* the only person who could bring an era of peace and order to the galaxy. "*Her* potential wasn't limited."

"Not in the way you mean. But could she ever win the confidence of *any* government?" Lumiya shook her head sadly. "She would always be tainted—at best suspected of being a Yuuzhan Vong agent, at worst of being a collaborator who helped them conquer so much."

Jacen sighed. "I imagine that's true." He was still unsure whether Lumiya was telling the truth, but he could find nothing in her explanations to prove she wasn't. "So that left me."

"I wouldn't say *left*," Lumiya replied. "You were clearly the best choice. Your reluctance to use Centerpoint against the Yuuzhan Vong demonstrated that you were capable of wielding great power responsibly. Your defeat of Tsavong Lah in personal combat proved you were not afraid to use great power when necessary. All that remained was for Vergere to recruit you."

"*Recruit* me?" Jacen scoffed, thinking of his long imprisonment among the Yuuzhan Vong. "You mean *capture*, don't you?"

"I mean *both*," Lumiya said. "Your uncle would have interfered with your training, so we had to isolate you. Vergere returned to the Yuuzhan Vong and helped them capture you, then maneuvered herself into a position to oversee your imprisonment."

"You mean my *breaking*," Jacen corrected. He was beginning to realize just how intricately the two had planned his fate. What had seemed like accident and coincidence at the time had been part of a much larger strategy—a strategy that he still did not fully comprehend. "Let's be honest. Vergere had to destroy what I *was* before she could turn me into what you needed."

Lumiya inclined her head. "Great strength demands great sacrifice. I have always been honest with you about that." She looked out the viewport and let her gaze linger on Hapes. "The question is: have you been honest with *me*? Are you willing to sacrifice all you love for the greater good?"

Jacen's stomach grew so hollow that he felt as if an air lock had opened inside him. Somehow, Lumiya *knew*. He started to demand how she had learned of the relationship . . . then realized that doing so would only reveal the depths of his feelings for Tenel Ka and Allana—and increase the likelihood that Lumiya would eventually demand their sacrifice in balance to his growing power.

He stepped to Lumiya's side. "I'm growing weary of being asked how much I'll sacrifice," he said. "I've already proven—"

A soft chime sounded from a small screen in the corner of the ceiling, then Ben's voice came out of the intercom speaker. "Special Agent Skywalker, sir. The packages have arrived."

"They're not packages, Ben," Jacen said. "They're our guests. Show them to their cabins and—"

"We would prefer to join you *now*." Tenel Ka's voice was less distinct than Ben's, but still very recognizable. "We'll freshen up later."

"That would be fine, Your Majesty." Jacen glanced over to find Lumiya studying him thoughtfully. "Will Ben be a satisfactory escort?"

"Quite," Tenel Ka replied. "We will see you directly."

The intercom crackled off, and a knowing twinkle came to Lumiya's eyes. "No need to worry, Jacen—I know when my presence would be a problem."

She went to the corner of the salon and touched her palm to a hidden pressure sensor. A meter-wide panel of wall popped forward and slid aside. She stepped through the opening into a narrow white corridor, then looked back over her shoulder. "When you need me, I'll be in my cabin."

"Good." Jacen went to the intelligence station and began to study the data Lumiya had gathered on Tenel Ka's nobles. "I'll let you know what else the Queen Mother can tell us about these suspects."

"I'm sure that will be very useful," Lumiya said.

As soon as the wall panel closed, Jacen summoned his

Tendrando Arms security droid, SD-XX, and asked him to do a security sweep of the entire cabin. He did not really suspect Lumiya of planting an eavesdropping device, but he was not going to take any chances. Lumiya clearly knew too much about his relationship with Tenel Ka already, and he was determined to keep her from learning any more.

By the time Jacen finished reviewing the files Lumiya had pulled, SD-XX had completed his sweep and was standing next to the intelligence station. With thin armor and blue photoreceptors set in a black, skull-like face, he resembled a scaled-down version of his progenitor line—the mighty Tendrando Arms YVH battle droid.

Jacen looked away from his display and nodded. "Report."

"No eavesdropping devices detected by preliminary and standard sweeps." The droid's voice was thin, raspy, and just a bit menacing. "Consent to proceed with a comprehensive sweep?"

"No," Jacen said. "We don't have time for that, Double-Ex."

"A standard security sweep is only ninety-three percent effective," the droid said. "If there is reason to suspect—"

"There isn't," Jacen said, rising. He had only a few moments before Ben arrived with Tenel Ka and Allana. SD-XX was designed to look menacing and ominous, and he did not want the droid giving his daughter nightmares. "Dismissed."

SD-XX remained next to the intelligence station. "Can you be certain, Colonel? In my experience, there's *always* reason to be suspicious."

"I'm *certain*." Jacen pointed toward the hidden exit Lumiya had used. "Leave the back way. I'm about to have visitors, and they don't have clearance to see you."

SD-XX leaned forward at the waist, then fixed his blue photoreceptors on Jacen's face and said nothing.

"Go," Jacen said. "That's an order."

SD-XX's voice grew cold. "Acknowledged."

He pivoted and stalked to the corner in utter silence, then touched the pressure sensor and vanished down the corridor. A moment later the feminine voice of Jacen's reception droid sounded over the intercom speaker.

"Special Agent Skywalker is here with your guests, Colonel Solo."

"Send them in."

Jacen rose and stepped out from behind his intelligence station. The door hissed, and Tenel Ka strode into the Command Salon with Allana at her side. Mother and daughter alike were dressed in tailored flight suits of gray eletrotex, a nanoweave material better known for its opalescent luster and outrageous cost than its effectiveness as an all-purpose armor.

Behind them followed Ben in his black GAG utilities, and an older woman with a long aquiline nose whom Jacen recognized as Tenel Ka's personal aide, Lady Galney. Bringing up the rear was DD-11A, a large Defender Droid with a cherubic face, synthskin torso, and weapons-packed arms. The droid served Allana as both bodyguard and nanny.

Jacen started to bow to Tenel Ka, but as soon as Allana saw him, she pulled her hand free of Tenel Ka's grasp and raced across the deck with her arms thrown wide.

"Yedi Jacen!"

Jacen laughed and leaned down to scoop her into his arms, and all trouble left his thoughts. She was a beautiful little girl with her mother's red hair and a button nose, and suddenly he knew that his long struggle was worthwhile, that he could *never* stop trying to bring peace and order to the galaxy . . . that Allana and all the children like her deserved to grow up on worlds untroubled by war and injustice.

Allana leaned back, studying Jacen with a pair of big gray eyes. "Jacen, some bad men twied to kill us but Mama's guards chased them off so now we can't have no more parties—"

"*Any* more parties," Tenel Ka corrected. She had stopped three paces from Jacen. Despite the worry circles beneath her eyes, she was as radiant as ever, with high cheeks and a long braid of red hair hanging over one shoulder. "Let Colonel Solo put you down. You're such a big girl now that you've grown too heavy to hold for long."

That wasn't true at all, of course. Jacen could have held Allana in his arms forever, because inside he was terrified of the sacrifice Lumiya kept hinting at. He *wanted* to hold his daughter forever, to keep her pressed safely against him and stay in constant touch with her through the Force—but doing *any* of those fatherly things would only place her in even more danger. Even this small display of Allana's affection had put thoughtful expressions on the faces of both Ben and Lady Galney.

"The Queen Mother is right," Jacen said, holding Allana out where he could look at her. Though he usually managed to sneak a visit three or four times a year, this was the first time he had noticed the same fiery sparkle in Allana's eyes that he had so often seen in his own mother's when he was growing up. "May I return you to the deck now?"

Allana frowned. "Yedi are supposed to be stwong!"

"I *am* strong," Jacen laughed. "But I need to save my strength for when I find the bad men."

Allana's eyes grew wide. "You're going to fight the bad men?"

"Of course," Jacen said. "Hunting bad men is my job."

Allana considered this a moment, then said, "Very well, Jacen—you can put me down . . . for now."

"Thank you." Jacen lowered Allana to the deck and watched her return to Tenel Ka's side. Then he turned to Ben, who was still studying him carefully, and said, "I'd like you to escort Lady Galney to the guest suite. Stand by during her inspection."

"Okay." Ben's voice betrayed his disappointment. "I mean, as you'd like, Colonel."

Jacen would have preferred to let Ben stay for Tenel Ka's briefing. But Ben had been present when Jacen learned that he was Allana's father, and Jacen worried that seeing them together would overcome the memory rub he had used to alter Ben's recollection of the incident.

Next, Jacen turned to Lady Galney. "Ben will see to anything you require to ensure the Queen Mother's comfort."

"Actually, I'll be staying." Galney flashed him a cold smile. "As I'm sure you can appreciate, times have been rather trying for the Queen Mother."

"I'll be *fine*, Lady Galney." Tenel Ka kept her gaze fixed on Jacen as she spoke. "Colonel Solo's suggestion is an excellent one—and I'd like you to take DeDe and Allana along. Ben—I mean, Special Agent Skywalker—can watch the Chume'da while DeDe does a security sweep."

Galney's green eyes flashed anger in Jacen's direction, but she inclined her head to Tenel Ka. "As you wish." She held her hand out to Allana. "Come along, Chume'da."

Allana stepped past the offered hand to Ben, then took his hand and pulled him toward the exit. "Are you a Yedi too, Ben?"

"Yes." Ben cast a guilty glance over his shoulder, then amended, "Sort of. I'm in training."

"Mama was a Yedi once," Allana said. "She still has her lightsaber and pwactices with a wemote . . ."

Allana's narrative grew inaudible as she led her small entourage deeper into the anteroom. Once the door had slid shut behind DeDe and Galney, Jacen and Tenel Ka stood facing each other in uncertain silence, their eyes meeting, but their bodies still three paces apart.

Finally, Jacen felt sure no one would be returning unexpectedly. "It's okay," he said. "I just had a security sweep."

Tenel Ka did not smile, but a look of relief flashed across her face. She was in Jacen's arms almost before he could open them. "It is good to have you here, Jacen. Thank you for coming."

"I'm glad you asked me." Jacen held her to his chest, then said, "You didn't need to come up here, though. I would have been happy to come to the palace."

"No. This is better." Tenel Ka pulled back far enough to look up into his eyes. "I needed to bring Allana someplace safe."

Jacen cocked a brow. "And your palace *isn't*?"

"Not at the moment." Tenel Ka took his hand and led him over to the viewport, where the shadowy crescent of the planet's night side was just rotating into view. "Someone poisoned the witnesses."

"Witnesses?" Jacen asked.

"To the coup attempt," Tenel Ka explained. "I had everyone who saw the attack isolated in the Well."

"The Well is your detention center?" Jacen asked.

Tenel Ka nodded. "My *secret* detention center," she explained. "Comfortable, hidden, and very secure. My ancestors have used it for more than twenty centuries to detain troublesome nobles, and no one has *ever* escaped from it."

"They still haven't, if I understand what you said correctly." Jacen flashed a lopsided Solo grin. "Unless the Hapan definition of *escape* is broader than it is in most parts of the galaxy."

Tenel Ka frowned at him. "Your joke is not funny, Jacen. Most of the men who died were innocent bystanders. I was only holding them until I could determine who was and was not involved in the attack."

"Bystanders? Why would anyone poison . . ." Jacen let the question trail off, then said, "Tenel Ka, whoever killed the prisoners is trying to do more than silence co-conspirators."

Tenel Ka nodded. "If all they wished was to protect their own identity, they wouldn't have poisoned *all* the prisoners." She turned and stared out at the darkening planet below. "The usurpers want it to appear that I am killing the innocent as well as the guilty. They are trying to turn my nobles against me."

"We won't let that happen. We'll find out who these usurpers are and stop them." Jacen placed his hands on her shoulders. "You said the Well is secret. Who knows about it?"

"Only one company of my personal guard and a few members of my inner circle."

"It *could* be someone in the guard," Jacen said. "But chances are—"

"Yes—it always seems to be the ones closest to you."

Jacen looked toward the salon exit. "Lady Galney?"

"That's not what I mean," Tenel Ka said. "Lady Galney's family members are among my strongest supporters. Her sister will rally to my cause the moment Jaina delivers my summons."

Jacen frowned. "Jaina was here?"

"Yes." Tenel Ka took Jacen's hand and led him toward the salon's conversation area. "Your sister arrived shortly after your parents."

"My *parents*?" Jacen was growing more perplexed every moment. "What are *they* doing here?"

"Nothing, any longer. They've fled." Tenel Ka sat on the couch and pulled Jacen down beside her. "I'm afraid they may have been involved in the assassination attempt."

"*Involved?*"

"Participated," Tenel Ka clarified.

For a time, Jacen was too stunned to reply. He knew his parents had taken Corellia's side in the conflict—that was one of the few things that made him question the Galactic Alliance's position—but assassination was just not their style. At least, he had *thought* it wasn't, until he started to read the intelligence reports describing his father's role in the murder of Thrackan Sal-Solo.

Finally, Jacen turned to Tenel Ka. "You're sure?"

"I am sure they were here," Tenel Ka explained. "They arrived on the day of the Queen's Pageant and insisted that they had an appointment to see me. At first, I thought there had been a miscommunication, but my security staff is now convinced that their assignment was to cause a break in my security routine."

"Your security staff is convinced." Jacen stood and looked into the corner, trying to make sense of what he was hearing, trying to picture the people who had raised him—the good-hearted scoundrel and the principled diplomat—setting up Tenel Ka for an assassination attempt. "What do *you* think?"

"Jacen, I don't know what to think," Tenel Ka said.

"Some preliminary reports suggested that they may have been trying to warn me about the assassins, but . . ."

Jacen continued to face the corner. He was beginning to feel almost relieved. Maybe Allana was not the sacrifice Lumiya kept talking about. Maybe his *parents* were what he would be required to surrender, and maybe their deaths would not be a coldhearted act of betrayal after all. Maybe he would be serving the Balance, merely delivering a final and terrible justice to one more pair of murdering terrorists.

"But what?" he asked, not looking away from the corner. "Go on."

"But they were seen leaving with the leader of the assassins," Tenel Ka finished. "She even went to their aid when my guards pinned them down."

"I see." A terrible sense of sadness came over Jacen, and a sense of inevitability. Had his parents really drifted across the thin line that separated heroes from murderers? Had they *really* slipped into the murky realm of terrorism? He turned to face Tenel Ka. "Is there any reason to think we should place our faith in the reports suggesting they were trying to warn you?"

Tenel Ka lowered her eyes. "Not really."

"I didn't think so." Jacen crossed the cabin to his comm station. "It appears my parents have become part of the problem in this war."

"Jacen, what are you doing?" Tenel Ka asked, following. "Please remember that as bad as it looks, we don't know the whole story yet."

"But we need to." Jacen slipped into the chair and activated the data display, then began to scroll through a long list of electronic forms. "That's why we need to find them."

"Do we?" Tenel Ka came around the desk and stopped

behind him. "After the *Millennium Falcon* left Hapes, she vanished into the Transitory Mists. As long as she stays vanished, I'm willing to give your parents the benefit of the doubt . . . in fact, I *want* to."

"Tenel Ka, we just can't do that." Jacen found the form he was looking for—a GAG SEARCH AND DETAIN WARRANT—and began to enter the names of his parents. "But thank you for offering."

"Jacen, stop." Tenel Ka used the Force to pull his hands away from the keyboard. "If you're angry with them because Allana was threatened, that's not fair. Your parents don't even know that Allana is their granddaughter, and there would have been an assassination attempt anyway."

Jacen lowered his guard so that Tenel Ka could sense his emotions, then said, "I'm *not* angry. I'm sad."

He pulled his hands free of her Force grasp and resumed entering his parents' data on the warrant.

"But this is bigger than me—and it may even be bigger than the Hapes Consortium." He entered a description of the *Millennium Falcon,* then hit a key and sent the warrant to the dispatch center. "Whatever the terrorists are planning, my parents are a part of it—and GAG needs to know how."

chapter twelve

The *Falcon* had reverted into the deepest, darkest space Leia had ever seen. The handful of stars she could see through the cockpit canopy were mere ghost twinkles, and the frequency with which they kept vanishing and reappearing made her think she might be imagining them.

"Who dimmed the blast-tinting?" Han asked, complaining more than inquiring. "Check that flash detector. It must be on the blink."

Leia pulled a glow rod from the emergency kit next to the copilot's seat and shined a light into a thumb-sized dome that sat on top of the instrument console. The ghost stars vanished instantly as the canopy darkened.

"The flash detector is fine," she reported. "We must have stumbled into a bank of Transitory Mists."

"*Stumbled* is not how I would describe it," said their passenger, Nashtah. The assassin was slouched in the navigator's seat, rolling an unsheathed vibrodagger between her long fingers. Her hair remained in its bushy topknot, and she was still dressed in her sleeveless bodysuit. "The mists absorb light and block long-range sensor readings."

"I see," Leia said. "So you were expecting this?"

"Always a good idea to blind your pursuers." Nashtah's black-rimmed eyes shifted to the back of Han's head. "We can take our time plotting our next jump. They won't find us in this."

"I like your thinking," Han said, watching her reflection in the canopy. "After the way things went back at the palace, we'll be leading a fleet of Battle Dragons around the galaxy if we're not careful."

Nashtah shrugged. "No worries. They'd have to be right on top of us to plot our next vector."

She continued to slouch in her seat, rolling the vibrodagger between her fingers and waiting for the Solos to start plotting jump coordinates they did not have. In the silence that followed, Leia began to think it might not be such a good idea to try tricking the assassin into revealing the identity of the coup leader. There was a cold hunger in Nashtah's Force presence that suggested she was just looking for an excuse to plant her vibrodagger in the back of Han's neck.

When the long silence began to stretch from uncomfortable to alarming, Leia unbuckled her crash webbing and rose.

"I don't know about you two, but I'm famished." She gave Han's shoulder an affectionate squeeze, then turned toward the rear of the cockpit; the last thing she wanted was to fight this assassin—but if it *had* to happen, she wanted room to maneuver. "Why don't I fix us something to eat while you do the sweep?"

"Sweep?" Nashtah asked.

"For homing beacons," Han said, smoothly following Leia's lead. "We *always* do a sweep after a scrape like that—a habit we picked up fighting Imperials."

"Ah." Nashtah's sunken eyes shifted from Leia to Han's reflection. "Very clever."

Han seemed to wilt a little beneath her scrutiny. "Uh, yeah." He unbuckled his crash webbing and started after Leia. "And count me in for the grub. I'm hungry enough to eat a rancor."

"Yes, eating would be nice." Nashtah sheathed her vibro-dagger and followed, clearly determined not to let the Solos out of her sight—especially together. "A good fight always whets my appetite."

They traveled down the cockpit access corridor to the main cabin. Han went to the engineering station to scan for unauthorized signals, and Leia went to the galley. The Noghri remained out of view, though Leia could feel them nearby, one hiding just inside the forward hold, the other lurking a few paces down the main corridor. Thankfully, C-3PO was in the rear of the ship, supervising a routine check of the backup life-support systems.

Instead of offering to help either Leia or Han, Nashtah took a seat at the table, where she would be in a good position to watch them both. None of them removed their weapons belts.

Leia called up a list of stores, then turned half toward Nashtah. "What would you like? We have brogy stew, gorba melts—"

"Do you have nerf steaks?" Nashtah interrupted.

"Sure," Leia said. Nerf steaks were more dinner than lunch, but who knew what timetable Nashtah was on? "How would you like it?"

"*Them,*" Nashtah corrected. "I need three. Just defrosted will be fine."

"*Three?*" Leia gasped. She did not mean to be rude, but even Saba would have trouble eating that much meat—and Saba was a *Barabel.* "Perhaps you're accustomed to smaller steaks than we stock. These are half a kilo apiece."

Nashtah's eyes flashed as though insulted. "Make it four," she ordered. "My species has an . . . *unusual* metabolism."

"I think the word you're looking for is *ferocious*," Leia said. "Defrosted it is."

She punched an order into the galley's multiprocessor, requesting two gorba melts for her and Han, and the four steaks for Nashtah. Then she returned to the table and sat across from the assassin.

"What *is* your species?" Leia asked, trying to sound casual and polite. "You have a youthful appearance, but I sense that you've lived a long and interesting life already."

"You *sense*?" Nashtah's face remained as severe and unreadable as ever, but the Force around her began to warm with resentment. "Be careful what you *sense*, Jedi. The dark side can be catching."

Leia frowned, suddenly feeling even more cautious and curious about the assassin than before. "Are you saying you were a *Jedi*?"

Nashtah laughed—a dry, humorless croak—then promptly changed the subject. "Why don't you and Captain Solo know where we are going?"

"I'll take that as a *no comment*," Leia said, automatically buying time. An abrupt change of subject could be just as effective for eliciting a candid reply as for avoiding one and, even without the tingle racing down her spine, Leia knew that her next answer would be a dangerous one. "Does that mean you don't want to talk about your species, either?"

"My mother was human. My father was a ghost in the night, and I doubt even my mother knew his species—but it was obviously a long-lived one." Nashtah drew her lips back in an indifferent smile. "If I ever find out who he was, perhaps I'll be able to hunt him down and kill him." Her hand drifted toward the swinging holster she wore on her hip. "So how come you and Captain Solo don't know who our employer is?"

Leia's danger sense turned to a sinking feeling. "Han and I don't work for your employer." She cautiously moved her hand to the hilt of her lightsaber. "We're agents of the Corellian government."

"That's right," Han said from across the cabin. He had stopped work and was facing Nashtah, his hand propped on the butt of his own blaster. "Prime Minister Gejjen asked us to go to the palace and lure Tenel Ka into a public area. That's *all* we knew about your plan."

"And you *agreed*?" Nashtah asked. It did not seem to trouble her that if a fight was to erupt, she would be caught in the middle of Han, Leia, and their Noghri— whom Leia felt sure the assassin could sense watching them. "My information says Tenel Ka is a Solo family friend."

"She is—and she's on the wrong side of this war." Leia put some durasteel in her voice. "I've seen one Empire rise in my lifetime. I don't want to see another."

"We'll do whatever it takes to stop it," Han said. "My own *son* is torturing Corellians."

"He does seem to be following his grandfather's example, doesn't he?" Nashtah kept her eyes fixed on Leia, and for the first time her smile appeared genuine. "That must make you very . . . unhappy."

"Unhappy isn't the way I'd put it." Despite the obvious enjoyment Nashtah took in her pain, Leia answered honestly; if they were to have any hope of tricking the assassin into revealing the identity of the coup leader, they had to win her trust. "It terrifies me."

Nashtah actually licked her lips. "Truly?"

"Yes." Leia took a deep breath, then continued, "When Han and I married, I didn't want children because I didn't want to take the chance that one of them would grow up to become another Darth Vader."

Han frowned across the cabin at Leia, clearly unhappy at having their family life revealed to an assassin.

"Then something happened to change your mind," Nashtah surmised. "You hardly strike me as the careless type."

"I'm not," Leia said. "We were on a mission to Tatooine. I started to have Force-visions, and then someone gave me my grandmother's vid-diary. When I began to see my father through her eyes . . ."

Leia let her sentence trail off, unable to help wondering if she had misinterpreted events all those years ago—if she should have seen Jacen's dark future in the burning eyes of the Force-vision she had experienced, if she should have heard the menace in its cruel-voiced message: *Mine . . . mine.* She had concluded at the time that the Force was trying to tell her that *she* belonged to it, that she needed to entrust it with her future. But now . . . now she could not help wondering if the vision had been something darker, some unseen evil laying claim to her issue.

"You changed your mind," Nashtah said, finishing Leia's sentence. "You began to think the danger was not real?"

Leia nodded.

"And *now* what do you think?" Nashtah's eyes were sparkling with delight. "Was your fear justified?"

"Just hold on a blasted second." Han started across the deck toward the assassin. "If you think we wish we never had kids—"

Leia raised a hand and used the Force to stop Han from

coming any closer. "If Han and I had never raised children, there would have been no Anakin Solo to save the Jedi from the voxyn, no Jacen Solo to show us the way to victory against the Yuuzhan Vong, no Jaina Solo to lead the fight. So what I *think* is that it's unwise to oppose the will of the Force."

"I see," Nashtah said. "So if it's the will of the Force for your son Jacen to follow in the path of his grandfather, you won't oppose it?"

"It's too early to tell how far down that path Jacen will go, but I *won't* let him become another Darth Vader." Leia saw the alarm her reply raised in Han's eyes, but to give any other answer would have been to step into Nashtah's trap—to admit that the reasons she had given for turning against Tenel Ka were false. "Whatever it takes to stop that from happening, I'll do."

Nashtah continued to study Leia. "*Whatever* it takes?"

"You heard her." Han said. He had stopped in the middle of the cabin, with his hand still resting on the butt of his blaster pistol. "Not that it's any business of yours how we feel about the way our kids turned out."

"It might be, when you realize that you can't handle him yourself." Nashtah slowly looked from Leia to Han. "I *specialize* in Jedi, you know. That's why they recruited me for Tenel Ka."

"Yeah?" Han replied. "Well, leave us your contact data and we'll think about it."

The multiprocessor chimed three times, announcing that lunch was ready.

Han unsnapped the keeper strap on his holster. "Are we gonna eat, or what?"

Nashtah's gaze dropped to his hand and stayed there for a moment. Then she let out a snort of derision and slowly moved her hand away from her blaster. "Eating sounds good," she said.

"Wonderful," Leia said. Trying to keep her sigh of relief relatively inaudible, she went to the multiprocessor and prepared a tray with the two savory-smelling gorba melts and Nashtah's four defrosted steaks. "Would you like something to drink, Nashtah?"

"Not necessary," the assassin said. "But I will need an empty glass."

Resisting the temptation to ask why, Leia added the empty glass to the tray, then returned to the table and distributed its contents.

To Leia's astonishment, Nashtah took one of the raw nerf steaks and rolled it tight. Holding it over the empty glass, the assassin wrapped her long fingers around the meat and sank her sharp nails into it, then carefully squeezed the blood out.

Suddenly Leia's gorba melt no longer smelled quite so savory.

Nashtah smiled at Leia's obvious look of revulsion, then said, "I saw your father race once."

"Race?" Han echoed. Though his eyes were fixed on Nashtah's slowly filling glass, he was gobbling down his sandwich and had to speak around a full mouth. "You mean *Podrace*?"

"Yes. It was the Boonta Eve Classic. He was good . . . *very* good."

"So I've heard." Leia found herself feeling resentful of Nashtah. As much as she still hated the memory of Darth Vader, over the years she had come to think of her father as the little boy she had glimpsed in her grandmother's vid-diary, and it seemed somehow unfair that this assassin had been there at the high point of his life when all Leia had known were the low ones. "He won, I believe."

"That's right. It was when he earned his freedom." Nashtah put the shriveled steak aside, then took a drink from the glass and smacked her lips in approval. "Do you know what always amazed me about that race?"

"Wait a minute." Han swallowed a mouthful of gorba melt. "You expect us to believe you were *there*?"

"*I* believe her, Han." Leia pushed her uneaten gorba melt aside, then asked, "What amazed you, Nashtah?"

"That he didn't cheat," she replied. "All that natural Force ability, and he ran an honest race in a contest that has no rules."

"Your point?" Leia asked.

Nashtah gulped down the contents of her glass, then picked up another steak and began to refill it. "Do I need to have a point?"

"Yeah." Han scowled. "It helps move the conversation along."

Nashtah arched her brow—somehow making even that simple gesture seem menacing.

"Then I suppose my point is this." The steak made a soft bursting noise as she tightened her grasp, forcing all the juice from it at once. Nashtah looked back to Leia. "Your father was as full of surprises as you are. I suppose I *do* believe your story."

"Good." Leia started to reach for her vitajuice, then caught a glimpse of what was in Nashtah's glass and thought better of it. "Then I hope you'll allow us to take you wherever you need to go."

Nashtah nodded. "Telkur Station."

"Telkur Station?" Han asked doubtfully. "You expect us to believe a bunch of *pirates* hired you?"

Nashtah eyed Han coldly. "Did I *say* we were going to meet my employers?"

chapter thirteen

The pincer-shaped silhouettes of a dozen Miy'til starfighters rose above the hill behind Villa Solis, then shot skyward on pillars of blue efflux. Jaina craned her neck, watching in silence as the fighter squadron arced toward a cluster of bright points already drifting across Terephon's night sky. She estimated the number of points at nearly thirty, and even as she watched they were arranging themselves into the open-diamond formation of a battle fleet deploying for a jump to hyperspace.

"Something's just not right about that," she said, still looking at the fleet. Having been denied hangar access by the flight chief, she and Zekk had landed outside the front gate only a short time before. "*We're* supposed to be the ones delivering mobilization orders for Tenel Ka. To ready a fleet this fast, Ducha Galney would have had to know about the coup attempt before we left Hapes."

"Well, her sister *is* Tenel Ka's chamberlain." Zekk was referring to the haughty Lady Galney, who had seemed so convinced in the aftermath of the coup attempt that Jaina's parents had participated in the attack. "Maybe Lady Galney told the Ducha what happened."

"How?" Jaina asked. "Terephon is in the Transitory Mists. There's no HoloNet here, remember?"

Zekk merely grunted and turned to study the spike-topped domes rising above the villa wall. Jaina did not need the Force to tell her that he was less interested in the villa's simple architecture than in avoiding a conversation with her. During the long and complicated journey from Hapes, he had allowed no more Force contact than was necessary to coordinate their hyperspace jumps, and his only words so far had been about seeing the Ducha.

Jaina grabbed his arm and turned him to look at her. "Look, we've got a mission to do. So whatever's kinking your air hose—get over it!"

Zekk pulled his arm away, but spoke in a mild voice. "I think I *am* over it."

"Good," Jaina said. Then she frowned, realizing that for the first time in years, she had no idea what Zekk meant. "Over *what*, exactly?"

"Jaina, stop," Zekk said. "You don't do coy very well."

"*Coy?*" Now Jaina was really confused. She could almost always tell what Zekk was thinking—at least until now. "Zekk, I don't know what you're talking about. I really don't."

Zekk studied her a moment, then arched his dark brows. "Come on—we're not *that* un-Joined." He shook his head. "You've wanted this for years. Stop hiding from it."

He secured his StealthX and started toward the villa, leaving Jaina alone. She was so accustomed to his blind approval that she could not quite believe he was talking to her as though she were a spoiled little girl. She returned in her mind to the last time things had seemed normal between them, shortly after they had arrived at the Fountain Palace and discovered that her parents were suspected of involvement in the coup attempt.

Zekk had tried to comfort her, suggesting that assassination just was not her parents' style, and she had snapped at him. He had stalked off to the other side of the room, and though he had continued to defend her parents to Tenel Ka and Prince Isolder, toward *her* he had remained silent and withdrawn.

"By the Force!" Jaina secured her own StealthX and caught up to him. "Is *that* what this is about? What I said in the sitting room? I was worried about my parents! You can't hold that against me."

"I *don't*," Zekk replied. "I just finally realized what . . ." He caught himself and softened his tone. "Look, Jaina, I just realized that you've been right all along. We're better as friends than we would ever be as lovers. I know you've been saying it for years, but I guess part of me really didn't believe it until now."

Jaina was so astonished that she stopped walking and simply stood there staring at Zekk's broad back. She had broken off their romance when they were teenagers, and she had been trying to get him to stop pursuing her ever since. So why did it suddenly feel like she had lost something?

Now that she understood what had happened, Jaina realized she could still feel Zekk's presence in the back of her mind. He was strong and certain and independent . . . and so over her. He had finally granted her wish.

And that was a good thing—it really was.

Jaina hurried to catch up, then fell in at Zekk's side. "It's about time," she grumbled. "Now maybe I can stop waiting until you're asleep to take my sanisteams."

Zekk laughed. "It didn't work anyway," he said. "I kept having these dreams . . ."

"You did?" Jaina glanced over to find a mischievous glint in Zekk's eye, but now that she had located their connection again, she *knew* he was telling the truth. "And you didn't say anything?"

Zekk shrugged and flashed an embarrassed grin. "I thought they were just . . . well, dreams."

Jaina started to accept his explanation, then had the sudden realization that he was mocking her.

"Liar!" She punched him in the shoulder. "Let's just deliver Tenel Ka's message."

"Sure," Zekk chuckled. "That's what I've been *trying* to do."

Jaina strode ahead, taking the lead as they crossed the last few meters to the gate. Villa Solis was a cluster of squat round buildings, constructed of white gratenite and located in the heart of the planet's remote moorlands. It was surrounded by two hundred kilometers of bog country, and the only practical way to reach it was by air. All in all, it was one of the most isolated and inaccessible retreats Jaina had ever visited—but she supposed that was the point. Lady Galney had warned them that the only thing her sister the Ducha enjoyed more than privacy was hunting, and there would certainly be plenty of both available at Villa Solis.

As they drew nearer, Jaina kept expecting a panel to slide open in the tarnished crodium gate so a sentry—or at least a security droid—could issue a challenge. But the villa remained eerily silent, with nothing stirring but the dank bog breeze.

"Too quiet," Zekk said. "They *must* know we're here."

"Yeah," Jaina said. As elusive as StealthXs were, even they created a sonic boom when they sliced down through an atmosphere at many times the local speed of sound. "Maybe we scared 'em."

Once they had stopped in front of the gates, a brass-sheathed tentacle shot up to each side of them. Jaina and

Zekk both snapped the lightsabers off their belts and pivoted so they were standing back-to-back, and Jaina found herself looking into the bobbing, dark blue lens of a Serv-O-Droid gatekeeper's eye pod.

"You have one minute to leave the essstate." The gatekeeper's voice—emitted by a small vocabulator hidden behind its eye pod—had been customized to sound sibilant and menacing. "Failure to obey will be dealt with harshly."

"We're here with a message for the Ducha," Jaina replied.

"You're not on the schedule." It was the gatekeeper on Zekk's side that spoke this time, in a voice that was sugary and feminine. "You should have requested an appointment."

"How?" Zekk asked. "The HoloNet doesn't reach Terephon."

"Our message is from Queen Mother Tenel Ka," Jaina added. "It's important."

"Then you'll have to make an appointment and return when you're on the ssschedule," the first gatekeeper said. "The Ducha is not in residence at thissss time."

Jaina frowned. "The Royal Intelligence Service says she *is*," she retorted. "And they haven't been wrong about the whereabouts of any of the *other* nobles we've visited."

The two gatekeepers reared back on their motility tentacles. "You have thirty secondsss to depart," the first said. In a sweet voice, the second added, "Termination procedures are already under prepar—"

Jaina activated her lightsaber in the same instant Zekk's blade snapped to life. They lashed out together, not so much slicing through the eye pods as incinerating them, then reversed their strokes in perfect unison, cut the motility tentacles off at the ground, and pivoted to face the gate.

"Better mission partners than we would be lovers, too," Jaina observed.

"No surprise," Zekk grunted. "We've actually been on missions together."

When the attack the gatekeepers had threatened did not materialize, Jaina asked, "Why would the Ducha be so reluctant to hear a message from Tenel Ka?"

"Don't know," Zekk said. "Guess we'll have to ask her when we track her down."

Jaina glanced up into the night sky, eyeing the bright flecks of the Ducha's gathering fleet. "I think there are a couple of things we'll need to ask her about."

She reached out in the Force and was a little surprised to feel only a single sentient presence on the other side of the gate.

"Open up!" she demanded. "We're not here to hurt anyone."

There was no response.

After a moment, Zekk glanced at Jaina and cocked a questioning brow. Jaina shrugged and stepped into position behind him, prepared to counter any attacks they were about to draw. Zekk plunged his lightsaber into the seam where the gate met the wall, then began to drag the blade slowly downward, cutting the internal locking bars.

A muffled voice sounded from the other side. "Stop!"

They heard a loud *clunk,* then the gate retracted into the wall with a pneumatic *whoosh.* On the other side stood a brawny, moon-faced woman wearing a grimy leather apron over a much-stained tunic. Her eyes were narrow and puffy, her nose was wide and flat, and her thick lips were curled into a permanent sneer. All in all, she was probably the ugliest Hapan whom Jaina had ever seen.

The woman frowned at Jaina. "It wasn't necessary to have your man cut the Ducha's gate," she said. "I would have let you in."

"Then you shouldn't have taken so long to make up your mind." Jaina deactivated her lightsaber, but continued to glare at the woman. "What's your name?"

"Entora," the woman replied. "Entora Zar."

"Well, Entora," Jaina said, "the next time a Jedi Knight addresses you, you might want to answer."

She and Zekk stepped through the gate into an eye-boggling mass of domed, white-gratenite structures, packed so tightly that at first glance it looked impossible to squeeze between them. Every window was shuttered, every door closed, and, aside from the ugly woman, there was no one in sight.

Jaina extended her Force-awareness a few dozen meters deeper into the compound and felt only the furtive presences of tiny vermin creatures.

"Where is everyone?" Zekk demanded.

"Gone," Zar said. "Your poor piloting was an affront to the Ducha's sensibilities."

Jaina was too astonished by Zar's audacity to be offended. "Our *piloting*?"

"Your entry angle was too steep," Zar said. "You couldn't decelerate fast enough to make a graceful approach. I'm surprised you didn't rip your wings off."

"We weren't *trying* to make a graceful approach," Jaina said through gritted teeth. "And I don't recall asking your opinion."

"Our craft have unique flight characteristics," Zekk explained. "They don't handle like XJ-Sevens, especially in the atmosphere."

"I doubt you could do any better with an XJ-Seven," Zar replied. "You obviously need more simulator time in *anything* you fly."

This was too much for Jaina. "Listen, rodder, I started flying XJs into combat before I was old enough to sign my own contracts. How many hours have *you* logged?"

"In an XJ?"

"No, in a pedal car!" Jaina retorted. "Of *course* in an XJ."

Zar looked away. "None, actually."

"None?" Jaina could not believe what she was hearing; no decent pilot would presume to know the proper atmospheric entry angle for a craft she'd never flown. "Then what *do* you fly?"

"A lot of different stuff," Zar answered with pride. "The Naboo Royal N-One, the Mark One Headhunter, the Xi Char DFS—"

"Those are antiques, not starfighters!" Jaina objected.

"And the DFS was a droid fighter," Zekk said, scowling suspiciously. "Where have you been flying those craft?"

Zar glared at Zekk, clearly offended that a mere male would dare question her credentials. "The same place I do all my flying," she said. "On my holosimulator. I'm a rated instructor."

Jaina's jaw dropped. "Are you crazy? There's a . . ." She felt a Force-nudge from Zekk and realized that she was allowing herself to be distracted by what was at best an irrelevancy and at worst an intentional delaying tactic. "Never mind. Just take us to the Ducha."

But Zar wasn't ready to drop the holosimulator debate. "In fact, I'm probably a better pilot than you, since my unit—"

"You're *not*," Jaina interrupted. "And we're done arguing about it."

Jaina pushed past on one side and Zekk on the other, both ignoring Zar's protests that they had no permission. As the daughter of a famous stateswoman, Jaina had learned early that it was always best to ignore blowhards and idiots.

There were no human presences in any of the nearby buildings. Jaina extended her Force-awareness deeper into the villa and was surprised to feel nothing there, either. But when she reached beyond the compound itself into the surrounding area, she did detect a knot of frightened people deep under the hill, in the vicinity of the villa's underground hangar.

"You feel that?" Jaina asked Zekk. "They're *hiding* from us."

Zekk nodded. "Probably an emergency shelter under the hill with the hangar."

"That would make sense," Jaina said. "But why would they be afraid of *us*?"

Zekk shrugged. "Guess we'll have to ask them."

He did not bring up the possibility of asking Zar, and Jaina did not suggest it. Another conversation with the woman would only cause further delay, and Jaina doubted they would learn anything useful. Zar was hardly the type of woman a shrewd Hapan noble would trust with any information not meant to deceive.

They continued deeper into the villa, with Zar trailing along and protesting. Now and again a mouse droid zipped across a nearby intersection, and once they came across a cleaning droid carefully polishing the gratenite blocks that paved the walkway. Otherwise, the interior of the villa remained as deserted as the entrance had been.

Given that the buildings were all locked and they were simply here to deliver a message, Jaina refrained from breaking in. But from the evidence she noticed as they passed—scarred door frames, an outdoor roasting pit, the sour smell of tanning vats—the villa certainly appeared to be the favorite hunting retreat of a very wealthy noble. The only odd part was that the Ducha would feel compelled to take her entire household into hiding because two Jedi had arrived with a message from Tenel Ka.

A few moments later, they reached the hill at the back of the compound, where an artificial cliff indicated the source of the gratenite that had been used to build Villa Solis. A pair of white towers stood tight against the cliff, one on each side of a large pit. The pit was surrounded by a chest-high wall, and from its interior rose a faint stench of decay and muskiness.

After confirming that both towers were sealed as tightly as had been the other buildings, Jaina went to inspect the pit. It was about three meters deep from the foot of the wall, with a muddy bottom littered by crushed bones and animal skulls. Pressed into the thin mud were the impressions of dozens of huge paddle-shaped feet, always arranged in pairs on either side of a long serpentine depression.

The back of the pit extended beneath the cliff, creating a large cave beneath the hill. Deep within the cave, Jaina sensed a cluster of semi-intelligent presences.

Zekk came to her side and peered over the wall, then made a sour face at the smell. "I hope that isn't the only way in."

"Can't be." Jaina pointed at the strange tracks pressed into the mud at the bottom of the pit. "No people feet."

"And I don't see the Ducha crawling through the mud just to avoid *us*, either." Zekk turned his attention to the towers beside the pit. "The entrance must be in one of those."

He started toward the nearest tower, holding his light-saber and clearly intending to cut his way inside.

"Hold on," Jaina said. "Let's not do any more damage than we have to—Ducha Galney is *supposed* to be one of Tenel Ka's most loyal allies."

She turned to Zar, who had finally stopped protesting but was continuing to follow the two Jedi through the compound. "How do we get into the emergency shelter?" Jaina asked. "You can help us, or you can explain to Ducha Galney why we had to cut our way in."

Zar frowned in confusion. "Emergency shelter?"

She had barely spoken before a chorus of shrill squeals rang out from the pit. Jaina and Zekk spun around to find six creatures—at least that was the number of *mouths* Jaina saw—spilling out of the cave in a slimy gray tangle. They were about as long as speeder bikes, with thick tubular bodies, stubby legs, and flipper-shaped feet.

As soon as they saw Jaina and Zekk, they launched themselves against the side of the pit. They hit belly-first and clawed frantically at the stone, dragging themselves up high enough to thrust their round-nosed heads over the wall, snapping and screeching at the two Jedi.

Jaina and Zekk retreated a step and ignited their lightsabers—then were nearly knocked over as Zar pushed between them, placing herself between the lightsabers and the creatures from the pit.

"No! Please!" She spun and faced the two Jedi, extending her arms to protect the strange creatures. "I'll tell you anything you want—just don't hurt my babies!"

The creatures began to squeal more excitedly than ever, their heads bobbing up and behind Zar as they licked at her ears and arms, coating her head and shoulders with stringy yellow slime.

Jaina wrinkled her nose in disgust. "Your *babies*?"

"They're the Ducha's favorite hunting murgs," Zar said. "I'm their handler."

Zekk deactivated his lightsaber. "Don't worry," he said. "We're not going to hurt—"

"As long as you help us," Jaina interrupted. She sensed Zekk's immediate disapproval, but stepped closer to Zar anyway. Sometimes Zekk was just too kriffing honorable for his own good. "Why is the Ducha hiding from us?"

"She's *not* hiding," Zar said. "I told you. She was so offended by your arrival that she decided to leave."

"She decided to leave *after* we arrived?" Zekk asked. "You're sure?"

"Of course I'm sure." Zar continued to hold her arms out protectively. "After your sonic booms intruded on her serenity, she summoned me to say that she and the rest of the household would be departing. I was to stay and care for my babies—the murgs—and see to it that you didn't steal anything."

"*Steal* anything?" Jaina began to have a sinking feeling. "Did the Ducha know who we were?"

"She said 'the Jedi.'" Zar's arms began to tremble, and her gaze fell on Jaina's still-ignited lightsaber. "Please don't hurt my babies. It's not their fault."

"Nobody's going to hurt your murgs," Zekk said. He frowned at Jaina. "Right?"

Jaina deactivated her blade. "I guess." To Zar, she said, "But you've got to show us how to reach the hang—"

A low rumble sounded from deep inside the hill. An instant later the almond-shaped silhouette of a Hapan luxury yacht shot into view and began to climb skyward on a pillar of blue efflux. Jaina stretched her Force-awareness into the hangar and felt only emptiness.

"Zar," she asked, "is it customary for the Ducha to take the *entire* household when she departs Villa Solis?"

"Not at all," Zar replied. "About twenty of us stay here all the time. There's a lot to care for besides the murgs."

"I was afraid you'd say that." Jaina uttered a silent curse, then asked, "Have you noticed the fleet orbiting Terephon?"

"A good pilot always keeps one eye on the sky," Zar said indignantly. "Besides, they've been sending fighter squadrons down to be refitted all week."

"*All week?*" Zekk repeated.

Zar frowned and started to count days on her fingers. "Yes, all—"

"Never mind," Jaina said. She turned to Zekk. "*Before* she could know about the coup attempt."

"There was a coup attempt?" Zar asked. "We *never* hear anything on Terephon."

Zekk put a hand on her shoulder and turned her toward the nearest tower. "Go. Find someplace safe."

Jaina frowned. "You think the Ducha is going to hit her own villa?"

"I *know* she is." Zekk tipped his head toward Zar, who had so far refused to leave. "If you needed to leave a decoy behind, who would it be?"

"Me?" Zar shook her head emphatically. "Never. I'm the Ducha's favorite riding companion!"

Jaina ignored Zar's protest and nodded to Zekk. "I see your point," she said. The Ducha had started to mobilize her fleet before the coup attempt, which meant *she* had been one of its architects, and that was clearly a secret worth protecting—especially since Tenel Ka still seemed to think the Galney family was loyal. "But I don't know that she'd level her own hunting villa just to get us."

"We're *Jedi*," Zekk countered. "And you know what it would mean to her if we get away. She has to be sure."

"Okay." Jaina had only to recall a few HoloNet accounts of miraculous Jedi escapes to know Zekk was right. The Ducha would be terrified that if they survived any attempts to kill them, they would warn Tenel Ka of her involvement in the coup. She turned to go. "Let's get back to the—"

Jaina stopped when two hulking forms stepped out from behind a dwelling. They had wedge-shaped torsos, massive systems-packed arms, and gray laminanium armor. With red photoreceptors gleaming from the socket mountings of their distinctive death's-head faces, there was no mistaking the droids' make.

"*Why-Vees!*" Jaina's heart leapt into her throat. Even Jedi were a poor match for the accuracy and ferocious firepower of YVH battle droids. She and Zekk ignited their lightsabers. "Uncle Luke better have a talk with Lando about who he's selling those things to."

Zar frowned at their hissing blades. "No need for that, Jedi Solo. They're just watch droids." She stepped forward, blocking the droids' line of fire. "You two stand down. These guests were just leaving."

"Negative." The closer droid raised the arm containing its blaster cannon. "Please clear an attack lane. Intruders are designated targets."

Zar placed her hands on her hips. "*I* decide who the targets are around here, Two-Twenty. I'm the one the Ducha left in charge."

"Uh, Entora," Jaina said. "Maybe you'd better listen—"

Jaina was cut off by the rapid whomping of a blaster cannon, and suddenly there was blood and hot light everywhere. Knowing better than to allow the droids to concentrate their ferocious firepower, she and Zekk sprang away in opposite directions, tumbling through the air in a wild helix of twists and flips, relying on the Force to stay one eye-blink ahead of the droids' targeting computers.

A tremendous cracking echoed through the compound as cannon fire struck the wall around the murg pit, spraying rock chips and superheated dust everywhere. Jaina came down four meters away and rolled into a somersault, then launched herself into a long, arcing spiral. There were so many bolts the air seemed about to burst into flame, and twice she had to use her lightsaber to deflect attacks that came so close she thought half her face would melt.

A cacophony of ear-piercing shrieks sounded behind her, almost as loud as the droids' blaster cannons. Jaina hit the ground rolling and somersaulted into cover behind the wall of the first building she could find.

She spun to face her attackers and was surprised to glimpse a string of slimy gray forms clambering through a smoking breach in the murg pit wall. The creatures' eyes were open wide, they were trailing long strings of yellow drool, and—given their ungainly form and misshaped legs—they were slithering into the compound with a speed Jaina could only think of as astonishing.

A volley of cannon bolts tore into the building she was using for cover—then abruptly went wide. She peered around the corner and saw that the pack of fleeing murgs had slammed headlong into the battle droids. Most had clamped their powerful jaws around a droid's leg or arm and were struggling to drag it down, but the smallest was holding what remained of Zar's lifeless body in its mouth and circling the melee, apparently trying to carry her to safety.

Jaina glanced across the courtyard at Zekk, who was also crouched behind a building, studying the situation. She reached out to him in the Force and knew instantly they were both thinking the same thing: *Go while the going is good.*

Zekk nodded toward her, then rolled in the opposite direction and disappeared behind the building. Jaina did likewise, racing down a twisting pathway that led more or less in the direction of the gate.

She pulled her comlink and opened a direct channel to Sneaker. "Hardfire those engines! We're coming back hot and need to be at takeoff power *fast.*"

Sneaker replied with an irritated whistle.

"No time to explain—just do it!" Jaina ordered.

Though Jaina couldn't really understand beep code, it was easy enough to guess her astromech's objection. Because they were running low on fuel, Jaina and Zekk had shut their StealthXs down without burning off the supply in the preheating cell. Hardfiring the engines now meant forcing cold fuel into the combustion chambers, and *that* would mean a complete overhaul—assuming, of course, the engines lasted long enough to return to base.

Jaina was about halfway back to the gate when the murgs flashed across an adjacent intersection, now chortling and squawking in excitement. A moment later she heard hissing servomotors and knew one of the battle droids had found her. She dodged around a bend, barely escaping death as a flurry of cannon bolts blasted a meter-wide hole through a gratenite wall.

The battle droid pounded after her, its blaster cannon continuing to punch black stars into the building at her back. When Jaina came to the next intersection, she used the Force to send a rock clattering down the walkway toward the gate, then deactivated her lightsaber, ducked around the opposite side of the building, and dropped to her belly on the cold walkway.

It seemed to take the battle droid forever to arrive.

Jaina began to worry that despite her precautions, it had detected her heat signature with a thermal-imaging sweep, or had perhaps picked up the pounding of her pulse through an acoustic analysis. She concentrated on her breathing, trying to quiet her heart with a relaxation exercise she rarely used.

From the other side of the compound came the sound of Zekk's battle against his own pursuer—his lightsaber droning in muffled counterpoint to the rapid crump of the battle droid's blaster cannon. Even more troubling was the fear and uncertainty Jaina felt through the Force, the growing desperation as the droid continued to press its assault. She began to fear Zekk was not going to make it; that the time had come to see if she could slip away from her own attacker and take Zekk's by surprise.

And that was when the distant roar of an atmospheric entry crackled down from the sky. Jaina craned her neck and quickly found a dozen bright efflux tails streaking from the stars. She thought for a moment the Ducha was sending a squadron of Miy'tils down to support the battle droids—but realized there was another, more important target for the starfighters.

Jaina pulled her comlink, intending to warn her astromech that the StealthX was about to come under attack, then heard servomotors hissing around the bend—exactly as she had planned.

But the battle droid was being uncharacteristically cautious, taking time to sweep the area with its sensors, alert to the possibility of an ambush. Jaina held her breath and pressed herself tighter to the ground, trying to stay calm, trying to slow her breathing and her heart. The droid had probably switched from an attack routine to a stalking routine, and if she could not control her bodily responses, they would give her away.

For the next few moments, Jaina could do nothing but lie on the ground and listen to the roar of the Miy'tils grow louder. The sound of Zekk's lightsaber began to fade as his fight drifted toward the gate, and she could sense his growing desperation through their combat-meld. By now, he had to be using the Force to keep himself going. Soon his skin would begin to nettle with the effects of drawing on the Force too heavily . . . and then he would simply stop.

Zekk would rather die than risk a brush with the dark side, and that was one of the things that frustrated Jaina about him. To him, a thing was either right or wrong, good or evil, and that made every choice simple. Either you loved someone or you didn't. There was no room for uncertainty, no room to be confused about how you felt—to wonder where the boundary lay between a life-long friendship and love . . . or even if there *was* one.

Finally a pair of metallic footfalls sounded from the other side of the building. Jaina remained where she was, working harder than ever to quiet her heart and her breathing. The droid would be going into a flushing routine now, and it would be alert to the possibility of attack.

Another trio of footfalls sounded from the other side of the building, then a whole series. Jaina rose as quietly as possible, then slipped around the bend and saw the battle droid moving down another walkway toward the gate. She started after it, running as silently as was possible, her lightsaber still deactivated but cocked to strike.

She was almost there when the droid pivoted, presenting its flank and fixing its red photoreceptors on her face. Its arm came up, and Jaina's throat cramped with fear as she found herself looking down the barrel of a blaster cannon.

She dropped into a slide, and a stream of colored bolts

crumped past so close she felt her skin blistering beneath its heat. The droid lowered its arm, blasting head-sized craters out of the walkway as it tried to track her. Jaina activated her lightsaber and slammed the blade into its knee as hard as she could.

The leg came off in a shower of sparks and hydraulic fluid, and the droid crashed down almost on top of her, jamming the cannon barrel against the ground and blowing its own arm apart as it continued to fire.

A spray of hot shrapnel sliced into Jaina's back and neck. She continued her slide, using the Force to pull herself free, then switched off her lightsaber and sprang to her feet a couple of meters down the walkway. She raced around the bend just ahead of a mini missile that reduced five meters of gratenite wall to crashing rubble.

Once Jaina's ears had stopped ringing, she was relieved to hear the *boom–boom–boom* of a grenade volley coming from the other side of the villa. She reached out to Zekk through their battle-meld and sensed his presence somewhere ahead, near the gate. There was no way to tell exactly what had happened, but from the sounds of it he, too, had found a way to cripple the droid chasing him. They were going to make it back to the StealthXs, after all.

Then a long series of sonic booms shook the villa, and Jaina looked up to see the Miy'tils streaking down toward the StealthXs. She pulled her comlink and opened a channel to her astromech.

"Sneaker, bring up the shields. And tell—"

She was interrupted by a negative chirp.

Of course—with all that cold congealed fuel in the system, even hardfiring the engines would not have them at full power yet. "All right, Sneaker. Just do your—"

The astromech's acknowledging tweedle vanished in

the thundering crash of a missile detonation. A brilliant flash lit the sky outside the villa, then several more detonations came, each brighter than the last—and all in the approximate area of the StealthXs.

By the time the explosions stopped, Jaina had reached the front courtyard of the villa. The gate had been closed, and the murgs were clawing at it in such a panic, they had gouged the hard crodium. Zekk was standing atop the wall, staring out toward a plume of black smoke. Even had Jaina not sensed his frustration, she would have known by the angry cloud on his face that their starfighters had been destroyed.

A distant roar sounded out over the bog, and Jaina looked up to the see the Miy'tils wheeling around for another pass. She raced forward and Force-sprang over the murg pack, then came down atop the wall next to Zekk. Where their StealthXs had been, there were now six smoking craters.

"We'd better get out of here," Jaina said. She turned her attention back to the sky and saw that the Miy'tils were already diving back toward the villa. "You were right about the Ducha—when it comes to Jedi, she doesn't think there's any such thing as overkill."

"There isn't," Zekk said darkly. "And when we find a way off of this mudball, I'm going to hunt her down and prove it."

Instead of jumping down outside the wall and running for cover in the bogs, he dropped back inside the wall and shoved through the screeching murgs toward the gate controls.

"Are you crazy?" Jaina cried from the top of the wall. "Those Miy'tils will be dropping bombs in about five seconds."

"Then help get these gates open!"

Jaina started to protest, then realized she would just be wasting time. Whatever else he was, Zekk was as kind and courageous as Jedi came, and nothing was going to change that—not even her.

"Zekk, sometimes you're a real pain in the neck." She used the Force to pull a pair of murgs out of his way, and he finally reached the gate controls. "And I can't believe I'm saying this, but I'm kind of starting to like it."

"*Now* you tell me." Zekk pulled the lock slicer out of his equipment belt and started to work on the gate controls. "Let me know when we're out of time."

"Why?" Jaina turned toward the approaching Miy'tils. "Would it make any difference?"

"Not really," Zekk said. The lock slicer surprised Jaina by beeping a success signal after only a couple of seconds. The gates hissed open, and the murgs shot out toward the bog. "But it's good to know you waited."

chapter fourteen

With dim blue lighting and the sweet taint of rekka smoke in the air, Telkur Station Cantina was the kind of place where smart customers kept their backs to as many walls as possible. Its only ceiling was a disorganized web of ventilation ducts suspended in the murk above, and there was a half-concealed entrance somewhere along every one of its eight walls. The patrons were clustered in groups of three and four, sitting around corroded steel tables and openly studying Han and his companions.

"What are we waiting for?" Nashtah demanded from behind Han. "I'm thirsty."

"Just being sure," Han said. The cantina's clients were exclusively human and near-human, with no droids, and roughly balanced between handsome men with scroungy three-day beards and beautiful Hapan women dressed to look tough but available. C-3PO and the Noghri were back in the *Falcon*, so Han thought he and his two female companions would fit right in—unless someone recognized him or Leia from an old HoloNews broadcast. "I can't believe Hapan Security wouldn't cover this place."

"They will—but there won't be many." Nashtah pushed

past Han and started toward the bar. "If they cause us any trouble, we'll kill them."

"Yeah, *that's* a great plan," Han retorted. "We wouldn't want to cause a scene or anything."

But Nashtah was already halfway to the bar, no doubt far more aware of the gazes furtively following her progress than she let on. Having rebuffed Leia's suggestion that they all wear disguises—claiming her contact would not show up unless both she and the Solos were easily recognizable—she now seemed determined to draw the entire station's attention.

"I don't like it," Han said to Leia. "She's testing us."

"Clearly," Leia said. "But she's our only lead. What are we going to do?"

"How about not going along?" Han took Leia's arm and turned toward the grimy access corridor. "We'll head back to the *Falcon* and let her come to *us*."

Leia pulled him back into the cantina entrance. "And take the chance that she'd just disappear?" She freed herself from his grasp. "We can't. Too much depends on her."

Leia started after their companion. Han cursed under his breath, then reluctantly followed the pair toward the bar. The cantina was almost certainly being watched by Hapan Security, and Nashtah was deliberately exposing the Solos to see what happened. If someone tried to kill or capture them, she would probably accept their story and let them fly her the rest of the way to her employers. On the other hand, if nothing happened—or if the capture efforts appeared insincere—she would either slip away quietly or try to kill them herself. Han was betting on kill.

At the bar, an aproned bartender with a cleft chin and dark eyes came over to take their orders. Han was immediately suspicious of the fellow's athletic build and clean-shaven face, but if he was a Hapan agent, he was a well-prepared one. He fixed Leia's Fogblaster and even Nashtah's Red Cloud without having to consult the data-pad behind the bar for a drink recipe.

He placed the two drinks on the counter, along with a Gizer ale for Han, then said, "Thirty credits."

"Thirty credits?" Han objected. "I see why they call this a pirate station."

The bartender merely pointed at Nashtah's Red Cloud. "Blood ain't cheap."

"Blood?" Han made a sour face, but removed a pair of credit chips from his pocket and laid them on the counter. "At that price, I hope it's yours."

They took a seat in the nearest corner, at a rust-stained table that looked as if it hadn't been wiped down in a month. Leia refused to set her glass down, and even Han refrained from resting his elbows on the surface. If Nashtah noticed the filth, she didn't show it, simply dropping onto the bench opposite the Solos with her back against the wall, then resting one arm along the table.

Han took a sip of Gizer and frowned at how flat it was. "I hope we don't have to wait long." He glanced around the cantina casually, trying to decide whether Nashtah's contact was the guy in the new utilities or that classy-looking brunette in the syntex vest. "I can't bring myself to drink two of these. It was brewed back when Ta'a Chume was Queen Mother."

Nashtah shrugged. "It may take awhile—you are unexpected companions, so my contact will be careful." She took a long sip of her Red Cloud, then raised it toward Han. "But you can always try one of these. They're fresh."

Han made a sour face. "No, thanks. I'd rather drink water."

"From here?" Leia glanced at the filthy table. "Don't you dare."

They sat for a time, waiting for a contact that probably did not exist to approach. Han and Leia only sipped at their drinks—Han because his Gizer barely tasted like ale, and Leia because she hated Fogblasters and only ordered them when she wanted to nurse a drink without having to think about it. But Nashtah drank more steadily, draining half her glass within the first quarter hour.

After another couple of minutes, she leaned across the table to Leia. "Someone is watching you."

"Yes, I have that feeling, too," Leia said.

"Probably a Hapan surveillance team," Han said wryly. "Maybe we should get out of here before the backup arrives."

Nashtah shook her head. "He doesn't look Hapan. And you may know him. He's trying very hard to keep out of your sight line."

Han turned toward Leia, straddling the bench as though he were going to face her . . . and sneaking a glance toward the corner where Nashtah was looking. He glimpsed a square-shouldered man with a thick beard and a mop of dark hair hanging in his eyes. The fellow quickly turned toward the wall to hide his face, but failed to change his upright posture . . . or the military precision of his movements.

"You know, something *does* look kind of familiar about him," Han said. "He's trying to hide it, but that guy is a soldier—and I have this crazy feeling we *do* know him."

"We should," Leia said. She was still looking across the table toward Nashtah, but Han could tell by her unfocused gaze that her concentration was on the Force. "I think he almost married our daughter."

"What?" Han spoke loudly enough that, despite the raucous buzz of scrak music, he drew glances from several nearby tables. He lowered his voice and leaned closer to Leia. "Come on. You *can't* be telling me that's who I think you mean."

"I don't understand, either," Leia said. "But his presence feels *very* familiar."

"You know him?" Nashtah asked. "Then we *must* go say hello."

Before Han could stop her, Nashtah rose and started across the cantina, weaving just enough to suggest it was not an act.

"Uh-oh," Leia said. "This looks like trouble."

The Solos rose and started after her. Han was surprised at Nashtah's condition. Whatever else she was, she was clearly a top-notch assassin, and top-knotch assassins did not let themselves get intoxicated on a job—and probably not many other times, either.

They arrived at the bearded man's table just as Nashtah sat on the bench opposite him. ". . . me why you are following my friends," she was saying, "and your death will be a painless one."

"You'll have to forgive our friend," Leia said, sliding onto the bench on the bearded man's side of the table. "I'm afraid she doesn't hold her spirits very well."

"Yeah, she'll probably miss." Han slid onto the bench next to Nashtah, positioning himself close enough that she would have to push him out of the way before she could reach the blaster in her thigh holster. "At least the first time."

"Then let's hope it doesn't come to that." The bearded man reluctantly looked away from the wall. Though the hair hanging over his brow concealed the crooked scar running up his forehead, there was no mistaking the steely green eyes. "Because I *never* miss the first time."

Nashtah tensed, but Han slapped a hand on her thigh—

blocking access to her holster—and smiled across the table.

"Jagged Fel!" He was genuinely pleased. "Glad to see we didn't kill you after all."

Leia frowned. "What Han means to say is we're happy to see you well. We inquired about you many times, but Aristocra Formbi kept claiming your status was a military secret."

"Because I had yet to be recovered." Fel's voice was polite, but reserved. "After you shot me down, I was marooned for two years."

"Two *years*?" Leia touched his forearm, drawing a flinch visible even across the table. She quickly withdrew her hand. "Jagged, I *am* sorry. Before we departed Tenupe, Aristocra Formbi led us to believe your recovery was imminent."

"Tenupe can be a very dangerous planet, as you know," he said. "The recovery team vanished, and the decision was made to risk no more lives on behalf of one pilot."

"Sorry, kid—that was a tough break," Han said. "So how *did* you get out of the jungle?"

"My family hired a private rescue company, and one of their search parties met a—" Fel stopped, picking his words carefully. "They met an unfortunate end. I repaired one of their commsets, and when the next party arrived looking for *them,* I was able to make contact."

"Telkur Station is a long way from the Unknown Regions," Nashtah said suspiciously. "What are you doing *here*?"

"Looking for the Solos, of course," Fel said.

Han raised his brow. "Kid, if this is about Jaina—"

"It *isn't,*" Fel said, a little too forcefully. "Jaina has caused the Fel family enough problems for one lifetime."

"All right," Han said, wincing inside at the sharpness

of Fel's voice. He had always kind of liked Fel, and there had been a time when he would have gladly welcomed him as a son-in-law—except for the part about dragging Jaina off to live in the Chiss Ascendancy. "I was just saying that if—"

"I'm here because of Alema Rar," Fel said, cutting him off.

"Alema?" Leia furrowed her brow. "I don't understand. She's dead."

"No more than I am," Fel said.

Han looked over at Leia. "You said some kind of spidersloth ate her!"

"I *said* I was fairly sure," Leia corrected. She looked back to Fel. "It had half her body in its mouth. I can't imagine she escaped—much less survived."

"I assure you, she did both," Fel said. "The creature . . ." He let his sentence trail off when the bartender suddenly appeared carrying the drinks Han, Leia, and Nashtah had left on their first table.

"One table at a time," the bartender said. He banged the drinks down and turned to Fel. "You drinking or leaving?"

Fel's eyes went to the mug of ale sitting in front of Han. "I'll have one of those."

The bartender grunted an acknowledgment and departed.

Han eyed the glasses. His drink and Leia's were still about three-quarters full, but Nashtah had emptied almost all of hers. "That bartender seems pretty determined to see us finish our drinks."

"I wouldn't indulge him, if I were you," Fel said.

Nashtah narrowed her eyes. "Why?"

"Because drinking can be bad for your health," Han said, resisting the urge to look around. He was pretty sure now that the bartender was part of a Hapan Security team, and he wanted to hear the rest of Fel's story before the fighting started. "Didn't anyone ever tell you that?"

Nashtah turned to glare at the bartender, but said nothing.

Fel pretended not to notice and shifted his gaze back to Leia. "I was preparing to tell you about Alema," he said. "She killed the creature before it had a chance to eat her."

"You found its carcass?" Leia asked.

Fel shook his head. "Bodies decompose too fast in the jungle."

He reached inside his jacket, causing Nashtah to reach for her thigh holster again.

"Whoa, there!" Han said, managing to clasp the assassin's arm before she could draw the blaster.

Nashtah squinted at him in disbelief. "How'd you do that?"

"Old smuggling trick," Han said casually. Something was definitely wrong with their drinks. He had seen how fast Nashtah was, and he should never have been able to stop her—not on his best day thirty years earlier. "Jag isn't going to hurt anyone here. He just wants to show us something."

Nashtah squinted across the table, but she pulled her hand away from her holster. "Don't try anything stupid."

"You have nothing to fear from *me*, I assure you," Fel said. Once it was clear she would not be trying to blast him, he pulled a coil of braided hide strips from inside his jacket. He held it in front of Leia. "You know what this is, I assume?"

Leia nodded. "A Twi'lek memory cord—a long one."

"Correct. I found it on Tenupe, shortly after I discovered the bodies of the commercial search party I mentioned." He laid it on the table. "But their vessel was missing, and I followed the tracks of a lame female back to a cave where she had been living."

"And that's where you found this?" Leia asked.

Fel nodded. "My family had it researched. The first part seems to recount how she saved herself by cutting the spidersloth's throat from the inside. It bit down just as you described, but the creature was already dying and didn't do as much damage as you led Aristocra Formbi to believe."

"Her lightsaber *was* activated when the creature took her," Leia said. "I just didn't think she'd kill the thing quickly enough to survive."

"She nearly didn't," Fel said. He pointed to the next set of knots. "These describe her wounds and recovery. Her arm and six ribs were fractured, and she had several deep wounds in her abdomen and back. Fortunately for her— and unfortunately for us—when the Killiks evacuated after the battle, they left thousands of stragglers behind. She was able to summon a small group to care for her."

"Wait a minute," Han said. He was doing his best to keep an unobtrusive eye on the rest of the cantina, and so far the Hapan Security team seemed willing to wait for them to finish their drinks and pass out. "Are you saying the Killiks are still there?"

"I doubt it," Fel said. "They were castaways, just as I was. I had regular, um, *encounters* with them during the first year. But they were always from different nests, and by the second year they were beginning to disappear. I think they lived out their lives and died."

"That makes sense—Killiks have short life spans," Leia said. "But a year would have been enough to nurse Alema back to health."

"Indeed. She records each of their deaths in detail." Fel paused, then indicated a set of knots that seemed to repeat themselves every four or five centimeters. "But these knots are the reason I'm here. They appear to be a recurring list of injuries received at your hands, and the knots between appear to be lists of possible retaliations."

"What are you getting at?" Han demanded. "Are you saying that crazy trollop is coming after Leia?"

"I'm telling you what I found in her cave," Fel replied evenly. "What you make of it is your business."

Leia's eyes flashed a warning at Han, then she turned back to Fel. "Thank you for telling me, Jagged. After what happened on Tenupe, I know it couldn't have been easy for you."

"*Easy* doesn't matter." Fel's gaze grew distant and perhaps a little hard. "You warned me to eject, and I had a debt to repay. Now I have."

"I see." Leia's expression turned sad. "So now you'll be heading back to the Ascendency?"

Fel shook his head. "No, I'll be watching you."

Han would have asked why, except that was when the bartender returned. He set Fel's ale on the table, then frowned at Nashtah, who was slumped in the corner with the same unfocused gaze that Leia often assumed when she entered a Force trance.

"Is Baldy all right?" he asked. "I don't want nobody dying in here."

"She'sh fine." Han slurred his words deliberately, but he truly *was* feeling a little warm and drowsy. "Jush forgets to closh her eyes."

The bartender scowled in suspicion. Han thought he might have overdone it, but Fel made a point of lifting his own mug to his lips and taking a small sip.

"Excellent." He smacked his lips with exaggerated pleasure, then set his mug on the table and wiped the froth away with his sleeve. "Very thirst quenching."

Han frowned. "Really? You don't think ish a little flat?"

"Not at all." Fel's eyes flicked away nervously. "But when it comes to ale, my tastes aren't very refined."

"That mush be it." Han raised his own mug to his lips and took another small sip, then nodded. "Yeah, the more you drink, the better it tashes."

The bartender grunted and returned to his bar.

Once he was gone, Han turned back to Fel. "So *why* are you watching us?"

"Because we're bait," Leia surmised. Her face was a bit flushed, but she seemed alert enough to finish the conversation and run. She turned to Fel. "Your assignment is to hunt down Alema and make sure she can't restart the Dark Nest, isn't it?"

"That's my intention, yes," Fel said. "But not my assignment. I'm no longer with the Ascendancy military."

Han frowned. "If you're not on assignment, what are you doing here?"

"I have nothing to hide." Fel pretended to take another long drink from his mug. "I'm in exile."

"Exile?" Leia asked. "Why?"

"As you know, I guaranteed Lowbacca's parole at Qoribu. When he participated in the attack on Supply Depot Thrago, my family became liable for the damage he inflicted on the Ascendancy from that point on."

A look of sorrow suddenly came over Leia's face, and Han's stomach began to feel a bit hollow. It hadn't been him who tricked Lowbacca and the others into attacking Supply Depot Thrago—but it *had* been his son, Jacen.

"As I'm sure you know, Wookiees can do a lot of damage," Fel continued. "Especially *Jedi* Wookiees. When my family couldn't cover the expenses, I was forced to leave the Ascendancy."

Leia's chin dropped. "Jagged, I'm sorry. If there's anything we can do—"

"There isn't," Fel said, a little sharply. "There's nothing any Jedi—or *Solo*—can do that would change the decree of the ruling families."

"I know things look bad now, but give it some time," Leia said. "After you find Alema, I'm sure the Ascendancy will reconsider—"

"Then you don't know the Ascendancy," Fel snapped. "Finding Alema will redeem my family's honor and give it the means to rebuild its fortune. But *my* situation will remain the same; if ever I return to the Ascendancy, my entire family will be dishonored."

"Well, whatever we can do." Han didn't like the tone Fel was taking with Leia, but the kid *did* have a pretty good reason to be angry. "Use us as bait all you want—everyone else does."

He cast a meaningful glance over at Nashtah, who was still slumped against the wall, staring off into space.

"I *am* using you as bait." Fel pushed his mug to the table center and started to rise. "And now, if you'll excuse me—"

"Not so fast." Han took a quick glance around and was dismayed to notice half a dozen pairs of eyes turned in their direction. "There's one thing about your story that bothers me."

Jag did not return to his seat. "That's really not my problem, Captain Solo."

"For old times' sake," Leia said. She grabbed Fel behind the elbow and, using the Force, pulled him down onto the bench. "I think Han is saying that your account doesn't add up."

"Yeah," Han said. "That's *exactly* what I'm saying. There's no way you found us on your own."

"Actually, it wasn't difficult at all," Fel said. "The HoloNews is filled with stories about your defection to Corellia."

"This isn't Corellia," Han said.

"True, but I happened to see a communiqué from Admiral Bwua'tu." Fel glanced nervously around the cantina, then continued, "He was convinced that Corellia's next move would be an attempt to persuade Hapes to enter the war on her side."

"You're lying," Han said, with more hope than conviction. Despite his fury over Gejjen using them to set up the assassination attempt on Tenel Ka, his heart remained with Corellia—and it alarmed him to think that the Galactic Alliance was good enough to predict Gejjen's desperate ploy. "*Nobody* sees that kind of communiqué."

"There are plenty of officers in the Galactic Alliance who value honor as highly as the Chiss," Fel said. "Is it too much to believe that one of them would assist me with the hunt for Alema Rar? Especially since it was the *Alliance* who asserted that she was dead?"

"He's got a point," Leia said to Han. "And I don't feel like he's lying."

Han understood what she was saying—that she could sense through the Force that Fel was telling the truth. But he remained suspicious. "It's still a long way from that message to Telkur Station."

"Not as long as you think, Captain Solo," Fel said. "You two have known the Queen Mother since she was a child. Who else was Corellia going to send?"

"Which gets you *halfway* here," Leia pointed out. "But nothing you've said explains how you went from Hapes to Telkur Station."

"That was the simplest part of all." Fel glanced across the cantina. "I followed *him*."

Han followed Fel's gaze to the bartender, who was pretending to wipe down the counter—but watching *them*.

"Of course," Leia said quietly. "Hapan Security."

Fel nodded. "His team departed the Fountain Palace a few hours after your attack on the Queen Mother."

"That right?" It irked Han to let Fel believe he and Leia had actually tried to kill Tenel Ka—clearly, the kid had already come to the conclusion that none of the Solos had any honor—but Han could hardly set the record straight with Nashtah sitting beside him. "And you just happened to slap your homing beacon on *their* ship?"

"Not really." Fel rose to his feet again. "I picked his team because I heard a hangar tech say it was going to the vilest den of corruption and degeneracy in Consortium space. Naturally, I knew *you* would show up sooner or later."

"You might want to be careful how you put that next time." Han was getting tired of Fel's bitter-exile act, but he had to admit the kid's logic was pretty good. Telkur Station was *exactly* the kind of place where an outlaw ship hanging around this part of the Consortium would eventually put in for supplies. "But thanks for warning us about the drinks."

"You're welcome—though I suspect you were *expecting* trouble." Fel's gaze slid over to Nashtah, who was now sitting up and blinking. "Now, you'll have to excuse me. This fight really won't be any of my concern."

Fel started toward the exit, leaving Han and his companions to locate the security team. It was hardly difficult. They were the ones trying too hard to mind their own business, appearing more interested in their drinks or conversation than in what was happening around them. Han quickly counted a standard surveillance team of six agents, including the bartender. They were scattered around the cantina near the exits, with a clear line of sight to the Solos, and well positioned to cut off any escape attempt.

It took longer to locate the team leader. Han was expecting a woman to be in charge and initially paid no attention to the scrawny fellow seated alone at the end of the bar. But the second time he looked, the man was studying their half-filled glasses and muttering into his drink.

"We just ran out of time." As Han spoke, he was swinging his legs out from beneath the table and dropping his hand toward his blaster holster. If he wanted to convince Nashtah that he and Leia were for real without a lot of bloodshed, he had to act *now*. "I think they're mad because we don't like the drinks."

The leader looked away and muttered into his drink more urgently. Han flipped the power setting on his blaster to stun, then drew and fired twice without standing.

The first bolt only grazed the leader's abdomen, melting a dark line across the front of his tunic and causing him to hunch over in pain. The second caught him full in the flank, knocking him to the floor in a convulsing mass.

In the instant of stunned silence that followed, Han thought his plan might succeed, that he and Leia and Nashtah might actually disappear into the station's tangled corridors before the surveillance team recovered from its shock.

Then he stood. His knees went weak and his head began to spin, and he had to brace himself on the table.

"Han?" Pulling her lightsaber from beneath her robe as she moved, Leia rose and started to reach for him—then had to put a hand down to catch herself. "Whoa. Strong stuff."

"Yeah," Han said. The security team was already recovering from its shock and drawing weapons. "Really hits you."

"Renatyl—a bounty hunter favorite," explained Nash-tah. Suddenly she seemed alert and ready to fight—clearly a result of the Force trance she had entered. "You don't notice it until you try to stand—then you fall flat on your face."

"Thanks for the warning," Han griped, starting to feel even more queasy and dizzy.

Half the security team—two tall burly men and a stony-eyed woman with high cheeks and thin brows—were already bringing blaster pistols to bear and shouting orders to surrender. Leia's lightsaber came to life with a sharp *snap-hiss*, but Nashtah showed no sign of rising to go with the Solos.

Han frowned at her. "You coming?"

"Not yet." She drew a long-barreled blaster from her thigh holster. "I *hate* being drugged."

"Then you'd better come with us *now*," Han said. He stepped in front of her, extending a hand as though to help, but actually trying to block her line of fire. "If you think this is bad, wait until the Hapan interrogators—"

Nashtah raised her blaster and squeezed the trigger, sending a bolt of blue heat screaling past Han's ear. He cried out in astonishment, then turned and saw the bartender tumbling away behind the bar—a T-21 repeating blaster flying from his hands and a wisp of smoke rising between his eyes.

Han dropped his head. "I really wish you hadn't done that. Now things are going to get—"

Before he could finish, the cantina broke into an uproar of shouting voices and screaming weapons. Leia's lightsaber growled as she brought her blade around to defend.

"Han!" she yelled. "A little help?"

Han whirled around to find Leia frantically batting aside full-power blaster bolts, doing her best to avoid hurting anyone by directing the attacks up into the web of ducts that served as the cantina ceiling. But the Renatyl was having its effect on her, slowing her reflexes enough that some bolts ricocheted off a wall or the floor instead, and a couple even slipped through and went screaming past Han's head.

Keeping his own blaster set to stun, Han began to return fire, concentrating on a trio of agents between them and the exit. He dropped one, and Leia started toward the exit, staggering and weaving.

Blaster bolts began to pour in from behind. Han spun around to lay covering fire, but the cantina slipped into a Renatyl-laced spin, and he could see nothing but whirling blurs of color. He pointed his blaster into the stream of blue bolts and held the trigger down—then cried out in shock as something hot slammed into his shoulder.

Han was on the floor before he knew he was falling, his nostrils burning with the smell of scorched flesh, one side of his body throbbing in searing pain. To his surprise, he was still holding his blaster pistol, pouring fire toward a pair of amorphous forms that were fast taking the shape of charging security agents.

"Han?" Leia cried. "Are you—"

"He'll be fine!" Nashtah called. Finally deciding to help out, she slipped off the bench and knelt at Han's side. She fired twice, and both agents went down with scorch holes in their faces. "Perhaps I believe your story after all."

"Too . . . late," Han groaned. "If we get out of here, you're on your own."

"Oh—you're angry?" Nashtah patted him on the cheek, then turned to face Leia's direction. "How cute."

She fired a dozen times, and suddenly the only sound in the cantina was the drone of Leia's lightsaber. Han rolled to his knees, nearly passing out from the pain and the Renatyl, and spun around. Leia was standing two meters ahead, holding her lightsaber at her side and staring at the motionless bodies of several Hapan Security agents.

When it grew obvious they were all dead, Leia deactivated her lightsaber and knelt beside Han. "How bad—"

"I'll live. We've got other things to worry about." Han shifted his eyes toward Nashtah, who was still kneeling on the floor beside him. "That was just a surveillance team, but—"

Han winced in pain as Leia pulled him to his feet.

"—they had to have called for backup the minute they identified us," she said, finishing his sentence. "You're right—we have to get out of here."

"Before we meet my contact?" Nashtah asked.

"*What* contact?" Han demanded. "You were just testing us."

But Nashtah was already staggering toward the back of the cantina, clearly feeling the effects of the Renatyl even more than the Solos. Though most of the bystanders were evacuating as quickly as possible, a classy-looking brunette in a red syntex vest was standing just inside the rear exit, her eyes darting around nervously as Nashtah approached.

Han's shoulder was killing him, but he was beginning to think this might have been more than a test after all.

"What do you think?" he asked Leia.

"I think we passed," Leia said. "Are you up to this?"

"For Tenel Ka, I'm up to anything."

Han led the way after Nashtah, grimacing inside as he and Leia stepped around wounded bystanders and motionless security agents. He was sickened by the thought of so many people getting killed just because Nashtah was too lazy to adjust the power setting on her blaster, but the stakes were too high to let his feelings show. The lives of Tenel Ka and her daughter depended on finding out who was behind the coup—and so did the stability of the Hapes Consortium.

By the time Han and Leia arrived, Nashtah was already talking to the woman.

". . . come alone?" she was asking.

"That was the agreement." The woman eyed the Solos and frowned. "For *both* of us."

"Those agents just *proved* that the Solos are on your side," Nashtah said, waving a hand at the dead Hapans. "And I needed a ride. Your assassination plan was a setup."

"That's impossible," the woman retorted. "If you think the council is going to accept the blame for your failure—"

Nashtah placed a hand over the woman's mouth, then slammed her against a durasteel wall and leaned in close.

"It is not a matter of what the council will accept, Lady Morwan." Nashtah's voice was cold and menacing. "It is a matter of what *I* am going to do."

The woman's eyes slid toward Leia as though seeking help.

"She's right, Lady Morwan," Leia said. "They were waiting for us. Someone on your council is a spy."

Morwan's eyes widened in alarm, and Han had to force himself not to smile. They had learned a lot about the coup already, but Leia had done something even more important—she had started to sow suspicion and discord within the organization itself.

After a moment, Morwan nodded, and Nashtah removed her hand.

"What are you going to do?" Morwan asked. "Spy or no spy, the council has paid you a Hutt's treasure. They expect you to earn your fee."

"I will—*my* way."

Morwan considered this for a moment, then said, "Very

well—but the Council wants you to attend to the Chume'da first."

"The child?" Nashtah frowned. "What about the Queen Mother?"

"After," Morwan said. "We will always be able to find the Queen Mother. But now that we have made our intentions clear, the Chume'da will be sent into hiding."

Nashtah did not even hesitate. "I'll require another fee."

"Of course—once you have eliminated the Chume'da," Morwan said. "Your first fee will be payment for that."

Nashtah considered this, then nodded. "Agreed." She stepped back and smoothed Morwan's vest. "What kind of vessel did you come in?"

"A Batag Skiff." Morwan lowered her brow, clearly confused. "Your instructions said to come in something small and anonymous."

"And you did well," Nashtah said. "Give me the security code."

Morwan frowned. "The security code?"

"I need transport." Nashtah glanced at Han. "The *Falcon* is not very anonymous, even with the false transponder codes."

"But how will I—"

"*You* are not my problem." Nashtah jabbed her thumb into Morwan's larynx. "The code!"

"Alophon!" Morwan gasped. "That's the hatch code."

Nashtah eased the pressure on Morwan's throat. "And the pilot's code?"

"Remela."

Nashtah smiled. "Was that so hard?" She lowered her hand and turned to Han and Leia. "I trust we won't meet again . . . I suspect it would be more pleasant for me than you."

"That's it?" Han asked. "You're just going?"

Nashtah thought for a moment, then raised her brow as though remembering something. "Ah—the problem with your son." She pulled a datachip from her utility belt and passed it to Han. "Contact instructions. Leave a message when you're ready."

She started through the exit, then stopped and looked back, smiling. "I hope you *will* contact me. I'm looking forward to working with you on that."

"Not going to happen," Leia said, snatching the chip from Han. "Jacen is our son."

"And Tenel Ka was your friend," Nashtah countered. "Yet here you are."

She disappeared out the exit, leaving Han and Leia to stand there fuming. Han caught Leia's eye, then glanced after Nashtah, silently asking if they should try to take the assassin out now. Leia gave a quick shake of her head. With him already injured, Han knew, their odds were poor. Besides, there was a good chance that Tenel Ka and her security team—not to mention the Star Destroyer's— would stop Nashtah on their own. What they would *not* be able to do, however, was find out who was on Morwan's mysterious "council."

Leia slipped a hand under Han's arm. "Come on, flyboy—we'd better get you back to the *Falcon* and take a look at that blaster burn."

She turned him toward the opposite side of the cantina and started away, then suddenly stopped and looked back over her shoulder as though she had just remembered something.

"Forgive my rudeness, Lady Morwan. Can we give you a lift somewhere?"

"*Please.*" Morwan started after them, not even attempting to hide her relief. "I was afraid you'd never ask."

chapter fifteen

After a hasty departure from Telkur Station, the *Falcon* emerged from her first hyperspace jump in a pocket of realspace listed on the charts as "Knot Holes." As far as Leia could tell, the name was a reference to the dozens of narrow hyperspace lanes that punched through the black depths of Transitory Mists, creating a torn-curtain tableau of jagged, star-filled shapes. Han, who was seated in the copilot's seat while Leia did the flying, pointed toward a crescent of stars hanging on the starboard side of the viewport.

"That . . . way." Han was sweating with pain and unable to move his wounded shoulder, but he refused to go back to the medical bay until they were a safe distance away from Telkur Station. He glanced back toward Lady Morwan, who was sitting behind Leia at the navigator's station, then added, "We're heading back to the Interior?"

"Correct," Morwan replied. Her voice grew a little louder as she addressed the rest of her reply to the back of Leia's head. "I hope that won't be an inconvenience, Princess."

"Not at all." Leia turned the yoke in the direction Han had indicated and caught him watching the S-thread display, no doubt checking signal strength. Once they figured out whom Lady Morwan was working for, they would need to access the HoloNet and pass the intelligence on as quickly as possible. "We're entirely at your service. We've been operating on our own initiative since the first assassination attempt failed."

"*Assassination.*" Morwan's voice held a definite tone of remorse as she repeated the word. "*Depose* sounds so much better . . . but I suppose assassination is more honest, isn't it? If the Council didn't want the Queen Mother killed, it wouldn't have hired Aurra Sing."

The name made Leia lift her brow. She knew from historical records that Aurra Sing had been a ruthless killer of Jedi Knights during the Old Republic. Before she could ask if that was Nashtah's real name, Han twisted around to look squarely at Morwan.

"Don't tell me you're growing a conscience all of a sudden?"

"I'm as dedicated to the Consortium's independence as you are to Corellia's." Morwan's voice had grown just cold enough to show her displeasure at being questioned by a man. "That doesn't mean I relish the deaths of the Queen Mother and the Chume'da."

"Of course not," Leia said. She glanced at Morwan's reflection in the canopy, wondering the same thing she knew Han was: were Morwan's misgivings strong enough to make her change sides and simply reveal the identity of the coup organizers? "Decisions like these are never easy."

"Perhaps I can be of some assistance," C-3PO offered. "If you're talking about the woman who accompanied us on our escape from Fountain Palace, I have some data suggesting she couldn't possibly be Aurra Sing."

"Just because she said her name was Nashtah doesn't mean it was," Han said. "If that's your data, forget it."

"I'm well acquainted with the use of aliases, Captain Solo," C-3PO replied. "Why, I have an entire sector of memory dedicated to the identities you and Princess Leia have assumed."

"We're more interested in Aurra Sing," Leia said. "If Lady Morwan says she was, I'm inclined to believe her."

"I'm afraid Lady Morwan must be mistaken," C-3PO said. "According to the records Master Skywalker found aboard the *Chu'unthor*, Aurra Sing was a nine-year-old Jedi trainee who was captured by pirates more than seventy-five standard years ago. She seems to have felt rather betrayed by the Jedi order's failure to rescue her, because she returned years later as a bounty hunter who specialized in hunting and killing Jedi. She was finally captured by Jedi Aayla Secura, then imprisoned in the penal colony on Oovo Four. There is no record of her release."

"Maybe that's because there *are* no records from Oovo Four," Han replied. "When the Yuuzhan Vong leveled the place, they were incinerated along with the guards, the confinement domes, and probably most of the prisoners."

"Perhaps," C-3PO replied. "But the warden was an excellent administrator. He maintained an offworld backup—"

"Threepio, Han's trying to say there wouldn't *be* a release record," Leia explained. The crescent of stars that Han had pointed out was in the center of the canopy now, shining through the black curtain of the Transitory Mists like a tipped smile. "If Aurra Sing escaped during the attack, there would have been no one left to report it."

C-3PO fell silent for a moment, then said, "Oh. I hadn't considered that."

"I *am* curious about how you chose Aurra," Leia said. "She's hardly a well-known killer of Jedi anymore."

"And even if she was, this isn't the kind of job you'd look up an eighty-year-old woman for," Han pointed out.

"Actually, she found *me*," Morwan explained. "When the Heritage Council assigned me to find someone capable of removing the Queen Mother from her throne, I began by assembling a history of known Jedi deaths. When I came across the story of Aurra Sing, I decided to research her as well, hoping to learn something that would help me choose my assassin wisely.

"I must have tripped an alarm gate," she continued. "Sing showed up a couple of weeks later, demanding to know why I was investigating her. After that, it was hire or die."

"Sounds like you didn't have much choice," Han said sympathetically. "I hope that doesn't mean you're having second thoughts now."

"I'm not." Morwan's tone grew defensive. "But I don't see why you are so concerned about *my* feelings, Captain Solo. I'm not even a member of the Council. The coup will go on no matter how *I* feel."

"Okay—don't get all touchy on me." Han turned forward again, grunting as the motion aggravated his wound. "I'm just trying to figure out who set us up at the palace, that's all."

"It wasn't me." Morwan stood and stepped between the pilot's and copilot's seats, then gently slipped a hand under Han's injured arm. "Time for you to go to medbay."

"Not yet." Han tried to pull his arm free, but managed only to cause himself so much pain that he gasped. "Not until we're in the Interior."

"By the time we reach the Interior, you may have an infection," Morwan said. Clearly unaccustomed to hearing no from a mere man, she continued to pull, slowly drawing Han to his feet. "And the way your arm won't move isn't good. The blaster wound may have fused— Are you *insane?*"

This last remark Morwan screeched as the barrel of Han's blaster suddenly appeared beneath her nose.

"*No* means *no,*" Han warned. "Didn't your mother teach you that?"

Morwan released his arm but refused to back down. "You aren't *that* tough, Captain Solo. When the numbspray wears off, you'll be screaming in pain."

"Probably," Leia said. "And he'll be sitting right there doing it. I've met rontos who aren't as stubborn."

Morwan turned to Leia, her mouth agape in surprise. "And you put up with that?"

"I have a shock collar," Leia replied, "but it just makes him drool."

Morwan's brow shot up in alarm. "Be careful. Turning it up that high may affect his performance . . ." She finally seemed to realize Leia was joking and let the sentence trail off. "Please forgive me. It's sometimes hard to remember that the rest of the galaxy has a more tolerant view of men."

"Sometimes, I find it hard to believe myself." Scowling at Han's blaster, Leia assumed the high-pitched voice a mother might use with a child. "Han, dear, why don't you put that nasty blaster away? Maybe See-Threepio will take the lady back to the medbay and help her find some bacta salve and bandages, and then you can stay in the cockpit with the grown-ups."

"All right—you don't have to go all sarcastic on me." Han holstered his blaster, then dropped back into the copilot's seat and winced. "I was just trying to make a point."

"You've succeeded beyond your wildest dreams, Captain Solo," Morwan said. "Next time, please feel free to yell."

She turned away and followed C-3PO down the access corridor. Once the protocol droid's metallic steps had died away, Han leaned closer to Leia and spoke in a soft voice. "Once we know who she's working for—"

"—we need to access the HoloNet and see that our intelligence reaches Tenel Ka," Leia finished. "I know."

"Good. Because we might not have much—"

"—time," Leia finished again. "I *know*, Han. Maybe you should activate the medbay monitoring cam."

Han lowered his brow. "Not yet. No one's sticking me in medbay until we've handled—"

"It's not *you* I want to watch," Leia said. "What if Lady Morwan isn't using her real name?"

"Oh—yeah." Han settled back into the copilot's chair and activated the medbay cam. "I guess a picture could be kind of useful."

"Kind of," she said in a wry voice.

Given even a moderately clear image, Leia felt certain that the Hapan Intelligence Service—one of the finest in the galaxy—would be able to identify Morwan and her superiors.

Han brought the medbay feed up on his display. "Great—Threepio's blocking the angle."

Leia glanced over to find the golden droid standing in front of Morwan, his head canted sideways as he pointed to a drawer. On the bunk was a tray where she was gathering supplies.

"Be patient," Leia said. "She'll lean into view when she opens the salve drawer."

Han grunted an acknowledgment and slumped back in his seat, looking more exhausted and discouraged than he had in years. It was as though all the struggle and loss they had endured through four decades of service to the galaxy had finally grown too heavy for even Han Solo to bear.

Leia reached over and touched his arm. "How are you doing?"

"Don't worry about me." He nodded at the crescent of stars outside the canopy. It was growing larger and more distinct by the moment, the black edges of the Transitory Mists seeming to pull away more quickly as the *Falcon* drew nearer. "I just need to hold on another ten minutes. Once we're in the mouth of that passage, we'll have a good signal."

"I'm not talking about your shoulder, Han. I mean, how are *you* doing?" With Nashtah—or rather, Aurra Sing—a constant presence since the failed assassination attempt, this was the first chance they'd had to talk over their decision to protect Tenel Ka, and Leia wanted to be sure Han realized what it would mean for Corellia. "No matter how you look at it, we're working against Corellia's interests here. I can sense how that troubles you."

Han frowned, and Leia thought he was about to object for the thousandth time to having his "mind read" by his own wife. Instead, he let out a weary sigh and dropped his chin in frustration.

"It's not what *we're* doing that bothers me," he said. "It's Gejjen. I *hate* being played."

Leia nodded sympathetically. "Me, too—but this is bigger than our feelings. If we're doing this just because Gejjen played us, we're doing it for the wrong reasons. I'm sure he felt he had no other choice. Corellia *is* in a desperate situation."

"Desperate doesn't matter," Han said. He turned to face her. "When you let me talk you into this—way back when we still had a life on Coruscant—Corellia was supposed to be in the right."

"We agreed Corellia was entitled to her independence," Leia said cautiously. "But she had to declare herself *totally* independent. She couldn't demand the benefits of Alliance membership without obeying Alliance law."

"Right," Han said, barely paying attention. "But Thrackan was playing games from the start, building secret fleets and trying to reactivate Centerpoint. And now Gejjen used *us* to try to expand the war."

"What are you saying, Han?" Leia studied his pupils, looking for dilation or disparate size or some other sign that he needed another stim-shot to keep him out of shock. "That we should go back to the Alliance?"

Han looked at her as though she had just asked him to step through an air lock naked. "And help Omas choke the last dregs of independence out of the galaxy?" His face grew angry. "No way. He doesn't get to use Corellia as an excuse for *that*."

"Okay—so what *do* you want to do?"

Han shrugged the one shoulder he could still move. "I think we're doing it, Leia."

"You're sure?" Leia already knew the answer—Han was never *unsure* about anything—but she wanted to hear him say it. "You know that keeping the Consortium out of the war might be the difference between survival and defeat for Corellia."

A defiant light came to Han's eye. "Don't underestimate Wedge. Niathal hasn't seen tricky until—"

"I'm not saying Corellia doesn't have a chance, Han," Leia interrupted. "Just that it's a small one—and we're about to make it smaller."

"Yeah, but what choice do we have? Let Gejjen arrange the assassination of Tenel Ka and a four-year-old kid?" Han shook his head sharply. "I don't want Corellia to win her freedom that way. If she can't do it without dragging Hapes and the rest of the galaxy into a big civil war, she shouldn't do it at all."

"I guess you *are* sure," Leia said.

"You aren't?"

"Oh, *I'm* sure," Leia said. "I'm fine with this."

Han looked confused. "Then why are we talking it to death?" He turned back to his display and remained silent a moment, then spoke in a sad voice. "I just wish *somebody* in this galaxy could be trusted."

"Somebody can." Leia smiled. "I'm sitting next to him."

A look of mild surprise flashed across Han's face, but he continued to watch his display and pretended not to hear. Even after all he had done to help overthrow the Emperor and win the war against the Yuuzhan Vong, he still refused to think of himself as one of the good guys. In his mind, Leia suspected, *good guy* was just too close to *sucker*.

On the display, Morwan finally leaned out from behind C-3PO, presenting a clear profile as she reached for the salve drawer. Han captured the image, then another of her full face as she turned to ask 3PO a question. The droid pointed at another drawer, and from this one Morwan pulled a sonic scalpel.

Han sat up straight. "What's *that* for?"

"Probably to cut away dead tissue," Leia said.

"Up here?"

"You aren't giving her much choice," Leia said. "I wouldn't worry about it. From what I've seen so far, she knows her combat medicine."

"Great," Han said. "She'll know right were to cut when she slits my throat."

Leia lowered her chin, giving him a *don't-be-ridiculous* look. "With a Jedi and two Noghri aboard?"

Han considered this a moment, then said, "She's still not getting near me with that scalpel. You *know* how she feels about men."

"It has to be done, or you could develop a necrotic infection," Leia said. "I'm pretty sure you can trust Lady Morwan, but you can always ask Threepio to do it instead."

"Thanks," Han grumbled. "I'd rather kiss a Hutt."

"No, you wouldn't," Leia replied quickly. "Take it from me."

On Han's display, Morwan finally picked up the supply tray and started forward again. Han saved the images he had captured, then deactivated the monitoring cam and replaced the image on his display with a drive nacelle temperature readout.

Once he had finished, Han leaned toward Leia again. "You know, maybe you're right about trusting Morwan," he said quietly. "She's not exactly happy about killing Tenel Ka and Allana. Maybe we could convince her—"

"Not going to happen," Leia said, cutting him off. "She's a true believer in Consortium independence. She may regret the necessities of the coup, but we'll never *talk* her into betraying the ringleaders."

Han dropped back into his chair, exhaling in frustration. "So we're back to doing this the hard way."

"I'm afraid so," Leia said. "We keep playing spies."

C-3PO's metallic steps rang up the access corridor, punctuating the sharp tones of Morwan's indignant voice. "I'm a field surgeon by training, Threepio," she was saying. "I think I can remember how to use an irrigation bulb."

"I'm certain you can," C-3PO replied. "It's really quite simple, as long as you use the proper antibiotic."

"I *know*, Threepio," Morwan said. "Does the Alliance program all its male-pattern droids to be as condescending as you are?"

"I'm afraid your question is based on an erroneous assumption, Lady Morwan. I don't even *have* a condescension module." C-3PO paused a moment, then added, "But please don't feel bad about it. Most female humans make the same mistake."

Morwan's only reply was a groan of exasperation. A moment later she led C-3PO onto the flight deck.

"I don't know how you live in a gender-equal society, Princess Leia," she said. "Even your droids have insufferable egos."

"You get used to it." Leia nonchalantly turned her gaze forward again. Their destination now filled most of the canopy, with a frame of dark mist swirling around the edges of the star crescent. "Did I hear you telling Threepio you're a field surgeon?"

"*Was*," Morwan corrected. "I, um, *moved on* after the Qoribu escapade."

Leia's brow rose. "You were at Qoribu?" The Battle of Qoribu had been short but vicious, the result of a misunderstanding during the Dark Nest crisis between a Hapan commander and his Chiss counterpart. "Aboard the *Kendall*?"

Morwan hesitated before answering, just long enough to suggest that she realized she had given away more information about herself than was probably wise.

"As a matter of fact, I did serve aboard the *Kendall*," she finally said. "How did you know?"

"I recognized you from when we transported the Kil-liks," Leia lied. The truth was that she had just tossed out the name of the Hapan flagship, hoping to trick Morwan into revealing the name of the vessel she'd served on. "So you served with Aleson Gray?"

"I wouldn't say *with*." The pitch of Morwan's voice was just a touch higher than normal, but it was enough to confirm the ripple of anxiety that Leia felt through the Force. "I wasn't part of the command staff."

"Lady Morwan, didn't anyone ever tell you it's impos-sible to lie to a Jedi?" Leia caught Han's gaze in the canopy reflection and held it, making sure he understood the significance of the question. Hapan officers tended to draw their command staffs from their own houses, so chances were good that they had just identified the coup ringleader. "But don't worry. Your Ducha's secret is safe with us."

"Yeah," Han said. "Who are we going to tell?"

chapter sixteen

Luke woke with the same troubled spirit he did every time he dreamed of the face, his chest heavy with the weight of a duty unanswered, his stomach churning with premonitions of failure. The face always came to him half hidden beneath a raised hood, betraying only a hint of its appearance—a mouth frozen into a lopsided grimace of anguish, a jagged brow fixed in a permanent scowl of disapproval, a pair of ebony eyes shining with perpetual malice. He never saw enough of the face to know whether it was the same one each time, but the emotions always came in order: pain, condemnation, spite. Luke had no idea what the pattern meant, but he felt sure it was a storm warning.

A beckoning whistle sounded from the far side of the *Jade Shadow*'s elegant master cabin, where R2-D2 stood in the hatchway, rocking back and forth on his support arms. Luke allowed himself the fantasy of using the Force to push the little droid back into the corridor and closing his eyes again. Since learning of Lumiya's involvement with GAG, he had been so worried about Ben that he had barely been able to sleep—and even when he did, he was so troubled by dreams that he never woke feeling refreshed.

R2-D2 let out an impatient bleat, then extended his charging arm and started across the floor.

"All right—no need for the ronto prod." Luke swung his feet around and sat on the edge of the bunk. "I'm awake."

R2-D2 issued a doubtful whistle, but stopped and retracted the charging arm as Luke pulled on his boots. The steady thrumming in the deck suggested that the *Shadow* had emerged from hyperspace and was decelerating hard, presumably on its final approach to the planet Hapes. Luke could sense Mara's impatience through their Force-bond, though not the cause. Perhaps she was having a hard time securing approach clearance from the Hapan defense forces—or perhaps she was simply eager to get Ben away from any influence Lumiya might be exerting over Jacen and GAG.

Once his boots were fastened, Luke grabbed his robe and started forward through the observation salon. The cratered faces of two silver moons were sliding past outside the *Shadow*'s starboard viewport. Outside the other, the ion tails of half a dozen starships were crawling across the star-flecked velvet. In the distance hung a white motionless disk—no doubt one of the Battle Dragons that would be screening Hapes after the attempt on Tenel Ka's life.

Luke continued forward onto the flight deck, where the cloud-mottled disk of the planet itself hung dead ahead. Its sparkling oceans and forested islands were as beautiful as ever, but Luke was more interested in the thumb-sized wedge slowly drifting toward the center of the canopy. Instead of the customary white, the Star Destroyer's hull was matte black, with the telltale dome of a gravity-well generator bulging beneath its belly and a cloaking cone rising midway down its spine.

It was the first time Luke had seen the new GAG Star Destroyer. He didn't much like it—and he really didn't like that it had been named the *Anakin Solo,* after his dead nephew.

A canopy section opaqued into a mirror, and Mara's face appeared in the reflection, looking focused and worried. The *Shadow* had a drop-deck helm, with the pilot seated down in the nose of the cockpit, so she had to tilt her head slightly upward to meet his gaze.

"We just received a very interesting holorecording," she said.

"From Jacen?"

Mara shook her head. "From Han, relayed over the HoloNet from the Jedi Temple."

"Really?" Luke lifted his brow; before leaving the Jedi Temple, they had been briefed on the Solos' "participation" in the assassination attempt. "Explaining how they're being impersonated by clones and weren't even on Hapes when someone tried to kill Tenel Ka? Because that's the only thing that makes sense."

"Not exactly," Mara said. "And it only gets more confusing. Han and Leia are spying on the coup plotters."

"*Spying?*" Luke frowned, trying to work out the course of events that would lead the Solos from Corellia to the assassination attempt to becoming spies for the Galactic Alliance. "You're right, it is confusing—but whatever Han and Leia do usually *is*. What was in the message?"

"They've learned the identity of one of the ringleaders," Mara said. "Han wants us to pass the information to Tenel Ka as soon as possible."

Luke looked out the front of the canopy, where the

Anakin's silhouette now hung dead ahead of the *Shadow.* "Then why are we heading for the *Anakin*?"

"I tried to relay the message to Tenel Ka. My signal was routed to Prince Isolder. He suggested I try again after we were aboard the *Anakin.*"

"The *Anakin*?" Luke closed his eyes and expanded his Force-awareness toward the Star Destroyer. It did not take long to find the familiar, levelheaded presence of Tenel Ka. "What's she doing there?"

"Protecting Allana, I'm sure. I doubt she needed Han to tell her there was a traitor on her staff—*or* that her daughter is just as much a target as she is."

"So she turns to Jacen," Luke said. He was struck—as he so often was—by how lonely and sad Tenel Ka's life had become, how much she was sacrificing to ensure a stable and humane government for her father's people. "I guess that makes sense."

Mara nodded. "When you can't trust your new friends, you go to your old ones." She fell silent a moment, then added, "Especially if one of them happens to be a very *close* friend."

Luke raised his brow. "You think Jacen and Tenel Ka are lovers?"

"He sneaks off to see *someone* every few months," Mara said.

"Tenel Ka?" Luke frowned, trying to imagine Tenel Ka having secret trysts with someone as dangerous to her throne as Jacen, then shook his head. "If she weren't the Queen Mother, maybe. But there's no future in it."

"And you think that would stop them?"

"Maybe not Jacen," Luke said. "But a Jedi lover would cause too many problems for Tenel Ka. She wouldn't take such a foolish risk—no matter how she felt about him."

Mara's expression remained doubtful. "Tenel Ka has to

have *something* for herself. She's giving everything else to the Consortium."

"Okay, it's *possible*," Luke said. He did not understand why he found the idea so alarming; was it merely because of his fears concerning Jacen? Or did his misgivings go deeper than that? Perhaps it made him fear that Lumiya's corruption was spreading faster than he could contain it. "And that's all the more reason we shouldn't speculate. We could be putting Tenel Ka's life at risk."

"All right," Mara said, taking the point. "But aren't you even a little curious about Allana?"

"Of course," Luke admitted. "But Jacen *can't* be the father. The timing is just wrong."

Mara put on a pout that looked completely out of place on her strong face. "Spoilsport."

"I'm just saying that it's impossible." Suddenly Luke felt the need to spell out his reasoning—perhaps because now Mara had *him* wondering about Allana's paternity. "For six months after the Battle of Qoribu, Jacen was confined to the academy on Ossus, along with the rest of the Jedi Knights involved—and *that's* when Allana had to have been conceived. If Jacen had been slipping off to visit Tenel Ka, we would have known."

Mara let out an exaggerated sigh of disappointment. "Killjoy."

"Okay, okay." Realizing that Mara was teasing him now, Luke smiled and raised his hands. "I surrender. I'm sure we can think of another explanation. We know he visited Tenel Ka when he asked for the fleet she sent to Qoribu. Maybe Allana's gestation took a whole year."

Mara winced in empathic discomfort. "Now you're just being cruel." She flicked her gaze toward the reflection of the copilot's chair. "Take a seat. You look like you've been wrestling rancors in your sleep."

"I wish." Luke slipped into the copilot's seat behind her. "It was the face again."

Mara's expression grew serious. "Jacen?"

Luke shrugged. "Maybe. I never see it clearly enough."

"Then you can't be sure."

"It was male," Luke replied. He could feel through the Force how worried Mara was about Ben, how alarmed she was by the relationship they had discovered between GAG and Lumiya—so he did not understand why she still refused to see what was happening to Jacen. "Who else could it be?"

"That's the point, Luke," Mara said. "We don't *know*. So far, the only connection we have between Jacen and Lumiya is some evidence suggesting she's been working with GAG."

"And you don't find that alarming?"

"Like a gundark in a petting zoo," Mara replied. She turned her gaze back to the *Anakin Solo,* which was steadily growing in the center of the canopy. "But there's a big difference between suspicion and fact. What if Lumiya wasn't working for GAG? What if someone in GAG is working for *her*?"

"You think she subverted one of Jacen's subordinates?"

"I *think* we need to be open to the possibility," Mara corrected. "You don't like what Jacen's doing with GAG, so you're predisposed to assume the worst. All I'm saying is we can't let emotion color our judgment."

Luke fell silent a moment, then let out a long breath. "You're right—maybe I'm assuming the worst because I don't like Jacen's methods. But your advice is good for both of us, you know. I think you blind yourself to what's happening with Jacen because he's the one who convinced Ben not to hide from the Force."

Mara nodded. "Guilty as charged," she said, keeping

her eyes forward. "That's why we have to work together on this, Skywalker. We need to keep each other honest . . . and if we don't like what we find, we're going to need each other more than ever."

Her tone made Luke frown. "What are you saying?"

"You know what I mean, Skywalker," she replied. "If you're right—if Jacen has been making a fool of me—he won't be easy to handle. It'll take both of us."

Luke raised his brow, surprised by the ice in Mara's voice. "What about that sense of certainty you experienced back at the Sparring Arena? You said we had to let Ben follow his own path, that you thought the Force had drawn him to Jacen for a reason."

"I still think that," Mara said. "But *we* have a path to follow, too. Maybe this is where all our paths converge— where Ben's path finally joins ours."

"Only Ben's?" Luke asked. He was beginning to sense some of the old ruthlessness in Mara, some of her old assassin instinct—and it scared him. "What about Jacen?"

"If I'm wrong, Jacen won't *have* a path," Mara said. "We'll have to end it."

"Now I think *you're* the one who's assuming the worst," he said. "I'm worried about Jacen, but I'm not ready to kill him."

"Then you're not being realistic," Mara said. "If he *is* working with Lumiya, we won't have a choice. I won't let him take Ben down that path with him."

"Of course not—but whatever Jacen has become, it's due to what happened after he was captured by the Yuuzhan Vong—and *I'm* the one who sent him on that mission." Luke paused, still struggling with the decision that had cost the life of his nephew Anakin and so many other young Jedi Knights—still wondering what else he could have done to save the Jedi. "I won't give up on Jacen just because he's lost his way. If he *has* fallen under Lumiya's sway, I'm going to bring him back under mine."

Mara's gaze strayed back to Luke's reflection in the mirrored panel. "Why doesn't that surprise me?"

Luke flashed an innocent smile. "Because you're used to me doing the impossible?"

Mara sighed. "Something like that." She looked back to the *Anakin*, which was now an arm-length wedge silhouetted against the sparkling waters of a Hapan ocean. "But you'd better not be intending to redeem Lumiya, too. I draw the line at ex-girlfriends."

"Don't worry," Luke said. "Even *I'm* not that naïve. Lumiya is going down."

The comm channel squawked as a traffic controller issued approach clearance for the *Shadow*. For the next few minutes, as the dark mass of the *Anakin* continued to swell in the canopy, they were kept busy making course corrections and providing identity verifications. A pair of XJ5 ChaseXs flew by to confirm their identities visually, then irritated Mara by looping around to fall into the kill zone directly behind the *Shadow*.

Finally, when the *Shadow* had drawn so close they could see nothing ahead except the dark tiers of the Star Destroyer's blocky superstructure, the traffic controller gave them clearance to berth in the Command Hangar. Mara dropped beneath the sky of black durasteel that was the *Anakin*'s belly, then angled aft to a small launching bay defended by two quad cannon laser turrets.

She used the attitude thrusters to rise through the barrier shield into the hangar, where a set of beacon lights led her to the designated berth.

No sooner had the *Shadow* set down than an honor guard of twenty GAG troopers emerged from an access hatch. They arrayed themselves in two columns and came to attention facing each other, and a moment later Jacen appeared and strode down the aisle between them. A black cape billowed from the shoulders of his black colonel's uniform.

"Oh, boy," Mara said, unbuckling her crash webbing. "Does he *know* who he looks like?"

"He does if he bothered to look in a mirror." Luke was disappointed to see that their son was not accompanying Jacen, but hardly surprised. He had not felt Ben's presence when he reached out to see if Tenel Ka was aboard the *Anakin*. "I just hope that's not the point. He might as well be a recruiting holo for Corellian terrorists."

As they shut down the *Shadow*, Luke expanded his Force-awareness to the entire Star Destroyer, searching for any hint that Lumiya was aboard. He felt a second presence near Tenel Ka's that seemed very strong in the Force—her daughter, Allana, he suspected—but nothing dark enough to be Lumiya. Of course, that didn't mean much. Jacen was standing right there in front of him, and Luke couldn't sense *his* presence, either.

Once all systems had been placed on standby, they went aft and found Jacen waiting at the bottom of the boarding ramp. His face was gray and furrowed, and the purple circles beneath his eyes suggested that he had not been sleeping well, if at all. He bowed first to Mara, then to Luke.

"Masters Skywalker, welcome aboard the *Anakin Solo*." Jacen's voice sounded genuinely warm, though it was impossible to read his true feelings. "What a pleasant surprise."

"You might want to reserve judgment on that," Mara said. "We need to talk."

"Of course." Jacen remained at the foot of the boarding ramp, making no move to allow them any farther aboard. "Is something wrong?"

"You'd be safe to assume that," Luke said. "Where's Ben?"

"On a mission," Jacen replied. "He's in a comm blackout zone at the moment, but if it's important, I could dispatch—"

"We'll talk about that later—in private." Luke had to struggle to keep his voice even; with Lumiya on the loose, he did not like the thought of Ben being on a mission *anywhere*. "First, we need to speak with the Queen Mother. We have an urgent message for her."

Jacen's eyes widened with surprise. "Tenel Ka?"

"*Now,* Jacen," Luke said. "And we'll need a holoprojector."

Jacen let out his breath. "Very well." He stepped aside and led them and R2-D2 up the aisle between the honor guard. "I'm sorry for hesitating, but she asked me to keep her presence confidential. Aside from the chamberlain she brought along, Prince Isolder is the only Hapan who knows she's aboard."

They passed through a hatchway into a small foyer, where four GAG troopers stood guard over a bank of lift tubes. Most of the tubes had a small sign next to them listing a destination such as ENGINEERING or COMMUNICATIONS, but at the far end of the foyer a tube large enough for five people remained unlabeled.

"It descends to the Detention Center," Jacen explained, apparently noticing what Luke was looking at. "We find that prisoners are less likely to resist if they don't realize they've reached the end of the journey."

"Very . . . practical," Luke said, trying not to be alarmed by how proficient his nephew had become at the art of imprisonment and interrogation. "I assume it results in fewer injuries to the prisoners."

Jacen nodded. "That, too."

A shudder of revulsion ran down Luke's spine, but if Mara was alarmed by Jacen's apparent indifference to his prisoners' welfare, she did not show it. She merely followed him across the foyer to a lift labeled BRIDGE, then stepped into the tube and rose out of sight.

Jacen turned to Luke. "After you."

Luke waved R2-D2 into the lift ahead of him, then followed without replying. His stomach sank as the tube walls blurred past. A moment later he came to a stop and stepped out into a sparse durasteel anteroom, where another detail of GAG sentries stood guard over several hatchways leading into a maze of blue-white corridors.

A single transparisteel wall, the only one without any openings in it, overlooked the flight deck one level below. Most of the officers there still wore the blue-and-gray uniforms of a normal Galactic Alliance Star Destroyer complement, but Luke could not help noticing the sense of pride and purpose that they radiated into the Force. Whatever Jacen's other faults, he was clearly a good leader.

Jacen stepped out of the lift behind Luke and spoke to an ebony-skinned trooper standing directly across from them. "Sergeant Darb, take an escort detail to the Situation Room and inform the Queen Mother that the Masters Skywalker would like to speak with her. We'll be waiting in the Briefing Cabin."

"Very well, Colonel."

The sergeant saluted sharply and left to obey. Jacen turned away from the flight deck, leading R2-D2 and the Skywalkers down a short corridor into a state-of-the-art Briefing Cabin with a large holocomm unit at one end of a sunken speaking stage. The area was enclosed by a circle of flowform chairs, each with a panel built into the arm to control individualized comm units, vid displays, and even automatic caf dispensers.

Jacen went to a chair at the far end of the oval, then turned to face Luke and Mara. "I'm afraid it will be a few minutes before Sergeant Darb arrives with the Queen Mother. After the attempt on her life, I'm insisting on Level Five security protocols even aboard the *Anakin*."

"It certainly won't hurt anything," Mara said. "Though from what I've sensed so far, your crew seems exceptionally focused and alert—almost fanatic. It's hard to imagine an assassin remaining undetected long enough to defeat security."

"Thank you. Coming from you, Aunt Mara, I take that as quite a compliment." He sat down and motioned the Skywalkers toward a pair of nearby seats. "There's a beverage menu in the arm display, if you'd like something to drink."

Luke remained standing. "Thanks, but we're not thirsty."

"I see." Jacen's expression turned from pleasant to disappointed, and he shifted to the edge of his seat. "Then why don't we get whatever is bothering you out in the open? I know you disapprove of my methods, but the hostility I sense runs deeper than that, and it pains me. You and Ben are the only family I have left."

"That's hardly true," Mara objected. "What about Jaina and your parents?"

"You know how strained my relationship with Jaina has been," Jacen said. "I'm afraid her insubordination at Corellia finally snapped it. We're not speaking, and I suspect things are going to stay that way."

"Maybe things would be different if you hadn't brought her up on charges," Luke pointed out.

"What *should* I have done? Looked the other way because she's my sister?" Jacen's voice was cracking, but his expression remained confident and his gaze steady. "The Galactic Alliance can't survive if her leaders keep playing favorites. That kind of thing is why Corellia thinks she doesn't have to live by the same laws as the rest of the Alliance. The rules apply to everyone or to no one."

Luke did not need the Force to sense the conviction behind his nephew's words. It was pouring off Jacen like heat from a star, bathing everyone near him in its glow—no doubt burning those who came too close.

"What about your parents?" Mara asked. "Are you turning your back on them because they don't share your beliefs?"

"Not at all. I'm turning my back on them because they tried to assassinate the ruler of an Alliance member state—someone who's always been a friend to them." Jacen stood. "My parents are terrorist scum, and *that* is why I have turned my back on them."

The fire in Jacen's eyes was as anguished as it was intense, and Luke finally began to understand just how alone his nephew really was. He had lost his younger brother during the last pan-galactic war and renounced his sister and parents in an attempt to prevent another one, and in his unwavering battle against the evil he saw threatening the galaxy, he was clearly ready to surrender his relationship with his aunt and uncle, as well.

Like the Yuuzhan Vong who had once held him captive, Jacen had become capable of any sacrifice—and just as intolerant of those who did not share his commitment. Jacen Solo had fallen not because he was selfish, Luke realized, but because he was *selfless*.

"Jacen, I know your parents' actions are confusing," Mara said. "But you need to trust your—"

"Let Jacen judge his parents for himself," Luke interrupted. Their only hope of bringing Jacen back was to shock him—to let him discover for himself just how wrong he was. "At the moment, I'm more interested in where Ben is."

"He's aboard a reconnaissance skiff," Jacen replied. "I'd offer to holocomm him for you, but they're in the Transitory Mists."

"What's Ben doing in the Transitory Mists?" Mara demanded.

"Looking for Jaina and Zekk," Jacen answered. "They went to Terephon to deliver a message for Tenel Ka and haven't returned yet. I sent the reconnaissance skiff to investigate, and Ben went along to see if he could help find them through the Force."

Mara's voice grew sharp. "Alone?"

"Of course not. As I told you, he's aboard a reconnaissance skiff—with an excellent crew." A concerned frown came to Jacen's face. "What's wrong?"

"Didn't I warn you that Lumiya had returned?" Luke's tone was just as sharp as Mara's. "That I was worried she would come at me through him?"

"Yes," Jacen said. "But that was back on Coruscant. I don't think there's any reason to worry out here."

"Why not?" Mara demanded. "Because you're sure Lumiya *isn't* interested in him?"

Jacen's frown turned indignant. "How would I know *that*?"

"Jacen, we found Lumiya's apartment," Luke said. "We know she's been working for GAG."

Jacen's eyes widened. It was not an unreasonable reaction, given the subject matter, but Luke still wished his nephew wasn't so good at hiding his feelings in the Force.

"You might think you've been using her for your own ends," Luke continued. "But you're fooling yourself. Lumiya always has an agenda of—"

"Working with GAG *how*?" Jacen interrupted. "I certainly haven't seen her in uniform."

"Don't insult us by denying it," Mara said. "She was living in a GAG safehouse, and she had been accessing GAG files on the True Victory Party."

"Then *she's* the one who's been assassinating the Bothans?" Jacen asked. "Why? What could she stand to gain by spreading the war?"

"You won't get out of this by changing the subject," Luke said. It was impossible to say whether Jacen's surprise was genuine or feigned—so Luke assumed it was feigned. "We know she came with you. She left her apartment the same day the *Anakin* left Coruscant."

"You think she *followed* us?" Jacen dropped into his chair and punched a button. "The *Anakin* needs to remain here in support of Queen Mother Tenel Ka, but I'll take a skiff personally—"

"We'll be handling that *ourselves*," Mara said. "Ben will be returning to Coruscant with us after this is finished."

"Do you think that's wise?" The comm light on the arm of Jacen's chair blinked on, but he ignored it and continued to speak to Mara. "It will only interrupt Ben's training, and if Lumiya *is* trying to get at him, she'll have an easier time stalking him on Coruscant."

"Ben is done with GAG," Luke said. "I don't understand yet why Lumiya is involved with GAG, but I *do* know she is. My decision is final."

Jacen's face fell. "Very well." He deactivated the comm unit, then composed himself and continued. "There's a refueling depot at Roqoo, just outside the Mists. You can rendezvous with him there."

"Thank you," Mara said.

Jacen nodded absentmindedly, then said, "I hope you'll

at least share the details of your investigation. If someone in my command is using Lumiya as an agent, I need to know."

"Of course. Tresina Lobi had been trying to track Lumiya down for some time." Luke was giving a slightly altered version of events, in part because he wanted to learn how much Jacen *did* know about Lumiya's relationship with GAG. "Apparently, she succeeded, because we found her body in Fellowship Plaza the morning you left for Hapes."

"Fellowship Plaza?" This time, Jacen's shock was real; Luke felt it through the Force. "Master Lobi is dead?"

"That's right," Mara said. Though her answer was casual, Luke could sense through their Force-bond how closely she was studying Jacen. "She had already commed the Temple with the address of Lumiya's apartment."

Mara's account of events was even less accurate than Luke's—and far more distracting to Jacen, who barely managed to reply with a murmured, "How . . . *unfortunate*."

Luke was trying to decide how best to proceed—how best to keep Jacen off guard so they could continue pressuring him—when the cabin door hissed open. Tenel Ka entered, wearing an eletrotex flight suit tailored tightly enough to suggest that her physical training remained as intense as ever. She crossed to Luke and Mara, her radiant smile at odds with the aura of tension and worry that hung about her in the Force.

"Master Skywalker! Thank you for coming." She embraced Luke, then did the same with Mara. "You are unexpected, but very welcome. We can use all the help we can find."

"Thank you, Your Majesty," Luke said. "Unfortunately, we're here on a different matter."

"But we do have a message that I'm sure will prove very useful," Mara added.

"I hope it includes word of when the Alliance reinforcements will arrive." The woman who said this was still in the cabin doorway, trailing half a dozen steps behind Tenel Ka. She was tall and pretentious looking, with a long nose and a mouth turned permanently downward at the corners. "After lending so many of our fleets to the Galactic Alliance, our enemies have us at a terrible disadvantage."

Tenel Ka's face reddened, but she turned and politely motioned at the woman. "Masters Skywalker, allow me to present my chamberlain, Lady Galney, younger sister to the Ducha Galney of Terephon."

Luke noted that the name was the same as the planet to which Ben had been sent, but merely bowed to Galney and did not remark on the coincidence.

"Chief Omas and Admiral Niathal are assembling a sizable defense fleet," he said. "It should be able to depart Coruscant in a week."

"A week!" Lady Galney burst out. "By then the usurpers will have mined the hyperspace lanes and be attacking Hapes itself."

"There's no need to worry about the mines, Lady Galney," Mara said. "Alliance fleets are well equipped to deal with them. Once the defense fleet is under way, the usurpers won't delay it for long."

"Of course they won't." Tenel Ka's voice carried more confidence than Luke sensed in her through the Force. "Is that the message you mentioned?"

"Actually, no," Luke said. "*That* message is for your ears alone."

He threw a tactful glance in Lady Galney's direction, but she merely smirked and remained where she was.

"I'm the Queen Mother's highest-ranking adviser. To perform my duties properly, I *must* hear whatever she hears."

"Then I'm sure she'll fill you in later." Mara took the woman by the arm and started her toward the door. "But our instructions were explicit."

Jacen rose. "In that case, perhaps I'd better go as—"

"No, you stay." Luke motioned him back into his chair. "You need to see this more than Tenel Ka does."

Jacen raised his brow, but returned to his seat. Mara pushed Lady Galney out the door with instructions to Sergeant Darb to have her escorted back to her quarters.

"I'm sorry about that, Your Majesty," Luke said to Tenel Ka. "But it's possible that someone close to you is a traitor."

Tenel Ka nodded. "Yes, I have been having premonitions of that myself—though I don't believe it is Lady Galney." She smiled. "I can still sense when someone is lying to me, you know. She is a fool—but she is an honest one."

"That doesn't mean she can be trusted with your secrets," Mara said, returning to Tenel Ka's side. "Anyone with that much interest in another person's business won't keep it private."

"I am counting on that. With the *Anakin Solo* in orbit around Hapes, I need someone with me who will report to the rumormongers that I have *not* been sleeping with her Jedi commander." Tenel Ka glanced in Jacen's direction and smiled again. "Besides, her sister, the Ducha Galney, is one of my most devoted nobles. It serves my purpose to cultivate the illusion of a special relationship with Lady Galney."

Luke snorted in amazement. "Your life is a maze, Your Majesty. I don't know how you live it."

"Because I was well prepared, Master Skywalker," Tenel Ka said solemnly. "And I thank you every day."

Luke actually blushed, but he remained composed enough to reply, "And you've always made me very proud, Tenel Ka."

"Though we are disappointed that we haven't met Allana yet," Mara added sternly. "I trust *that* will change before we depart today?"

Jacen started around the chairs, clearly alarmed. "That won't be—"

"Perhaps," Tenel Ka said. "But, as Jacen was about to say, Allana has been very upset by the assassination attempt—particularly since there was a Jedi involved. It might be best if we put it off until another time."

Luke and Mara exchanged baffled glances. Maybe Allana really *had* been traumatized by the attack, or maybe the rumors of deformity were true; in any case, they had no choice but to accept Tenel Ka's excuse.

"I'm sorry to hear that," Luke said. "I was looking forward to meeting her."

"But the message may clarify a few things about Leia's involvement." Mara's voice had just a hint of petulance, as though she felt Tenel Ka should have known better than to think the Solos would really try to kill her. She used the Force to lower R2-D2 into the speaking area, then said, "Play Han's message."

R2-D2 acknowledged the order with a chirp, then went over to the holocomm unit and inserted his interface arm into a data socket. A rosy blur appeared over the projection pad and quickly resolved itself into an image of Han's face. His skin was pale and waxy with shock, and his mouth was hanging in a lopsided grimace of pain.

Luke immediately felt a pang of concern—Mara hadn't warned him that Han was wounded—but when he glanced over at his nephew, Jacen's eyes were hard and narrow.

"Listen up, kid." Han's voice was low and raspy, as though he was trying to avoid being overheard. "I don't have long—we've got someone aboard who can't know about this—but I need you to relay this holo to Tenel Ka . . . and *only* to Tenel Ka. Someone close to her is a traitor, and it could go bad on us if this message got back to the wrong people."

The image changed to the profile of a beautiful Hapan woman with long brunette curls and high cheeks. She seemed to be leaning over something—Luke thought it might be a bench or table, until he saw her remove a tube of bacta salve from a drawer in the *Falcon*'s medbay.

Han's voice continued, "This is a woman named Morwan, but that might be an alias. She was a flight surgeon aboard the *Kendall* at the Battle of Qoribu. We're fairly sure she's in service to the AlGray family of the Relephon Moons, and she's the contact between the Heritage Council—that's what the nobles behind the coup call themselves—and the assassin who escaped with us."

The woman's image changed to full face, and she looked even more striking, with full lips and soft, slanted eyes.

Han kept speaking. "We heard her tell the assassin to take care of Allana first."

The woman's image vanished, then Han's face reappeared, looking even more distressed than he had a moment earlier. "Luke, Tenel Ka needs to take this threat seriously. The assassin's name is Aurra Sing . . ."

Luke was so shocked that he temporarily shut out Han's voice. He knew Aurra Sing's name from records of the old Jedi order that he had gathered and studied over the years.

". . . thinks she might have been some sort of Jedi about eighty years ago," Han was saying. "That's all we know, but there's something else. Keep an eye out for Alema Rar. We bumped into Jag Fel out at Telkur Station, and—"

Han stopped and glanced over his shoulder, then his voice dropped to a whisper. "Gotta go. Tell Tenel Ka we're sorry about that mess in the palace. Gejjen was using us to set her up, and we didn't know."

The hologram vanished, leaving them to stand there in silence. Though Luke was intrigued by the mentions of Alema Rar and Jagged Fel, he didn't give it much thought. He was more interested in his nephew's reaction to what they had just seen.

Jacen was keeping his Force presence buried and unreadable, but he was scowling at the floor and taking long breaths. Luke resisted the temptation to suggest that it had been wrong to doubt the Solos in the first place. If Jacen was going to break the dark side's hold, he had to rediscover for himself that a Jedi trusted his feelings as much as his eyes.

After a few moments of silence, Tenel Ka said, "Thank you for showing us this message. It is certainly easier to believe the Solos were being used than that they were trying to kill me."

Jacen surprised Luke by nodding. "And it explains some of those witness conflicts you mentioned," he said. "If my parents *were* being used by Gejjen, once they realized what was happening, they would have tried to prevent the attack."

A warm sense of relief rose inside Luke. Not only was Jacen open to the idea that his parents were innocent, he was *looking* for reasons to believe they were. Luke grew even more confident that he would be able to turn Jacen away from the dark side, whatever his nephew's relationship with Lumiya.

"I hate to be a wet blanket," Mara said. "But to me, this smells like they're inviting us to a Hutt's banquet."

Luke lowered his brow. "What are you saying?" He wanted to tell her to stop planting doubts in Jacen's mind, but he sensed through their Force-bond that Mara was only trying to be certain Jacen understood his mistake—to be sure that Jacen believed in his heart that his parents were not only innocent of aiding the assassination attempt, but *incapable* of it. "That this might be misinformation?"

"I'm saying their message is convenient." Mara addressed her comments to Jacen. "If they *were* involved, the message would be a good way to throw off suspicion—and feed us misinformation."

Jacen's eyes widened. "I'm surprised to hear you say that, Aunt Mara." There was a note of resentment—perhaps even anger—in his voice. "I thought you had a better opinion of my parents than that."

Mara's gaze did not waver. "I have a very high opinion of Han and Leia—which is why we have to consider the possibility that they they're deceiving us." She paused, then, with perfect timing, turned to Tenel Ka as though she were dismissing Jacen's opinion. "This is war, and the Solos are fighting for the other side. We have to be careful."

"We also have to take into account who they are," Jacen said, also turning to Tenel Ka. "You know my parents. They're not murderers. I think we should trust this message."

Luke's heart filled with joy. Clearly, Jacen remained in touch with his emotions—and that meant there was still hope of guiding him back to the light side.

After a moment's thought, Tenel Ka nodded to Jacen. "So do I." She turned to Mara with an apologetic air. "You don't know of the discrepancies in the witness accounts, but there was some question of whom the Solos were fighting during the attack. Their message clears that up."

"Well, it's your decision." Despite Mara's reply, Luke could sense that she was as happy as he was about the results. "I just wanted to be sure you had considered the possibility."

"And I'm grateful for that—it could not have been easy." Tenel Ka turned back to Jacen. "Obviously, this means we both need to cancel the orders regarding your parents."

"Orders?" Luke asked.

"Capture and detain," Jacen explained. He thought for a moment, then shook his head. "But we can't. If they're right about a traitor in your court—"

"And that much seems obvious," Tenel Ka interrupted.

"—then canceling the orders would give them away," Mara finished. "You have to let the orders stand."

Jacen nodded. "Anything else could be a death sentence."

"Very well—they've proven quite adept at eluding us so far." Tenel Ka fell silent for a moment, then said, "Now we must consider what do we do about AlGray and her Heritage Council."

"There's only one thing to do," Jacen said.

"Exactly." Tenel Ka went to his side. "I have no right to ask you to do this—"

"Of course you do," Jacen replied. "You don't know which of your own fleet commanders you can trust, the Hapes Consortium is a loyal member of the Galactic Alliance, and it's my duty to aid you any way I can. But I'm afraid the *Anakin Solo* won't be enough—as I recall from the intelligence file, House AlGray has a dozen Battle Dragons of its own."

"Correct—and I will provide you with a large enough flotilla to assure your victory," Tenel Ka said. "But that isn't what I was talking about."

"It isn't?"

"No." Tenel Ka took his hand. "I must stay here to command the Home Fleet. With Aurra Sing coming after Allana, however, I want her away from Hapes. Until this is over, she will be safer with you aboard the *Anakin*."

"Are you sure?" Mara asked, alarmed. "Jacen may be going into battle."

"And I *will* be," Tenel Ka replied, almost sharply. "AlGray is not alone on this 'Heritage Council.' When we move against her, the others will move against me—and Hapes will become a far more dangerous place for Allana than the *Anakin*."

Mara nodded, a bit taken aback by Tenel Ka's tone. "Of course. I didn't mean to question your judgment."

"Of course you did." Tenel Ka's tone softened. "And I thank you—it is not something I am very accustomed to these days. Besides, Jacen will not have much of a battle. He will have twice the fleet and far better weapons, so he is my best option." She paused, as though an idea had just occurred to her. "Unless you and Master Skywalker will be returning directly to Coruscant?"

"Sorry," Mara said. "Allana wouldn't be any safer with us."

"I'm afraid we have to track down Ben," Luke explained, "and then take care of some unfinished business with Lumiya."

chapter seventeen

It was not the dark silence of the Missile Hold that Alema found so troubling, nor even all those cylinders packed with detonite and baradium and propellant. It was the cold. The caves of Ryloth, where she had spent the first years of her life, had been hot and dry and dusty, and the Gorog nest, in which she had lived as a Killik Joiner, had been warm and humid and close. But the Missile Hold of the *Anakin Solo* was frigid, even with a pair of bulky GAG utilities pulled over her own customary robes. Her nose was numb; her lekku were tingling, her teeth chattering, her old wounds aching; and her breath rose in curtains of steam.

"Alema, if you don't keep that glow rod on the cut, we're *both* going to be sorry." Lumiya was kneeling in front of a missile rack, using her cybernetic hand to carefully run a fusioncutter down the nose-cone welds of a baradium missile. "This isn't something I do every day."

"You are not making us confident." Alema shined the light on the missile just ahead of the fusioncutter's beam. "Why not tell Jacen to have a trained technician remove the . . . whatever it is you're after?"

"The proton detonator charge," Lumiya said. She was not wearing her face scarf, so her disfigured jaw instilled in Alema a feeling of kinship and togetherness. "And Jacen can't know about this."

"We should have guessed." Actually, Alema *had* already guessed, and she was simply seeking confirmation. Even after she had prevented Master Lobi from exposing what Lumiya was doing with Jacen, Lumiya remained secretive about her goals and plans—almost as though she did not truly understand the nature of her partnership with Alema. "But we have told you—Jacen is important to the Balance. We need him alive."

Lumiya continued to work, moving down the side of the missile toward the point of the initial cut. Alema counted to five. Then, when she had still received no reply, she moved the light away. The fusioncutter strayed from the weld, causing a shrill hum as it sliced into the skin of the missile cylinder.

"Crazy bugslut!" Lumiya snapped off the cutting beam. "You could blow the whole ship apart!"

Alema shrugged. "What does it matter? If Jacen dies, he does not become a Sith. If Jacen does not become a Sith, Leia's suffering is not equal to mine. If Leia's suffering is not equal to mine, the galaxy remains out of—"

"—Balance. You've *told* me." Lumiya reignited the fusioncutter, but continued to hold it away from the missile. "I'm doing this to *help* Jacen, not hurt him."

Alema continued to shine the glow rod away from the missile. "How?"

"Jacen asked me to rendezvous with Ben at Roqoo Depot," Lumiya said. "He's about to lead a task force to capture one of the coup leaders at the Relephon Moons, and he wants me to make certain Ben rejoins the *Anakin* safely."

Alema frowned. "But Ben is aboard a reconnaissance skiff," she said. "They can find their way to the Relephon Moons."

"Exactly." Lumiya motioned at the missile. "If you don't mind, the *Anakin* will be making her first jump within the hour, and I need to be gone before then."

Alema swung the light back toward the missile, but kept the beam focused on the floor. "It sounds suspicious."

Lumiya sighed in exasperation. "It sounds suspicious because it *is* suspicious. Jacen came to me as soon as the Skywalkers ended their little visit. I fear I've become a liability."

Alema returned the light to Lumiya's work. "You think Jacen is sending you into a trap?"

"I *know* he is. He's arranging a fight between me and Luke." Lumiya returned the fusioncutter to the weld and resumed work. "If I kill Luke, it creates an opening for Jacen to take over leadership of the Jedi order. If Luke kills *me*, then it will look as though I've been stalking Ben all along. Luke will assume that his original fears were correct, and the veil of suspicion will be lifted off Jacen."

"Jacen is no better than any Solo!" Alema was boiling with outrage. "Leia spawned a pack of lyleks."

"Oh, I think she did better than that," Lumiya replied. "I'd say Jacen is more of a thernbee—sly, ruthless, and deadly. I couldn't be more proud."

She completed the cut, and the nose cone came free. Alema caught it with the Force lest it jar the impact trigger and detonate the proton charge.

"Proud?" Alema carefully lowered the nose cone to the floor. "For betraying you?"

"Oh, *very* proud," Lumiya said. "I was growing worried that Jacen lacked the strength and cunning to fulfill his destiny. His betrayal proves that I was wrong. Jacen is very capable."

"We do not understand."

"Jacen's destiny doesn't allow him the luxury of loyalty," Lumiya explained. She deactivated the fusioncutter and set it aside. "If he were unwilling to betray *me*, how could we expect him to betray his entire family?"

Alema had no answer for that. Even in the ryll dens of Kala'uun, where a dancer's loyalty was strictly to herself, the one person she had never betrayed was her sister, Numa.

Lumiya began to sort through the tangle of wires and filaments surrounding the missile's proton detonator charge.

"Master Skywalker is not someone to trifle with," Alema said. "You could be killed."

"I'm aware of that." Lumiya found a bundle of wires leading into the head of the detonator housing and began to sort through them. "I *have* fought him before, you know."

"What about Jacen's destiny?" Alema asked. "Without you to guide him—"

"Jacen has the knowledge to complete his journey." Lumiya separated out an orange wire that ran from the detonator housing into a relay box on the head of the missile cylinder. "All that remains for him is to make his sacrifice."

"Then he hasn't?"

"Not yet." Lumiya pulled a pair of wire cutters from the pocket of her utilities and slipped the jaws over the orange wire. "But he will."

Alema's heart leapt into her throat. "Not the safety delay!"

Lumiya looked up, her brow furrowed in irritation. "Orange isn't the safety delay. It's the proximity sensor."

"It was on *Imperial* missiles," Alema said. "On Alliance missiles, it's the safety delay. There's only one wire—see?"

Lumiya studied the bundle, then reluctantly shifted the wire cutters to the first of a handful of gray wires.

Alema breathed a sigh of relief, then asked, "How can you be sure?"

"I *assume* you'd tell me if I was wrong again," Lumiya replied sharply.

"We mean Jacen." Alema explained. "If he doesn't make his sacrifice and you are already dead—"

"He *will* make his sacrifice," Lumiya snapped. "Now, about these wires—"

"Cut," Alema said. "What are you waiting for?"

Lumiya cut the first wire, then—when the *Anakin Solo* did not vanish in a white flash—began to cut the other gray wires.

"We are not sure we like this plan," Alema said. "If you are killed, his uncle will try to draw Jacen back to the light side of the Force—"

"He won't be able to," Lumiya said. "Because whether or not I return from this fight, *Luke* won't."

She cut the last of the gray wires, then exchanged her wire cutters for a hydrospanner and began to unbolt the detonator housing.

"That is what the proton detonator is for?" Alema asked, finally comprehending Lumiya's plan. "A combat fail-safe?"

Lumiya nodded. "As you said, I might be killed."

"It seems to us you are planning on it," Alema replied.

"Planning *for*, not *on*." Lumiya removed the last fastener from the detonator housing. "But I will admit that being killed is a more likely outcome than I would prefer."

"Then why go?" Alema asked. Although she would never admit this to Lumiya, she did not like the idea of Luke dying so soon. The Balance would be better served if he were forced to watch Jacen's decline, if he struggled to redeem his nephew before ultimately falling on his blade. "Killing Master Skywalker is no good if you don't survive to enjoy it."

Lumiya set the hydrospanner aside, then looked up at Alema with an expression approaching pity. "I'm not doing this for *me*, you silly dancing girl," she said. "But there's no use explaining. You wouldn't understand."

She turned her attention back to the missile, grabbing the detonator housing with both hands.

Alema, seething at Lumiya's put-down, deactivated the glow rod. There was a metallic click as the housing contacted the proton detonator.

"Are you mad?" Lumiya whispered. In the silence that followed her question could be heard the soft, nearly inaudible clicking of an electronic timer counting off second-tenths. "Turn on the glow rod!"

"We're trying." Alema slapped the glow rod against her crippled arm a couple of times. Assuming the housing had activated one of the impact triggers, they had about five more seconds to deactivate before the safety delay expired and allowed the charge to detonate. "But we aren't smart enough to understand. We're just a silly dancing girl."

"I *apologize*!" Lumiya snarled. "Now turn on the kriffing light!"

Alema tapped the glow rod against her arm again. "We're still not sure we understand."

"All right," Lumiya said. "Have you ever been part of something bigger and more important than yourself?"

"Our nest."

Alema reactivated the glow rod. Lumiya quickly removed the detonator housing the rest of the way from the proton charge, then reached out with the Force and pulled the trigger plunger away from its contact.

Alema continued her answer. "Individuals died, but Gorog lived on. Gorog was more important than we were."

"Exactly." Lumiya exhaled slowly, then used the Force to levitate the detonator casing while she retrieved the wire cutters and reached inside to snip the rest of the wires. "My situation is not so different."

Alema frowned. "How is it not different? You are the . . . last of . . . the . . ." She stopped, suddenly realizing why Lumiya might be willing to risk dying before Jacen completed his sacrifice . . . why Lumiya seemed so confident he *would,* even without her to guide him. "There are *more* Sith?"

Lumiya floated the housing down to the floor, revealing a head-sized wafer of bright metal with a small tube of liquid deuterium sunk into the center.

"There is a *plan*—a plan that will be carried out whether or not I survive." Lumiya reached over and followed two wires from the top of the deuterium tube to a small circuit board, then unclipped them both. "That's all you need to know."

"We don't believe you." Alema did not bother moving the glow rod away, since they were no longer at a crucial point in the disarming process. "Aren't there only *two* Sith at a time?"

Lumiya picked up her hydrospanner and began to unbolt the proton charge. "Do you really want me to answer that?"

There was a cold edge in Lumiya's voice that rocked Alema back on her heels, and she realized she had probably heard too much already. If there really was a secret organization of Sith—and that was the only reason she could think of for Lumiya's willingness to sacrifice herself—they were obviously *very* serious about keeping their existence secret.

"No, there is no need," Alema said. "We have heard enough of your lies for now."

An amused twinkled came to Lumiya's eyes. "That is probably for the best."

Lumiya removed the proton charge from the missile, then pulled a black combat vest from her tool satchel and slipped the device into a chest pocket. She checked to be sure that the actuation wires would reach from the deuterium tube to a small sensor pad located about where the wearer's heart would be, but did not affix the clips.

"Very clever," Alema said. "You win even if you lose."

"It *is* the Sith way." Lumiya scooted her tool satchel down the floor to the next missile on the rack. "Bring the light—we're running out of time."

"We don't understand." Alema began to have a sinking feeling, but she did as Lumiya asked and shined the light on the nose cone of the missile. "How are you going to wear *two* proton charges?"

"*I'm* not." Lumiya reignited the fusioncutter, then looked up at Alema. "This one is for *you.*"

chapter eighteen

Ribbons of smoke were still seeping from the hangar mouth and rising into the downpour, but the rest of Villa Solis had obviously burned out long before the rains came. A couple of proton bombs had reduced the site to a smear of rubble and melted stone, leaving only a few ghostly foundation circles to mark where the habitation domes had once stood. To Ben's surprise, he felt only a hint of death in the Force. Either the attack had occurred a very long time ago—which seemed unlikely, given the fumes still rising from the hangar—or very few people had died in it.

The lilting voice of the skiff's pilot and commander— a Duros junior lieutenant named Beta Ioli—came over Ben's headset, which he and the rest of the crew were wearing to muffle the roar of the oversized engines.

"Something bad happened here," she said. "Chief, you picking up anything?"

"Negative, ma'am," Tanogo replied. A Bith chief petty officer who had been in the space navy since before Ben was born sat three meters back in the *Rover*'s cramped cabin, operating the "snoop station" used to locate and

evaluate enemy targets. "There aren't any signals origi-
nating within three hundred kilometers—but we do have
a bogey squadron headed our way from Warro Field."

"Miy'tils?" Ioli asked.

"Negative. Looks more like Headhunters."

"Headhunters?" Ioli grunted. "You're kidding."

"The planetary militia still uses Headhunters," Ben
said, quoting the intelligence file Tenel Ka had provided
when Jacen assigned him the mission. "They're probably
curious about us."

"Nobody sends twelve fighters on a look-and-report,"
Tanogo repeated. "That's an attack squadron."

"Can't blame them for being cautious," Ioli replied.
"Somebody did just level their Ducha's place. Identify us
and see if they know what happened."

Tanogo acknowledged the order, and a moment later
Ben noticed the weapons systems running through a test
pattern. Either the skiff's young Twi'lek weapons tech
had taken it upon himself to bring up the systems, or—
more likely—the seasoned petty officer had quietly suggested it.

After the *Rover* had descended to an altitude of two
hundred meters, Ioli circled around to the front of the
ruins, where a cluster of flooded craters sat in what had
once been the villa's foreyard. Ben suddenly experienced a
sensation of frustration, so faint and muted that he
thought at first he might be imagining it. As they swooped
over the craters, however, the feeling grew stronger, and
he recognized it as a reverberation in the Force.

"They were here," he said.

"Who?" Tanogo demanded over the headset. "Be pre-
cise, son!"

"Sorry," Ben said. "Jaina and Zekk. Those craters were
a big problem for them."

"I'll say." Tanogo's voice was sarcastic. "Getting blasted back to your molecules is always a big problem."

"Chief!" Ioli brought the skiff's nose up and wheeled around to land. "That's his cousin you're talking about."

"It's okay—death isn't what I'm sensing," Ben said. As they swung back toward the villa ruins, the feeling of frustration and anger began to grow weaker. "Turn back to our old heading, Lieutenant. I think that's the way we need to go."

Ioli started to swing the skiff back around.

"Ma'am, we don't have time for the kid's guessing games," Tanogo said. "If we're going to look around, we need to get on the ground now. That squadron is only twenty minutes out, and it just went from bogey to bandit."

"Why?"

"The squadron leader answered your inquiry about what happened here," Tanogo said. "She's saying a pair of Jedi bombed the place."

Ioli glanced over at Ben. Her Duros face remained unreadable, but he could sense her uncertainty through the Force.

"We need to resume our previous heading," Ben said. "Jaina and Zekk aren't here. I'd feel them if they were."

"Even if they're dead?" Tanogo's tone was not cruel, just pragmatic. "Ma'am, if we can't locate these two Jedi, our orders are to determine what happened to them."

"And to use Ben as a resource," Ioli said, continuing to bring the skiff's nose around to the heading Ben had requested. "Are you going to be the one who tells Colonel Solo we didn't trust his apprentice's instincts?"

Tanogo fell instantly silent, suddenly pouring uncertainty and worry into the Force. Ben felt both secretly thrilled and vaguely unsettled by the response—thrilled to realize that he had been invested with a certain measure of power simply by being associated with Jacen, unsettled to realize that the reaction to this power was fear instead of respect.

Once the *Rover* had returned to her original heading, the sensation of frustration and anger grew more discernible in the Force. Ben twisted around in his seat and looked back at Tanogo's age-flaked face.

"I'm not imagining this, Chief Tanogo," he said. "The Force is real."

Tanogo rippled his cheek flaps in what seemed to be amusement. "It's your call, son. You don't have to explain it to an old spacecan like me."

"Okay," Ben said, still wondering whether he had smoothed things over. "Thanks."

He turned back around to find a rain-blurred plain of mud and grass sweeping past beneath the skiff. It was impossible to see how far the terrain extended ahead, but Ben knew from the intelligence file that the bog extended for more than three hundred kilometers in every direction—farther than even Jedi could trudge through soft mud in so short a time.

He closed his eyes and pictured Jaina's face, at the same time focusing his attention on the frustration he felt in the Force. The ripples grew stronger almost instantly, striking him more noticeably from a direction about twenty degrees to their starboard. Without opening his eyes, he pointed. "That way."

Ioli hesitated for only an instant before swinging the craft in the direction he indicated. The ripples grew even stronger, but now it seemed to Ben that they were coming from about ten degrees to port. He pointed back in that direction.

"More that way."

Tanogo's snort came over the headset, and Ioli hesitated a little longer before correcting their course. Ben tried not to let their doubts trouble him, but the ripples began to grow weaker and more difficult to sense.

"Back the other way, I think."

This time, Ioli did not correct the course at all. "Ben, you're moving us back and forth," she said. "If you don't know where they are, we need to go back to the villa."

Ben opened his eyes and frowned at Ioli. "Trust me, Lieutenant. It's not like I'm seeing a waypoint, but they are out there."

Ioli stared at him for a moment, then slowly nodded. "As you wish, Special Agent Skywalker."

They made two more course corrections before the ripples strengthened again. This time, Ben extended his Force-awareness as far as he could in that direction, picturing Jaina in his mind and trying to touch her through the Force.

Then, suddenly, she was there in his mind with him, full of surprise and joy and relief—and urgency. Something was terribly wrong, and she needed Ben to help her correct it.

"They're straight ahead." Ben tried to open his eyes—maybe he did—but Jaina would not release her grip on his mind. All he could see in front of him was her face, looking at once happy and worried and exhausted. "I think they might be in trouble."

"When you say straight ahead—"

"I mean straight ahead." Ben extended his arm toward the image of Jaina in his mind. "There."

The skiff banked . . . hard.

"I said straight—"

"I see them!" Ioli snapped back. "But I'm not flying into a hillside, no matter who orders me to!"

Jaina's image vanished, and a pair of tiny colored blades appeared in the rain at about the same altitude as the *Rover*. They were some fifty meters ahead, on Ben's side of the canopy and slowly sliding starboard as Ioli turned away.

Through the heavy weather, it was impossible to see the figures holding the blades, but Ben could feel Jaina's concern as the skiff continued its turn. He reached out to her in the Force, trying to reassure her that her lightsaber beacon had been noticed, and then the blades passed out of sight.

Ioli's voice came over the headset. "Tanogo, how long before those bandits—"

"We've been flying toward 'em, Lieutenant," Tanogo reported. "The interceptors will be in missile range in two minutes, and they'll be on top of us in five."

"Then we're in trouble," Ioli said.

"No, we're not." Ben unbuckled his crash webbing and stood. Fortunately, the headset was wireless, so he did not have to remove it before starting aft. "They're Jedi. Just get us within ten meters."

Ioli brought the skiff around so hard that Ben had to Force-stick himself to the deck to keep from being flung into the fuselage. She decelerated hard and began to creep forward on the repulsor drives, at the same time issuing engagement orders to their weapons tech.

By the time Ben reached the rear air lock and opened the outer hatch, Ioli had the skiff hovering alongside the hill. For a moment, nothing was visible outside but rain, fog, and mounds of mud and grass. Then one of the mounds suddenly flew off the hillside and landed inside the air lock, spraying tear-shaped mud drops across the viewport of the inner hatch. A moment later the *Rover* rocked noticeably as a second, heavier weight landed inside.

"They're in!" Ben reported. "But take it easy. They haven't had time to—"

"Missile range," Tanogo reported. "Launch!"

The skiff tipped its nose up and shot skyward so fast that Ben had to catch a grab handle to keep from tumbling back into the Twi'lek weapons tech. A pair of dull thumps reverberated from inside the air lock, and for a moment he thought Ioli might have lost Jaina or Zekk.

A moment later the inner hatch slid open and the two Jedi stepped into the flight cabin, sagging in exhaustion and coated head-to-toe in mud. They were covering their ears against the roar of the engines, but even that did not prevent a torrent of questions that Ben could only half understand by reading Jaina's lips.

"What's . . . hurry?" she asked. ". . . nearly lost . . ."

Ben led them to the only passengers' seats available in the flight cabin—midway between Tanogo's snoop station and the weapons station at the aft bulkhead—and motioned them to sit. Zekk obeyed gratefully, buckling himself in and donning a headset hanging on a hook behind his seat.

Jaina took the headset hanging behind the other seat, but continued to stand and fire questions at Ben. "What are you doing here?"

The skiff bucked as the weapons tech deployed chaff and decoys.

Jaina's eyes went round and, before Ben could answer her first question, she demanded, "Are we under attack?"

Ben nodded. "The Terephonians sent some Headhunters—"

"Those lungworms!" She started to step past Ben toward

the snoop station. "How many? Are they on a chase vector or an intercept—"

Zekk caught her arm. "Jaina, you don't have rank here." He pulled her back to her seat. "And we've just been rescued, remember?"

To Ben's surprise, Jaina did not jerk her arm away or tell Zekk she wasn't asking or even flash him a dirty look. She simply sat down and reached for her crash webbing. "Sorry," she said. "Guess I'm not used to being a civilian."

"I need to return to my station," Ben said into his microphone. "Lieutenant Ioli will want to jump as soon as we're clear of the gravity well, and I'm the navigator."

Jaina nodded and waved Ben toward the cockpit. "Go. Let us know if we can help."

Ben started forward, shaking his head in amazement. Jaina was acting like she actually liked Zekk. Maybe Ben's mother was right about those two after all—clearly, something had changed between them.

The skiff shook as the first concussion missiles fell prey to the countermeasures and began detonating. Ben sneaked a glance at the threat display as he passed Tanogo's station, then slipped into his own seat feeling immensely relieved. The wily chief had been exaggerating their danger just enough to assure a safe escape. The Terephonian missiles had begun to burn out and drop away almost as soon as they had reached the chaff wall, while the old Headhunters would not even leave the atmosphere until long after the *Rover* had entered space and hit maximum acceleration.

After strapping himself in, Ben activated the navi computer display and brought up a schematic of the route they had taken to Terephon. "Retrace our inbound jumps, Lieutenant?"

"Do we have a choice?" Ioli asked.

Ben studied a maze of narrow, twisting hyperspace lanes that disappeared into the Transitory Mists with no indication of where they led. "We've got a gazillion choices," he said. "There's just no way to tell where any of the others lead."

Ioli nodded. "That's what I thought," she said.

Ben plotted a bearing to their first jump and transferred it to Ioli's display, then set up a course retracing their route out of the Transitory Mists. By the time he finished, the *Rover* had entered space and escaped Terephon's gravity well. Ioli sounded the jump alarm, then a faint shudder ran through the skiff and the stars stretched into lines.

"I can handle it from here, Ben," Ioli said. "Why don't you get our passengers cleaned up and debriefed? Colonel Solo will expect a full report as soon as we can make contact again."

Ben removed his headset—the *Rover*'s engines had fallen silent the moment they left Terephon's atmosphere—and collected Jaina and Zekk, leading them through a bulkhead into the crew quarters. This cabin was as cramped as everything else aboard the little skiff, with a small galley and a sanisteam unit tucked into the two front corners and four bunks stacked behind a sleeping partition in back.

Ben motioned Jaina and Zekk to the small table in the center of the cabin. "You must be hungry," he said, turning to the galley. "What do you want?"

Jaina raised her brow—dislodging several flakes of mud—then looked down at her filthy jumpsuit and snorted. "I'm glad to see Jacen hasn't trained the teenage boy out of you completely," she chuckled. "Until I have a chance to clean up, a cup of caf will be fine."

"Then you can have first sanisteam," Zekk said, rising.

"Because I'm starved. I'll have anything—as long as it's hot and there's plenty of it."

He stepped into the sanisteamer to clean his hands and face, squeezing Jaina's shoulder as he slipped past behind her. She did not wince or roll her eyes or anything—until she caught Ben staring at her shoulder.

"What?" she asked.

"Uh . . . nothing."

Ben turned to the caf dispenser.

"We're just friends," Jaina said.

Ben shrugged. "It doesn't matter to me."

"He's not even in love with me anymore."

"Sure," Ben said, filling her cup. "Whatever you say."

He turned to give Jaina her caf and found her staring at the sanisteamer's closed door. Wishing the cup had taken a little longer to fill, he turned back around and reached for one of the sipper lids the crew used at their duty stations.

"Ben—I don't need a lid." Jaina's tone suggested she knew exactly why he had turned away. "What are you doing out here, anyway?"

Ben put the caf on the table. "Jacen sent us."

"No kidding," Jaina deadpanned. "Why?"

"Because you disappeared after you went to Terephon," Ben said. "And then Tenel Ka started to feel like she couldn't trust anyone, so she asked Jacen to send us out to see what happened."

"Then at least we gave her some warning," Zekk said, emerging from the sanisteam unit. His face and hands were clean, but he smelled more than ever like a bog. "Good."

"Warning about what?" Ben asked. He punched an order for a nerfloaf sandwich into the multiprocessor— then remembered how low Zekk had needed to duck when he stepped out of the sanisteam unit. He added a bowl of brogy stew to the order and turned back around. "Terephon's not exactly on Tenel Ka's side, is it?"

Jaina shook her head. "The Ducha was already mustering her fleet when we arrived," she explained. "And when we asked to see her, she tried to have us killed."

"She must have thought we were coming to arrest her," Zekk added, keeping a watchful eye on the multiprocessor.

"And that's why you bombed her villa?" Ben asked.

Jaina frowned. "We didn't bomb anything. Her Miy'tils did that after the battle droids didn't work."

"The Ducha bombed her own villa?" Ben asked. "She really must have wanted you dead!"

"It was the only way to protect the sister she has spying on Tenel Ka," Jaina said. "She could strand us here by destroying our StealthXs, but now that Tenel Ka is the Queen Mother, I'm sure the Ducha has done enough research on Jedi abilities to realize we can touch each other through the Force across great distances."

The multiprocessor dinged, but Ben barely heard it. He was too confused by what Jaina had said. If he understood the Hapan kinship system correctly—and he kind of doubted he did—the Ducha Galney's sister was Tenel Ka's chamberlain, Lady Galney.

"Ben?" Zekk asked, studying the multiprocessor with a worried expression. "Doesn't that chime mean my snack is ready?"

"Uh, sorry." Ben placed the "snack"—it was two standard ration packs—on a tray and set it in front of Zekk. "But that doesn't make any sense. Tenel Ka used to be a Jedi Knight, right?"

"A very good one," Jaina said.

"Then wouldn't she be able to tell when someone was

lying to her?" Ben asked. "She'd know if Lady Galney was spying on her."

"Are you saying she doesn't?" Zekk asked. Without rising, he leaned toward Ben and began opening drawers beneath the counter. "Where are the spoons?"

Ben retrieved a set of silverware from the sterilizing bin and handed it to Zekk. "Lady Galney was still with Tenel Ka when Jacen sent me on this mission."

Jaina's expression grew alarmed. "Then Tenel Ka doesn't know the Ducha is a traitor?"

Ben shook his head. "I don't think so," he said. "The last I heard, she was counting on the Galney fleet to bolster her defenses."

"Blast it!" Jaina pounded the table so hard a gob of purple stew slopped out of Zekk's bowl. "That's why the Ducha didn't want to talk to us—she's pretending to be on Tenel Ka's side, and she knew two Jedi would sense the lie."

"So Tenel Ka will think she's rushing to the defense—and then the Ducha can attack from inside. That makes sense." Zekk nodded, then frowned. "What I don't get is why Tenel Ka can't sense that her chamberlain is a spy."

"Maybe Lady Galney can hide it when she's lying," Ben said. "If Jedi can do it—"

"Most can't," Jaina said, frowning at Ben. "At least not from each other."

Ben cringed inwardly, realizing too late that hiding lies was one of those special techniques that Jacen probably did not want him talking about.

"Well, maybe Lady Galney can," he countered. "She wouldn't need to be a Jedi. All she has to do is make herself believe she's telling the truth when she isn't."

"Or not know she's lying at all," Zekk added between mouthfuls.

Jaina turned to Zekk and asked, "You think Lady Galney's not in on it?"

Zekk shrugged. "You don't have to be a spy to be a security leak," he said. "Carelessness is all it takes."

"Yeah," Ben said, growing excited. "Sort of like the Blind Woolamander, only in reverse."

"The Blind Woolamander?" Jaina asked.

"You know—when you use someone innocent to put out false intelligence," Ben explained. "Only this way, you're collecting the information from someone innocent, and since she doesn't know what's happening, she's her own cutout, too. It's a perfect setup against someone like Tenel Ka."

Jaina looked vaguely worried. "Where are you learning all this stuff?"

Again, Ben winced inwardly. Weren't other apprentices learning anything Jacen was teaching him?

"It's part of my GAG training." Ben drew a veneer of calm over his Force presence so Jaina and Zekk would not sense his lie. "We need to know all that spy stuff."

"Well, you must be studying hard," Zekk said. "Because I think you're right."

Jaina nodded. "It makes sense. The real spy is probably one of Galney's consorts. Tenel Ka would have no reason to talk to them anyway." She glanced back to Ben. "And Hapan noblewomen have a bad habit of underestimating male duplicity."

The comment sent a bolt of alarm shooting through Ben, but he did his best to stay calm, reminding himself that during their practice sessions, not even Jacen could always tell when he was lying. "I'm glad that stuff finally came in useful. To tell the truth, I was beginning to wonder if those instructors were making it up." He turned his attention to Zekk, who had already devoured most of his "snack" and was using the bread to wipe the stew bowl clean. "You know how to use the multiprocessor if you're still hungry?"

Zekk studied the unit with a ravenous gleam in his eye. "Oh, yeah."

"Good." Ben pointed to the locker beneath his bunk. "My spare flight utilities might fit you, Jaina, but Zekk—"

"Don't worry," Jaina said. "I'll stick Zekk's in the cleaner while he's sanisteaming."

"Then I'd better go talk to Lieutenant Ioli," Ben said. Ioli had not told him to report, but the last thing he wanted to do was say anything else to arouse Jaina's scrutiny. "She'll want to send a report to Jacen as soon as we're out of the dead zone."

"Ask her to send one to Tenel Ka, as well," Jaina requested.

"I don't know if that's a good idea," Zekk said. "We know she's surrounded by spies—even if Lady Galney isn't one of them."

"We're just going to have to take that chance," Jaina said. "Tenel Ka needs to know about this as soon—"

"The Queen Mother will know about it as soon as Jacen does," Ben said. "She's aboard the *Anakin* with him."

Jaina frowned. "The *Anakin*?"

"The *Anakin Solo*—our new Star Destroyer," Ben said proudly. "She's in orbit above Hapes, and Queen Mother Tenel Ka is hiding—"

"*Our new Star Destroyer?*" Jaina echoed. She stood and leaned across the table toward Ben. "Jacen named a GAG ship for Anakin?"

"Yeah, he thought—"

"What did he think?" Jaina demanded. "That he would

drag our little brother's name into the poodoo pit with him?"

"Uh, you'll have to ask him," Ben said, realizing there was nothing he could say to calm Jaina down. "I gotta go."

He retreated through the bulkhead and escaped forward. He was aware of the bad feelings between Jaina and Jacen, of course, but he had not understood the reason until now. Jaina was just as volatile and unreasonable as Jacen claimed. It was a wonder she had lasted in the military even as long as she had—but then, the standards of the old New Republic forces had not been nearly as high as they were now that Jacen and Admiral Niathal had reorganized the military. These days, someone as hotheaded as Jaina would never even make it into flight school—and he couldn't imagine how she had *ever* become a Jedi Knight. Jacen was always telling him that a good Jedi used his anger—not the other way around.

Ben returned to his duty station and reported to Ioli, then coded a burst message to be sent over the HoloNet as soon as they left the Transitory Mists. After a few minutes of thought, he also included a warning about Jaina's reaction to the *Anakin*'s name. With a little forewarning, maybe Jacen would be able to avoid another blowup like the one that had opened the rift between them in the first place.

After Ben finished the message, he remained in his seat, afraid to go back and give Jaina something else to be angry about. He really did not want to cause any more tension between her and Jacen, but his motives were also selfish. With his father already threatening to end his apprenticeship with Jacen, the last thing he wanted to do was give Jaina any reason to suggest to his parents there might be reason for concern.

Fortunately, avoiding Jaina and Zekk turned out to be

easy. Their long trudge across the bogs had left them so exhausted that as soon as they had cleaned up and eaten, they climbed into bunks and fell asleep.

The pair still had not stirred nearly a standard day later when the *Rover* finally emerged from hyperspace in the star-spangled vastness outside the Transitory Mists. Tanogo quickly brought up the holocomm and sent Ben's message.

To their astonishment, they received a response almost immediately—even before Ben had finished plotting their course back to Hapes.

"That was fast," he said.

"Too fast," Tanogo answered. He set to work decoding it. "It's a CU message. Has to be."

This drew a groan from the usually silent Twi'lek weapons officer.

"CU message?" Ben asked.

"See you later," Ioli explained. "When a Star Destroyer has to change posts while her scouts are out, she drops a message beacon with rendezvous coordinates."

"Okay," Ben said, not seeing the problem. "So I don't plot a course until we have the new coordinates."

"That'd be too easy, son," Tanogo said.

"It's pretty rare that a Star Destroyer moves toward the scout ship," Ioli said. "And since reconnaissance skiffs don't carry a lot of fuel or provisions—"

"And since we have half again our normal complement," Ben added, beginning to understand.

"Right," Ioli said. "It can be a problem."

They waited in silence while Tanogo finished decoding the message. Then Ben felt a ripple of relief in the Force.

"It's not so bad," Tanogo announced. "We might even get in a little R and R, if the lieutenant is feeling generous."

"That depends on how long you intend to keep me waiting," Ioli said.

The message appeared on the cockpit display almost immediately. RECON SKIFF ROVER PROCEED TO ROQOO DEPOT FOR REFUELING AND RESUPPLY. AWAIT RENDEZVOUS OR ORDERS.

"What about our message?" Ben asked.

"The *Anakin* is probably in hyperspace herself," Tanogo said. "We'll have to keep trying and hope we catch her between jumps."

"That's not good enough," Jaina said from the back of the cabin.

Ben turned in his seat and saw her and Zekk emerging from crew quarters. Their faces still had pillow lines and their hair was still sleep-tousled, but they appeared completely rested—as Jedi usually did after a recovery trance.

"We have to go to Hapes," she said, continuing forward.

"Those aren't our orders," Tanogo objected. "When Colonel Solo tells us to go somewhere—"

"Colonel Solo doesn't know about our message," Zekk interrupted. "Or the importance of getting it there now."

Jaina slipped past Tanogo's station and stopped behind Ioli's seat. "You know how important it is to deliver our intelligence to the Queen Mother in time, and you have the authority to act on your initiative."

Ioli nodded. "Of course. But the Queen Mother is aboard the *Anakin*—"

"Not if the *Anakin* left Hapes, she isn't," Jaina said.

"A leader of Tenel Ka's courage and integrity is *not* going to leave her capital world while it's under threat of attack," Zekk added. "Wherever the *Anakin* went, the Queen Mother will be staying behind to oversee Hapes's defense."

"So I suggest you act on your own initiative," Jaina said. "Or we'll act on ours."

Ioli's small jaw clacked shut, then she let out a snort of irritation and turned to Ben. "What do you think Colonel Solo would want?"

Ben glanced over his shoulder at the uncompromising faces of Jaina and Zekk. "Well, that message is pretty important," he said. "And I don't think Jacen would want you to get your crew killed by the two Jedi Knights he just sent you to rescue."

Jaina smiled at Ben, then winked. "Good answer," she said. "Maybe Jacen's teaching you something after all."

chapter nineteen

The task force had emerged from hyperspace in perfect crescent formation, and the luminous green disk of the planet Relephon was already swelling in the *Anakin*'s bridge viewport. The world was one of those truly massive gas giants on the verge of becoming a star itself, the tremendous pressures in its core releasing enough energy to bathe its horde of moons in a life-sustaining blanket of heat and light.

Jacen did not notice the tiny saucers of any Battle Dragons silhouetted against the pale glow, nor see the blue slivers of even one efflux tail streaking in to intercept the task force Tenel Ka had sent to arrest AlGray. Still, he had a cold prickle along his spine and an uneasy emptiness in his stomach. The minutes after a fleet emerged from hyperspace were always its most hectic and vulnerable, with the sensor officers struggling to calibrate their instruments and the hangar chiefs rushing to launch a fighter screen. It was the ideal time for an attack, and Jacen could feel one coming.

Unfortunately, he had no idea from where. The advance scouts had reported only an alarming inability to locate the enemy fleet, and AlGray's commander was certainly in no rush to reveal her position.

"Major Espara, I find this odd." Jacen was addressing Major Moreem Espara of the Hapan royal guard, whom Tenel Ka had assigned to serve as his adviser and command liaison. Along with a handful of aides, they were standing together on the observation balcony overlooking the *Anakin*'s busy bridge. "Wouldn't Ducha AlGray be deploying her fleet by now?"

"She would if it were here." A tall woman with silky black hair and alabaster skin, Espara was dressed in a pale blue uniform that managed to look both military and stylish. "Even if she were innocent, she'd be troubled enough by our arrival to make a show of force."

Jacen remained silent, concentrating on what he was feeling through the Force. He could not sense the source of the danger, but the prickle along his spine felt as if it was about to erupt into hives.

"We're too late," Espara continued, as though Jacen were not astute enough to understand what she had said. "The coup must be moving faster than the Queen Mother realized. The usurpers are going into open revolt."

Jacen began to expand his Force-awareness rapidly, but the population of the Relephon Moons was too scattered to glean anything useful. The planet was ringed by at least thirty major population centers and hundreds of smaller concentrations, and none of them felt particularly hostile.

"Colonel Solo?" Espara asked. "Did you hear what I just said? The AlGray fleet is probably on its way to Hapes!"

"Your aides," Jacen asked, still troubled by his premonitions. "How many did you bring?"

"You think someone betrayed our mission?" Espara

glanced toward the two female officers behind her. "I assure you, Beyele and Roh are above suspicion—"

"How many?" This time, Jacen put the power of the Force behind his words.

Espara shrank back. "Just Beyele and Roh."

"What about your pilots?" Jacen demanded. "Were they personal staff?"

Espara shook her head. "They were from the Royal Transportation Pool."

The empty feeling in Jacen's stomach turned to a cold void. Whatever had gone wrong, it had started with the pilots.

"But I don't see how they could have betrayed us," Espara continued. "Even if they were traitors, all they did was ferry me into orbit. They might have noticed the *Anakin* making preparations to get under way, but they wouldn't have known to where."

"That might have been enough," Jacen said. He turned to his aide, a Jenet named Orlopp. "Ask Commander Twizzl for a threat report."

"I've been monitoring that continuously." With a pink snout, wet nostrils, and smirking upper lip that did not quite cover his yellow fangs, Orlopp cut a menacing figure in his black GAG uniform. "There don't seem to be any threats. A junior garrison commander is demanding to know our intentions, though she hasn't deployed her defenses yet."

"She wants to avoid giving us an excuse to attack," Espara surmised. "That confirms the main fleet has departed. Colonel Solo, we must return to Hapes at once. If the Queen Mother is not under attack already . . ."

Jacen did not hear the rest of Espara's complaint, for he had turned away and was rushing off the observation balcony. The threat seemed more immediate than ever—and if it was not coming from outside the *Anakin,* then it had to be coming from inside.

"Colonel Solo?" Espara called, following behind. "We're in the middle of an action here!"

Espara's confusion was understandable. Even she did not know that Tenel Ka had left Allana aboard the *Anakin,* and she certainly didn't know that Jacen's parents had provided intelligence suggesting that Aurra Sing's primary target would be the child.

As he raced for the lift tube, Jacen's comlink chimed for attention. He pulled it off his belt and opened the channel.

"You know who this is?" asked a wispy voice.

"Double-Ex," Jacen replied. "What is it?"

"You ordered me to report if anyone attempted to enter the girl's cabin," the security droid replied. "I'm reporting."

Jacen's stomach sank. "I was afraid of that."

"What are my orders?" SD-XX asked. "Evaporate them?"

"No," Jacen said. His briefing on Aurra Sing had suggested that "evaporating" her would be beyond the security droid's capabilities. "Stay out of sight and frustrate her attempts to enter. I'm on my way."

Jacen opened a channel to Bridge Security. "Execute a Level One lockdown." He did not bother identifying himself, as his name would already be displayed on the duty officer's datascreen. "This is not a drill."

"Level One, Colonel?"

"Affirmative." Jacen reached the lift tube and stepped inside, not bothering to acknowledge the crisp salutes from the two GAG sentries stationed there. "Now!"

"I'm sorry, sir," the officer replied. "We can't lock down while we're at battle stations. The crew needs to move freely."

"Then go to Level Two!" Jacen ordered.

He would have canceled battle stations, except the order would have to go through Commander Twizzl, who would demand a confirmation and an explanation Jacen had no time to provide. The assassin—assuming Sing was the danger he had been sensing—had chosen her moment well, when the priorities of a Star Destroyer ready to enter battle took precedence over the safety of even her most important passenger.

Alarm horns began to beep over the *Anakin*'s intercom, indicating that the Level Two security protocols Jacen had ordered were now in effect. Armed guards would be posted at every lift tube and bulkhead hatch with orders to detain anyone lacking proper identification; anyone who resisted would be blasted. Jacen did not think those precautions would make the slightest difference to Aurra Sing.

When he arrived at the Commander's Deck, he found the lift sentries lying on the floor with smoke rising from their blaster-scorched faces. A dozen paces down the corridor, two more guards were down outside the Sovv Stateroom—the quarters assigned to visiting dignitaries—and there was smoke pouring from the cabin. He unclipped his lightsaber and rushed forward.

Jacen's mind was whirling with dark fears and black furies. For the first time since his imprisonment by the Yuuzhan Vong, he truly wanted to hurt someone, to make them pay in agony and anguish for their vile actions. And if Allana were to die, he did not see where he would find the strength to carry on with his mission. Who would want to save a galaxy that could abide the murder of his own innocent daughter?

As Jacen approached the Sovv Stateroom, one of the guards began to moan for help. The fellow's torso had been cleaved at an upward angle by something hot and long, and his fading Force presence suggested he would die if he did not receive help soon. An abandoned lock slicer hung on the keypad above his head, and a still-crackling arc had been cut through the double doors.

Leaving the stateroom uninspected and the guard to die where he lay, Jacen continued down the long corridor. The low hum of a lightsaber cutting metal was droning around the corner ahead, where the entrance to his own stateroom was located. He extended his Force-awareness into his own quarters and was relieved to feel the presence of his daughter somewhere near the back of the cabin, approximately where the refresher was located. She seemed curious and not at all frightened.

Suddenly Allana responded to Jacen's contact, filling the Force with surprise and delight. She seemed to recognize his touch and be happy about it, and that filled him with pride and joy and an even greater determination to catch Sing before she found his daughter.

But their contact was shattered by the intrusion of a cold presence, gleefully pouring its murderous intent into the Force. Allana reeled back in shock and vanished, leaving Jacen alone with the assassin's presence. Then the humming of the lightsaber suddenly assumed a higher pitch, and a loud clang sounded as a freshly cut panel of security door fell to the floor.

In the next instant a brilliant orange flash lit the corridor ahead, accompanied by the crashing *whumpff* of a concussion grenade—launched, no doubt, by Allana's Defender Droid, DeDe. Jacen paused a moment to be sure there would not be another grenade, then rounded the corner when he began to hear the shrieking of DeDe's blaster cannon.

The corridor ahead was so filled with smoke and

blasterfire that it looked like the inside of a thunderstorm. Sing was a pale ghost in a red bodysuit, battling through the hole she had cut in Jacen's door, surrounding herself in crimson snakes of light as she used her lightsaber to bat aside DeDe's attacks.

Jacen drew his sidearm and fired on the run, hoping to blast the assassin in the back while she was too overwhelmed to defend herself. Sing dropped into a forward roll and vanished through the door. An instant later her lightsaber whined half a dozen times, and DeDe's blaster cannon fell silent.

Aurra Sing was alone in Jacen's stateroom—and with her Force abilities, it would take her only a second to find his daughter. He stopped a few paces from the door and reached out to the assassin in the Force.

Wait.

Jacen spoke the word with his mind instead of his mouth. At the same time, he was expanding his Force presence into Sing's mind, opening himself fully to the Force and using its power to push himself deeper into her mind, to crush her own presence and force it deep down into the bottom of her being.

"Wait," he repeated.

Sing fought back, trying to push him from her mind, but Jacen had taken her by surprise. He had the power of his anger and his fear and his hatred behind him, and she simply was not strong enough.

Jacen started forward again, then dropped his blaster pistol and retrieved his comlink.

"Double-Ex, open—"

The doors to his stateroom slid open, grating loudly as the damaged area scraped past the jambs. Jacen stepped into the foyer of his suite, where beads of molten durasteel were still popping and hissing on the stone decking.

To his right, the walls above the galley and dining area were pocked with scorch marks. Allana's Defender Droid lay to his left, a heap of severed limbs and smoking circuits scattered along the edge of a sunken conversation area.

Sing stood with her back to Jacen, about five paces beyond the droid, on the other side of a smoldering couch. In one hand, she held her still-ignited lightsaber. In the other was a class-C thermal detonator with a disintegration radius large enough to kill herself, Jacen, Allana, and probably half the personnel on the decks directly above and below.

As Jacen started toward her, she looked over her shoulder with an expression in her pale eyes that seemed equal parts hatred and awe.

"Don't ever touch me like that again."

Jacen did not reply. Sing was still struggling to free herself of his domination, and all his concentration was focused on keeping the pressure on until he drew close enough to strike.

Sing flashed him a cold smile. "But then, I don't think you'll have the chance."

Her thumb twitched.

The activation light on the thermal detonator began to blink, and that was enough to shatter Jacen's concentration. He felt Sing slip free, and suddenly he was completely outside her mind, watching in horror as she pitched the detonator toward the refresher where Allana was hiding.

Jacen's heart dropped through the bottom of his stomach. His arm shot out without conscious thought, and the detonator floated into his hand almost before he realized he had summoned it.

Sing was already whirling, leaping toward him with her

crimson blade coming around at neck height. Jacen brought his lightsaber up automatically and blocked, then pulled the detonator's thumb slide back.

He never saw whether the activation light darkened. Suddenly Sing's knee was sinking into his stomach, driving the breath from his lungs and sending him tumbling over a couch. The detonator clattered to the floor somewhere in the galley. He came down on a beverage table, smashing it apart, then Sing was over him, her crimson blade arcing down.

Jacen whipped his lightsaber around to block, catching her blade about halfway up the shaft and filling the air with a sizzling shower of sparks. Sing grabbed her hilt with both hands and began to push, slowly driving the tip of her lightsaber down toward his eye.

The glow was as blinding as the heat was searing, and Jacen's vision blossomed into a fiery red blur. He brought his free hand up to brace his weapon arm and tried not to worry about whether his eyeball would melt, not daring to turn his head or even look away for fear that he would slip.

Sing kicked him in the side. The tip of a small, wedge-shaped blade scraped against his ribs and sent a blazing bolt of pain shooting into his body.

"Never—" She kicked him again, sending another bolt of pain deep into his stomach. "—violate—"

She kicked again.

"—my—" Another kick, more pain. "—mind!"

Sing kicked again, this time catching him near a kidney. A wave of fiery anguish rolled through his body, stealing his breath, so hot he could not even scream. The pain would have paralyzed anyone else, left him on the floor praying to die before he drew his next breath.

But pain was an old friend of Jacen's. He had learned to

embrace it during his imprisonment among the Yuuzhan Vong, and now it no longer troubled him. Now it served him.

He turned the palm of his bracing hand toward Sing and pushed with the Force.

The move did not surprise her as much as he had hoped. As she flew away, Sing rolled the tip of her blade over his, and his lightsaber went flying. He held his Force shove until he heard her thud into the wall opposite, then sprang to his feet.

A fiery blur continued to blind one eye, and his sight in the other was still splashed with crimson blotches. But he could see clearly enough to be worried. Sing had landed near the refresher where Allana was hiding—close enough to fulfill her contract, if she was willing to risk Jacen attacking her from behind.

Jacen did not give her that chance. He opened himself fully to his fear and anger, using the power of his emotions to bring the Force flooding into him, and his body began to crackle and burn with dark energy. He raised his arms in Sing's direction, hands held level and fingers splayed wide.

That was when the door to the refresher hissed open, and a pair of small gray eyes peered out. They were wide open and locked on Jacen with an expression that might have been awe or fear or both.

"No, Allana!" Jacen could not bring himself to release the Force lightning while she was watching; even if Tenel Ka had not yet taught her that the dark side was evil, his own childhood training remained strongly enough ingrained that he did not want his daughter to see him using it. "Close the . . ."

Jacen had to let the order trail off when Sing took advantage of his hesitation to leap at him. Allana screamed from inside the refresher, then Sing was three paces away, lightsaber coming in for a midbody strike. Jacen lifted one foot as though to pivot away, and Sing took the bait and stopped, dropping one leg back as she continued her swing.

Instead of spinning past as he feinted, Jacen cartwheeled over her blade and came down on the other side. Sing reversed her attack so fast he barely had time to grab her wrist, much less turn her own weapon against her as he had intended.

So Jacen kicked her in the knee as hard as he could.

The joint dislocated with a sickening pop, and Sing collapsed to the floor shrieking. But she did not release her lightsaber. She did not even stop fighting, rolling into him in an effort to break his grasp and slash him open. Jacen started to pivot out of the way, intending to bring her arm around for a clean break behind her back.

But Allana suddenly appeared on the other side of Sing, charging forward with her dark brows lowered and what looked like a small recording rod clutched in her hands.

"Allana, no!"

Allana kept coming.

Determined to keep Sing from striking out at his daughter with any of her weapons, Jacen Force-leapt backward, dragging the assassin away from his daughter. Allana took two more steps and raised the silver rod over her head . . . then dived.

Sing raised her uninjured leg, cocking her foot to kick Allana with the stubby knife in the toe of her boot.

Jacen screamed and whipped Sing's arm around, twisting her away from his daughter. Her lightsaber flashed by so close he nearly lost an ear, but the assassin's legs spun around with her body, and the kick-knife flashed past half a meter above Allana's head.

Allana landed on Sing's other leg and jammed the silver rod into her injured knee. The hiss of an autoinjector sounded from its tip, and Sing cried out in astonishment.

"You little shrew!"

Sing drew her leg back again to kick . . . then let it drop to the floor. Her eyes widened in anger—or perhaps it was fear. She craned her neck around, staring at Allana, and began to convulse. Jacen quickly pulled Sing's lightsaber from her unresisting hand, then held the still-ignited tip to the assassin's neck.

"Allana, what—"

"She'll be awright, Jacen." Allana sat up and straddled the assassin's leg, no longer afraid—if she ever had been. "It was just my safety stick."

"Okay." Jacen was too numb and relieved to ask more— or to chastise Allana for not staying in the refresher. He simply waved her off Sing's legs. "Get off. She could still be dangerous."

"That's not what Doctor Meala says." Despite her protest, Allana climbed off Sing's legs. "She says the bad person won't be dangerous again until someone gives her the antidope."

Allana came to Jacen's side, then squatted and looked into Sing's hate-maddened eyes.

"But don't be scared," she said. "Yedi never kill help-less people—even bad ones like you."

"That's right." Jacen took Allana's hand and, surprised by how right her words felt, pulled her up to stand at his side. "We just put them in a confinement facility for a very, very long time."

chapter twenty

Outside the *Falcon*'s canopy hung a streaming veil of blue and white brilliance, so intense that it made Han's eyes hurt like a Fogblaster hangover. He hesitated at the back of the flight deck, trying to make some sense of what he was seeing, half convinced that it was the efflux tail of some Death Star–type megaship.

And if it was some big new superweapon, Han knew he and Leia would end up trying to destroy the thing before it blew up Tenel Ka's throneworld or something—and he had no doubts about how that would turn out. Han was already older than Obi-Wan Kenobi had been when he'd died aboard the original Death Star, and on crazy missions like that, wasn't it always the wise old man who got killed first? If it happened, Han only hoped his kids would figure out he and Leia had been no part of the assassination attempt on Tenel Ka. Dying, he could take—he just didn't want to go out with people thinking he was some kind of terrorist.

But the longer Han studied the blazing sheet ahead, the more he realized he could not be looking at any kind of efflux tail. There were actually two bright streams, one broad and curving and fan-shaped, the other thin and straight and braided.

He finally realized what he was seeing.

Scowling toward the pilot's seat, which had become Leia's until his shoulder was healed enough to fly, Han stepped onto the flight deck. "Are you flying my ship into a comet?"

"Yes, dear." Leia met his gaze in the canopy reflection, then shot him a brief frown—one he knew was meant to remind him that they still had a lot to learn about Morwan and the usurpers. "We agreed to return Lady Morwan to her Ducha, remember?"

"Of course I remember." Han glanced at Morwan, who was in the copilot's chair, then dropped into the navigator's seat behind Leia. "But no one lives on a comet."

"Actually, a surprising number of beings inhabit comets," C-3PO offered from the communications station. "Hermits, pirates, fugitives, political exiles—"

"AlGray's no hermit," Han grumbled. "And even if she was, she must own a dozen empty moons already."

"Actually, all of the Relephon Moons are inhabited," Morwan said. "But we're not meeting Ducha AlGray at her residence."

Han glanced down at the navigation display and saw that they weren't anywhere near Relephon—far from it, in fact. "The Hapan system?" he asked. "What are we doing here?"

"The answer to that is obvious," Morwan replied. "And you shouldn't be out of medbay. You need that hydration drip to keep your electrolytes in balance. Blaster burns remove a lot of fluids from your system."

"My fluids are just fine." Han had the sinking feeling that he knew exactly why they were in the Hapan system, and he was fairly sure that Tenel Ka could not be ready.

With so much of her Royal Navy assigned to the Galactic Alliance, she would need support from the nobles still loyal to her—support that would take time to arrive. "And stop changing the subject."

"Fine," Morwan replied. "Your health is no concern of mine. If you're truly having trouble figuring out the situation, just look through the viewport."

Han squinted out at the comet. Once his eyes had grown accustomed to the glow, he saw a dark crescent of empty space at the starboard edge of the canopy, just in front of the boiling brilliance of the comet's head. Clustered close behind the head were about seventy tiny black ovals, arranged in a three-dimensional diamond commonly used to attack planetary defenses.

"Oh, that," Han said, trying to conceal the alarm he felt at how fast the usurpers were moving. "I meant what are we doing here? You can't intend to be a part of this fight."

Morwan scowled over her shoulder at him. "You doubt my devotion?"

"That's not what I said." Han raised his hands defensively. "But the *Falcon* ain't much of a warship."

"I won't be aboard the *Falcon* after we rendezvous," Morwan replied. "And I suspect you won't be, either."

"Is that a threat?" Han demanded, starting to worry that she'd discovered he and Leia were spies. "Because if it isn't, you'd better clear things up real fast."

"Even if it were a threat, you're hardly in any condition to do anything about it," Morwan replied. "But all I mean is I'll be aboard the *Kendall,* and you'll most likely be with your friends from Corellia."

"Corellia?" Han glanced back toward the battle formation and realized that the three silhouettes in front were several times the size of the others. "I was wondering if those were our Dreadnaughts."

As Han said this, he tried to catch Leia's gaze in the canopy reflection. But her eyes had that distant, unfocused look they got when she was caught up with something in the Force. With any luck, she was reaching out to Tenel Ka, trying to warn the Queen Mother about the trouble coming her way.

"Dreadnaughts?" Morwan repeated. "I really don't know what they are, only that Corellia promised to send a fleet that could defeat Hapes's defenses."

"They did," Han assured her. "Those Dreadnaughts will punch through in no time. By this time tomorrow, AlGray will be the new Queen Mother."

"That's not the reason she organized the overthrow," Morwan said. "Her only concern is for the Consortium's independence."

"Whatever you say," Han said. "It doesn't matter to me."

He switched the navigator's display to tactical. None of the vessels in the usurpers' fleet was broadcasting a transponder code, but the *Falcon*'s threat computer had used a combination of mass and energy bleed-off patterns to classify the contacts as Battle Dragons. The three egg-shaped vessels at the head of the fleet—the Corellian Dreadnaughts—it had designated UNKNOWN, assigning them an estimated threat level approximately twice that of *Imperial*-class Star Destroyers.

The Dreadnaughts were surrounded by a screen of light frigates configured for fighter defense, and the Battle Dragons had a number of Nova battle cruisers interspersed among them. After a moment of study, Han noticed that the Battle Dragons were grouped in clusters with nearly identical masses and energy bleed-off signatures. It only made sense; the noble houses would be operating as sub-units within the larger formation, and their vessels would tend to have standard configurations.

Han stored a screen shot of the tactical display—then noticed that one of the Nova cruisers had dropped out of formation and was turning to intercept them.

"Anyone in that fleet know we're coming?" he asked. "They're sending out a welcoming party."

"Ducha AlGray won't be expecting me to arrive in—" Morwan paused to glance around the flight deck. "—a common freighter," she finished.

"Then maybe we'd better turn this freighter around," Han said, bristling at the disdain in her voice. "Because they're not going to look in the windows before they open fire."

"That won't be necessary, Captain Solo," Morwan replied. "Open a ship-to-ship channel. I'm sure the Ducha will understand if I break comm silence to avoid being fired upon."

"Yeah—I suppose so," Han said, reasoning that a comm wave was a lot less noticeable than a turbolaser volley. "Go ahead, Threepio."

C-3PO opened the channel. "Just activate your microphone, Lady Morwan."

Morwan checked the comm status panel—no doubt to make sure the channel was on a tight beam—then activated her microphone. "Heritage Fleet Nova. This is Lalu Morwan, a true guardian of Hapan independence, arriving aboard alternate transport . . ." She glanced down to see what transponder code the Falcon was using. "*Longshot*. Request clearance to join formation and rendezvous with the *Kendall*."

"*Longshot* acknowledged as our fellow guardian,"

came the cruiser's reply. "Continue approach, stand by for instructions."

Han studied Morwan with a raised brow.

"Don't say it," Morwan warned. "I've heard all the 'lulu' jokes I care to."

"Han dated a lot of lulus before he met me," Leia said, finally returning from wherever her attention had been. "I think he's just surprised you gave us your real name earlier."

Morwan shrugged. "I didn't have much choice—Aurra Sing found *me*, remember?"

"Pardon me," C-3PO said. "But we're being hailed by the *Kendall*. Shall I put it on?"

"Of course!" Morwan replied.

C-3PO tapped a key, and a crisp, middle-aged voice came over the cockpit speakers. "You're late!"

"I apologize," Morwan replied. "It's Lalu, your fellow guardian."

"Yes, yes, we're both true guardians of Hapan independence," AlGray said, clearly irritated at having to use the recognition phrase. "Now tell me why you're late—and why you're arriving in that wreck."

Han scowled and would have objected, except that he was busy with his tactical display, attaching the designator KENDALL to the Battle Dragon from which the comm signal was coming.

"Actually, this is the *Millennium Falcon*," Morwan explained. "I was forced to turn my yacht over to . . . our agent, and Princess Leia was kind enough to offer me a ride."

AlGray paused before answering. Han stored another screen shot of his tactical display, this one detailing the *Kendall*'s location and designating her the flagship. He could almost hear AlGray wondering whether her plot had been exposed—but the sad truth was that so far, he and Leia had managed to warn Tenel Ka of precious little.

AlGray finally seemed to reach the same conclusion. "How did that come about?"

"It's a long story, given our comm restrictions," Morwan replied carefully. "Perhaps I could fill you in once I'm aboard?"

"You won't be aboard," AlGray replied. "The Heritage Fleet is preparing to make the attack-jump. Fall in at the back of the formation. You can explain after the battle."

"After?" Morwan asked, clearly not happy about the prospect of riding out a major space battle aboard the *Falcon*. "Ducha?"

"I'm afraid the *Kendall* has closed the channel," C-3PO said. "Shall I attempt to reestablish contact?"

"Absolutely not." Morwan turned to Leia. "Princess Leia, I truly hate to ask this, but the Ducha's orders were clear."

"Of course, we'll obey." Leia was already pushing the throttles forward. "We're old hands at staying out of trouble in big battles like this."

As Leia spoke, the nav computer beeped to announce that it had received jump coordinates. A moment later the usurper fleet—Han refused to think of it as the Heritage Fleet—began to accelerate under the head of the comet.

While Leia chased after the fleet, Han performed the jump calculations—taking the time to look up Hapes's rotation cycle so he could plot exactly where the fleet would revert to realspace relative to the planet. After double-checking his answers, he copied the information to a datafile, then attached the two screen shots he had captured identifying the fleet's flagship and composition. As field-intelligence dossiers went, it was neither very thorough nor very timely, but it was the best he could do under the circumstances.

The *Falcon* passed under the comet and pulled ahead. A moment later the canopy blast-tinting paled, revealing the blue circles of hundreds of ion engines spread across the darkness in front of them. The circles were accelerating toward the tiny white ball of the Hapan sun, but still growing rapidly larger as the *Falcon* overtook the fleet.

"Blast!" Han said. He needed an excuse to make Leia delay a few seconds when the usurper fleet jumped into hyperspace—and he had to keep Morwan distracted at the same time. "The sensor dish is sticking again. Lady Morwan, can you shut down the sensor suite just before we jump?"

"Won't that be dangerous when we revert?" she asked. "We won't be able to tell where the rest of the fleet is."

"Not if Leia waits a bit after everyone else jumps," Han replied. "And if you bring the sensors up again right after we jump, we won't be blind for more than fifteen or twenty seconds."

"Twenty seconds?" C-3PO squawked. "Eighty-seven percent of all fleet-maneuver accidents occur within the first ten seconds of exiting hyperspace!"

"Better that than being blind for the rest of the battle," Leia said, following Han's lead. "I can handle it, Three-pio. I have the Force, remember?"

"Of course—pardon me for doubting you," C-3PO said. "It's impossible to assign a safety coefficient to the Force, but I'm quite sure we're as safe with you flying blind as we are even when Captain Solo has all his instruments."

Han would have reminded the droid that he had not gotten them killed yet, except that the blue circles ahead had begun to swell more slowly as Leia matched the fleet's velocity. He quickly formatted his intelligence dossier for transmission, then watched in silence as the *Falcon* slid into position at the rear of the formation.

Finally, the voice of a female maneuvering chief came over the cockpit speakers. "Jump in three."

Leia put her hand on the hyperdrive actuator, and Lady Morwan reached for the sensor controls.

"Two."

Han turned to C-3PO and held his finger to his lips, then cranked their S-thread unit to maximum transmission power and switched to a general hailing channel.

"Mark."

Space ahead flared blue as the usurper fleet accelerated to jump speed.

"Deactivate sensors," Leia ordered.

Morwan used both hands to pull the sensor suite glide-switches to their off positions, and space went dark again as the usurper fleet entered hyperspace.

Han hit the TRANSMIT key.

Leia waited another second, then shoved the throttles to maximum and activated the hyperdrive. The stars stretched into a pearlescent blur.

Han returned the comm unit to its previous settings, then caught C-3PO looking at him with a cocked head.

"It was hardly necessary to do that yourself," the droid said. "I'm perfectly capable of—"

"Your timing's no good," Han interrupted, worried the droid was about to mention the S-thread message. "And that's the last I want to hear about it."

"But my timing is excellent!" C-3PO protested. "My reaction speed is less than two one-thousandths of a second, which is two magnitudes better than yours."

"Han means that it's a matter of judgment," Leia said.

"There were too many variables to define in the time available."

"Oh, I see," C-3PO replied, sounding calmer. "Captain Solo is having trouble expressing himself again."

"I'm going to trip your primary circuit breaker," Han said. "Is that clear enough?"

"That's hardly necessary." C-3PO retreated toward the far side of the flight deck. "If you want me to keep quiet, all you have to do is say so."

Morwan turned around in her seat. "Keep you quiet about what, Threepio?"

C-3PO glanced briefly in Han's direction. "I'm really not at liberty to say, Lady Morwan."

"Threepio isn't allowed to divulge anything concerning the *Falcon*'s operation," Leia lied. She kept her gaze fixed on the control panel chrono, counting down the seconds until they reverted to realspace. "It's a standard security protocol."

"But there's no big secret," Han added quickly. "The comm antenna retracts when the sensor dish reverses for the jump. And since the dish was stuck—"

"—you had to lower it manually," Morwan finished. She glanced at C-3PO, as though she could read the truth in the droid's expressionless face, then nodded. "Of course."

Morwan turned back to the sensor glides, leaving Han to wonder how high her suspicions had been raised. Even had she not believed before that he and Leia were spies, C-3PO's gaffe had clearly planted the seed.

The reversion alarm chimed, and an instant later the gray veil of hyperspace erupted into a wall of crimson energy. The cockpit speakers began to crackle with alarmed voices and shipboard explosions, then the invisible fist of a turbolaser strike glanced off the *Falcon*'s top shields, pounding her so hard that C-3PO clanged to the deck on his back.

"We've been hit!" the droid cried. "Shall I activate the abandon-ship siren?"

"No!" Han said. "That was just a graze. We're fine."

He peered over Leia's shoulder at the damage-control board and saw that he was only partially right. The forward cargo hold had sealed itself off because of a pressure leak, and a coolant line had burst somewhere in the aft engineering tunnel, but Han thought they would probably last out the battle—as long as they didn't take another big hit.

"Let's not do that again," he said, speaking into Leia's ear. "We don't want to scare the droid."

A turbolaser strike blossomed a hundred meters beneath the *Falcon*'s belly, bucking Han against his crash webbing and setting off a new round of alarms.

C-3PO emitted a surprised squeal and wrapped his arms around the comm officer's chair, then Leia flipped them into a tight spiral and even Han gasped in alarm. He ached to take the pilot's yoke—but with only one hand to hold it, that would have been foolish even for him. The crimson fury of a rolling barrage erupted ahead and began to advance toward the *Falcon*.

"Dive!" Han was straining against his crash webbing, yelling over Leia's shoulder. "Go beloooooooowww!"

Leia had pushed the yoke as far forward as it would go. "Trying!"

The barrage passed over their stern, bucking the ship hard enough to bang C-3PO against the floor—and to send a bolt of pain shooting through Han's wounded shoulder.

A glowing red disk appeared ahead, then quickly expanded into a sheet of half-molten metal that had once been the upper saucer of a Hapan Battle Dragon. Escape pods were spraying from the vessel like shooting stars, and momentary fists of flame kept punching out through breaches in the hull.

"Pull up!" Han cried.

Leia was already bringing their nose up, and the Battle Dragon began to swing out from beneath the *Falcon*. "Trying!"

They leveled off just above the Battle Dragon, so close to the half-melted hull that the temperature inside the *Falcon* began to climb.

"Give her some throttle!" Han ordered. "Get us out of this!"

Leia already had the throttles pushed past the overload stops. The *Falcon* leapt away from the Battle Dragon— only to find a slender Nova cruiser dead ahead, breaking apart midway down her long spine, pouring dark clouds of vapor and flotsam into space.

"Go left!" Han yelled half a second before the Nova's bridge exploded into a spray of superheated shrapnel. "Wait, go down!"

The Nova's stern weapons arrays began to fire at random, lacing space below with stabbing shafts of color and flame.

"No, go—"

"Captain Solo!" Morwan cried. She was clenching the arms of her chair with both hands. "Will you please shut up and let her fly? You're going to get us killed!"

Han bristled at Morwan's tone—then realized how right she was and began to feel a little ashamed. "With Leia holding the yoke?" he said. "No way! I'm a better teacher than that."

"Don't . . . brag!" Leia spoke through clenched teeth. "You'll jinx us."

She flipped the *Falcon* on her side and continued in the only direction she could, straight between the two halves of the Nova's broken spine. The gap vanished behind a cloud of frozen atmosphere. Dark blurs began to flash past too quickly to identify, and the impact alarm sounded continuously as they plowed their way through the flotsam.

"I certainly hope the particle shields don't fail us now," C-3PO said, clanking to his knees. "One of those frozen bodies could cause a catastrophic hull breach!"

They emerged from the vapor cloud into a pocket of relative calm behind two wrecked Battle Dragons. The main part of the fleet was barely visible ahead, a field of blue efflux circles exchanging dashes of color with an enemy fleet too distant to spot visually.

Han let out a sigh of relief. "You see? Nothing to worry about."

"Nothing to worry about?" Morwan released her chair arms and turned to Han with a half-accusatory glare. "We were ambushed! The Royal Navy was waiting for us."

Han met her gaze with his best sabacc face. "Yeah, it's almost like they knew the reversion coordinates. Wonder how that happened?"

Morwan's eyes narrowed. "So do I, Captain Solo."

They passed the wrecked Battle Dragons, and the *Falcon*'s canopy darkened against fresh blossoms of nearby turbolaser strikes.

"I hate to interrupt," Leia said with her usual perfect timing. "But I need that tactical display back up. Even Jedi can't see through this much battle fire."

The suspicion in Morwan's eyes changed to fear, and her attention returned to the sensor panel. "I've been trying. All I get is one long burst of screen snow."

"It's all this turbolaser fire," C-3PO said from behind her. "You need to bring up the filters."

"Filters?" Morwan sounded confused. "How do I do that?"

"You call yourself a pilot?" Han grumbled. "How did you ever find Telkur Station?"

"I was flying a Batag Skiff," Morwan answered, as though the name explained everything. "The sensors have automatic filters."

"Automatic filters?" Han shook his head. "What will they put in spacecraft next? Heated seats and cockpit caf dispensers?"

He unbuckled and stepped into the gap between the pilot's and copilot's seats, then leaned in front of Morwan to activate the electromagnetic discharge filters. "They're on glide-switches, starting with radio waves and going all the way up to gamma rays."

As Han explained this, he pushed the glides up, reducing the amount of static. Gradually, a clear image appeared on the tactical display. The usurper fleet was in even worse shape than he had imagined, with large gaps in the assault formation and a quarter of the Hapan Royal Navy pouring fire into the *Kendall*.

"Looks like you lucked out staying with us," Han said, removing his hand from the filter glides. "AlGray's flagship is taking quite a pounding."

"Yes." Morwan caught Han's arm and held him in front of her. "I think we both know why that is."

Something small jabbed Han in the side, and he looked down to find a small hold-out blaster pressed to his ribs.

"You think I had something to do with it?" The anger in Han's voice was genuine—and mostly with himself for letting Morwan get the drop on him. "Of all the ungrateful she-Hutts—"

"Save it, Solo!" Morwan ordered. "You really don't want to heat my jets more than you have. I'm already furious with myself for not seeing through you two from the start."

"Seeing through us how?" Leia asked. The *Falcon* decelerated and banked as she turned away from the battle. "And I'd be very careful with that blaster. I've been known to lose my temper with people who shoot my husband."

"And you really don't want to see Leia lose her temper," Han said, doing his best to keep his body in front of Morwan's face. As soon as Leia had said *shoot,* C-3PO had started to creep toward the back of the flight deck, probably intending to sneak down the access corridor to fetch Cakhmaim and Meewalh. "Ever since she became a Jedi, when she gets mad, things just start flying at you from all directions."

"That shouldn't be a problem, Captain Solo. Your fate rests entirely in the Princess's hands." Morwan was speaking from under Han's arm, since she continued to hold him in front of her. "I won't blast you if she turns back toward the battle."

Leia continued to bank away. "What for?"

"Because she doesn't want it to look suspicious when we send Tenel Ka another message," Han said, glancing down at the tactical display. Protected by their powerful shields and multilayered hulls, two Corellian Dreadnaughts were continuing to press the attack, with what remained of the usurper fleet close behind. "She wants to tell Tenel Ka to tighten up and hold her position."

Leia was quiet for a moment, probably studying her own display, and the anger that Han had felt over being taken hostage began to give way to other emotions. Knowing that Leia would be sensing the change through the

Force, he only hoped she realized that the fear he was feeling was only for Tenel Ka. The last thing he wanted was for Leia to think a little thing like having a blaster stuck in his ribs was starting to bother him.

After a moment, Leia asked Han, "You think the Dreadnaughts can actually break through?"

Han nodded. "That's what they were designed for—to penetrate an enemy fleet and tear it apart from the inside. And if that strategy works—"

"—they'll go after Tenel Ka," Leia finished. "And it won't matter whether they win the ship-to-ship melee that follows. If they kill Tenel Ka, the monarchy will be shattered."

"And the Heritage Council will still be in position to put the Consortium back together again," Morwan said. "Very astute, Princess."

C-3PO reached the back of the flight deck and began to clank down the access corridor.

Morwan didn't even turn to look. "It sounds as though we're running out of time, Princess. Will you turn back now . . . or do I blast your man?"

"Hmmm," Leia said. "That's a tough decision. On one hand, I would inherit this old transport—"

"That's *classic* transport," Han corrected. "The YT-Thirteen-hundred is one of the most valuable—"

"Stop stalling," Morwan ordered. "Turn back now, or I pull the trigger."

Leia sighed, and the *Falcon*'s nose started to drift back toward the battle.

"Leia!" Han's fear had turned to embarrassment; could she really believe he would want her to risk Tenel Ka's life to save him? "The traitors have a spy!"

"It's okay, Han," Leia said. "I have a feeling it won't matter."

"Of course it'll matter!" Han objected. "They'll know what ship Tenel Ka is—"

"That's enough, Captain Solo." Morwan jammed the blaster harder into his ribs. "With a Jedi and two Noghri aboard, I don't expect to survive this anyway. On my way out, I won't hesitate to rid the galaxy of one more Alliance braintick."

"*Alliance braintick?*" Han pushed his wounded arm forward in the sling. "There's no call for insults!"

He clamped his hand over Morwan's hold-out blaster. As he pushed the tiny weapon away from his body, she squeezed the trigger, sending a flurry of bolts burning across his palm and ricocheting off the control board.

"Han, no!" Leia screamed.

But Han was already slamming the elbow of his good arm into Morwan's nose. He felt cartilage crumble and heard her scream, but the blaster bolts continued to come. He brought his elbow back again.

Morwan released the hold-out blaster and reached up to protect her nose. Han stepped away, moving the weapon to his good hand—and letting out a roar of pain as he finally realized just how much his scorched palm hurt.

"Han!" Leia reached out and gently pushed Han back so the lightsaber in her hand would have a clear path to Morwan's head. "What are you doing?"

"Taking my ship back." Han pointed the weapon at Morwan, who was now holding her face in both hands, bleeding between her fingers and groaning in pain. "What do you think?"

"I think you're getting yourself shot up again for no reason." Leia laid her lightsaber in her lap, then ordered, "Sit down and keep her covered until the Noghri get here."

Han dropped into the navigator's seat. "What do you mean, *no reason*?" A cloud of gray smoke was hanging over the control board, rising from half a dozen holes that Morwan had shot through the durasteel. "She was going to kill me!"

"I don't think so," Leia said. "She wouldn't have had any reason."

Han noticed they were still headed toward the battle. "Don't tell me you were going to send that message!"

"Actually, I still am," Leia said.

Even Morwan was surprised. "You are?" Her voice was muffled and nasal. "Why?"

"Never mind," Leia said. She cocked her head, looking into the canopy reflection, then raised her voice so it projected down the access corridor. "It's okay, Cakhmaim. We have things under control."

She had barely spoken before Cakhmaim and Meewalh rushed onto the flight deck, Cakhmaim holding a deadly fighting sickle and Meewalh a capture net. When they saw Han sitting in the navigator's seat with the blaster and Morwan hunched over with her head in her hands, their saurian faces looked almost disappointed.

"It's okay, guys—you get to lock her up." Han motioned for them to take her away. "And use the stun cuffs."

"After you see to her nose," Leia added. "We don't want her choking to death on her own blood."

Han looked down at the furrows charred across his wounded palm. "Speak for yourself."

"Han!"

Han shrugged. "You're the one who's always telling me to be honest about my feelings." He waited until the Noghri had taken Morwan away, then asked, "You're not serious about that message, are you?"

"I am—and we need to do it now." Leia nodded at the tactical display, which showed Tenel Ka's formations starting to fall back in preparation for a ship-to-ship free-for-all. "Open a channel."

Han studied his display, trying to see what Leia was talking about. Unfortunately, he was distracted by an irregular pattern of flickering and blinking.

"Blasted woman!" he said. "She hit something in the control panel."

"Which is all the more reason to send the message now, Han," Leia said. "Tenel Ka can't let this battle degenerate into a ship melee, or the Alliance won't be able to spring its trap."

"Trap?"

Something popped in the control panel, and smoke began to pour out of a hole in front of the copilot's station. Han cursed and, ignoring all the blood Morwan's broken nose had sprayed everywhere, slipped into the copilot's seat. The tactical display there was no better than the one at the navigator's station, but he could see clearly enough to tell it did not show any Alliance fleets.

"I don't see a trap."

Leia fell silent for a time, then said, "Listen, Han, if you can't do this, just say so."

Now Han was growing really confused. "Do what?"

"It's okay," Leia said. "I'll understand."

"Good," Han answered. "That makes one of us."

Leia dropped her chin and glanced over, giving him one of her patented *I-know-you're-lying* looks.

"Leia, what are you talking about?"

"Once you send the message, we both know our names will be Hutt slime in Corellia," Leia said. "Gejjen will know we were working against them here, and you'll be branded a traitor."

Leia's words hit Han hard, up near the heart, and he realized she was right. If they helped Tenel Ka now, it could only be in the open, and the Corellian High Command—Wedge, Gejjen, all of them—would know he had chosen Hapes over his homeworld.

But how could Han not choose Tenel Ka? Corellia was in the wrong here, trying to assassinate a sovereign leader and expand the war just to win a more favorable negotiating position—trying to plunge sixty-three worlds into a civil war that would make the Corellian conflict with the Alliance look like a spitball fight.

"Leia, my reputation doesn't matter," he said. "My conscience does."

Leia smiled in relief. "I'm so glad," she said. "That's what I thought, but I didn't want to make the decision for you."

"Great, I appreciate that," Han said. "But I still don't have any idea what you're talking about."

"I told you I had a feeling," Leia said. "And then you made a grab for Morwan's blaster."

Han frowned, remembering that Leia had said something about a feeling. "Oh, *that* kind of feeling. Why didn't you tell me that's what you meant?"

Leia rolled her eyes. "What could I say? Trust me?"

"I guess not," Han admitted. He felt a little foolish for missing the hint, but he couldn't be expected to read Leia's mind all the time—after all, he wasn't the Jedi. "But look, I can't just open a channel to Tenel Ka and say, *Hang tight, kid—the Solos are on their way.* What kind of trap did you sense?"

Leia shook her head. "I don't know exactly. Back at the comet, I sensed someone watching us."

Han remembered Leia's distant expression, when he thought she was trying to warn Tenel Ka. "A Jedi?"

Leia nodded. "I think it was Tesar, but he wasn't sure about me and closed down pretty fast."

Han frowned in concentration. "And since you felt Jaina watching us back at the Kirises—"

"Exactly," Leia said. "Chances are that whoever was watching the Kiris fleet there—"

"—followed it here."

Han switched the comm unit to the hailing channel, which they would need to use since they didn't have the codes or frequencies for Tenel Ka's fleet. Another streamer of smoke began to rise from the shield array panel, and when he tried to adjust the glides, the readout did not change.

"Uh, before I send this message, maybe you'd better put yourself into a Jedi flying trance or something."

"Han, I'll be open to the Force," Leia said. "But there really is no such thing as a Jedi flying trance."

"Too bad—because I think our shields are stuck." Han looked over at Leia and blew her a kiss, then activated his microphone and began to broadcast on the general hailing channel. "This is a message for Queen Mother Tenel Ka from Han Solo. Listen up, kid—I've got something important to tell you . . ."

chapter twenty-one

Outside the viewport of the depot cantina hung a glorious aurora, a luminous explosion of green and violet and scarlet fanning across the face of the Transitory Mists from the direction of the star Roqoo. The spectacle was a testament to the vast sweep of the mists and the ferocious power of a blue giant's solar wind, but today Mara found it more eerie than awe inspiring. Today its dancing beauty was only the barrier that prevented her and Luke from making comm contact with their son.

Mara turned away from the viewport and looked across the table, where Luke sat nursing his third hot chocolate of the afternoon. "We might as well face it. Ben's not coming."

Luke continued to gaze out at the shimmering curtain of light.

"He's way overdue," Mara continued. "And when I reach out to him in the Force, he doesn't feel anywhere near here. Either Jacen didn't send the rendezvous message, or Ben didn't get it. But something went wrong."

Luke nodded and took another sip from his mug. "And

something wrong is coming," he added. "Don't you feel it?"

Now that Luke had mentioned it, Mara *could* feel something. It wasn't much—just a faint prickle easily mistaken for a chill—but it *was* there.

Mara turned back to the viewport, but this time she studied the reflections in its corners instead of the aurora outside. Most of the customers she could see in the murky cantina were good-looking humans—typical Hapans—and without exception they seemed more interested in their meals or the Falleen glimmik singer on stage than in the Skywalkers. The nonhumans—a dozen blue-skinned Duros, some anvil-headed Arcona, and a couple of Mon Calamari—seemed transfixed by the aurora beyond the viewport. And the Twi'lek family who ran the place was being kept far too busy to pay attention to anyone not ordering something.

Mara looked back to Luke. "You think Jacen set us up?"

"I do." Luke's voice was steady, but their Force-bond was permeated by sadness—and by a sense of bewilderment and failure. "If Tenel Ka hadn't verified it, I wouldn't even believe he had sent Ben to find Jaina and Zekk."

Mara sighed. "I have to admit, I'm beginning to feel a bit like a fool for placing my faith in Jacen."

"Don't," Luke said. "We both trusted him—and I'm still not sure we were wrong. Jacen helped Ben overcome his fear of the Force. We can't forget that."

"How *could* I?" Mara asked. "But if he *has* set us up—if he's leading Ben into the dark side—"

"*Now* who's leaping to conclusions?" Luke leaned across the table and took her hands. In a low voice, he added, "Look, even if Jacen is working with Lumiya, I don't think it's been for long. And it doesn't mean he's becoming a Sith."

"It doesn't mean he *isn't*," Mara countered. "We can't know what's going on between him and Lumiya."

"I know *Jacen*," Luke said quickly. "Whatever he's doing, it's because he thinks it's right for the galaxy. Once he realizes he's mistaken, he'll be easy to bring back."

Mara considered this, trying to recall when she had *ever* seen Jacen do anything selfish, trying to think of *anything*—even after assuming command of GAG—that Jacen had done out of self-interest rather than for the good of the state.

After a few moments, she nodded. Her fear for Ben—and her anger at feeling deceived by Jacen—were beginning to affect her judgment.

"You're right," she said. "But we'd better work fast. Jacen is too powerful already, and if Lumiya has her hooks in him, it won't be long before he reaches the point of no return. We can't let that happen, Luke. We can't let him drag the galaxy down with him."

"We won't," Luke assured her. "We stopped Raynar, didn't we?"

"You're not inspiring much confidence," Mara said. After crash-landing near a nest of Killiks, Raynar Thul had joined their culture, eventually rising to become the leader of a powerful insect civilization. Under his guidance, the Colony had expanded to the edges of the Chiss Ascendancy, provoking a border war that Luke had averted only by capturing Raynar in personal combat. "Look how well that worked out. He's been locked in the Temple basement for how long?"

"Raynar *is* making progress," Luke said defensively. "He's accepted a prosthetic arm and is considering cosmetic surgery to repair the burn scars."

"That should come in handy when he escapes," Mara

said. "He won't scare so many little children on the way to the undercity."

Luke frowned at her sarcasm. "The surgery will help Raynar see himself differently," he said. "Cilghal says that will be a big step in his recovery."

"Okay—so maybe he'll be cured in another two or three years." Mara rose and hiked up her equipment belt, which tended to slip down on her hips now that she was carrying the extra weight of the shoto she had built in anticipation of meeting Lumiya. "Let's catch up with the *Anakin* and stick close to Jacen. Ben will show up there sooner or later."

"If he hasn't already."

Luke rose and started toward the door, and suddenly the uneasy prickle he had been feeling blossomed into full-blown danger sense. He glanced around the room, trying to locate the source of the threat. He felt nothing menacing from the other patrons, but that didn't stop him from pulling his lightsaber off his belt as casually as possible.

Mara already had her weapon in her hand, though, like Luke, she held it down at her side to avoid sparking a panic. "You feel it, too?"

"Let's go," Luke said. He weaved through the crowd toward the nearest exit hatch, and Mara stayed close on his heels. If they allowed a fight to start in here, a lot of innocent beings would suffer.

They were a few paces from the exit when a hunched figure appeared in the bare durasteel corridor outside the cantina, hobbling out of an intersection about six meters up the way. She was wearing a bulky black cloak with the hood pulled up, and she was being careful to keep her face turned away from the ceiling lights.

Luke had just enough time to realize that he did not feel

her presence in the Force before she brought her arm forward and sent a silver tube tumbling down the gray corridor toward him. A set of flashing diodes midway down its length confirmed the cylinder's nature. He raised his arm and used the Force to hurl the tube back up the corridor.

"Grenade!" he yelled.

The grenade was almost back to the intersection when the corridor erupted into silver brilliance. A tremendous bang shook the cantina, and Luke found himself tumbling backward over a table, ears ringing and spots dancing before his eyes.

He hit the floor amid a torrent of spilling drinks and flailing customers. His eardrums popped painfully as the air pressure dropped, and the exit hatch fell with a deafening clang. An instant later half the cantina's lights flickered out, leaving the stunned crowd bathed in shadows. A hull-breach alarm began to whistle overhead.

Luke reached out in the Force and sensed Mara lying about three meters away, surprised but unharmed and already recovering her wits. He sprang to his feet and saw that the area closest to the exit had taken the brunt of the explosion, with perhaps two dozen beings lying on the debris-strewn floor in various states of injury. Most of the yelling seemed to be coming from deeper in the cantina behind him, where the patrons had been far enough from the blast to become panicked instead of stunned.

Mara stepped to Luke's side. "Nice save." She nodded out the viewport, where a cloud of flotsam from the damaged corridor was already drifting past. Fortunately, there seemed to be only a few bodies—but none was dressed in a black cloak.

"That was just the opening salvo." As Luke spoke, the first frightened patrons began to crowd toward the cantina's other exit, their cries turning impatient and angry when everyone could not squeeze through the hatch at once. "There's a reason she attacked before we were—"

A long hissing crackle sounded from the second exit, drawing a frenzy of screams from fleeing patrons. Luke had not heard the sizzle of a striking lightwhip in decades, and the sound sent a hot prickle up his spine. He reached inside his robe and withdrew the shoto he had been carrying in anticipation of just this moment.

"Well, I'd say this proves it." Luke's heart ached with disappointment. "Ben's not here. Lumiya *is*."

"Yeah." Mara's voice was angry. "Jacen set us up."

She snapped the shoto off her own equipment belt and started for the cantina's inner wall, moving into position to flank their attacker. Luke started toward the hatch and saw snakes of light crackling into the crowd ahead. A leathery, anvil-shaped head went flying and two human arms dropped to the floor. A dozen voices cried out in pain as ribbons of bloody cloth flew from their tunics.

"Back, you kreetles!" The icy voice belonged to Lumiya. "Get back! Only one man can save you now!"

The whip struck again, and the confused patrons began to fall back. A dark-cloaked figure appeared in the hatchway. Her hood had been pushed back off her head, but her face was swaddled in black cloth. Her lightwhip trailed at her side, its half a dozen strands divided evenly among energy, leather, and crystal-studded metal. Luke started to push toward her, using the Force to subtly move people aside as he fought against the retreating crowd.

"You!" Lumiya pointed a long finger in Luke's direction. "Lay down your blades and kneel."

"Not a chance."

Luke ignited his blades—one short and one long, to counter the dual nature of her weapon—and watched the crowd part before him. It would have been quicker and safer to launch himself at Lumiya in a long arc of Force tumbling, but she did not seem to be aware of Mara sneaking up on her flank, and Luke wanted to keep her attention fixed on him until Mara was in position to strike.

Lumiya was in no mood to be patient. Her lightwhip crackled out again and shredded a Duros down one whole flank. Her victim fell, warbling in pain, and the blaster he had been trying to pull clattered to the floor in front of him.

The crowd froze in terror, staring gape-mouthed at the still-writhing victim.

"The *Jedi* has decided your fate!" Lumiya yelled over the screeching Duros. Her whip lashed out again, this time wrapping its tendrils around the waist of a lithe Hapan beauty and cutting her nearly in half. "Because of him, you *all* die!"

Cantina patrons began to whirl on Luke, many pulling blasters or vibroblades. Their eyes were distant and their mouths uniformly twisted into the same angry snarl, and Luke realized that Lumiya was using the Force to redirect their fear and anger toward him. Clearly, she did not intend this to be a fair fight . . . any more than he and Mara did.

Luke danced forward, shoving patrons out of his way with the Force and using his light blades to return the bolts of those who made the mistake of firing on him. He hated to wound Lumiya's unwitting minions and did his best to avoid injuring them seriously, but he had to defend himself. If he allowed the situation to get out of hand and they tried to mob him, a lot of people were going to lose arms, legs, and maybe worse.

Luke had closed to within striking range of the lightwhip when a Twi'lek male in a clean kitchen apron stepped out to block his way.

"You're a Jedi!" The Twi'lek's head-tails were twitching in anger, and if he was troubled by the two blades hissing in front of him, his lumpy face showed no sign of it. "You can't let my customers die just to save yourself!"

Luke used the Force to shove the Twi'lek aside. Though Mara was no longer in his line of sight, he could sense through their Force-bond that she was in position and ready to strike—and Lumiya continued to seem unaware of her.

The Twi'lek stepped out behind Luke. "Coward!" His voice grew a little muted as he turned toward the crowd. "Let's get—"

Luke silenced the Twi'lek with a bone-crunching back kick, then hurled himself at Lumiya, both blades striking for the kill. He knew better than to think victory would come so easily, but he had to keep her attention riveted on him until Mara struck.

Lumiya's counter was, of course, masterful. She flicked her whip at Luke's legs, forcing him into a high somersault that bought her half a second to spin away. He came down a couple of paces inside the cantina, framed in the hatchway and facing the murky corridor where Alema crouched, hidden inside her Force shadow.

Then Lumiya's lightwhip crackled in at Luke's flank, striking high, low, and in between all at once. He pivoted around to defend himself, filling the air with sparks and ozone and flying shards of Kaiburr Crystal as he blocked with the short blade and used the long to cut away one of the strands.

Alema could have taken him at that moment. She had the cone-dart in the blowgun and the blowgun pressed to her lips, and Skywalker was so focused on Lumiya that he would never have sensed the dart coming. That was what Lumiya would want, what she *expected*.

But where was the Balance in that? Luke Skywalker had taken so much from her—the use of her arm, her nest, her identity—and it would not be right for Alema to simply *kill* him. She had to destroy him, to let him watch Mara die first so that when *he* died, he would know that there was no hope—so he would know that Lumiya had won, that the Sith would have his nephew and his son, and that the Jedi order would die with him.

So Alema held her dart, waiting motionless while Lumiya's lightwhip flashed again and again, keeping Skywalker framed in the hatchway for her, striking at his flanks and head to keep him from pivoting or somersaulting or simply advancing out of her line of sight.

Finally Skywalker feinted a leap for the hatchway. When Lumiya made the mistake of trying only halfheartedly to block his "escape," he made an unbelievable parry across his body with his short blade, then spun into a slashing, whirling advance with his long blade.

Lumiya had no choice except to retreat. Skywalker vanished from the hatchway and out of Alema's sight, then the last of the lightwhip's metallic strands whirled past the hatchway. A fresh chorus of screams arose, and a jet of blood arced out of the cantina to splat down in a line of elongated red beads.

When Alema looked back into the cantina, it was to find Mara crouching opposite her, just inside the hatchway and facing away. Half a dozen meters beyond her, Skywalker and Lumiya were fighting a frantic battle in the midst of the crowd, Skywalker trying to remain in clear areas so no bystanders would be injured, Lumiya working to keep those same bystanders in front of her so Skywalker could not attack without cutting his way through them first.

Now was Alema's chance—but it would not be enough to simply kill Mara. Alema was a *Jedi,* and Jedi served the Balance.

As she filled her lungs, Alema was also reaching out to Skywalker, sharing with him all the sorrow and loneliness and despair he had caused her—the shame and hopelessness and unending anguish.

A bolt of surprise shot through the Force. Skywalker's eyes widened and slid toward the hatchway—and that was all the opening Lumiya needed.

The lightwhip cracked again, wrapping Skywalker in a fiery cage of light and leather. The short blade went flying, taking along the hand that had been holding it, and Skywalker's robe fell away below the armpits in ribbons, leaving the air pink and smoky with blood and charred flesh.

Alema emptied her lungs, and the dart shot from the blowgun.

Mara heard Luke screaming and thought it was only because he had been so badly hurt, but then he touched her through their Force-bond and she realized he was frightened for *her,* that something was coming at her only slightly under the velocity of a blaster bolt. She dived away and felt her skin prickle as something tiny and dark shot past her shoulder.

A female Twi'lek cried out in astonishment, and when Mara rolled back to her feet, it was to find one of the cantina owner's wives standing a couple of meters in front of her, staring back through the hatchway as she plucked a tiny cone-shaped dart from her thigh. Clearly, Lumiya had brought backup, but Mara had no time to think of likely candidates. The Twi'lek suddenly began to tremble

and gasp for breath, then her leg buckled and she collapsed in convulsions.

Poison.

Mara whirled around to charge through the hatchway—
only to find it blocked by a swarm of terrified Hapans trying to flee. She deactivated her weapons and rushed into
their midst, Force-shoving the leaders into the dark corridor ahead of her. Luke was badly wounded and she knew
it, but she was not going to save him by giving the dart
blower another shot. As soon as she was through the
hatchway, she reignited her blades and spun toward the
dark corner from which the dart had come.

There was nothing but shadow.

Fleeing patrons continued to jostle past behind Mara,
cursing her for blocking their escape. Thinking the attacker had already fled up the corridor, she turned to
follow—then wondered why the corner had still been in
shadow with the glow of two light blades shining into it.

Mara pivoted around to face the corner—but had to deactivate her lightsaber when a salt-drunk Arcona nearly
impaled himself on her blade, whistling in panic and
slamming into her so hard she had to use the Force to
avoid being bowled over.

"Get off!" she ordered.

Instead of Force-shoving the Arcona back through the
hatchway, she stepped back to let him continue up the
corridor—and that was what saved her life when a deep
blue, almost black, lightsaber blade came shooting out of
his chest, so close to her throat she was afraid to drop her
chin.

Reacting even before she understood what was happening, Mara whipped her left hand around behind the
shrieking Arcona and felt her shoto's blade rub across
something. A female voice cried out in surprise, then

the dark blade vanished from the Arcona's chest, and he dropped to the floor gurgling and wailing.

Standing behind him was a twisted figure in a black Jedi robe. She held herself slightly hunched, as though it would pain her to stand upright, and one arm hung atrophied and limp beneath a sagging shoulder. The far lekku had been seared off just above the shoulder, while the near one had a smoking wound across the back where it had been grazed by Mara's blade.

"Alema?"

Mara was not so astonished that she forgot to defend herself when the Twi'lek reignited her lightsaber. She caught Alema's attack on her shoto, then swept the Twi'lek's blade aside and brought her long lightsaber around in a killing slash.

Alema used the Force to hurl herself into a backward somersault, crashing upside down through the line of still-fleeing cantina customers. She alit on both feet on the other side of the corridor. An angry din began to build in the cantina as fleeing patrons stopped in the hatchway rather than run through the middle of a lightsaber fight.

There were a dozen questions Mara would have liked to ask Alema. Was she Lumiya's apprentice? How had she escaped Tenupe? How long had she been back?

But Mara could feel through her Force-bond that Luke was fading fast. His energy was dwindling and his concentration slipping, and he was drawing heavily on the Force just to keep his pain in check and his body moving.

Mara stepped into the middle of the corridor, bringing herself within striking range of Alema. The Twi'lek stepped away from the wall, buying herself room to maneuver and betraying the limp caused by her half foot, and Mara added one more question to her list: why had Alema helped kill Tresina Lobi?

Mara leveled her long blade at the Twi'lek's throat. "I don't have much time, so I'll give you one chance to surrender," she said. "After that, this is to the death—and it doesn't look like you're in condition to last long."

Alema glanced toward the cantina, where the crackle of Lumiya's lightwhip was growing both louder and more frequent, and the sneer that came to her lip was surprisingly confident.

"You *could* let us limp away," she said. "We *promise* to go."

Mara grew cold and angry inside. "*That* was your chance."

She leapt in, attacking with both hands, beating Alema's defense down with her lightsaber and thrusting for the torso with her shoto. Normally she would never have risked such an all-out attack, but Alema was not much of a challenge and Luke was running out of—

As overconfidence always does, Mara's proved costly. Alema dropped her lightsaber and stretched out her arm, driving her sharp Twi'lek finger talons into Mara's throat and twisting aside so that the short lightsaber slipped past without hitting anything.

Mara's breath stopped instantly, and she felt herself choking on something wet and warm. She started to bring her arms together, intending to cross her blades through Alema's body, then realized they had dropped to her sides. She started to bring them up, but Alema's eyes had grown dark, and tiny forks of energy were crackling across her blue face.

Mara did not have the half a second it would take to raise her arms again, so she simply threw herself backward, pulling her throat off the talons and bringing her legs up to either side of Alema's. A bolt of blue lightning crackled past above her face so close she saw it even through closed eyes.

Mara was already scissoring her feet, catching the Twi'lek below the knees with one leg and above the knees with the other. The two foes hit the floor in the same instant, Alema coming down hard on the back of her head.

The Twi'lek went instantly limp, her arms and body flopping to the floor as though her robe were filled with warm gelmeat. Mara sat up, already bringing her lightsaber around to lop off Alema's head—then stopped the blade just centimeters above the Twi'lek's throat. She could not kill an unconscious foe, even one who had betrayed the Jedi order . . . even when she was in a hurry to help Luke.

Having knocked out enough beings to be certain Alema was not faking her unconsciousness, Mara put away her weapons and spun to her knees. She could sense that Luke's strength was continuing to fade and that he was starting to doubt his ability to prevail, but leaving the Twi'lek armed and free—even when she was unconscious—was not an option.

As the exodus of patrons resumed through the hatchway, Mara bound Alema's hands behind her back and collected her lightsaber and blowgun from where they had been dropped. Then she opened the Twi'lek's robe to check for concealed weapons and was suddenly very glad she had stopped short of killing an unconscious enemy.

Under the robe, Alema wore a black combat vest with a sensor pad blinking over the heart. A bundle of thin wires ran from the pad down into a chest pocket bulging with something shaped like a thick wafer. Very carefully, Mara opened the pocket and followed the wires to what she had feared she would find: a dead-man relay connected to the proton detonator from a baradium missile.

There was no question of returning to the cantina without disconnecting the relay. Head injuries were too unpredictable. The Twi'lek could die at any moment, and even if she lived, one of the fleeing patrons might trigger the device accidentally. Unfortunately, the wires had to be disconnected in a specific sequence to keep from triggering the detonator. Mara only hoped that Luke could hold Lumiya off until she finished. Even with the Force to guide her, this was going to take time.

And time was something Luke did not have. He could feel that in the fire eating his lungs, in the raw nettling of his flesh. His breath came in inadequate gasps, and his blood was bubbling from his side in a pink froth. He was calling on the Force to keep fighting, drawing it through himself faster than his body could endure, literally boiling his own cells. At most, he had another minute of fight in him . . . maybe less.

Luke had to end this *now*.

He blocked a pair of crackling energy strands with his lightsaber and flung them aside, then launched himself across a claqball table toward Lumiya. She countered by pivoting away, bringing between them a Twi'lek serving girl. He could have continued the attack, slicing through the chests of both shield and captor, but even desperate, he could not kill a hostage. He threw himself into an aerial cartwheel and came down on a slick, utensil-strewn floor squarely facing Lumiya.

Her hand flicked, and the lightwhip came arcing toward his head. Luke dropped to his haunches and let it crackle past overhead. Then, when Lumiya started to back away from the expected lunge at her midsection, he hit her hard with a Force shove and spun her half around. She crashed into a drink table and nearly fell, but quickly brought her hostage around to protect her from an attack.

Luke smiled and raised his arm, pointing his lightsaber toward the serving girl, then using the Force to wrench her free of Lumiya's grasp, he sent her flying across the claqball table. She crashed down on the other side in a heap, screaming in terror but far safer than she had been a moment earlier.

By then Lumiya had recovered from her stumble, and the lightwhip was snaking back toward Luke. He sprang into a round-off, wrapping the tip of his blade into the crackling strands as he passed over upside down. He landed on the claqball table's squishy surface and jerked backward with all his might.

And that was when his mangled body failed him. Instead of yanking the weapon from Lumiya's hand, his lightsaber slipped out of his own grasp and went flying into the shadows.

Luke cursed in disbelief—then rolled off the table in a backward somersault.

Even *that* turned into a disaster. He landed on the body of one of Lumiya's original victims and—too weak to steady himself—hit the floor with an audible thump. He could sense Mara out in the corridor, concentrating intently on something, very frightened and urging him to wait for her, not to press the attack until she was there.

There was no chance of that. Luke's strength was failing so fast that he feared Jacen's betrayal would cost him his life. And when Lumiya was done with him, she would be free to go attack Mara, as well. His chest tightened with an emotion that might have been anger or sorrow or fear—and was probably all those things at once. Jacen had betrayed them . . . which could only mean that somewhere along the line, Luke had failed *Jacen*.

Lumiya must have suspected a trap, because when Luke failed to rise immediately, she did not rush to attack. Instead, she called, "It's not too late, Skywalker. Let me kill you now, and everyone else survives. Even Mara."

"Very generous." As Luke replied, he was inspecting the cantina floor, searching for the shoto he had lost when Lumiya took his cybernetic hand. "But I don't . . . think so. You can't have . . . Jacen."

"Jacen?" Lumiya let out a cold laugh. "What makes you think this is about *him*?"

"Your involvement with GAG." He wasn't having much success looking for his lightsabers; the blades had deactivated as soon as they left his grasp, and the cantina floor was too littered in debris and shadow for him to find anything. "Who else could give you . . . an apartment? Who else could give you access to . . . their files?"

Again, that cruel laugh. "Indeed." The lightwhip's crackling grew deeper as Lumiya shortened the strands for easier control. "Who else has access to Jacen's codes? Who *else* could give orders to GAG officers in Jacen's name?"

The questions caught Luke like a kick in the stomach. He knew that Lumiya was only trying to hurt him, that her implications were likely more false than true. But the possibility explained too much . . . and now that he thought back on Ben's behavior over the last several months, he had to admit that he had seen too much of that possibility himself.

Something crunched on the floor as Lumiya circled the base of the claqball table. Luke gave up his search for his shoto and began to look for another weapon. He had not brought his own blaster into the cantina, preferring light blades instead, but the body he had fallen on was almost certainly a spacer, and spacers *always* carried blasters.

"You're lying." Luke found the spacer's belt and followed it to a holster. "Just saying that . . . to hurt me!"

"Does that make it a lie?" Lumiya asked. "You've

caused me a lot of pain over the years, Skywalker. What better way to repay it than bringing your family legacy full circle?"

Luke knew she was only trying to twist the vibroblade, to hurt him as much as she could before she killed him—but he stuck his head up anyway.

"Stop it!" he yelled, with real anger. "You'll never make a Sith of my—"

Luke never had a chance to say *son*.

All he saw was the bright glow of Lumiya's lightwhip snaking across the claqball table barely centimeters above the surface, and he knew that his reflexes were just too slow right now, that he could not duck quickly enough to keep the whip from slicing into his brain.

So Luke simply fell backward, closing his eyes against the crackling glow as the strands swept past a finger's width above his nose, bringing up the blaster he had taken from the dead spacer's holster, allowing the Force to guide his hand, squeezing the trigger three times before he felt Lumiya's shock in the Force, then squeezing it twice more before he heard her body hit the floor.

And suddenly Mara was screaming at him from across the cantina, flooding the Force with alarm. "Stop firing!"

Luke sat up and glanced over long enough to see her in the hatchway, pushing past the last handful of stragglers—mostly wounded—who were still struggling to leave the cantina.

"You can't kill her!" Mara yelled.

Luke looked back to Lumiya and thought he had done a pretty good job of it. She was lying at the foot of the claqball table with three different columns of blaster smoke rising from her chest, her cybernetic life-support girdle sparking and sizzling with short circuits. Her lightwhip lay on the floor nearby, where she had dropped it when he blasted her. His own lightsaber lay a few meters beyond, where it had landed when she used the whip to disarm him. Luke used the Force to summon both weapons to him, then stood and went to check on her.

To his surprise, Lumiya's eyes were focused and alert—and horribly bugged out with pain. As soon as she saw him, they crinkled at the corners as though she were smiling. That tiny act made his spine ache with danger sense, but he tried not to let that show when he spoke.

"Mara's . . . coming," he gasped. "She'll try to save you—"

"Maybe not." Mara came up behind him and took one look at Lumiya, then said, "In fact, not a chance."

She grabbed Luke and tried to pull him away, but—still fighting his pain—he pulled back and remained where he was.

"Mara, we can't leave her—"

"Yes, Luke, we *can*." Mara leaned down and pulled open Lumiya's robe, revealing—aside from the blaster wounds and life-support girdle—a black combat vest with a sensor pad over the heart. The diodes were blinking weakly and erratically. "In fact, I think we'd better *run*."

chapter twenty-two

With a swarm of pincer-winged Miy'tils nibbling at the forward shields and a *Nova*-class battle cruiser chewing on the stern, Leia was jerking the pilot's yoke around at random, just trusting to the Force and blind luck to get the *Falcon* through the storm of enemy fire. How Han had done this for forty years without getting them blasted to atoms—or at least developing a nervous stomach—was beyond her imagining. She only hoped she was a good enough pilot to see them through until the Alliance's rescue fleet arrived . . . and that she had not been wrong about it coming.

Golden shimmers of dispersal energy began to appear a few meters ahead, a sign that the *Falcon*'s shields were overloading. Leia ignored the flashing maelstrom long enough to glance at the copilot's seat, where Han sat hunched over a disassembled shield-adjustment panel. C-3PO stood next to him, trying to hold the panel steady against the control board while Han worked.

"How are those shield repairs coming?"

"Even *I* can't splice a moving target," Han complained. "Hold still, Threepio!"

"It's not my fault," C-3PO replied. "Holding still is quite impossible while Princess Leia continues to evade enemy fire. The *Falcon*'s inertial compensators are simply inadequate for this kind of maneuvering."

The *Falcon* lurched forward as a turbolaser struck the rear shields, and then an alarm chime sounded from the control board, announcing a desperate need to redistribute the shield power.

"I'm *trying*," Han muttered to the chime. "I'm trying!"

Leia swung wide to avoid a flight of concussion missiles. The *Falcon* shuddered as the Noghri, operating the cannon turrets, cut loose with the quad cannons. The Miy'til that had launched the attack erupted in a boiling sphere of flame.

C-3PO squawked in alarm. "That's my hand, Captain Solo!"

"Stop whining," Han ordered. "It didn't even burn through."

"I'm still going to require a new metacarpal covering," the droid complained. "Perhaps we wouldn't need to evade so wildly if Princess Leia were to travel in a direction *opposite* the enemy."

"I *can't*, Threepio," Leia said. At the moment, she was flying away from the usurpers at a right angle, doing her best to keep the *Falcon* pointed toward the growing yellow crescent of Hapes's third moon, Megos. "We'll get caught in the crossfire."

"Crossfire?" C-3PO asked. "Between whom? I didn't see a friendly fleet exit hyperspace behind us."

"It *will* be here," Leia said.

"Sure, any day now," Han added.

Leia could hardly blame Han for his skepticism. The Alliance rescue fleet *should* already be attacking, and the brief brush of Force contact she had felt earlier was hardly confirmation of its existence. But nothing else made sense. She had sensed Jaina and Zekk watching as the *Falcon* departed the Kiris Asteroid Cluster, which could only mean that the Galactic Alliance had been waiting for the right opportunity to pounce on Corellia's secret assault fleet.

So why weren't they pouncing?

A turbolaser strike erupted close to port, throwing the *Falcon* sideways and slamming C-3PO into the back of Leia's seat. The droid bounced off and crashed to the deck, leaving a tangle of broken wires sparking in an empty control board socket.

"Oh, dear," C-3PO said from behind Leia. "I seem to have pulled the shield-adjustment panel away from the control board. Now it's going to take Captain Solo twice as long to make repairs!"

"Forget it, Threepio." The fusing pen gave a soft *snap* as Han deactivated it. "We never had a chance."

The resignation in Han's voice worried Leia more than any amount of yelling or cursing would have. It almost seemed as though he did not believe they would get out of this—as though he did not think she was a good enough pilot to save them.

"Sorry I missed your signal about the message thing," Han said to Leia. "Getting the control board shot up is going to cost us."

"No, Han, *I'm* sorry," Leia replied. With the tactical display still showing no sign of the Alliance Fleet, she was beginning to wonder if she had been right to urge Tenel Ka to stand firm in the first place. "But I'm *not* giving up." She put one hand on the throttles. "Do you see any reason I shouldn't push the engines hard?"

"You mean aside from the leaking coolant line and the number four vector plate getting sticky?"

"Yeah." Leia almost took her hand off the throttles—she hadn't noticed the sticky vector plate. "I mean aside from those two problems."

"Well, then—no, I don't." Han sounded a little more hopeful, as though taking a desperate gamble with their lives on the line was all he ever needed to cheer him up. "Let her rip, sweetheart."

Leia pointed the *Falcon*'s nose straight toward the dark interior of the crescent moon, then pushed the throttles past the overload stops and kept pushing until they would go no farther. She felt herself sink in her seat as the vessel's acceleration tested the already overburdened inertial compensators, and they shot forward into the swarm of Miy'tils that had been harassing them.

As the *Falcon* careened through their midst, the starfighters took close-range snap-shots, and space exploded into a wall of energy blossoms. The Noghri answered with the quad cannons, taking out four starfighters in half as many seconds. Then the *Falcon* was through the formation, with nothing but the crater-pocked sickle of Megos swelling rapidly in the forward canopy.

The Miy'tils launched a desperate volley of concussion missiles and turned to give chase—placing themselves between the *Falcon* and the Nova cruiser, exactly as Leia had hoped they would. Han activated the decoy launchers and the Noghri kept the quad cannons chugging, and the missiles started to vanish from the tactical display two and three at a time.

Fearful of hitting her own starfighters, the Nova quieted her turbolasers, and there was a moment of relative peace as the Miy'tils struggled to bring themselves back into cannon range and reacquire target locks. Leia kept their nose pointed straight ahead, adding gravitational pull to the ship's acceleration, and the gap between the

Falcon and Megos began to close more quickly than the one between the *Falcon* and the Miy'tils.

"Trying the old Solo Slingshot?" Han asked.

"A partial, anyway," Leia said. "Seems like a good time to learn it."

"Sure, why not?" Han replied. "You *do* know that it's a pretty tricky maneuver at full acceleration, right?"

Leia nodded. "I thought it might be."

"And if that vector plate sticks at the wrong time, you know the crater we drill is going to be about three kilometers deep?"

"I hadn't actually done the calculations," Leia admitted.

"I don't think Captain Solo has, either," C-3PO said from the deck behind her. "At our current acceleration and mass, the crater will be closer to five kilometers deep—assuming our nacelles don't overheat and vaporize us first, of course."

Leia was still digesting that cheery thought when a cold prickle ran down her spine. She glanced at the tactical display and saw that the Miy'tils were swinging hard to port, trying to open a clear firing lane for the Nova. She swung the yoke in the same direction, trying to keep the starfighters behind them and banking toward the center of the moon—in the *wrong* direction for the Slingshot maneuver.

"Uh, honey?" Han's voice was nervous and high. "That's—"

A boiling cloud of brilliance erupted to starboard, engulfing the position they had just abandoned.

"—a nice save," Han admitted. "Probably would have done the same thing myself."

"If you say so, dear."

Leia glanced at the tactical display and saw that the Nova had raised a wall of turbolaser fire alongside the

Falcon, cutting off the route she needed to follow to complete her maneuver. The Miy'tils were still close behind, steadily closing the gap. Leia cursed the competence of the enemy commander and pulled back the yoke. The number four vector plate did not respond, putting the entire ship into a dangerous, weld-cracking oscillation.

Leia reached over to back the throttles off.

"Too late!" Han warned. "Can't let them close the distance. We'll have to do a partial Reverse Slingshot."

"A partial *Reverse* Slingshot?" Leia asked. The bright side of the moon was slipping out of view, and now there was nothing but the pitch blackness of Megos's dark side ahead. "Never heard of it."

" 'Course not," Han answered. "It's new."

"New?" Leia had a sinking feeling. "Han, that vector plate is sticking again. Can't you feel the vibration?"

"Just keep the nose up," Han said. "You're doing great."

Doing great was no guarantee of survival, Leia knew, but hearing Han say it made her feel better about their odds. She continued to hold the yoke back, vibrating in her seat so hard she couldn't even read the nacelle temperature gauge—which was probably just as well, given the coolant leak and how long they'd been flying at maximum acceleration.

Too large and cumbersome to follow the *Falcon,* the Nova had to break off and turn in the opposite direction. But the Miy'tils continued to close the distance, and soon they began to pound the rear shields again. Leia could do little to stop them. With the *Falcon* shaking like a Neimoidian under interrogation and the moon's dark surface coming up rapidly, she had to concentrate all her efforts on simply retaining control of the ship.

Finally a sliver of star-dappled velvet appeared along the top of the *Falcon*'s canopy. Leia continued to hold the yoke back, her relief growing as the sliver slowly became a twenty-centimeter band of open space hanging above a dark and undulating horizon.

"Couldn't have done it better myself!" Han exclaimed, even more relieved than Leia. "Okay, now you can level off."

A staccato rumbling sounded from deep in the ship as the Miy'til laser cannons finally broke through the shields and began to hammer at the hull armor, then Megos's horizon suddenly grew jagged and stretched toward the top of the *Falcon*'s canopy again.

"A mountain range!" C-3PO cried. "*That* will certainly complicate our escape."

"*Complicate?*" Han turned to glare at the droid. "If it were *me* flying, you'd be back there yelling, *We're doomed, we're doomed!*"

"Quite likely," C-3PO admitted. "But Princess Leia is a *Jedi*."

Leia would have thanked the droid for his vote of confidence, except she was pretty sure it would seem misplaced in about three seconds. She continued to hold the yoke back, trying to will the *Falcon* to pull up faster— then noticed a jagged notch of starlight showing through the mountains ahead. She pushed the yoke to center position. The vector plate came unstuck, and the ship finally stopped vibrating.

"Uh, Leia," Han said. "That part about leveling off? You can forget—"

"Too late!" Leia swung the *Falcon* toward the notch, coming in at an angle so the nose pointed at the mountain on the far side. "Launch missiles!"

"Missiles?" Han looked forward and saw the gap opening before them, then reached out and flipped an arming switch. "Why not?"

He depressed a pair of LAUNCH buttons, and two blue circles appeared in front of the cockpit, then rapidly shrank as the missiles raced away. Leia rolled the *Falcon* up and banked into the notch with their pursuers still close behind. She was too busy flying to see what happened next, but by the time the *Falcon* reached the star-filled wedge at the other end of the gorge, the hammering on her stern had stopped.

As they shot out of the canyon, the moon's surface fell away, and Leia finally had time to risk a glance at the tactical display. The Miy'tils were gone, either destroyed when the missiles filled the gorge mouth with debris or momentarily outmaneuvered. Leia stayed within a kilometer of the surface for a few seconds to be certain no Miy'til survivors were going to pop up from behind the mountain range, then pulled the yoke back and pointed their nose away from the moon.

They had just started to climb when space ahead broke into crooked snakes of iridescence. The proximity alarm blared to life, and the viewport was suddenly packed with blue halos—all growing steadily larger.

"What the blazes?" Leia gasped.

"I think your fleet showed up," Han said. "And in the wrong place!"

Leia glanced down and found her tactical display growing more crowded by the moment. Frigates, cruisers, and Star Destroyers were reverting from hyperspace at the rate of two or three per second, all pouring starfighters into space and accelerating toward Megos at full power. The name ADMIRAL ACKBAR appeared under a Star Destroyer at the rear of the formation, and suddenly Leia understood why it had taken the Alliance so long to attack.

"That's Bwua'tu!"

"Figures," Han grumbled. "What Bothan makes a straightforward attack when he can try something tricky like coming out from behind a moon instead?"

"Well, at least they cared enough to send the best." Leia pushed the *Falcon*'s nose down and started back toward the moon. Continuing to approach a reverting fleet at this velocity was *not* an option. Even if Bwua'tu realized they were not on an attack run, the chance of a head-on collision with one of his capital ships would still force him to blast them to atoms. "What do you think? Find a crater to hide in?"

"At this velocity, we'd *make* a crater," Han said. "No time to decelerate."

"You mean—"

"Yeah," Han said. "We have to do the whole Slingshot."

"Back through the battle?" Leia asked. "With no rear shields?"

"Relax," Han said. "At this speed, we'll be on the other side of the fighting before the gunners get a lock on us."

"Which means they'll be firing at our stern," Leia pointed out. *"Where we don't have any shields!"*

"Well, yeah," Han said. "Got any better ideas?"

Leia had to admit she did not. They were in a bad spot. Of course, they had been in bad spots a hundred times before. But this time, *she* was sitting behind the pilot's yoke instead of Han . . . and he had never let *her* down.

Leia looked out the viewport and saw that they were already coming up on Megos's light side. "How are our nacelle temperatures doing?" she asked.

"Not bad," Han said. "We're only thirty-seven percent over spec."

"And you're *sure* we can go to forty?"

"Sure," Han said. "I just don't know how long we can stay there."

Leia considered reducing the throttles, but by then they were already crossing between Megos and Hapes, and a full view of the battle convinced her they would want all the velocity they could achieve. Space ahead was one big sheet of turbolaser fire, dotted by crimson knots of energy and the tiny slivers of distant ships jetting flame, vapor, and lives.

As the *Falcon* left the moon behind, a tightly packed screen of Battle Dragons—looking like stacked dashes at this distance—began to appear inside the conflagration. They were clustered in front of two thumb-sized eggs, slowly falling back toward Hapes and putting up such a wall of fire that the Corellian Dreadnaughts had been forced to abandon their penetration tactic and simply try to punch it out from short range.

"Looks like Tenel Ka trusted us."

"Yeah—I just hope it didn't get her killed," Han said. "Bwua'tu took too much time getting here. There are a lot of broken ships floating around out there."

Leia was too busy flying to check the display, but she felt certain the Bothan would disagree with Han's assessment. From a strategic viewpoint, saving Tenel Ka would be a secondary goal to destroying the Corellian fleet, since the latter would be such a crippling blow that it might well end the revolt. But Leia did not point this out to Han; it would only make him feel angry and betrayed—and the truth was, she already felt angry enough for both of them.

Seeing that it would be impossible to slip past the battle outside turbolaser range, Leia swung the *Falcon* around behind the usurper fleet and watched in horror and fascination as the combat grew larger and brighter. Within seconds the inferno filled Han's side of the canopy entirely, flashing and boiling so brilliantly that it was impossible to see the planet behind it.

The brilliance began to slip toward the back of the canopy, and still no one fired on the *Falcon*. Leia began to hope the usurpers were simply too busy to notice one little transport zipping past behind them—until her entire spine began to prickle with danger sense, and she knew they weren't that lucky.

"Seal the hatches!" she ordered.

Leia rolled them up on their side, and the ship began to vibrate violently as the sticky vector plate caught again. A meter-wide shaft of blue fire stabbed past beneath the *Falcon*'s belly, then another shot by just an arm's length above the canopy.

She pushed the yoke forward and felt it catch about halfway. The *Falcon* began to buck—then abruptly stopped when a turbolaser bolt hit the stern with a deafening clang.

Leia drew what she feared might be her last breath and turned to say good-bye to Han—then felt the yoke obey and saw stars whirling in front of them. A flurry of turbolaser bolts stabbed past harmlessly, growing thinner and more distant until they ceased altogether, and the sound of damage alarms filled the cockpit—which meant they still had air.

Leia drew back the yoke again. It was a bit sluggish, but the *Falcon* had stopped vibrating, and she quickly brought the ship under control.

Discovering that she was still looking at Han, she asked, "What happened?"

"Looks like a glancing strike to the starboard aft." His voice was steady but determined, and his gaze was fixed on the control board. "I don't think we even *have* the number three and four vector plates anymore . . . and maybe you'd better back off those throttles. We lost another coolant line."

Leia dutifully throttled back, then realized the turbolaser attacks had stopped. "Han, that's not what I mean. We're still alive."

Han finally looked up, smirking at the surprise in her voice. "Sure we are," he said. "You're a Jedi—remember?"

"Very funny," Leia replied. She checked the tactical display and saw the reason no one was shooting at them. Bwua'tu's fleet had finally rounded Megos and opened fire, ripping a hole in the flank of the usurper fleet that left no doubt about the final outcome of the battle. "But true. We just might survive this thing."

Of course, that was when the proximity alarm blared to life again. Ribbons of color danced across space ahead, then blue halos began to wink into existence and swell into the backlit forms of an oncoming fleet.

"*Another* one?" Han gasped. "What is this, a war?"

On the journey back from Terephon, the *Rover* had managed to beat the Ducha to Hapes by shaving safety margins and pushing hard between jumps. But Ben was still bringing up the comm systems when the Galney fleet slid out of hyperspace beside them and began to accelerate toward the battle. At this distance, the conflict was little more than a smudge of radiance flickering against the planet's jewel-colored face, but Ben could feel it tearing at him inside; could feel all those lives fluttering out. It reminded him of why he had tried to hide from the Force when he was younger—of the constant sensation of anguish that was all he remembered about the war with the Yuuzhan Vong.

Except now Ben was older. He knew it was not the

Force causing all that pain; it was people. He knew that people could be selfish and frightened and noble and brave, and when all those things got mixed up together, wars got started. That was why the galaxy needed someone like Jacen: to straighten things out so there wouldn't be so much suffering.

The comm system finally completed its postjump diagnostics, and Ben started to set it to Tenel Ka's command channel.

"Jedi Skywalker!" Ioli snapped. She turned her noseless face toward Ben. "What *are* you doing?"

His hand hovered above the input pad. "If Tenel Ka lets the Ducha come in behind her—"

"The lieutenant knows what will happen, son," said Tanogo, the chief petty officer who operated the snoop station behind Ben. "She asked what *you* were doing."

Ben glanced over his shoulder at the huge-headed Bith. "Opening a comm channel?"

"With the enemy so close we can read the names on the sides of their ships?" Tanogo riffled his cheek folds. "We wouldn't last ten seconds."

"But we've got to warn Tenel Ka!" Ben turned back to Ioli. "And we're not going to reach her before the Ducha does."

"Can't you do something with the Force?" Ioli asked.

Ben shook his head. "It wouldn't be specific enough. She'd know there was danger, and she might even sense I meant there was treachery. But it's still just a feeling, and in the middle of a battle—"

"She'll be feeling those concerns anyway." Ioli let her breath buzz out, then said, "Very well—but we'll do this with a voice recording. And bear in mind we'll be sending it over the hailing channel."

Ben frowned. "I don't understand."

"We have to be sure it gets to her," Tanogo said from behind Ben. "And since the traitors may still have someone close to the Queen Mother intercepting messages—"

"—we want *everyone* to hear the warning," Ben said, nodding. "It's the recording part I don't get. Why can't I just—"

"Jedi Skywalker, do you really expect me to explain my orders?" Ioli demanded. "Tenel Ka is running out of time, so make your report brief and to the point."

Ben cringed—more from the anger in her presence than the sharpness in her voice.

"Okay—sorry." He opened a recording file, then spoke into the comm microphone. "This is Jedi Ben Skywalker with an urgent warning for the Hapan Royal Navy. Ducha Galney is a verified traitor coming to launch a sneak attack on the Queen Mother. Repeat urgent warning: Ducha Galney is a traitor. Take all precautions."

Ben finished and looked over for Ioli's approval, but found her returning the intercom microphone to its cradle.

She hooked a thumb toward the rear of the skiff. "The others are getting ready to go EV. Join them."

"Copy." Still stinging from the last time he had questioned Ioli's orders, Ben unbuckled his crash webbing and rose—then realized what she intended to do and stopped between their seats. "Wait a minute—we have six people and only four suits."

"You think I don't know that?" she asked.

"Yes—I mean no," he said. "I know you do. But there has to be another way."

She looked at him with an expression that seemed more impatient than hopeful. "You have one?"

Unable to think while he was looking into her eyes, Ben let his gaze drop to the deck. Both she and the chief seemed so calm and focused, but he could feel their fear in his own stomach, a fluttering ball of Force energy that made him want to throw up.

When Ben did not answer quickly, Ioli said, "I didn't think so." She checked the chrono on the control panel. "The chief says I need to send your message in two minutes and twelve seconds to give the Queen Mother a fighting chance. It's going to take you three to put on that suit."

"What about a message beacon?"

"Great idea," Tanogo said. "If recon skiffs *carried* message beacons."

"Go, Ben." Ioli pointed aft. "And that's an order."

"I can't just leave you to die," Ben said, remaining where he was. "I'm a Jedi."

"You're going to be a dead Jedi, because I *am* going to send this report in exactly—" Ioli checked the chrono again. "—one minute and fifty-two seconds."

Tanogo grabbed Ben's arm. "We're *scouts*, son. This sort of thing goes with the shoulder patch." He pulled Ben out of the cockpit and pushed him aft. "Go on, now. We'll swing back and pick you up if we don't get vaped."

Ben stumbled aft, feeling guilty and confused, thinking it should be him and Jaina staying behind while the rest of the crew went EV. But after so many days sitting beside Ioli in the cockpit, he knew without asking that she would view any such offer as an insult to both her and her crew. Even with the Force, he and Jaina would not be able to handle the unfamiliar skiff as well as Tanogo and Ioli could. Besides, the *Rover* was *their* ship, so it was *their* duty to send the report—and in Admiral Niathal's new military, an officer simply did not hand off her duty to someone else.

Ben reached the back of the cabin, where Gim Sorzo,

the *Rover*'s Twi'lek gunner, was just sealing his neck ring. Jaina and Zekk—who had already been Force-hibernating inside evac suits to avoid straining the *Rover*'s limited life-support systems—were buttoned up and waiting outside the evacuation cabinet, where the last suit hung open and ready.

Ben stepped into the legs and shoved his arms down the sleeves, and Jaina depressed the emergency tab on the shoulder. As the suit sealed itself, Zekk slipped the helmet over Ben's head and closed the neck ring. Less than a minute later, the helmet speaker chirped to confirm the suit's spaceworthiness, and the three Jedi crowded into the air lock with Sorzo.

Ben had just closed the inner hatch when his own voice began to come over the helmet speaker. *"This is Jedi Ben Skywalker with an urgent warning—"*

"Line up," Jaina's voice cut in. "Blowing the hatch in three . . . two . . ."

As she counted, they hooked their tether lines to one another and arranged themselves for an emergency exit, with Jaina in front of the hatch and Sorzo behind her, wrapping his arms around her waist. Ben stood beside the Twi'lek, holding on to a grab bar with one hand. Zekk stood in the corner beside him, clutching the bar with both hands.

"One."

Jaina hit the emergency release, and the outer hatch tumbled away in a cloud of smoke and escaping atmosphere. Jaina and Sorzo were drawn out of the lock directly behind it. Ben's hold on the grab bar delayed him for the half a second it took Jaina and Sorzo to clear the exit; then his hand came free and he was sucked out the hatchway. His visor fogged instantly, and he felt the tether jerk as Zekk was pulled into the void behind him.

His stomach began to turn somersaults as they left the *Rover*'s artificial gravity behind, but all sensation of motion ceased. Ben listened as his own voice continued to come over his helmet speaker, urging Tenel Ka to *"Take all precautions."* Then a soft click sounded as the suit's comm receiver automatically switched to the *Rover*'s intercom channel.

"Watch your eyes," Ioli's voice warned. "*Rover* moving off."

"Thanks," Jaina said. "And may the Force be with you."

"Same to you," Ioli replied. "*Rover* out."

The skiff's ion engines flared to life, brightening space so intensely that Ben's eyes hurt even through a darkened visor and closed lids.

The glow diminished a couple of seconds later, and Ben opened his eyes to find the fog cleared from his visor. The star-dappled void was whirling by at dizzying speed, and every once in a while he caught a glimpse of battle flash, or of his companions twirling around on their tether pivots.

Ben activated his suit thrusters and brought his own tumble under control, then spun himself toward Hapes. The Ducha's fleet had already opened fire on Ioli and Tanogo, concealing the planet behind a wall of streaking energy. He could barely make out the *Rover,* a finger-length sliver of darkness trailing an efflux helix as Ioli tried to spiral her way to salvation.

A stripe of turbolaser fire touched the head of the spiral and blossomed into a boiling ball of flame. Ben could not tell whether the anguish he felt was in the Force—or in him.

chapter twenty-three

In the Command Salon holodisplay, it all looked so neat and orderly. The planet Hapes loomed at the back of the projection, a bulging wall of light with dull green islands scattered across basic blue ocean. The battle itself was an arrow-headed column of blue "friendly" symbols driving through a block of red "hostiles." The friendlies were trying to reach an amorphous mass—identified in blue as the HAPAN ROYAL NAVY—that was swarming a pair of ovoid symbols designated UNKNOWN. A reinforcing fleet labeled GALNEY was racing in from the periphery of the Hapan gravity well, its designator colors changing from friendly blue to hostile red as it traveled.

But Jacen knew what the battle was really like. He could feel it in the hundreds of life-presences winking out every second, in the waves of anguish rolling through the Force ever more powerfully. Most of all, he could sense it in Tenel Ka, in the carefully controlled anger he perceived when he reached out to her, in the fear and sadness she felt over the outcome. Was *this* what he had been fighting to protect all his life, a civilization that devoured itself?

Was *this* the higher purpose Vergere had shaped him to serve—a society that sent assassins to murder children?

A subtle pressure in the Force drew Jacen's attention to his aide, Orlopp. He turned to find the Jenet just looking up from the datapad in his hands.

"Yes?" Jacen asked.

Orlopp's big snout twitched uneasily. It always disconcerted him to be anticipated, but Jacen didn't care. Orlopp was monitoring two crucial situations on his datapad, and he had orders to interrupt immediately if the status of either changed.

When Orlopp took too long to compose his thoughts, Jacen snatched the datapad from his hands. "I can't wait all day, Lieutenant."

Jacen's eyes went first to the left corner of the display, which showed an image of his cabin, where Allana sat on the floor playing with a pair of simple rag dolls. Scattered around her was a GAG special assault squad with orders to kill anyone attempting to enter the room. The other corner of the display showed Aurra Sing lying unconscious on the floor of a durasteel cell, secured at the wrist and ankle by stun cuffs and fastened to the wall at three points by heavy chains.

Only then, once he was sure that his daughter was safe and her attacker was still incapacitated, did Jacen read the message on the lower part of the display.

"What's this about Alliance rescue beacons, Lieutenant?"

"The Signals Deck started to pick them up as soon as we reverted, sir. They're about . . . *here*."

Orlopp extended a finger into the holodisplay, indicating a position on the far side of Galney's reinforcement fleet. But Jacen's mind had wandered again, his gaze drifting back to the fight above Hapes. After the attack on his daughter, and with her mother in danger *now*, he was finding it hard to concentrate on his command duties. He wanted to be in a starfighter whisking Allana to safety on some anonymous world where this kind of danger could never find her.

But that would not save Tenel Ka. She was down there in battle, probably aboard one of the five Battle Dragons fighting from a standoff position at the rear of the Royal Navy.

"Colonel?" Orlopp flicked his finger, drawing Jacen's attention back to the question of the rescue beacons—which were located squarely on the opposite side of the Galney reinforcement fleet from the *Anakin Solo*. "I was debating whether to bother you with this at all, since any rescue vessel we dispatch will probably be destroyed. To retrieve the stranded personnel, we'd have to divert the entire fleet."

"Obviously." Jacen continued to study the hologram, wondering what could have caused an Alliance crew to go EV so far from the main battle. "Any idea who—"

"Colonel Solo." The interruption came from Major Espara, the pale-skinned woman Tenel Ka had sent along to serve as a liaison officer to the Royal Battle Dragons in his task force. "I *hope* you're not even going to consider diverting this fleet to rescue a handful of your people. The Queen Mother is already in danger, and if you allow Ducha Galney's reinforcements—"

"I assure you my understanding of the Queen Mother's danger is far clearer than *yours*," Jacen replied, rather sharply. He returned his attention to Orlopp. "Have the Signals Deck place a tracking lock on the beacons. We'll attend to them after the Queen Mother is safe."

Orlopp punched a button on his datapad, sending an

order that he had obviously prepared in anticipation of Jacen's decision.

When the Jenet did not look away, Jacen asked, "Is there something else, Lieutenant?"

"There is," Orlopp replied. "The message dinghy you dispatched to Roqoo Depot was waiting to be taken aboard when we reverted from hyperspace."

Jacen frowned. "And?"

"And the hangar chief is suspicious, Colonel," Orlopp said. "The pilot is requesting an immediate audience with you, and there's some question as to how she could have known our reversion coordinates."

"Commend the chief on his caution," Jacen said. "And tell him to get that pilot up here *now*."

For someone like Lumiya, foreseeing the *Anakin*'s reversion coordinates would have required only a little guesswork and some Force meditation. Jacen was far more surprised that she had returned at all, since he had felt nothing in the Force to suggest that either Luke or Mara had been killed.

It occurred to him that Lumiya might have foreseen his trap and avoided the confrontation entirely. He wondered briefly if her return ought to worry him, but—despite the reservations she had expressed recently about his ability to make the necessary sacrifices to bring order to the galaxy—he was well aware that Lumiya needed *him* more than he needed her.

In the holodisplay, the Galney fleet began to glow more brightly as the *Anakin Solo* closed to within range of its new, long-distance turbolasers. The usurper reinforcements continued toward Hapes at maximum acceleration, clearly convinced they could reach the battle and kill Tenel Ka before Jacen's task force caught up to them.

Jacen used the Force to depress a button on the wall, activating an intercom microphone. "Commander Twizzl, time to grab their attention. Attack at your discretion."

Twizzl's voice came over the speaker. "Very good, Colonel."

A few moments later the *Anakin*'s long-range turbo-laser batteries unleashed a salvo, causing the lights to flicker and the ventilation fans to slow. In less critical parts of the ship, the effects would be even worse, plunging corridors into temporary darkness and forcing electronic systems to switch to battery power. The new turbolasers were cutting-edge technology, but they required so much power that they were unlikely to become standard armament anytime soon.

A moment after the first volley, one of the Galney Battle Dragons started to flash with damage. The lights in the Command Salon flickered again, and then the vessel vanished from the holodisplay. Apparently, the *Anakin* had caught the target with her shields still balanced forward.

"Well done," Jacen said. He turned to Espara. "Would you give the Queen Mother's Battle Dragons clearance to open fire, as soon as they're within range?"

"Of course, Colonel."

As Espara spoke into her comlink, Jacen took the opportunity to glance over Orlopp's shoulder and confirm that Sing was still in her cell. Her door had been welded shut, she had not been given the antidote to Allana's paralyzing drug, and a constant stream of sleep-inducing coma gas was being piped into her cell, but Jacen had to be sure. She had already demonstrated that she understood the value of timing an attack, so if she was going to attempt an escape, it would be soon.

"Sir?" Orlopp asked.

"Just checking." Jacen glanced at the image of his cabin

and found Allana still playing on the floor. "You can't be too careful."

"No, sir, you can't." Orlopp's tone was routine, but he was pouring concern into the Force. "I'm keeping a very close eye on the situation, Colonel . . . you don't have to worry about *that*."

"Good," Jacen said, realizing that he was drawing concern from more people in the cabin than just Orlopp. "Thank you."

He returned his gaze to the holodisplay. Several Galney Battle Dragons were flashing with damage, and there were holes in the formation where two more had already been destroyed. It was far more damage than the *Anakin* could do with three long-range turbolaser batteries.

Jacen turned to Espara. "I didn't know the Queen Mother's Battle Dragons had been equipped with long-range turbolasers."

Espara granted him a rare smile. "I'm sorry, Colonel. Admiral Pellaeon was kind enough to share the technology after the Queen Mother assigned two fleets to the Galactic Alliance. The Royal High Commander instructed me to reveal the upgrade only on a need-to-know basis."

"I see." Jacen was irritated, but not surprised. Even among allies, secrets were not shared easily. "And how widespread is this technology in the Consortium?"

"It's not. So far, the only Battle Dragons carrying the new turbolasers are in our task force." Espara turned back to the holodisplay, where several more of the usurpers' vessels were blinking. "Perhaps that will change after the Queen Mother sees how effective they are."

"Don't count on it." Jacen nodded toward the holodisplay. The rear elements of Galney's reinforcement fleet were splitting off to meet the *Anakin* and her task force.

"Now that the element of surprise is gone, the new turbo-lasers will lose effectiveness fast."

Galney's ships were already pouring clouds of starfighters into space, trying to set up a defensive screen so the leading elements of the traitor fleet could continue the attack on Tenel Ka. Jacen's task force began to decelerate and spread out, preparing to launch its own starfighters and take advantage of their long-range turbolasers to soften up the enemy before fully engaging.

"Colonel Solo, we can't stop to fight," Espara said. She pointed at Tenel Ka's small flotilla. "The Queen Mother will be pinned against the planetary shields."

"I see that, Major." Jacen knew better than to suggest Tenel Ka could retreat planetside; there were too many enemy vessels nearby. If she had the planetary shields lowered, they would simply follow her through and take out the generator stations. "Are you suggesting a breakthrough attempt?"

Espara nodded. "We have no choice. If we slow down to fight here, by the time we reach the Queen Mother, she'll be in an escape pod trying to dodge Miy'tils."

Espara was right, and Jacen knew it. Even with half the Galney fleet hanging back to fight his task force, the Queen Mother's flotilla would still be outnumbered nearly three to one. What Espara did *not* know was that any breakthrough attempt would also put at risk the life of the Consortium's Chume'da, Allana—and Jacen felt certain Tenel Ka would not want that any more than he did.

Espara frowned. "Colonel Solo, you are wasting valuable—"

Jacen silenced her with a raised hand. "*Thinking* is not a waste of time." He activated the intercom microphone again. "Commander Twizzl, how many Battle Dragons would be required to have a reasonable chance of breaking through that screen? And bear in mind they'll need to have enough strength left to continue pursuit."

Twizzl's answer came immediately. "It would be better to send us *all*. That's our best chance."

"I didn't ask for our best chance," Jacen countered. "I need a *reasonable* chance."

Twizzl was silent for an instant, then said, "Eighteen, sir. Berda believes that strength would give the task force a sixty-three percent chance of disrupting the Galney attack on the Queen Mother."

"Then that's what we'll do, Captain," Jacen said. Berda was the *Anakin*'s tactical computer, a powerful mainframe operated by a squad of Bith programmers. "Have the other two Battle Dragons stand off with the *Anakin*."

"*Stand off?*" Espara echoed. "Colonel Solo, a sixty-three percent chance of saving the Queen Mother's life is not good enough. You may be too much of a coward to send in the *Anakin*, but I assure you every Hapan—"

"That's quite enough, Major."

Jacen made a pinching motion with his fingers, and Espara was suddenly too busy gasping for breath to continue speaking. Her accusation stung more than he cared to admit, in part because it was so true—at least when it came to Allana. He was too afraid of losing his daughter to risk her life in the middle of a pitched starship battle, and it really didn't matter that Tenel Ka *would want* him to make this decision. The simple fact was that there were some things he would never sacrifice—not even if it meant saving the galaxy.

When Jacen continued to hold his Force choke, Espara's gasping changed to a desperate gurgling, and her hands rose to her throat. Her two aides scowled in alarm, and they stepped forward to shield her, automatically reaching for sidearms they were not permitted to carry aboard the *Anakin.*

Jacen froze them with a glance, then turned back to Espara. "Your dedication is commendable, Major. But there are facets of the situation that you're unaware of, and I am doing *exactly* as the Mother Queen would wish. Is that clear?"

Espara nodded and braced her hand on the arm of one of her aides.

"I'm glad we understand each other." Jacen released his Force choke and allowed her to gulp down a long breath, then held out his hand. "I doubt it will be necessary for you to communicate with Her Majesty's Battle Dragons until after the battle. I'll take your comlinks now."

Espara reluctantly passed over her own comlink and nodded to her aides to do the same.

"Thank you." Jacen slipped the devices into his uniform pocket, then turned back to the holodisplay feeling worried and useless. The eighteen Battle Dragons he had dispatched to save Tenel Ka were already closing on Galney's defensive screen. Clouds of starfighters were pouring into space between them, and vessels on both sides were already blinking and starting to fall out of formation.

Jacen could not help thinking that the intelligence provided by his parents had so far been more of a curse than a blessing. It had not prevented Aurra Sing's attack on Allana, but it *had* sent him to Relephon with a sizable piece of the Royal Navy at exactly the wrong time—a blunder that might well end up costing Hapes her queen . . . and Allana her mother.

The *Anakin* and its two escorts were concentrating their fire along one flank, trying to help open a hole through the screen. But the usurpers adjusted quickly, sliding a fresh vessel into place each time an old one was destroyed, compressing their formation as their attackers drew closer. The pursuit detail was already down to fourteen Battle Dragons, and a third of those were blinking with various degrees of damage.

Jacen felt Orlopp's attention. He looked over and waited until the Jenet was actually looking at him, then cast a meaningful glance at the datapad.

"Everything all right there?"

"Nothing has changed." Orlopp's voice held a note of distress over Jacen's apparent obsession with monitoring the assassin and the girl in his cabin. "The pilot you asked to see has arrived."

"Good," Jacen said. "We'll need a few moments of privacy."

Happy to escape Jacen's presence, Espara and her aides left immediately, followed closely by his own staff. Only Orlopp lingered.

"Is there something else, Lieutenant?"

"There is," Orlopp said. "You probably don't need to be concerned, but we may not need to send anyone after those rescue beacons we detected. The Signals Deck reports a private transport headed their way."

"Good. Have Signals track the vessel, and we'll make contact after the battle."

"Very good, sir." Orlopp flipped the datapad up under his wrist and turned toward the exit. "I'll send the pilot in now."

"Thank you." Jacen extended his hand. "But leave the datapad."

Orlopp wrinkled his snout in concern, but passed over the datapad and departed. Jacen checked the display to make certain his daughter was indeed okay, as Orlopp had reported, then set the unit on a table and blanked the screen. His conversation with Lumiya was going to be difficult enough without having to explain his obsession with safeguarding Allana.

A moment later, a slender woman in a black flight suit appeared in the doorway, her face concealed behind a closed helmet visor. Jacen immediately had the sense that something was wrong—not dangerous, but not what he had expected, either. For a moment he thought the cause might be his own feelings. Perhaps he was merely nervous about meeting Lumiya after he had tried to set her up at Roqoo Depot. Or perhaps his real fear was that she had prevailed after all—that Luke and Mara were dead.

Then Jacen noticed how much taller and more slender this pilot was than Lumiya, how bulky her helmet was in back, how one shoulder sagged. He let his hand drop to his lightsaber.

"That's far enough until I see your face."

The pilot stopped, and a dark flutter of amusement rippled unevenly through the Force. Leaving one hand to hang useless at her side, she reached up with the other and released the neck ring.

"You mustn't kill us." Even modulated through a helmet speaker, her voice sounded silky and half familiar—and it definitely did not belong to Lumiya. "We have news of your Master."

"My Master?"

"Your *Sith* Master . . . Lumiya." The helmet rose, revealing a once-beguiling face that had gone hard and sharp. "Surely, you're curious about what became of her at Roqoo Depot?"

A pillar of fire rose inside Jacen. Alema Rar had been a Gorog Joiner, a member of the Killik nest that had tried to kill his daughter as a newborn—and now here she was aboard the same ship as Allana. Before he knew it, Jacen had ignited his lightsaber and grabbed her in the Force.

Alema allowed him to draw her closer, her eyes gleaming with unbalanced delight. "You would do it," she snickered. "You would kill us without a thought!"

Startled by the truth in her words, Jacen released her.

"Without *hesitation*," he corrected. How many times had Lumiya told him he could not be a servant to his emotions? If he wanted to restore order, his emotions had to serve *him*. "But I have been thinking about it. I've thought about it a lot."

"That is nice to know, Jacen." Alema's lip curled into an odd sneer, what she probably intended to be a coy smile that her haggard face could no longer muster. "We have been thinking about *you*, too."

"And that *still* sends a creep down my back," Jacen replied. "Now, since I really doubt you came here to fulfill a death wish, why don't you tell me about Lumiya?"

Alema raised one thin eyebrow. "You don't deny that she is your Master?"

Jacen shrugged. "I doubt there would be much use in it." He glanced at the holodisplay, where his pursuit detail was just crashing into the screen of Galney ships, then added, "And I'm kind of in the middle of something, as you can see."

Alema's gaze went from the holodisplay to his lightsaber, and she retreated a step.

"Go ahead and kill us, then. You *should*." Despite the Twi'lek's words, she seemed clearly less confident about her chances of leaving the salon alive than she had been a few minutes earlier. "We are the only ones who know Allana's heritage—aside from you and Tenel Ka, of course."

Jacen's hatred welled up inside him again—or perhaps this time it was alarm. He had always worried that the

Gorog had been told the secret of his daughter's heritage when they were engaged to assassinate her. Now Alema had confirmed his fears, and he ached to do exactly as she suggested and snuff the life from her twisted body.

But it had to be a trap—the Twi'lek would never have tempted him if protecting his secret were as simple as killing *her*.

"I've never liked threats," Jacen warned. "These days, I don't tolerate them at all."

"Then it is a good thing we were not making a threat," Alema replied coolly. "We were making a suggestion. Gorog tried to kill your daughter. We are all that remains of Gorog. You *should* kill us."

"And have gossipvids claiming that I'm Allana's father start popping up all over the Consortium?"

"Did we say that would happen?" Alema asked innocently. "We are concerned with higher purposes, Jacen. We serve the Balance."

Jacen knew better than to believe her. Alema Rar would never have come within a light-year of him without some means of assuring her safety, and the most likely form of that assurance was the very threat she had so skillfully avoided making directly. Were Alema to fail to leave the *Anakin* alive, he had no doubt that the secret of his daughter's heritage would quickly become public knowledge.

Jacen considered killing the Twi'lek anyway, thinking it might be better for the secret of Allana's paternity to come out now, while the Consortium was already in such disarray. But that decision was not his to make—at least not while Tenel Ka was still alive.

He glanced at the holodisplay and saw that the issue of the Queen Mother's survival remained undecided. Though the flotilla he had sent to save her was down to ten vessels, three Battle Dragons had penetrated deep into the defensive screen and were close to breaking through—provided they did not take much more damage. Their designators were already blinking rapidly.

Jacen deactivated his lightsaber and turned back to Alema. "As tempting as I find your invitation, I prefer to let you live for now. Tell me what happened at Roqoo."

Alema's face relaxed, and she said simply, "We failed."

"We?" Jacen asked. "Who is we? *You?* You and the Killiks? You and—?"

"Lumiya," Alema said. "We have been working with her for some time."

The Twi'lek risked taking one step closer, then went on to explain how she had stumbled across Tresina Lobi spying on Ben in Fellowship Plaza, and how she had helped Lumiya kill her. After that, Lumiya had agreed they should work together. Alema had gone on to assassinate several members of the Bothan True Victory Party, then boarded the *Anakin Solo* with Lumiya and accompanied her to Roqoo Depot to attack the Skywalkers.

"Wait," Jacen said. "Lumiya *knew* they would be there?"

"Of course—she knew the best way for you to deal with their suspicions was to betray her and send her to fight them." Alema reached for his forearm—then, when he jerked it away, pretended not to be bothered. "Your Master was very proud of you, Jacen. By betraying her, you proved that you have the strength to fulfill your destiny."

"I don't know which I find harder to believe," Jacen scoffed, "that Lumiya would work with *you*, or that she would be proud of me for setting her up."

"Believe both," Alema retorted. "We both worried that you were more committed to your family than to your mission, but your answer to Luke's suspicion convinced us we were wrong. You used everyone brilliantly—Lumiya *and* your aunt and uncle. It proved you are capable of anything."

"Thanks," Jacen said, more surprised than sincere. He was finding it hard to ignore the details Alema knew about his relationship with Lumiya, but something still wasn't adding up. "You said Lumiya *knew* she was being set up to fight the Skywalkers?"

"Of course," Alema said. "Lumiya was a Sith, after all."

"And she went? And *still* got killed?"

Alema nodded. "She knew that killing your uncle was the best way to ensure your success, but she couldn't be certain of her victory. So she wore a proton detonator on her chest. When her heartbeat stopped, the detonator exploded. We are sorry."

"You saw her die?"

Alema shook her head. "We're still here, are we not? But Lumiya couldn't have survived. The entire cantina was destroyed. Even your aunt and uncle escaped by only two minutes." The Twi'lek paused for a moment, then added, "That's why we came back—to warn you that they'll be returning to Hapes as soon as they make repairs."

"Repairs?"

Alema's eyes twinkled mischievously. "The *Jade Shadow* suffered a mysterious rupture of a containment line," she said. "The repairs won't be simple."

"And you arranged this because . . . ?"

"Because you needed time to prepare," Alema said. "The Skywalkers know that you set *them* up, too."

Jacen frowned. He was growing increasingly troubled by Alema's story, though only because he sensed that she was telling the truth—at least as *she* knew it. His plan *had* been to use the Skywalkers' own fears against them by making it appear that Lumiya had been following Ben. Clearly, something had gone wrong.

"What about Ben?" Jacen asked.

For the first time, Alema looked confused. "Ben?"

"Did he survive the explosion?"

Alema frowned. "Ben was never there," she said. "That's how the Skywalkers know you betrayed them."

Jacen's stomach sank. If Ben had never made the rendezvous, naturally the Skywalkers would have believed Roqoo Depot was a trap. But then where *had* Ben gone? The sinking feeling in Jacen's stomach grew cold, and he turned back to the holodisplay.

The rescue flotilla—or rather, the eight Battle Dragon designators still blinking on the holodisplay—had finally broken through. They would soon be in full pursuit of the Galney force moving against Tenel Ka. But Jacen's gaze went to a position on the far side of the battered defensive screen, where a blinking transport symbol labeled LONG-SHOT was gliding toward the tiny blue blips of four Alliance rescue beacons.

"What is so interesting there?" Alema asked, following his gaze.

Instead of answering, Jacen oriented himself toward the real, physical rescue beacons, then reached out in the Force and sensed four presences—three of them familiar. They seemed healthy, though perhaps a little impatient, frightened, and—at least in Jaina's case—angry. Jacen didn't bother even trying to guess why the three Jedi had returned the *Rover* to Hapes instead of obeying their orders to rendezvous at Roqoo Depot—or how they had gotten themselves blasted out of their skiff. He simply flooded his presence with reassurance and tried to project that to them, so they would know help was on the way.

Zekk and Ben responded by projecting feelings of gratitude toward him. Jaina simply shut down.

"Isn't the *Longshot* one of the *Falcon*'s false transponder codes?" Alema asked.

Jacen turned and found her frowning at the *Longshot*'s designator symbol. "It might be."

If Alema noticed the suspicion and hostility in his tone, she ignored it. "Do you think that is a good idea?"

"Do I think *what* is a good idea?" Jacen asked.

"Allowing your parents to take your apprentice hostage," she said.

"Don't try that on *me*, Alema," Jacen said, scowling. "I know how the Dark Nest worked—remember?"

"How could we forget?" Alema turned to him, the hatred in her eyes now open and honest. "We would never try to use our powers on *you*, Jacen. You have already proved that you are too powerful and smart for *us*."

"Just so we understand each other." Jacen waved her toward the door. "My parents are going to *help* Ben and the others, not take them hostage."

"If that's what you believe, then we're sure we are wrong," Alema said. "We are hardly as well informed as you are."

"Wrong about what?" Jacen asked. He knew this was how the Dark Nest had worked—by using a victim's own doubts against him—but Jacen would have *known* if Alema was using the Force. "You don't expect me to believe my parents would harm Jaina or Ben."

"They would never do *that*," Alema agreed. "Only, we thought they had taken Corellia's side in this war."

"They have," Jacen admitted. "That doesn't mean they're terrorists."

"Then we must have heard wrong," Alema said. "We

thought they had been involved in the assassination attempt on your daughter."

"They weren't," Jacen said tersely. "That was a misunderstanding."

"No doubt," Alema said. "After Roqoo Depot, we know you would never let a personal attachment prevent you from making a necessary sacrifice."

"I *wouldn't*," Jacen said.

"We believe you." Alema used the Force to retrieve her helmet, then turned toward the door. "Perhaps we should be going—if you are going to permit us to leave."

Jacen nodded. "Lieutenant Orlopp will arrange an escort for you." His hands ached to kill the Twi'lek, but he did not dare—not while he suspected it would expose the secret of Allana's paternity. "You may consider the message dinghy a gift from the Galactic Alliance."

Alema lifted her brow in surprise. "Thank you."

"But if my relationship to Allana is ever exposed, I'll hunt you down myself."

"Have no fear, Colonel Solo," Alema said. "Your secret is safe with us. We know it is the only reason we are leaving here alive."

Jacen nodded. "I'm glad we understand each other." He waited until she reached the door, then added, "There's just one more thing, Alema. If you ever come within a light-year of my family again, I won't be so forgiving."

Alema smiled and nodded. "Of course—we understand." She used one hand and the Force to lift the helmet onto her head. "The Balance must be served."

The Twi'lek lowered the visor and went out the door. Jacen activated the intercom and asked Orlopp to arrange an escort for her, then retrieved his datapad and checked to see that his daughter was still safe—and her assassin still locked away.

Orlopp's voice sounded from the door. "I've arranged the escort, Colonel. Would you like us to return now?"

"In a minute, Lieutenant. I need to think."

Jacen went to the holodisplay, where the six surviving Battle Dragons of his rescue flotilla were in full pursuit of the Galney attackers. The remains of the defensive screen—seven rapidly blinking Battle Dragons and a like number of Nova cruisers—were gathering to give chase, but Jacen had anticipated that possibility and had a plan to stop them. Tenel Ka's small force was already laying fire on the leading elements of the Galney fleet, and he thought it more likely than not that the Queen Mother would survive.

Jacen's gaze shifted to the tiny blue blips that represented Ben's and Jaina's and Zekk's rescue beacons. The *Longshot*'s designator was only a couple of centimeters away from them now. He *knew* Alema had been trying to make him doubt his parents' intentions, but she was gone, and those doubts remained. There were too many unanswered questions about his parents' role in the attempt on Tenel Ka's life—and the intelligence they had provided had been more harmful than useful.

The fact was, Jacen had begun to question his parents' motives *before* Alema ever boarded the *Anakin*—when he returned from Relephon to find Tenel Ka already under attack. Of course, he knew that the great Han and Leia Solo were capable of playing double agents. He had simply *refused* to believe they would participate in a cold-blooded assassination attempt against a friend.

Lumiya had been right. Jacen *had* put loyalty to family above his mission. He *had* balked at the necessary sacrifices. And that hesitation had nearly cost Allana her mother and Hapes a Queen Mother, had come close to costing the Alliance one of her most important member states . . . and maybe even the war.

Jacen motioned Orlopp and the others back into the salon, then activated the intercom. "Commander Twizzl, the time has come to smash the usurpers. Order the *Anakin* and her escorts to advance and engage—we need to wipe those Galney Battle Dragons off the tail of our rescue flotilla."

"Very good, sir." Twizzl's voice was happy. "And nicely done, if I may say so."

"You may, Commander," Jacen said. "And I have one other order. Have one of our long-range batteries target the *Longshot*."

There was a moment of silence, then Twizzl said, "But, Colonel, the *Longshot* is a false transponder code. That transport is really—"

"Stop wasting time," Jacen said. "I'd like the vessel destroyed *before* it reaches those rescue beacons."

There was a moment of stunned silence, then Twizzl said, "Colonel Solo . . . the *Longshot* is almost on them now."

"I *understand* the risks, Commander." Jacen checked the datapad one more time and found Allana smiling up into the cam. Her eyes were sparkling with confidence and trust, and he knew he was doing the right thing for her—and for all the children of the galaxy. "Assign our best gunnery team and fire away."

chapter twenty-four

The air lock had almost finished equalizing when a boom like a meteor strike resonated through the *Falcon*'s hull. The corridor dropped away, and Han hit the ceiling—or rather, it hit him. An instant later he found himself plastered to the deck with no memory of leaving the ceiling. His head was aching and his shoulder was throbbing, and his ears weren't ringing—they were *blaring*.

Han rolled to his side and lay there suffering, trying to sort out what had happened—trying to sort out the whole last couple of months, as a matter of fact, how he and Leia had gotten themselves involved in another war and what made this one worse than the others, so much more painful and confusing.

Then a scrap of flimsiplast tumbled past, bouncing along the deck past Han's nose, and suddenly it didn't matter what had happened. The blaring was not in his ears at all. It was coming from the intercom speakers, and it was slowly—though steadily—rising in pitch.

The cabin pressure was dropping.

Han scrambled to his feet, then stepped over to the control panel next to the air lock and silenced the emergency alarm.

Leia's voice came over the ship intercom instantly, backed by a chorus of chimes and buzzers that suggested the *Falcon*'s systems were sinking faster than a comet down a black hole.

"Han? You okay?"

"Yeah, so far." Realizing he would need both hands to make repairs, Han tried to pull his arm out of the sling—and nearly collapsed with pain. He was going to need help. "But I can't waste time talking about it. We've got a pressure leak somewhere."

"A *leak*?" C-3PO asked, also speaking over the intercom from the cockpit. "Captain Solo, you have only one functional arm. You'll never be able to—"

"I'll *handle* it." Han peeked through the hatch viewport and was relieved to see that Jaina and her companions were all on their feet and steady. "I've got help in the air lock."

"Just watch yourselves," Leia warned. The deck continued to tilt and buck as Leia put the *Falcon* through a serious of evasive maneuvers. "Some laserbrain in a Star Destroyer is taking potshots at us."

"Is that all?" Han asked. Seeing that the air lock pressure was almost within normal safety margins, he hit the safety override. "I thought you'd hit an asteroid or something."

A warning light flashed inside the air lock chamber, and the hatch hissed open a moment later. Jaina and the others—Zekk, Ben, and a Twi'lek stranger—emerged in the typical post-EV rush to free themselves of their claustrophobia-inducing emergency suits, pulling off gloves and opening closure rings. Han's heart soared at seeing Jaina—and his gut clenched because now she was in just as much danger as he and Leia were.

Once Jaina's visor was raised, she turned to Han and opened the bulky arms of her evac suit to embrace him. "I don't know what you're doing here, but whatever it is—"

"I love you too, kid," Han said, raising a hand to stop her. "But the hugs will have to wait. We've got a pressure leak."

Jaina's eyes dropped to the sling hanging in front of Han's chest, and her expression switched from relief to understanding. "How bad have we been hit?"

"Don't know yet," Han said. He turned back to the control panel and tapped the keypad, calling up a ship-wide damage report. "But it can't be that bad. We've still got—"

Han was interrupted when a hand appeared between him and the display panel. It took his eyes a second to focus, but when they did, he saw that the hand was holding a pair of Jedi wrist-restraints.

"What the frizz?" Han turned, running his gaze up an evac-suited arm to his nephew's face.

"I'm really sorry, Uncle Han," Ben said. "But you're under arrest."

"Arrest?" Han frowned at the boy, trying to decide whether he should explode in laughter or anger. "Kid, you've got one *lousy* sense of timing."

"It goes with the company he keeps," Jaina said. She turned on Ben with fire in her eyes. "Put those away before I—"

"It's okay, Jaina." Zekk reached over Ben's shoulder and gently pushed the boy's hand down. "I've got this."

To Han's amazement, Jaina merely nodded and turned back to the control panel, perfectly content to let Zekk take charge of Ben while she focused on the pressure leak.

Clearly, something had changed between the two of them—she was acting like she actually *respected* him.

"But there's a Search and Detain Warrant out on them," Ben protested. "We've *got* to arrest them!"

"You're training to become a Jedi, Ben," Zekk said. "That means you're supposed to use your own best judgment in these situations."

"I *am*," Ben insisted.

"I hope you don't really believe that." Zekk pulled his hand back, then said, "Put those away. We'll talk about this later."

Finding himself in no position to argue, Ben obediently returned the restraints to a utility pocket inside his evac suit, then scowled up at Han. "Nothing personal, Uncle Han—but I'm still bringing you in."

"Whatever you say, kid," Han answered. "Let's just get through this first."

Han turned away from Ben.

"I don't know, Dad," Jaina said. "This leak might be more than we can handle."

"You're kidding, right?" Han said. "Back in the Corporate Sector, Chewbacca and I used to get banged up this bad every week."

"Not *this* bad."

Jaina pointed to the damage schematic she had brought up on the control panel display screen, and Han's heart dropped into his gut. The upper cannon turret was gone—along with a substantial portion of the surrounding hull armor—and the lower turret was spread open like a flower blossom, clearly blown apart from the inside. The access tunnel that connected them was red, indicating a total pressure loss, and the surrounding compartments were quickly shading to pink.

Jaina must have sensed Han's shock, because she asked, "Cakhmaim and Meewalh were in the turrets?"

"Yeah—firing the laser cannons." Han's insides were knotting with sorrow; given the damage he had seen in the schematic, the only thing left of the two Noghri were the places they would always hold in the Solos' hearts. "I owe whoever's commanding that Star Destroyer a detonite sandwich."

"A *Star Destroyer* fired on you?" Ben asked. His lightsaber was hanging from a utility loop on his evac suit, but Zekk was being careful to remain at his side anyway. "What'd you do to deserve *that*?"

"Saved *you*," Han said sourly. "We can always throw you back, if you think it was a bad idea."

"We'll take care of Ben later." Jaina took Han's arm and started forward. "Right now we need to get you and Mom into evac suits."

"Evac suits? No way." Han started aft. "By then, the *Falcon* won't have any cabin pressure left."

"Dad, you took a turbolaser strike straight down your access core." Jaina waddled up beside him in her suit. "We might not be *able* to patch things up."

"Sure we will," Han replied. "This is a YT-Thirteen-hundred. The access core isn't that important."

He continued aft, bouncing off the walls as the corridor tipped and tilted around him. A deepening shudder in the deck hinted at a broken engine mount, while a steady serenade of muffled groans suggested how fiercely the *Falcon*'s damaged frame was straining under Leia's evasive maneuvers—and made Han wonder how long they had before a metallic bang deep inside the ship somewhere brought that final ear pop of decompression.

He rounded the corner to find the bulkhead hatch sealed and a stream of air whistling out through a tiny hole in the wall. The edges of the hole were smooth and puffy, as though the durasteel had been melted instead of punctured.

"*That's* bad news," Ben commented from a couple of meters behind Han. "It's a spatter breach."

"No big deal," Han said. Spatter breaches happened when a metal mass erupted in a molten spray, usually after being hit by a turbolaser strike. They were notoriously dangerous and difficult to repair because they caused so much damage in so many different places. "It didn't hit anything important, or we'd be dead already."

Han activated the control panel, then checked the pressure on the other side of the bulkhead and entered a safety override code. His ears popped painfully as the hatch retracted, and the whistle of escaping atmosphere became a scream. He stepped into the rear hold and turned toward the sound, and the first problem became instantly apparent.

The spatter had perforated a meter-wide circle of durasteel with literally hundreds of tiny melt holes. The metal was so weak that the air pressure was bowing the wall outward, and Han knew it wouldn't be long before the area simply tore free and sucked the atmosphere from the hold in a deadly *whoosh*.

"Okay, so it's *kind* of a big deal," he said. "Jaina, you and Zekk go to the repair locker and break out the patches and reinforcement strips. Ben, take your Twi'lek friend and—"

"We're not really friends," Ben interrupted, sounding as petulant as only young teenagers could at a time like this. "And his name is Spacer First Class Sorzo."

"Fine." Han looked over Ben to the Twi'lek. "Just take a look around the access core and see if there are any other spots this bad."

The Twi'lek—Sorzo—acknowledged the order with a salute and started off with Ben in tow. Han spent the next twenty seconds searching the immediate area for less obvious punctures—and finding plenty. Even if they did manage to patch this cluster, they would still have to track down dozens of tiny melt holes concealed behind places like the engineering station and medbay. It was going to mean sealing off the cockpit and spending hours in evac suits, but what else could he do—abandon the *Falcon*?

A tremendous bang rumbled up from somewhere belowdecks, and an odd chugging sensation began to accompany the ship's shuddering and bucking.

Leia's voice came over the intercom, barely audible above the screech of escaping air. "Han, what was *that*?"

"How should I know?" Han was actually beginning to feel overwhelmed by the *Falcon*'s problems, and that never happened. "Can't See-Threepio tell you?"

"There's no indication of a new problem on the damage reports," the droid reported. "But we *do* seem to be losing power in our sublight drives."

"Blast!" Han started to bang a fist against the wall—then took another look at the circle of spatter perforations and decided not to risk it. "Something must be pinching a feed line."

"Perhaps you could free it," C-3PO suggested.

"I'm kind of busy patching pressure leaks back here," Han responded.

"That won't matter if we take another hit," Leia said. "And if we can't maneuver—"

"We're going to take another hit," Han finished. "I *know*. Okay—let me get a flow report and see if I can locate the problem."

He stepped around the corner and found Ben already

standing in front of the aft engineering station, eyes glued to the display and fingers on the keypad. Thinking the boy had done something to cause the power loss, Han rushed to his side.

The screen had nothing on it but a tactical display feed, which showed a confused-but-improving situation near the planet Hapes. Admiral Bwua'tu's fleet was already starting to hammer the Corellian Dreadnaughts, and a task force of Royal Battle Dragons was tearing through the second usurper fleet from behind.

With the Royal Battle Dragons was an *Imperial*-class Star Destroyer with a designator symbol reading UN-KNOWN. While the vessel was directing most of her fire toward the usurpers, she had dedicated a single long-range turbolaser battery to attacking the *Falcon*.

"I thought I told you to look for pressure leaks," Han said, relieved he hadn't caught Ben actually trying to sabotage the *Falcon*. "I'm still captain of this tub, and that means you do what I say."

"I'm using my own best judgment," Ben retorted. He put a finger on the display, indicating the mysterious Star Destroyer. "And it tells me we're in big trouble. Our only chance of surviving is to make for that Star Destroyer."

"Are you crazy?" Han asked. "She's already firing on us!"

"Only because you're trying to escape," Ben countered. "She'll stop firing if you surrender. That's the *Anakin Solo*."

Han's jaw dropped. "The Anakin *what*?"

"The *Anakin Solo*," Ben said proudly. "Jacen's ship."

"*Jacen's* ship?" Han actually stumbled back, and not just because the deck had tipped again. He felt like a bantha had kicked him in the gut. "They named a GAG Star Destroyer for my dead boy?"

"Well, yeah," Ben said, clearly confused. "Anakin *was* a really great Jedi."

"I can't believe it!" Afraid he would lash out at Ben in his fury, Han turned and kicked the wall so hard he felt his toes pop. "The kriffing rodders!"

Ben cringed and began to back away. "It's an honor. Jacen said—"

"Forget what Jacen said," Jaina interrupted, returning with Zekk and the patching supplies. "He's living in his own galaxy these days."

Ben frowned. "But Admiral Niathal thought it was a good idea, too."

"Then Admiral Niathal is one dumb fish." Han snatched the reinforcement strips from Zekk's arms and nodded him toward the engineering station. "I think we've got a pinched fuel feed. See if you can clear it before the engines shut down and we turn into a target barge."

Without waiting for a reply, Han stepped around the corner. The pressure had fallen far enough now that the air was beginning to cool as it expanded. They had less than three minutes until the atmosphere grew so thin that breathing would become difficult. He dropped the strips on the floor in front of the spatter perforations, then turned one over and tried in vain to scratch off the flimsi-plast backing. It was not something that could be done one-handed—at least not when your only working hand was shaking in fear.

"Uncle Han, surrendering is our best chance of surviving," Ben said, following. "All I have to do is comm Jacen and tell him I'm bringing you in."

"So he can torture his parents like his *other* Corellian prisoners?" Jaina demanded. She knelt at Han's side and took the metal strip from his hand. "They're better off taking their chances in the *Falcon*."

"But *we're* not," Ben countered. "We're not traitors to the Alliance—at least *I'm* not."

"I'll forget you said that—because if I don't, we're *both* going to regret it." Jaina removed the strip's backing in one smooth pull. "Be careful how you apply this, or you'll just create more suction. Dad will show you."

She held the strip up for Ben and reached for another, but he was shaking his head and ignoring her. "No, not until Uncle Han promises to—"

The strip fluttered past Ben and plastered itself into the middle of the spatter perforations. The scream of escaping atmosphere grew shrill and urgent, and a crease shot across the damaged area.

Han's heart climbed into his throat. "Uh, Jaina—"

"Oh, kriff!" She jumped up, already peeling the backing off another reinforcement strip. "Ben, what's *wrong* with you?"

"Nothing—I'm just doing my duty." Ben snapped his lightsaber off his evac suit's utility loop. "If we help make repairs, they're just going to escape."

"And if we don't, we're *all* going to be sucking a vacuum in about thirty seconds." Holding the reinforcement strip in two hands, Jaina stepped toward the wall—then suddenly stopped when Ben ignited his lightsaber. Her jaw dropped, and she looked up and said, "Please tell me you *didn't* just pull your lightsaber on me."

"I'm sorry, Jaina," Ben said. "But you don't have any discipline—like Jacen says, you're always making up your own orders instead of following the ones you're given."

Jaina glared at Ben for an instant, then thrust the reinforcement strip at Han. "Hold this."

Ben retreated a step, bringing his blade up behind his rear shoulder. "Jaina, don't make me—*whaaaargggh!*"

Ben's threat came to a surprised end as Zekk slipped

around the corner and caught hold of his hands from behind, twisting his wrists forward and forcing the lightsaber blade down toward the deck.

And that was when the shock wave of a nearby turbolaser strike slammed the *Falcon*. The deck jumped so hard that Han's knees buckled, and he came down on his wounded shoulder again. Cries of astonishment rang out all around, and his body exploded into pain.

"How's that feed line repair coming?" Leia asked over the intercom. The air was so thin now that her voice was starting to sound tinny and faint. "If I can't accelerate, the flight is only going to get bumpier."

"Just keep us pointed out of here." As Han spoke, he realized that someone nearby was groaning in terrible pain. "We'll pass out of range *sometime*."

He rolled to his knees and saw Zekk curled on the deck, his hands clutched to a blackened slash in the side of his evac suit. Ben was kneeling next to him with a look of horror on his face, still holding an ignited lightsaber and shaking his head in despair.

"You shouldn't have grabbed me," he said. "Why'd you have to grab me, Zekk?"

"Because you were acting like a Jedi *wannabe*," Jaina said, coming up behind him. "Give me that."

She snatched the lightsaber from Ben's hand.

He looked up at her. "It wasn't my fault."

"Then whose fault was it, laserbrain?" She switched the lightsaber off. "I just hope you haven't killed us all. Now grow up, go help your uncle, and I'll—"

"No, Jaina." Han stuck a handful of reinforcement strips into his sling and turned to the damaged area. "You've got to get Zekk and Ben out of here."

"Out of here?" Jaina asked.

"Get into the escape pods." Without removing the

strip's backing, he held it up to the edge of the perforation circle and allowed the vacuum to suck it into place. "Zekk needs medical help, and I *really* don't want you sticking us with the brat."

"But what about—"

"The *Falcon*'s only carrying a four-person pod capacity right now," Han interrupted. "And even if we had more, Leia and I are *not* surrendering." He shot a look at Ben that could have melted frasium, then added, "Not to Jacen—or anyone else."

He held another strip to the edge of the circle and let the vacuum suck it into place. It would be a temporary patch at best, but it might hold long enough to save them. He placed another strip, then looked back to find Jaina kneeling beside Zekk. She had the fingers of one hand pressed to his throat, taking his pulse. But her eyes were fixed on Han, and there were tears running down her cheeks.

She nodded, then chinned a toggle switch in her collar, and spoke into the microphone of her suit's comm unit. "Sorzo, get back here. We're abandoning ship again."

"Good." Han had never been more proud of his daughter. He could see in Jaina's face how much she wanted to stay aboard the *Falcon* with him and Leia, but she was a seasoned spacer who knew better than to question a captain's orders aboard his own ship. "Don't worry about your mother and me. Until we get the *Falcon* patched up, it'll be good not to have so many noses breathing the air— but we'll be okay. We've been in a lot of fixes tougher than this one."

Jaina managed a smile, though her fear for her parents remained obvious. "I know, Dad—I've seen the holovids." She motioned Ben toward the rear hatch and used the Force to lift Zekk off the deck, then stepped to Han's side and gave him a little kiss on the cheek. "Let me know how it goes . . . and may the Force be with you."

"Yeah." Not wanting her to see the tears welling in his eyes—and to realize that he was afraid this might be their final good-bye—Han didn't look as she started after Ben. "You too, kid."

He turned back to the damaged area and started to lay the rest of the reinforcing strips in place. By the time he had finished, Jaina had everyone loaded into the escape pods and was sounding the departure alarm. The turbolaser strikes just kept coming. The *Falcon* was bucking and leaping like a wild ronto, and the cabin pressure had fallen to the point that Han was shivering and starting to lose his breath.

He didn't feel the escape pods go. The launch alarm simply fell silent, and he had a feeling like something had torn loose inside him.

"Han?" Even over the intercom, Leia's voice sounded as though it was cracking. "You still there?"

" 'Course I am." He started forward, sealing the bulkhead behind him. "You're not getting rid of me *that* easy."

"*Nothing's* easy with you, flyboy." Leia's tone was joking, but a little forced and frightened. "I just wanted to let you know we're ready to jump."

Another shock wave slammed into the *Falcon,* bouncing Han off the wall and eliciting a metallic screech of pain from the old ship. He gulped down a deep breath thinking it might be his last, then was amazed to still be in once piece when he reached the corridor's forward bulkhead.

"What are you waiting for?" He punched a safety override code into the control panel, then felt a blast of pressure as the hatch irised open. "The sooner we jump, the better."

"What about poor Lady Morwan?" C-3PO asked. "She's still locked in the forward hold!"

"And safer than *we* are," Han replied, stepping through the bulkhead.

He closed the hatch behind him and hurried across the main cabin into the flight deck access corridor. The jump alarm chimed—sounding higher-pitched than usual in the thin air—then the lights dimmed and an alarming purr rose from the engine compartments in the back of the ship. The *Falcon* began to chug and slow, and Leia's voice rolled down the corridor, cursing and yelling like an Aqualish spice smuggler on a bad day.

Han leaned close to the wall. "Come on, old girl," he whispered. "You're not ready for the scrap heap yet, are you?"

The purring intensified into a high-pitched whine, then the lights came back up, and Han was nearly knocked off his feet again as the *Falcon* leapt into a hard acceleration.

He smiled and gave the bulkhead an affectionate pat. "Me, neither."

He sealed the bulkhead, then made his way to the flight deck, where the engine whine had grown so high that it was no longer audible to human ears. The *Falcon*'s shuddering had settled into a teeth-tickling vibration, and C-3PO was at the navigator's station checking their jump coordinates. Leia was in the pilot's seat, with nothing ahead but dark, empty freedom.

Han went to her side and saw by her glassy eyes that there was no need to tell her about events in back. She had probably sensed Meewalh and Cakhmaim's deaths through the Force, and Jaina would have commed her to clear the escape pod launches. As for Ben and Jacen and the *Anakin Solo,* there would be time enough to tell her about that later . . . and if there wasn't, it would be just as well if she never knew.

Han leaned down. "It'll be okay." He kissed her cheek, then slipped into the copilot's seat. "You've still got *me.*"

Leia let out a shocked snort, then smiled and looked over. "I guess so." She reached across and squeezed his arm. "You'll do."

The hyperdrive finally kicked in, and the stars stretched to lines one more time.

epilogue

A lively murmur rose near the mouth of the *Dragon Queen*'s Royal Hangar, then built to a rousing cheer. Tenel Ka, Queen Mother of the Hapes Consortium and uncontested monarch of sixty-three worlds, turned from the newly arrived *Jade Shadow* toward the sound. Dozens of crewpersons in fireproof refueling suits and tool-draped utilities were looking out through the containment field, pumping their arms and shouting in joy.

But all Tenel Ka saw beyond the hangar mouth was the star-flecked darkness of the realm she ruled. It was strewn with the hulks of wrecked warships and laced with the ion trails of hundreds of rescue vessels, and she saw nothing joyful in *that*. She had retained her throne, but too many Hapans had died on both sides, and too much of the Consortium's strength had been squandered on someone else's fight.

And the ordeal was far from over. Soon, Tenel Ka's intelligence service would start bringing her names and prisoners, and she would be forced to deal the Queen's Justice. Her advisers would recommend that it be brutal and swift, and her remaining nobles would expect their loyalty to be rewarded with a redistribution of the usurpers' holdings. Tenel Ka would consider all their suggestions carefully, of course—but in the end, she would keep her own counsel . . . and that was bound to disappoint everyone.

After a moment, a GAG-black shuttle slid into view and began to nose through the containment field. The cheering grew even louder, and a marshaling officer stepped forward with a pair of signal batons to direct the pilot to a nearby berth. Tenel Ka reached out in the Force and was alarmed to feel the familiar presence of her daughter.

Jacen was returning Allana—and his timing could not have been worse. Tenel Ka turned back to the *Jade Shadow* and saw Mara and Jaina already carrying a stretcher down the boarding ramp toward her. It was too late to comm Jacen and warn him. Instead, Tenel Ka reached out in the Force, counting on him to sense her anxiety and figure out the reason. She felt a brief touch of warmth, then had to break off contact as Mara and Jaina reached the bottom of the ramp with their burden.

Lying on the stretcher was Zekk, pale, unconscious, and heavily bandaged around the middle. Tenel Ka's heart ached to see her old comrade-in-arms wounded so severely, but she forced herself to keep a blank face. It would not do for her ever-present retinue of "loyal" nobles to notice an arched brow or a quivering lip when she had just watched so many Hapans perish in stoic composure.

"Master Skywalker, Jedi Solo, welcome aboard." Tenel Ka stepped forward to greet them, followed closely by the medical team she had brought to meet the *Shadow*. "My surgeon is waiting in an operating theater. If you would entrust Zekk to the transport team, they will take him up immediately."

"That's very kind," Mara said. "We appreciate it."

"Yeah, thanks," Jaina added. "It means a lot."

They passed the stretcher to a pair of red-uniformed medics, who quickly placed Zekk aboard a small hoversled then zipped away toward the back of the hangar. Noticing how Jaina's gaze followed the sled all the way to the lift tubes, Tenel Ka stepped to her side.

"They'll take good care of him, Jaina." Tenel Ka could sense that Jaina was a little irritated by all the cheering going on behind them, but there was nothing to be done about it. Even if the Queen Mother called for silence, she doubted the order could be carried out anytime soon. "Once they have prepared Zekk for the operation, we can go up to wait in the infirmary."

"That'd be great," Jaina said. "But don't worry. Zekk's as strong as a bantha these days."

Tenel Ka smiled. "I'm glad to hear that—but I *am* a little confused. My surgeon said he had been told it was a *lightsaber* injury?"

Jaina glanced at Mara, then said, "It's a long story."

"Ben made a mistake," Mara said.

"*Ben?*" Tenel Ka gasped.

"It wasn't an attack." Mara's tone suggested she did not want to discuss Ben's "mistake" any further. "There was some confusion aboard the *Falcon*."

"The *Falcon*?" Growing more confused herself by the moment, Tenel Ka turned to Jaina. "But I thought the Masters Skywalker found you in escape pods?"

"The *Falcon*'s pods," Luke answered from the top of the boarding ramp. His cybernetic hand was missing, and his robes looked bulky around the middle—as though he, too, had a bandage wrapped around his chest. "We're still trying to figure that out ourselves."

"Master Skywalker, you're hurt, too!" Tenel Ka cried. "If you had told us—"

"I'm fine—I've just come out of a healing trance." Luke sounded as haggard as he looked. He glanced toward the GAG shuttle, which was now surrounded by jubilant Hapans, and asked, "Is that *Jacen* everyone is cheering for?"

"Yes, it is." Tenel Ka turned toward the shuttle, where Jacen had descended the boarding ramp and was beginning to make his way toward them through the cheering throng. Major Espara was with him, but Allana had apparently been left aboard with Espara's aides. "After destroying the Galney fleet and saving *me*, Jacen has become quite the hero of loyal Hapans."

"A *hero*?" Jaina asked. "You've got to be kidding!"

"Not at all," Tenel Ka said sternly. Given the warm reception Jacen was receiving from her subjects, she was considering whether it might be possible to reveal Allana's paternity. Not having the secret to keep would certainly simplify her life, and her nobles—at least the loyal ones—would never be more receptive to the truth than they were right now. "Jacen saved my life—and with it, the Hapan monarchy."

Jaina's face hardened as only Jaina's face could. "Does that give him an excuse to fire on his own parents?"

Tenel Ka frowned. "I'm not sure I heard you correctly. Did you really say that Jacen had fired on Han and Leia?"

"I'm afraid she did," Luke said grimly. He started down the ramp, followed by Ben and a Twi'lek in Alliance military utilities. "The *Falcon* had already jumped by the time we arrived from Roqoo, but it sounds like the *Anakin* hit her pretty hard."

"You're sure?" Tenel Ka could not believe what she was hearing. "It doesn't make sense."

"We're having trouble understanding a lot of what Jacen

has been doing," Mara said. As Luke reached the bottom of the ramp, she stepped to his side. "Now that matters are settling down in the Consortium, we're hoping to have a chance to work some of those things out."

The disapproving undertone in Mara's voice—and the bitterness in Luke's—made Tenel Ka's heart fall. After their meeting aboard the *Anakin Solo,* Jacen had told her that the Skywalkers were losing faith in him—that they even suspected him of working with Lumiya—and now she could see how right he was.

Tenel Ka turned to Ben. "What do you know about this? I find it difficult to believe Jacen would open fire on his own parents."

"He didn't have a choice," Ben said. "They're terrorists, and they were trying to escape."

"Terrorists?" Tenel Ka was crushed to hear the boy say such a thing. "Ben, that's just not true."

"I'm afraid it is," Jacen said, emerging from his throng of admirers. "The suspicions Aunt Mara voiced during our meeting aboard the *Anakin* were right after all."

Mara scowled. "They *were*?"

"Yes—and I apologize for not considering your point more carefully," Jacen said. "But events have certainly proven you correct. The intelligence my parents provided regarding Ducha AlGray did us more harm than good, and they were certainly involved in the attack on Her Majesty."

The cold anger in Jacen's voice made Tenel Ka even sadder, but she was beginning to understand what had happened, to see how he had misinterpreted events to reach a terrible conclusion.

"Jacen, you can't believe your parents would do such a thing."

Tenel Ka realized the crowd had quieted around them,

straining to hear, and she knew that whatever she said next might determine how the Solos would be viewed in galactic histories—whether they would be remembered as idealistic heroes or amoral terrorists.

"Han and Leia Solo had as much to do with saving the Crown as you did," she said, speaking evenly and clearly. "They risked their lives to provide me with the reversion coordinates of the AlGray fleet."

Jacen's eyes widened. "They did?"

"Yes," Tenel Ka said. "Furthermore, the Solos placed themselves at even greater risk to make sure the Royal Navy stood firm until Admiral Bwua'tu attacked."

Jacen's expression changed from shock to shame, and Tenel Ka's sadness began to lift. Clearly, the attack on the *Falcon* had been the result of a terrible misunderstanding. Jacen had made a grave mistake—but only because he was overcompensating, trying too hard to avoid letting his personal feelings influence his judgment.

That was certainly what Tenel Ka hoped—and what she chose to believe.

"I am sure your parents will be fine." Tenel Ka addressed this to both Jacen and Jaina, but in her heart she was speaking more to Jacen. He was the one who had made the mistake, and she knew how he would blame himself if any harm came to them because of it. "No one is more capable of taking care of themselves under difficult circumstances—and I'll issue orders for all Hapan vessels to aid them in every way possible."

"That can't hurt," Mara said. "But nobody's going to see them until they're a long way from here. They'll go stealth until they find someplace safe to land."

Luke nodded. "That's right. I'll reach out to Leia in the Force, try to let her know that help is available if they need it." He turned to Jacen, his brow lowered in disapproval. "But we need to talk. You're very quick to believe the worst about someone you love. That's a problem."

Jacen's eyes burned with resentment—and Tenel Ka understood why. After all, wasn't Luke assuming the worst about Jacen and Lumiya?

"That's not fair, Master Skywalker," Tenel Ka said. "Jacen's suspicions were based on the information available to him at the time."

"The difference is *our* suspicions haven't harmed anyone. Jacen has put his parents in mortal danger." Luke cast a meaningful glance at Tenel Ka's retinue, then added, "Perhaps we could talk about this aboard the *Shadow*?"

"As you wish." Though Tenel Ka made it sound as though she were granting a favor, she was relieved to have any excuse to get the Skywalkers and Jaina off the hangar deck so she could sneak Allana away from the shuttle. Given the schism of mistrust that had opened between Jacen and everyone else, revealing her daughter's paternity no longer seemed like a good idea. "I'll be along in a moment. There are a few things I need to attend to here."

"Of course."

Luke bowed and led the others back aboard the *Shadow*. Tenel Ka waited until they were gone, then turned to the crowd of crewpersons that had gathered around the confrontation.

"And you thought *Hapan* politics were treacherous!" she said in a light—if rather forced—tone. A self-conscious laugh rustled through the crowd, more in acknowledgment of the Queen Mother's attempt at humor than because Tenel Ka had finally learned to tell a joke. "But now your fun is over. Back to work with you."

She made a shooing motion, and the crowd began to disperse. Tenel Ka turned to the nobles who always accumulated around her, when she permitted it. She motioned

Major Espara forward, then frowned at the absence of one of the most familiar faces in her retinue.

"Where is Lady Galney?" she asked, frowning. "I *asked* her to stay close."

A nervous voice sounded from the back of the flock. "Here, Majesty."

As if by magic, an aisle opened through Tenel Ka's retinue. At the other end stood Lady Galney, her eyes fixed on the deck and her chin tucked to her chest. The Force grew electric with anticipation, and Tenel Ka knew that these raptors she called nobles smelled blood.

"Would you come forward please? There's something I need you and Major Espara to do for me."

"Of c-course, Majesty."

Galney shuffled forward, her legs shaking so hard they nearly buckled twice. Of course, her fellow nobles only watched and smirked, convinced their peer was going to receive the punishment she so richly deserved for having had the misfortune to be sister to the sneakiest of the Heritage Council's many traitors.

Galney stopped in front of Tenel Ka, then found the strength to look up. "If I may, Majesty, I would like to be heard before you speak."

"Very well," Tenel Ka said. "But we don't have much time. You know how pushy those Jedi can be."

This drew a genuine chuckle from the nobles, but Galney remained nervous and somber. "I—I know it won't change your decision, but I want to apologize."

Tenel Ka met the woman's gaze and frowned. "For what, Lady Galney?"

"For my role in all this," she said. "I never would have—"

"Milady Galney," Tenel Ka interrupted. "I may not be a member of the Jedi order any longer, but I assure you I still retain the skills of a Jedi Knight. Don't you think I would have *known* if you had meant to betray me?"

"Of—of course," Galney answered, confused. "Nevertheless, I did. My tongue was too free with my consort, and he was reporting everything I told him—"

"To your sister," Tenel Ka interrupted. "I *know*—and I'm quite sure that is a mistake you will never make again." She glanced toward the *Shadow*. "Now, may I make *my* request?"

Galney's chin dropped again. "Of course, Majesty."

"Thank you." She pointed at Jacen's black GAG shuttle. "Allana is aboard that shuttle, and you are a familiar face to her. I'd like you and Major Espara to retrieve her and take her to your cabin."

Galney's eyes widened. "*My* cabin, Majesty?"

"Yes—and allow no one inside until I arrive." Tenel Ka turned to Espara. "Is that clear, Major?"

Espara looked as confused as Galney, but she was too accustomed to taking orders to question them now. "Yes, Majesty."

"Good." Tenel Ka turned back to Galney. "I'll join you as soon as I'm able."

Galney continued to looked bewildered. "Majesty, if you're trying to spare me the pain of knowing—"

"Lady Galney, I am *not* my grandmother," Tenel Ka interrupted. "I don't execute my subjects for the crimes of their sisters. As for your consort—we'll talk about your choice in men some other time." She turned to Espara. "Are my instructions clear, Major?"

"Yes, Majesty."

"Then carry on." Tenel Ka started up the *Shadow*'s boarding ramp, but when her retinue broke into a drone of shocked voices, she stopped and turned around. "If you're aboard the *Dragon Queen,* there's *supposed* to be a reason. My advice to you all is to figure out what that reason is—and start attending to it!"

The retinue fell into stunned silence, then suddenly dissolved as noblewomen scurried for the hangar exits. Tenel Ka smiled to herself and, thinking she just might stand a chance of bringing Hapes into the modern galaxy, ascended the boarding ramp.

She entered the opulent passenger salon of the *Jade Shadow* to find the discussion already in full swing. Luke and Jaina were standing on one side of the central beverage table, with Jacen and Ben on the other and Mara caught between. She was addressing her nephew, but looking like she just wished everyone would take a seat and calm down.

". . . supposed to think, Jacen?" Mara's tone was reasonable, but pointed. "You sent us there to meet Ben. Instead, Lumiya ambushes us."

"That doesn't mean I sent her," Jacen responded. Tenel Ka knew how upset he was by the fact that she could not feel him in the Force; he always closed himself off when he grew angry. "You said yourself that you were worried she was after Ben."

"Ben wasn't *there*," Luke said.

"I was supposed to be!" Ben interrupted. "Jacen dropped a message beacon ordering the *Rover* to go to Roqoo Depot, but we ignored it."

"You *what*?" Mara asked, facing Ben.

"We ignored the order." Ben turned to Jaina. "Ask Jaina. It was her idea."

All eyes turned to Jaina, who reluctantly nodded. "I pretty much insisted on it. We needed to warn Ten—er, the Queen Mother—about the Ducha."

Ben turned back to Luke. "You see? It wasn't Jacen's fault."

"You ignoring an order *doesn't* explain how Lumiya knew we would be there," Mara pointed out. "Or why she's been working with GAG."

"And I wish I had the answer to that," Jacen said. "I'll be looking into it as soon as the *Anakin* returns to Coruscant. I want the answer more than you do, I can promise that."

"Can you?" Luke asked, keeping his gaze fixed on Jacen.

"Of course he can," Tenel Ka said, stepping to Jacen's side. "A few minutes ago, you rebuked Jacen for being too quick to believe the worst of those he loves. And here *you* are, doing the same thing."

Luke frowned, clearly irritated with her, but Mara sighed and looked at her husband. "She has a point, Luke. We really don't have any more evidence against Jacen than he did against Han and Leia. The battle's over—maybe it's time we all holstered our blasters and tried to work things out like family."

"That sounds good to me," Jacen said. "I'll be the first to admit that I've made some mistakes, but I *have* been working for the good of the Alliance—and I know you have, too."

Luke considered Jacen's words for a moment before speaking again. "What about your parents? They're family, too."

"I can't cancel the detention warrant, if that's what you're asking."

Jacen's words shocked Tenel Ka to the core. "Jacen, if not for your parents, I wouldn't be alive. Neither would Allana."

Jacen's face grew as sad as it was hard, and Tenel Ka knew that even *she* would not be able to change his mind about this. He was convinced that his duty compelled him to ignore his feelings for his family, and she found that terribly painful—and, when she remembered that she and Allana were his family, too, just a little frightening.

"I know that," Jacen said to her. "They risked their lives to save you, but they still have crimes against the Alliance to answer for." He returned his attention to Luke. "If Han and Leia Solo are having second thoughts about their political loyalties, we can negotiate a safe surrender and suitable confinement."

"*Surrender?*" Jaina exploded. "*Confinement?* They'll never—"

"Don't you think I know that?" Jacen replied, just as hotly. "But if I cancel the warrant on them, it will look like I'm giving my parents special treatment—and I can't do that. There's one law, Jaina, and it applies to everyone—even to Solos."

"They risked their lives to save Tenel Ka," Jaina objected. "They're not terrorists."

"I know," Jacen said. "But they're not innocent, either."

Jaina exhaled in frustration, then looked to Luke in silent appeal. Luke stared at the floor for a moment, then looked up to meet Jacen's eyes. "Okay, but I haven't changed my mind about Ben. He's still coming back to Coruscant with us."

"*What?*" Ben cried. "No way. Jacen is my Master!"

"That's not your decision, Ben," Luke said. "And Jacen *isn't* a Master."

"He is to me," Ben retorted. "No one's as strong in the Force—"

"It's your father's decision," Jacen said. He raised a hand to silence Ben, then turned back to Luke. "But is it really necessary? Now that Lumiya is dead—"

"What makes you think she's dead?" Mara asked.

"You do," Jacen answered, frowning. "Not five minutes ago, you said she was wearing a bomb—"

"A bomb that exploded *after* we left the cantina," Luke reminded him. "We don't know that Lumiya was still wearing it."

"And if I had to guess, I'd say she *wasn't,*" Mara added. "It took nearly two minutes for that bomb to detonate. Even with her chest wounds, that would have been plenty of time to escape."

"Which is certainly what we should assume," Luke said. "I won't believe Lumiya is dead until I slide her body into the crematorium myself."

"I see." Jacen's gaze dropped to the floor, growing distant and glassy. When he finally raised it again, he looked Luke straight in the eye, steady, calm, and collected. "Then I guess I should trust your judgment. After all, I've never even met the woman."

Luke held Jacen's eyes. "I hope that's true, Jacen."

Jacen's expression darkened, but before he could speak, Ben stepped between the two men and scowled up at his father.

"Of course it's true!" Ben exclaimed. "Jacen is trying to *protect* the galaxy. Why doesn't anyone understand that but me?"

"*I* understand it, Ben," Tenel Ka said, trying to divert the storm she felt gathering. "And I am sure your father does, too."

Tenel Ka cast an expectant look in Luke's direction, but he only continued to study Jacen, and Tenel Ka felt the tension continuing to build.

So did Mara, apparently. She stepped closer to Ben and laid a hand on his shoulder. "Ben, we're *all* trying to save the galaxy," she said. "But we don't always agree on how it should be done."

"And *that's* why I can't stay with Jacen?" Ben demanded. "That's ridiculous!"

"The reason you can't stay with Jacen is because I'm ordering you to return home with us," Luke said sternly. "And the reason I'm doing that is because Lumiya told me *you* were the one helping her in GAG."

"*What?*"

Tenel Ka exclaimed the word at the same time Jacen and Ben did, then watched Jacen's expression turn from shocked to angry to enigmatic. Ben merely seemed confused.

"And you believe her?" he demanded.

"No," Luke answered. He glanced back toward Jacen. "But somebody has been helping her, and until I know who that is—"

"—you need to stay away from GAG," Jacen finished. "Your father is right to be cautious, Ben."

"But *you're* my Master!" Ben objected.

"And I'm asking you to stay with your parents until I've sorted this out." Jacen looked up at Luke, then added, "I'm sure we'll be working together again much sooner than you expect."

Tenel Ka's heart fell at the challenging tone of Jacen's voice, but Luke seemed to accept the statement without animosity.

"I hope we'll *all* be working together again soon." Luke reached across and clasped Jacen's arm. "I know better than to think you'll accept my help, but let me know how the investigation goes. I'll be very interested to learn more about Lumiya's involvement."

"Of course," Jacen replied. Though he was not allowing his feelings to seep into the Force, Tenel Ka could tell by the slight tightening of his lips that he had taken Luke's comment as something of a threat. "And now, if you'll excuse me, I really should return to the *Anakin* and get started on that."

Jacen said his farewells to the Skywalkers, then turned to Tenel Ka. "Your Majesty, if all is well—"

"It is," Tenel Ka said. She took his arm and, heart breaking, started toward the hatch with him. "Jacen, what can I say? We are in your debt."

"No," Jacen said. "The Alliance is in *yours*. Thanks to the Consortium's courage here, we may have broken the Corellians' ability to make war."

They stopped just inside the hatch, where they would be hidden from the hangar floor but still be visible from the passenger salon of the *Shadow*. It would be, Tenel Ka knew, the most privacy they were likely to find for a long, long time. She took Jacen's hand.

"All the same, we are grateful," she said. "Please let us know if there is anything we can do for you—and feel free to visit us again when you have time. You will find a warm welcome among our subjects."

"Thank you, Majesty." Jacen bowed. "I will."

"Good. We will be looking forward to it."

Tenel Ka kissed Jacen on the cheek, then fought to keep back the tears as she watched him step through the hatch and once more vanish from her life.

Read on for a sneak preview of Aaron Allston's

EXILE
The fourth novel in
the thrilling new *Star Wars* epic!

IMPERIAL STAR DESTROYER **ANAKIN SOLO**
OUTSIDE CORELLIAN SPACE

It wasn't exactly guilt that kept Jacen awake night after night. Rather, it was an awareness that he *should* feel guilty, but didn't, quite.

Jacen leaned back in a chair comfortable enough to sleep in, its leather as soft as blue butter, and stared at the stars.

The blast shields were withdrawn from the oversized viewport of his office, and the office itself was dark, giving him an unencumbered view of space.

His office was on the port side, the bow was oriented toward the sun Corell, and the stern was pointed back toward Coruscant, so he'd be looking toward Commenor, Kuat, the Hapes Cluster, the length of the Perlemian Trade Route . . . But he did not try to pick out these stars individually. Astronomy was a lifelong occupation for people who spent their entire existences on only one planet; how much harder must such a study be for someone like Jacen, who had traveled from star to star throughout his life?

He let his eyelids sag. But his mind continued to race, as it had every day since he and his task force had rescued Queen Mother Tenel Ka of the Hapes Consortium from an insurrection, instigated by treacherous Hapan nobles aided by a Corellian fleet.

Believing that Han and Leia Solo had been among the conspirators, Jacen had ordered the *Anakin Solo*'s long-range turbolasers brought to bear against the *Millennium Falcon*. Later, he had heard compelling evidence that his parents had had no part in the plot.

So where was the guilt? Where was the horror he should have

felt at an attempted act of patricide and matricide? What sort of father could he be to Allana if he could do this without remorse?

He didn't know. And he was certain that until he did know, sleep would continue to elude him.

Behind his chair, a lightsaber came to life with its characteristic *snap-hiss,* and the office was suddenly bathed in green light. Before the intruder's blade could have been fully extended, Jacen was on his feet, thumbing his own lightsaber to life, gesturing with his free hand to direct the Force to sweep his chair out of the way.

On the other side of the desk stood his mother, Leia Organa Solo. But the lightsaber she was holding was not her own. Jacen recognized it by its hilt, its color. It was the lightsaber Mara Jade Skywalker had carried for so many years. Luke Skywalker's first lightsaber. Anakin Skywalker's last lightsaber.

Leia wore black Jedi robes, and her hair was down, loose. She held the lightsaber in a two-handed grip, point up and hilt back, ready to strike.

"Hello, Mother." This seemed like an appropriate time for the more formal term, rather than *Mom.* "Have you come to kill me?"

"I have," she said.

"Before you attack—how did you get aboard? And how did you get into this office?"

She shook her head, her expression sorrowful. "Do you think ordinary defenses can mean anything at a time like this?"

"Perhaps not." He shrugged. "I know you're an experienced Jedi, Mother, but you're not a match for any Jedi Knight who's been fighting and training constantly throughout his career . . . because you haven't been."

"And yet I'm going to kill you."

"I don't think so. I'm prepared for any tactic, any ploy you're likely to use."

Now she did smile. It was the smile he'd seen her turn on political enemies when they'd made the final mistakes of their careers, the feral smile of a battle dog toying with its prey. "Likely to use," she said. "Don't you know that the whole book of tactics changes when the attacker has chosen not to survive the fight?"

Her face twisted into a mask of anger and betrayal. She released her grip on the lightsaber hilt with her left hand and reached out, pushing. Jacen felt the sudden buildup of Force energy within her.

He twisted to one side. Her exertion in the Force would miss him—

And then he realized, too late, that it was *supposed* to.

The Force energy hurtled past him and hit the viewport dead center, buckling it, smashing it out into the void of space.

Jacen leapt away in the fraction of a second he had before escaping atmosphere would have drawn him through the viewport. If he could catch the rim of the doorway into the office, hold on there for the second or two it took for the blast shutters to close—

But Leia's own leap intercepted his. She slammed into him, her arms wrapping around him, her lightsaber falling away. Together they flew through the viewport.

Jacen felt coldness cut through his skin and deaden it. He felt air rush out from his lungs, a death rattle no one could hear. He felt pain in his head, behind his brow ridge, from his eyes, as they swelled and prepared to burst.

And all the while Leia's mouth was working as though she were still speaking, and for one improbable moment he wondered if she would talk forever, rebuking her son as they twirled, dead, throughout eternity.

Then, as in those last seconds he knew he must, he awoke, once again seated in his comfortable chair, once again staring at the stars.

A dream. Or a sending? He spoke aloud: "Was that you?" And he waited, half expecting Lumiya to answer, but no response came.

He turned his chair around, found his office to be reassuringly empty. With a desktop control, he closed the blast shutters over his viewport.

Finally, he consulted his chrono.

Fifteen standard minutes had passed since the last time he'd checked it. He'd had at most ten minutes of sleep.

He put his booted feet up on the desktop, leaned back, and tried to slow his racing heart.

And to sleep.

CORUSCANT
GALACTIC ALLIANCE TRANSPORTATION DEPOT, NEAR THE JEDI TEMPLE

The *Beetle Nebula* settled down to a landing on an elevated docking platform the size of a city stadium adjacent to the blue, mushroom-shaped transportation depot. The landing was smooth and gentle for a craft so large. At two hundred meters, the *Freebooter*-class transport, built by Sienar Fleet Systems—the firm that had once been most famous for its TIE fighters—was an awkward-looking vessel anywhere but in space. From above, she looked like a crescent moon bisected by a knife blade, the blade point oriented in the same direction as the crescent tips, and her wide, curved stern put observers in mind more of fat-bottomed banthas than of sleek, stylish vessels of war.

But that wide stern could carry large volumes of personnel and matériel, and in the moments after the ship settled onto her landing pylons, a dozen loading ramps came down and began disgorging streams of uniformed soldiers—many on leave, others riding repulsorlift-based medical gurneys, being guided to hospitals.

From a much smaller platform fifty meters from the *Beetle Nebula*'s starboard bow, Jedi Master Kyp Durron watched the event unfold. At this distance, he could barely see facial features of the new arrivals, but he could distinguish enough to see expressions light up with happiness as they recognized loved ones in the crowd below.

And through the Force he could feel the emotion of the day. It swelled from the *Beetle Nebula* and her surroundings. Pain radiated from shattered bones and seared stumps that had once been connected to organic limbs. Pain flowed from remembrances of how those injuries had been sustained and of how friends had been lost forever to battle.

But more than that, there were sentiments of relief and happiness. People were returning home, to rest and recover. They were veterans of the extraordinary space battle that had so recently been waged in the Hapan system. Some of the veterans knew pride in their role in that battle, some knew shame or regret, but all were glad it was over. All were glad to be here.

For a few quiet moments, Kyp relaxed, letting the emotions from the other platform wash over him like a cool, refreshing stream in summertime. The muted nature of the sounds of welcome from that platform, of Coruscant air traffic not too far away, of transport and commerce from the adjacent depot, allowed him to stay comfortable, detached.

Then he felt new presences in the Force, specific presences for whom he had been waiting. He glanced away from the depot and up, toward the origin of that sensation, and saw the *Jade Shadow* on an approach angle, coming straight at him.

The craft approached the depot at a slightly faster-than-safe approach speed, then rapidly decelerated and dropped to a smooth repulsorlift landing atop the platform, mere meters from Kyp. He grinned. Whoever was piloting—probably Mara—had either playfully or maliciously made the approach as intimidating as possible, the better to spook him into sudden retreat. Of course, he hadn't budged. He waved a hand at the shapes within the cockpit, indistinct behind its viewscreens, and waited.

Soon enough the boarding ramp descended, and down trotted Luke Skywalker and Mara Jade Skywalker. They were dressed simply, Luke in black, Mara in the standard two-shades-of-brown Jedi robes.

Kyp offered a smile and extended a hand to Luke. "Master Skywalker."

Luke took it. "Master Durron."

"And Master Skywalker."

Mara gave him a nod of greeting, but Kyp detected a trace of irritation or impatience. "Master Durron."

"That's a new hand, I take it." Kyp released his grip. "I heard about your injuries. How does it compare with the old one?"

Luke held up his right hand and looked at his palm. "The neural matrix is more sophisticated, so it feels even more like flesh and blood. But—you know how a droid whose memory is never wiped tends to become more individual, more idiosyncratic?"

Kyp nodded. "You're not suggesting that a prosthetic hand does the same thing. It doesn't have enough memory."

Luke shrugged. "I don't know what I'm suggesting. Maybe through the Force my brain developed a familiarity with the old hand that exceeded what's normal. Regardless, this one doesn't feel right yet."

"Meaning," Mara said, "that he's dropped from being the most accomplished lightsaber artist in the galaxy to, well, still being the most accomplished, just a little less so for the time being."

"Aunt Mara? Oops. Hello, Kyp. Master Durron." The voice was Jaina's, and Kyp looked up to see the diminutive Jedi at the top of the boarding ramp.

"Jaina." Kyp gave her a friendly nod. He steered his thoughts away from the time, years ago, when he had fixated on her, when she'd been a teenager and he a younger, more self-centered man who hadn't recognized that his interest in her was more about loneliness and self-appreciation than it was about anything else.

He again pretended that she had never meant anything more to him than the daughter of his oldest surviving friend should. She, perhaps, didn't have to pretend. Giving Kyp a brief smile, she returned her attention to Mara. "So can I take Zekk and Ben back to the Temple now?"

Mara nodded. "I think so. Kyp, any reason to delay?"

"No." He glanced to the left, where the Jedi Temple, nearby, was clearly visible just past the *Jade Shadow*'s stern. "Unless you'd like to save your engines—I can just pick you up and set you down over there." He reached out with his hand, palm up, an overly dramatic gesture, and the *Jade Shadow* vibrated for a moment, moving under the pressure he exerted with the Force.

Jaina gave him a reproving look. She turned around and the boarding ramp lifted into place, concealing her.

"How *is* Zekk?" Kyp asked.

"He'll make a full recovery," Luke said. "The surgeons on Hapes were very proficient. But he'll be out of action for a while."

Mara's expression became concerned. "How many people know how it happened?"

"Just me, for the moment." Kyp gestured to the far side of the platform, adjacent to the depot. "My airspeeder's over here." Once they were all moving toward his vehicle, he continued, "I was assigned the investigation on this one." All lightsaber accidents that caused any harm to a living being had to be looked into, and any Master on duty at the Temple might be randomly assigned the duty of investigation.

Mara's face set. "Everybody who witnessed it said it was an accident."

Kyp nodded. "Of course, and Luke's report makes it pretty clear what happened. So I should dispense with our customs, not investigate at all, take the day off?" They reached the platform edge and Kyp's airspeeder, a long, narrow yellow vehicle with comfortable seats in front and a backseat that looked as though it was scaled for children. Kyp hopped into the pilot's seat and extended a gallant hand for Mara.

She gave him an admonishing look and leapt past him into the front passenger's seat. "No, of course not." She sat. "I'm just a little touchy about it, I suppose. *My* son has a lightsaber accident. Suddenly I feel the eyes of all the Jedi in the galaxy on me."

Luke stepped into the backseat and settled behind Kyp. "So what is this all about?"

Kyp sank into the pilot's seat, activated the speeder, and pulled straight back in a speedy reverse that put them within meters of the nearest cross-traffic stream. "You don't want to sit right behind me. Trust me." He swerved so he was pointed in the direction of the traffic stream's travel and accelerated, as though he were playing a *Millennium Falcon* simulator, to merge with the stream.

"Why not—oh."

Caught by the wind, Kyp's hair was pulled out of the hood of his Jedi cloak and stretched back to full length. The ends whipped mere centimeters in front of Luke's eyes and tickled the tip of his nose.

Luke slid sideways to the center of the seat. "You've grown it out."

Kyp reached up to give his hair an indulgent stroke, then grinned at his simulated display of vanity. "I've been seeing a lady who likes it long. And doesn't mind all the gray in it."

"Congratulations. So again. What is this all about?"

"Chief Omas and Admiral Niathal wanted to see you on your return from Hapes. They asked me to bring you. You can opt out if the timing isn't good."

Mara gave him a puzzled frown. "Is this about what happened on Hapes?"

"Sort of." Kyp gave her a broad, trouble-loving smile. "This time, *they* want Luke to make Jacen a Jedi Master."

CARGO VESSEL **BREATHE MY JETS** OUTSIDE THE CORELLIAN SYSTEM

Captain Uran Lavint was an heir to the tradition of Han Solo.

That's how she saw herself, at any rate, and she was indeed a smuggler, and not a small-scale one. Her cargo ship, *Breathe My Jets,* had hold space large enough to carry several *Millennium Falcon*s. Nor did she always make solitary smuggling trips—some missions, like this one, were small fleet operations.

Still, she was not rich, not even financially comfortable. Creditors—more successful smugglers, members of organized crime—now demanded their due whenever they could contact her, whenever they could catch up to her during *Breathe My Jets*'s brief stays in port. She'd been threatened, she'd taken a beating at a landfall on Tatooine, and rumor had it that one creditor had given up and hired a bounty hunter to eliminate her—to demonstrate the folly of not paying on time.

She needed this mission to go well. If it did, she could pay everyone off, start over. If it didn't, she might find herself in a position to describe *explosive decompression* firsthand.

She looked at the distant star Corell through the bridge's forward viewport as she sat slumped in her captain's chair. She sagged not out of defeat, but from habit and a deliberate attitude of indifference that gave her a reputation for being cool under fire. Though born to well-fed, well-tended middle-manager parents on Bespin, she now had skin like Tatooine leather and a craggy face that might have benefited from a drooping mustache.

Grudgingly, she sat upright. Glancing at the undersized, youthful Hutt in the specially designed copilot's couch beside her, she nodded. "All right, Blatta. Put me on," she said.

Blatta flipped a switch on the control panel before him. A display there lit up and showed Captain Lavint's face, a live holocam feed. In typically deep, gooey Hutt tones, he said, "Broadcast in five, four, three . . ." He held up two fingers, silently signaling the continuation of the countdown, then one, then closed his fist to indicate they were broadcasting.

Uran stared into the holocam recorder. "Captain to fleet," she said. "In a minute I will broadcast the nav data for our final jump. That jump will bring us as close as the planet Corellia's gravity well will allow, and then one of two things will happen—we'll be jumped by Galactic Alliance forces, or we won't.

"If we're not, congratulations—the armaments and bacta we're carrying will earn us tidy profits. If we are, our instructions are clear: break and run, straight down into Corellia's atmosphere. It's every ship for herself. You see your best friend being assaulted, you wish him well and get down to ground. Don't hang back and fight to free him.

"Good luck." She gave her viewers a brisk nod, and Blatta cut the transmission.

"Nav data?" he asked.

"Send it."

He did. A one-minute chron timer appeared on both cockpit displays, counting down. It was just enough time for the fleet's captains and navigators to load the data and test it, not enough time for them to waste, and increase their jitters.

More or less as a single body, the thirty-odd ships and vehicles of the fleet accelerated, pointing straight for the distant, unseen planet. Those who had defensive shields activated them. And at exactly the same moment, each cockpit crew saw the stars before them lengthen and begin the axial swirling that was the visual characteristic of hyperspace entry.

This jump would take only a few seconds—

It took less than that. They'd been in hyperspace half the time they should have been when the stars stopped spinning and snapped back into distant points of light. Corell was larger, closer, but not as close as the sun should be, and there was no comforting sight of the planet Corellia directly ahead of them. Instead, there was empty space decorated with the occasional fast-moving colored twinkle of light.

Uran swore, but her invective was drowned out by Blatta's shout: "Enemy ships! Chevron formation. We're toward the point, and the two flanks are falling in on our formation."

"Which one's the Interdictor?" One of the enemy ships had to be some sort of Interdictor, a capital ship carrying gravity-well generators—devices that would project a gravity field of sufficient strength to yank ships right out of hyperspace.

Blatta highlighted a point of light on his display, and it began blinking on Uran's display as well. It was just at the point of the chevron, directly ahead of Uran's ship.

Uran keyed her comm. "Captain Lavint to fleet. Maintain formation, match speed with me. Our only chance—"

On the sensor display, the crisp line of her fleet was blurring as each member craft vectored in a different direction.

"No, no, maintain formation!" She couldn't keep the desperation out of her voice. The original orders to scatter only made sense if every craft was a short distance from the safe haven of Corellia—didn't the idiots see that? "We've got to run this gauntlet at high speed—"

"Belay that," came a voice over the comm. It was female and a bit rough, a close match to Uran's own. "This is the real Captain Lavint. Follow your orders. Scatter." *This* voice was calm, self-assured.

"Sounds just like you," Blatta said.

"Shut up." Uran put her cargo ship on a new course, vectoring downward relative to her current orientation.

Blatta offered up a sigh that sounded like a bantha passing gas. "At least they can't know which vessel is carrying which cargo. Since we're not the biggest ship in the fleet, they might not pay us special attention—"

Breathe My Jets shuddered so hard that Uran's teeth clacked together and Blatta shook like a plateful of Corellian spice-jelly. The cockpit lights dimmed for a second.

Frantically, Uran wrenched the controls around in a new direction, but *Breathe My Jets* was not a small, nimble craft. In the agonizing seconds it took the cargo vessel to take a new bearing, she heard Blatta calmly describing their situation: "The Destroyer at the port tip of the chevron formation is firing on us. The first hit was against our engines. If it hits again—"

Breathe My Jets shuddered a second time, hard enough that Uran would have been thrown from her seat if the restraining straps hadn't been buckled in place. The cockpit lights dimmed again, and the displays all showed static for a second.

The lights did not come up again, and the cargo ship stopped responding to Uran's handling. The displays cleared of static. Running on emergency power, they began scrolling a list of damage sustained by the ships.

"Engines out," Blatta said, imperturbable.

"Thank you for that holonews update."

Blatta shrugged. "It's been good working with you, Captain. I only wish—"

"Wish what?"

"That you weren't half a year behind in what you owe me." He switched his main display over to follow the progress of the battle now raging all around them.

OUTSIDE THE CORELLIA SYSTEM

In the Command Salon of the *Imperial*-class Star Destroyer *Anakin Solo,* Jacen Solo stood staring through the forward viewports. He could see the last few twinkles and flashes of laserfire as this abortive space combat drew to a close.

He chose not to follow the events more closely on the readily available computer displays. Instead, he reached out through the Force, sampling the ships and vehicles he could see, looking for oddness, discrepancy, tragedy.

He found none. The smugglers, outmaneuvered and outgunned, gave up almost to a ship. A few nimble craft got away, making the jump to lightspeed before the warships of Jacen's task force could cripple them, but most did not; the majority of the smugglers floated, helpless, their engines destroyed by laserfire or their electronics systems rendered inert by ion cannons. Shuttles were now moving from ship to ship, picking up smuggling crews, dropping off the personnel who would bring the captured craft back to GAG facilities, directing tractor beams. In another hour or two, this section of space would be empty of everything but a few debris clouds that had once been engine housings.

"Our agent would like to speak with you," said Ebbak. A dark-haired human with skin the color of desert sand, she was short and unremarkable of appearance but had been of considerable use to him since he had been assigned the *Anakin Solo.* A civilian employee aboard ship, assigned to data analysis, she had demonstrated a knack for knowing what sort of information Jacen would need, and for supplying it at useful times. He was considering whether she would be interested in trading her civilian's post for a commission with Galactic Alliance Guard; he could benefit from someone with her skills if she proved as loyal as she was dutiful.

She had not *quite* materialized beside him—he had felt her walk up. Her approach had been silent. Perhaps she would also prove to be adept at stealth work.

"Why would I want to speak with her?" Jacen asked, his mind still elsewhere. "And please don't call her our *agent*. She betrayed her comrades for money. She is our temporary hireling. She is their traitor. She is nobody's agent but her own."

Ebbak paused, then evidently decided not to address those last few comments. "She didn't say what she wanted. But since she's already proven that she had one piece of information useful to us—"

"Yes, yes." Jacen nodded. "Where is she?"

"Your office."

Jacen followed her back through the bulkhead doors aft of the Command Salon. Once in the main corridor beyond, they moved through a port-side door into the office that served as Jacen's retreat aboard the *Anakin Solo*.

Waiting there were two people—a large man, dressed in the uniform of ship's security, standing, and a woman, seated . . . though she rose as Jacen and Ebbak entered.

Jacen looked into the weathered face of Captain Uran Lavint. "Yes?" he said.

Uran paused, apparently put off by his distant, brusque manner. "I simply wanted to find out if you had any requests or, more to the point, assignments before I left."

Jacen repressed a sigh. "First, I'd never prolong a business relationship with someone who sells out her fellows. Second, you're lying."

Uran flushed, but her expression did not change. "All right," she said. "I mostly just wanted to meet you."

"Ah." Jacen paused, carefully considering his next words. "Lavint, you now have all the time in the galaxy available to you. In betraying thirty-odd fellow smugglers, you have earned enough credits to pay off all your debts and start over, whether as a smuggler or something legitimate. You can cruise, you can frolic, you can relax. I, on the other hand, don't have time to spare. And you have now wasted some of it. I don't appreciate that." He turned to the security officer. "Take her down to Delta Hangar, put her on her ship, and get her off *my* ship."

Uran cleared her throat. "*Breathe My Jets* is on Gamma Hangar. And the engines won't be repaired for a couple of standard days at least."

"That's right. I'm claiming *Breathe My Jets* for the current military crisis." Jacen pulled his datapad from a pocket and consulted it. "Your ship is now the *Duracrud*."

"*Duracrud?*" Uran practically spat the name. "That's a stock why-vee six-six-six older than I am. It's a brick with wings and a hull that leaks gases like a flatulent Hutt. It's a fraction the size of *Breathe My Jets*."

"And exactly the sort of vessel needed by a smuggler starting a new career."

"Our agreement—"

"Our agreement was that you would receive a sum of credits—Ebbak, you showed her the transfer proof and gave her the data to claim it from the Bespin account? Yes—and that you would be allowed to depart on your ship, minus her cargo. The agreement did not specify which was to be your ship." He fixed Uran with an impassive stare. "Now would you care to waste any more of my time?"

The glare she turned on him was murderous. He understood why. He'd just taken her ship, her beloved business and home, and given her a hovel in its place. His father, Han Solo, would have felt the same way.

But Uran Lavint was no Han Solo, and Jacen didn't worry that she might someday return to cause him grief. Her record made it clear that she had no goals, no drives other than the acquisition of credits. She was nothing.

Uran turned away, her body language stiff, and marched to the door, her security man behind her. As the doors slid open, though, she paused. Not turning back, her voice quiet, she asked, "What's it like to have once been a hero?" Then she left, and the door hissed closed behind her.

Jacen felt himself redden. He forced the anger away. It wouldn't do to let an insect like Lavint bother him. But clearly, additional punishment was in order. To Ebbak, he said, "My father used to have endless trouble with the *Millennium Falcon*. The hyperdrive would fail all the time, and he'd tell the universe that it wasn't his fault, and then he'd fix it and be about his business." He nodded toward the closed door. "Delay her in transit to the hangar bays. Have *Duracrud*'s hyperdrive adjusted so that it will fail catastrophically after one jump."

"Yes, sir." Ebbak considered. "Since she's a smuggler, she's not going to go anywhere with a single jump. Her first jump will always be to some point far away from planetary systems or traffic lanes. She'll be stranded."

"That's right. And she'll become intimately acquainted with her hyperdrive."

"She might die."

"And if she doesn't, she'll be a better person for the experience. More polite, probably."

"Yes, sir." Ebbak moved to the door. It slid open for her. She said, "Your meeting with General Antilles is in one hour."

Jacen consulted his chrono. "So it is. Thank you."

"And, Colonel, if I can make a personal remark—"

"Go ahead."

"You're not looking well."

He gave her a humorless grin. "Crisis will do that to a man. I'll be fine."

The door slid shut behind her.